SORENSON

by

P. Dersen

AVON BOOKS
1 DOVEDALE STUDIOS
465 BATTERSEA PARK ROAD
LONDON SW11 4LR

This book has been sold subject to the condition that it shall not, by way of trade or otherwise, be lent, re-sold, hired out, photocopied or held in any retrieval system, or otherwise circulated without the publisher's consent in any form of binding or cover other than that in which this is published and without a similar condition including this condition being imposed on the subsequent purchaser.

Printed and bound in the U.K.
Avon Books
London
First Published 1998
© P. Dersen 1998
ISBN 1 86033 517 9

Characters

Edward Sorenson
Emily Sorenson
Sven Sjogren
Mrs. Brown
Maggie Brown
Felicity Brown
Rory Mcleod
Tam Richards
Mrs. Mcgregor
Bjorn Bengtson
Nils Thorenson
Ignatius Lucius Chancitt
Harry Macsween
Lady Margaret Mackaskill
Judge Cedric Simpson
Mussel Meg
Einer Wevling
Norma Wevling
Hr. Thorvaldson
Fr. Thorvaldson
Jessie Mathieson
Doctor Mathieson
Steve Allrock
Punchy Rush
Oskar Petterson
Alastair Ross
Ove Magnusson
Sergeant Mcillwraithe
Doctor John Broad

Chapter 1

He was a young man, less than thirty; he had the fair skin of the Nordic races tinged with the golden hue which indicated a prolonged exposure to wind, sun and sea. Small fair brown curls peeped from below his seaman's hat. His eyes, as blue as the sea, were full of mischief, but reflected an experience of life well ahead of his years. He was not tall, barely five feet eight inches, and in modern boxing terms would have weighed in at light middle weight. In physique, he tended to the athletic, but in posture he resembled a cat, too lazy to bother, but ready to spring into action in an extreme emergency.

Our hero had travelled down to the Port of Leith and was now standing perilously close to the edge of the Imperial Dock. Deep in thought, he seemed unaware of the close proximity of danger. He leaned back ever so slightly against his bicycle, using the machine as a prop.

Staring down into the murky depths, a smile flitted across his face as his mind flashed back some ten years or so. The year was 1901, the place the Kattegat and his ship, the Panskerskibet Danmark, the pride of the Danish Navy, had anchored just off the island of Samso.

It was a warm day in July and he, together with other young sailors, lined the deck. The guard rails had been removed and the Deck Officer was issuing commands.

"Survival practice today men, take up stations, swimming instructors Svenson and Olsen. On the command 'commence', the rest of you will step forward one at a time at five second intervals and take the plunge."

"I'm number five," sighed the young man, "another half minute before I sink or swim."

The officer was speaking again. "When you enter the water, you will effect a clearance by immediately swimming to the left or right so that there is no hold-up in the drill."

"Or straight to the bottom if you are a non-swimmer!" whispered the young man.

"Number five forward to the edge."

He ran forward, hesitated and then opened his mouth to explain.

"Mouth shut," snapped the officer and helped him on his way with an almighty heave.

He shot well clear of the ship away out into space. In years to come he would, in retrospect, sum up this most unfortunate experience in the words of the old song, appropriately amended of course.

'I float through the air with the greatest unease,
A despairing young sailor on the Danish high seas
My actions, disgraceful, old salts I'll displease
And my lifebelt they've all thrown away.'

He came down with such a thump that the air exploded from his body and the space was obligingly filled with sea water, compliments of the Kattegat. The shock caused such choking, coughing and spluttering he felt that he would never breathe again. His frenetic attempts at swimming would have been comical if the situation had not been so serious. I will not add to his ignominy by describing them.

Some seconds later, he was dragged by the hair to the comparative safety of an outstretched oar and clung ever so lovingly to this piece of wood until he was half-dragged, half-hoisted over the gunwale of the rescue launch.

Like all healthy young men, he recovered rapidly and was summoned to appear before the officer of the day.

"Name."

"Sorenson, Sir."

"You come from a seafaring family, I believe."

"Yes, Sir. From Laeso, not far from Frederikshavn."

"I see. Do you know that the men from your island have achieved much and have gone far in His Majesty's Navy? This seems out of character, Sorenson, surely your father advised and instructed you in what would be expected when you entered the service."

"He did, Sir."

"Well, what did he advise?"

"He said, 'Keep your eyes open and your mouth shut.'"

"Now, he was right, was he not? If you had kept your mouth shut, you would not have swallowed so much salt water. In future remember that an officer today, and that includes the deck officer, is like a father. He is there to look after you and as long as you do as you are told, you will be safe and progress in the service of His Majesty. Now, did he not say, 'Keep your mouth shut' just as your father advised?"

"Yes, Sir, he did, but my thoughts then were with my mother, whom I love dearly."

"What do you mean? Explain yourself."

"Well, my mother was against my joining the Navy and told me that if I joined and I was drowned, she would never speak to me again."

A wicked look came into the eyes of the officer, followed by what could best be described as a leer.

"So now we have another Danish comedian. If you carry on like this, my little ugly duckling, you will find that it will most definitely be your swan song!"

Edward could not help but smile.

"You will not smile when you find out what happens next. Your first name is Edward, I believe." His tone was ominous. "Look here, Edward," snapped the officer - his voice was certainly not reassuring but

Edward seemed unaware and was still smiling in a most angelic fashion.

"Edward!"

The voice rose to a crescendo with such intensity that he was catapulted out of his reverie back to reality. It was no longer the Kattegat he saw, but the water of the Imperial Dock. The shock was sufficient to make him step back so quickly that the bicycle, which till then had been a prop, was now transformed into an obstacle which he immediately fell over in a hydrophobic panic.

He was, however, a very resilient young man and bounced back onto his feet. Within a moment he had retrieved his bike and looked around sheepishly to see if his misfortune had been observed.

It had been; a docker passing by had seen his dilemma and asked kindly if he could be of assistance.

"No, thank you," replied Edward. "I am all right."

"Aye, laddie," the docker remarked, "you were lucky. If you had tumbled the other way I'd be shouting 'man in the dock!' by now. Oh, by the way, there's a man shouting 'Edward' from the ship that's just drawn away from the quay. He's been bawling this last half minute. I take it that he knows you?"

Suddenly Edward realised that his day-dreaming had obscured what he was really here for. He had cycled down from the 'Grange', a place further up on the East coast of Scotland so that he could bid farewell to his former shipmates.

He waved to the sailor who was shouting his name and pointed in the direction of the lock gates, indicating he would see him there when the ship passed through. He then mounted his bicycle and rode down to the rendezvous. A minute later he reached a red brick building, which it appeared housed the hydraulic machinery used for operating the lock gates. He took up a position on a raised doorstep, but then decided to move forward to the safety chain near the edge of the quay, taking the precaution this time of having his machine in front of him.

It should not be thought that, because he had not majored in swimming, he was not a good sailor. He was, in fact, a fine sailor and although the last two years had been a new experience on steam vessels, most of his young seafaring life had been spent with iron men on wooden ships.

He had seen much of the world and during his peregrinations had experienced a way of life that would have been by normal standards considered unique. In the main he had enjoyed life to the full aboard ship and ashore.

His inclination towards a career at sea had never been paramount in his thoughts. At its best, it had provided good company and the opportunity to mix with and enjoy the companionship of men of different races. And, of course, for a man of natural charm, the company of women had proved interesting, intriguing and a delectable relaxation, classified as highly recommended.

He had, however, despite an indifference to reaching the top, become *hovmester* at the age of twenty four and if he had really been serious, he might well by now, at twenty-eight years of age, have been a Ship's Master.

Edward could never be serious for long, it was not his nature. 'Life should be fun,' he would say. This did not mean that he lacked feeling or a deep understanding of life. He was in fact a kind and humane man and would help anyone in trouble, particularly if it meant deflating some pompous ass vested with too much authority.

The title 'Ship's Master' did not in any case appeal to Edward as he, in common with many Danes, disliked the word 'master', and if the connotation in any way indicated a master and slave or servant relationship, then they will have none of it. Their philosophy is that no-one should be permitted to function as a master; a Lutheran could concede to Christ, the others to no-one.

However, this did not exclude accepted leadership and no doubt Edward would have considered a go at the Captain's ticket had he felt so inclined.

Although he was fond of fun and had a gregarious nature, he was by no stretch of the imagination a sluggard. The time and energy which might have been spent in studying navigation and allied subjects was used in learning languages and acquiring a knowledge of the habits and culture of the various races with whom he came in contact.

As Hovmester and later as Chief Steward, he had taken the trouble to acquire a Swedish Manual on the maintenance and provisioning of ships. He had also, in the course of his duties, gained experience as a butcher and that, added to the culinary arts he had developed over some years, qualified him as a valuable asset on any ship.

He always made sure that the men were properly fed and properly led. After all, a well-fed and healthy crew will respond more readily to the inevitable discipline required when facing hazards at sea. Always approachable by the crew, he had in turn their respect and they would take an instruction readily, knowing that Edward would never ask a man to do anything that he was not capable of doing himself.

Suddenly the ship's siren sounded and Edward realised it would now only be seconds before the ship would pass slowly through the locks and he would see the lads possibly for the last time. Peter Larsen was the first to greet him from a position of advantage on the starboard bow, just above the words S.S. Vestero.

"Jump aboard, Edward, you'll never make it home on a bike!"

Then Edward spotted Elsa Langstrom, the skipper's daughter, standing half way up the steps leading to the bridge; she had always encouraged him to believe that she was just a demure young girl and Edward, kind soul that he was, had acquiesced, despite her forty years.

Forever gallant, Edward shouted up, "Hallo, Elsa, you are as pretty as ever."

She smiled and waved her hand. His blandishments had of course never deceived her, but the kindly nature of the man filled her breast with the appreciation that this man understood her true value of womanhood.

She invoked him, "Come home soon, Edward, and in the meantime, you watch out for those Scottish girls!"

As the vessel moved through the locks, he spied the bulky physique of Olaf Jacobsen standing amidships.

"Good afternoon, Hovmester," he hailed. He was met by the rejoinder, "Good afternoon to you - jump aboard if you want a trip to Frederikshavn."

"Ah, so that's where you're headed," replied Edward.

"Yes and then we are off to Aalborg after that."

"Send me back some Akvavit when you get there."

"You are far too young for strong drink," shouted Olaf. "I'll get your father, old Lars Villem, to send you some of his lobsters, put some back into you, do you far more good."

Edward had to shout louder now the ship was all but past the lock gates. Edward's final message rang out: "You are probably right. Anyway, tell him that I am safe and sound and that I will write home soon."

As he watched the ship move out towards the Roads, the words on the stern 'S.S. Vestero. Kobenhavn.' stirred in him a feeling of nostalgia. The word Copenhagen would obviously evoke a feeling for home in any Dane, but it was the word 'Vestero' which meant much more to Edward.

His childhood had been spent on Laeso, an island in the Kattegat lying approximately halfway between Frederikshavn on the Danish coast and Gothenburg in Sweden. On Laeso, his home had been in the district known as Vesterohavn. So Vestero conjured up country capers and sea escapades as a boy, assisting his father at the fishing and helping his mother in more ways than one when she was cooking.

Edward always insisted that his mother's smorrebrod was the best in Denmark and no one could equal her frugtgrod. Yes, the word 'Vestero' symbolised happiness. Vestero translates into Western Isle and it was the Western Isles of Scotland which had so enthralled Edward that he had developed a liking for the country and its people. Here he was, watching the old Vestero sailing away, and in his mind he was fervently hoping that the new-found Vestero would adequately fill the gap.

It was not just the breathtaking beauty of the West Highlands which had influenced him to stay in Scotland; he had also frequently called at the East coast ports and had found in general that the Scots were kind and friendly people. These last few months, realising that there was a lot more to life than perpetually sailing the high seas, his mind had more and more been occupied with a desire for change. There was the recurring urge to settle down on terra firma and try something original; hopefully something that would give him a comfortable financial return.

He had no illusions regarding the amassing of great wealth, he felt that the role of "whizz kid" or "shooting star" was not for him. He had no desire for the hectic life where ascendancy is rapid, followed only too frequently by a descent of greater velocity, terminating ultimately in complete oblivion. In his own whimsical way, he reckoned you could not build up great wealth without acquiring many enemies on the way up. It mattered little whether they were competitors beaten in the 'rat race' or some simple folk trampled upon during the process of exploitation.

It was surely better, and certainly safer, to build up friendship by dealing fairly and helping others. What he wanted now was the opportunity which would reward him for effort, maintain and expand his interest in life, preferably an occupation that entailed meeting people. Channelling his thoughts into such spheres of activity, he was just considering his next move and was so engrossed, that the sound of a voice at his side so startled him that he almost gave a repeat performance of the bike incident.

"Edward Sorenson, what are you doing here?" the stentorian voice asked. Turning round, he saw a big blond man - in one hand he held his hat and in the other he clutched a rather big briefcase.

"Sven Sjogren!" ejaculated Edward. "I must ask you the same question."

"Oh, I have been here for almost a month. I am no longer an engineer," said the big Swede. "In fact, you are now looking at the Scottish Representative of the Anglo Swedish Trading Company."

Not to be outdone, in mock seriousness, Edward responded, "Oh, you are, are you? Well let me tell you that you are looking at the Chief Representative of Richards & Son, Butchers at Grangemouth."

"How many representatives are in the company?" asked Sven.

"At present one, myself," answered Edward with a wry smile.

The lock gates had now closed and the two friends were able to cross the bridge.

"Let's go to my lodgings and then we can discuss matters which interest us over some Swedish schnapps."

Edward indicated, however, that he had booked bed and breakfast and that the landlady would be expecting him within the next half an hour.

"I made an arrangement with the lady this morning that I would return at a certain time for my tea and of course I cannot disappoint a lady."

"And as you know, Edward," said Sven, "I would be the last person to ask you to break an appointment, but I am sure that we can arrange to meet very soon."

"Our reunion could take place at six o'clock tonight outside the Customs House."

"Splendid, I see you know your way about already. Six o'clock it is then. *Farvel, Edward, farvel.*"

Chapter 2

After the two friends parted, Sven walked through the shore gate and, turning left, he entered the Sailor's Home to collect a small parcel sent to him from his parents in Stockholm. He then proceeded along the shore to his lodgings.

Edward, meantime, had cycled through the docks, crossed over a swing bridge and had left by another gate, finding himself ultimately in Sandport Street. It was not long before he reached the tenement stair where Mrs. Brown, the landlady, lived with her husband and family.

It was she who had agreed to give him bed and breakfast after he had cycled down from Grangemouth during the earlier part of the day. He rang the bell and waited for the door lift operating. Within seconds the stair door jolted open and he walked into the well of the stair and a voice immediately above welcomed him.

"Come on up, Mr. Sorenson. I've no doubt that you will be ready for your tea."

On walking upstairs and reaching the landing, he was confronted by a large woman of ample proportions. Smilingly she beckoned him into the house and then ushered him into what she called the parlour.

"Do sit down, make yourself comfortable."

He did as she indicated and sat down on a small sofa. Sank down would be more accurate, for the piece of furniture was barely a foot from floor to seat, a low dive in fact and it was anyone's guess who had knocked the stuffing out of it. It was rather superfluous for Mrs. Brown to add, "Just lie back and relax, Mr. Sorenson."

Edward found that the force of gravity obliged him to do just that.

Mrs. Brown was now in complete command and ready to make Edward aware of the realities involved in the role of a housewife.

"You will be tired, Mr. Sorenson. I know I am: while you were away seeing off your seamen friends, I was busy about my chores."

She sat down on a high chair, folded her arms in front of her ample bosom and then resumed her story.

"Early this morning I visited my aunt, Mrs. McFarlane. She's a widow, you know, getting on for eighty and she is not too well, so I did her housework, cooked her a meal and after that I had to go for her messages. I did my own at the same time of course and got a nice bit of fish for the tea. And then off to see Mary McIver, she's got a sore leg and likes a wee bit of company. Then when I got home, I tackled a big wash and just before you arrived I finished off the ironing. But there I go, telling you all my troubles and you no doubt starving and wanting your tea. Now don't say another word, Mr. Sorenson, I'll away into the kitchen, see you in ten minutes."

Edward had never said a word, his early naval training had taught him that there are times when you keep your mouth shut.

"Ah there now, Mr. Sorenson, come into the living room, your tea is on the table. Now if you require anything just you say the word. I know you won't have a guid Scot's tongue in your heid, but I have no doubt you will make yourself understood."

"Thank your Mrs. Brown, I think I will manage."

She showed him his position at the table, but he pulled out what he considered to be her chair and insisted that he would sit down once she was seated.

"No, just you sit down, Mr. Sorenson, I won't be taking my tea until the family come home."

Once seated she served him his meal and at the sight of a large plaice with fried potatoes, garnished

12

with tomatoes and a tartare sauce, obviously a Mrs. Brown concoction, he relaxed, smiled in anticipation and settled down to the serious and delightful task of demolition.

With an expertise gained over many years, he demonstrated his consummate skill by leaving only the cleaned, picked skeleton on his plate. He rose from his chair, an expansive smile on his face, exuding an aura of sublime 'bonhomie' and with obvious enthusiasm and sincerity indicated in the best Danish tradition, "That was excellent, Mrs. Brown, *tak for mad*."

"What does that mean Mr. Sorenson?"

"Well," explained Edward, "when you are finished at the table you excuse yourself in the proper fashion and suitably compliment the hostess or mother of the family. *'Tak for mad'* means thank you for the food and it recognises that the effort of the mother in the preparing and serving of food to the family is of extreme importance and no one must take that for granted."

"And does the mother say anything after such a nice compliment?"

"Yes," replied Edward, "she usually says *'Velbecommen'*."

"You don't need to translate that bit, Mr. Sorenson, and as far as I am concerned, you are indeed very welcome."

"I should like you to know, Mrs. Brown, that the fish was a delight, what name do you give it in Scotland?"

"That fish you've just eaten, laddie, is called a plaice and seeing that it had red spots on it, in this part of the country we call it a flounder."

"That's interesting, we call it a *flunner* and of course, like you, we know the fish by its red spots and refer to it as *rodspotten*. In fact, Frederikshavn, near my home, is called the Flunner Town and the people there hang out flounders like so much washing, allow them to dry and then store them for future use."

Mrs. Brown decided that she liked this young man and her maternal instincts indicated that he might well be worth protecting, but first she must know something of his background.

"Have you any brothers or sisters, Mr. Sorenson? Mother and father in good health? Don't you feel a little homesick at times? Where you come from, are they all seafaring folk? I suppose in common with most folk who have men at sea, they are very religious. There must be many farms in Denmark when you consider the number of boats that come here crammed with butter. Is there much industry in your part of the country? Maybe there isn't and that is the reason you have decided to stay in Scotland. Oh, by the way, are you married, Mr. Sorenson, or could it be that you have already got your eye on some bonnie lassie over here? Believe you me, as far as women are concerned, your best friend is your mother. I do hope you write to her often. Mothers, remember, are always concerned when anyone leaves the nest."

The interrogation of Edward had been fully comprehensive and the peroration at the end held an ominous portent, all the more effective when Edward considered that she had been able to set table for her husband and three girls at the same time.

An academic, listening to Mrs. Brown formulating her laws on social and domestic behaviour, might well, for his own peace of mind, have classified her as an expert in social jurisprudence. However, her neighbours would have been more down to earth and less charitable, and had been known to regard her as a 'nosy besom'.

Edward was not yet committed to either view, but was impressed at the number of questions asked and the speed with which they were delivered. He had just sat back with a fixed smile, not daring to interject, but towards the end the realisation that the husband and three young women would shortly appear, plus the inference that he might be looking for a suitable wife, sent a shiver down his back and effectively wiped the smile off his face.

Seizing the opportunity to speak when she was about to draw breath for further development of her subject, Edward rose to his feet and apologised for the interruption, hastily adding that he had an appointment with a friend and that he had been so interested in what she had been saying, that he had quite forgotten the time.

"I wonder, Mrs. Brown, would it be any trouble if I gave myself a shave and brush up before I go out?"

"No trouble at all, Mr. Sorenson. I will show you where you will be sleeping tonight. There is a jug and basin in the room and if you will just allow me a few minutes, I will see that you get the hot water you require."

Edward was agreeably surprised that he had been able to terminate a rather irksome experience so speedily. Almost immediately he had second thoughts and felt that his behaviour had been rather boorish; after all Mrs. Brown was obviously a kind person and had only been giving vent to her matriarchal views to her immediate audience. It did not take him long to shave and complete his toilet. He then indicated to Mrs. Brown that he would be on his way and asked her to outline the routine of the establishment.

"Take these keys, Mr. Sorenson. The big one opens the stair door and the small one is the house key, you know your own bedroom, now away and enjoy yourself. Should you be late, be as quiet as you can. Oh! and by the way, your breakfast will be on the table at half past eight in the morning. Now, if you wish, you are welcome to come back soon. I am sure that the family would be pleased to see you."

"Thank you for everything Mrs. Brown. I am off now to see my friend."

Edward left the house in high spirits, feeling that he had possibly avoided becoming involved in a relationship which, at this stage, would have severely cramped his style. Although his English was passable, he was nevertheless a foreigner who had resided in the country for barely a week, with not much money and prospects which were questionable, all of which indicated a lone role, not to be jeopardised by three eligible young women and a mother who, to say the least, would have proved a powerful advocate of family life.

With the air of a free man, he strolled happily down Sandport Street until he reached St. Bernard Place. Pausing momentarily to orientate himself to his surroundings, he saw slightly to his right, just across the road, the imposing building he was looking for and recognised it as the Customs House.

Sure enough, as promised, Sven had arrived and was standing on the pavement outside the Customs House and was conversing with a man in navy blue.

As he approached, Sven turned and, on recognising Edward, he immediately introduced them to each other in real Swedish style, using their proper titles.

"Hovmester Edward Sorenson, this is Prevention Officer Rory McLeod of His Majesty's Customs and Excise."

They shook hands and Edward, always one for a bit of fun, responded with, "I am pleased to meet your Majesty, I trust that you will not prevent Sven and myself from having a drink together and I am sure Sven would wish you to join us."

Mr. McLeod looked quizzically at the man who had addressed him in such an unusual fashion and wondered, "is he an eccentric, or just a mischievous rascal?"

He was not given much time to reach an assessment because Edward had spied on his right, in front of a bridge, an alcoholic dispensing establishment with the intriguing name, the Sailors' Rest.

"Let us seek rest and refreshment, gentlemen, and quaff the local brew, trusting that it will meet with our approval."

Without further ado, Edward led the way into the saloon bar, followed by two rather perplexed men of the sea. While Edward ordered the drinks, Mr. McLeod quizzed Sven about his friend.

"Edward is a good man, Rory. I have known him for a number of years, but you must remember he is a Dane. They are not serious like the Swedes, they laugh a lot, they are kind, but find it very hard to show respect for authority."

When Edward returned with the drinks, he set down whiskies and carlsbergs and commented that although the place was clean and respectable, it was uncivilised and they had no akvavit. Rory Mcleod's retort was significant.

"You will get your akvavit, Mr. Sorenson - never fear."

"What's all this Mister or Herr business? For that matter, we are friends are we not? Sven has been my friend for years and as you are his friend, then you can be my friend. I am Edward, you are 'Rawry' and he is Sven."

"Not Rawry, Edward," interjected Sven. "You must call him Rory, like the word roar."

"Ah, Rory, just like the roar of a lion."

"Chust so," said the big West Highlandman in a mollified tone.

"Your second name interests me," exclaimed Edward. "It appears that in Scotland they call the men after their mothers. In Jutland where I come from, our names are handed down from our fathers."

Before the big man could answer, he carried on in his sublime innocence and recounted something that had happened two days earlier.

"It was up at the Grange that I met this young girl. We were dancing, you see, and the house, she called the place the Hall, was very hot and we decided to come out and enjoy a walk in the cool evening air. Now, Sven, you know me, I did what she wanted and she was ever so happy and invited me home to meet her mother."

"That was fast work," said Sven. "You've only been in the country a week."

"Fornicator," murmured Rory, who was thinking that the quicker this young Viking was de-horned, the better for all concerned.

"And," Edward concluded, "she kept on saying 'My Ma says this and my Ma says that', so as she always pointed to her mother, I realised that Ma in Scotland signifies leader, or, I believe you would call her Clan Chief."

"Bl-y blether!" snorted Rory.

Nothing daunted and obviously enjoying himself, Edward carried on. "Therefore, Rory, you are the son of Ma Cloud, which means that your ma's ancestors came from the sky; this I think is wonderful."

Rory broke his silence. "Little man, if you are finished with your blethers, I will chust put you in your place. We Scots are like all men, we take our names from our fathers. My mother does however come from Skye, but not the sky of the clouds where your mind seems so firmly embedded. As for yourself, you are a Sorenson which means, I think, that you are a son of sorrow and probably a source of sorrow to your mother also, God rest her soul."

The challenging attitude of the big man seemed in no way to affect the young Dane. A radiant smile lit up his face, his mischievous blue eyes twinkled as he offered his hand to Rory.

A rather perplexed Rory seized the hand in front of him and determined to teach the upstart a lesson. He squeezed the hand very hard and found, to his surprise, that although the hand was smaller than his own, it was the hand of a sailing ship seaman and was as strong as his own. The more he squeezed, the harder Edward reacted and it was obvious that stalemate would be the ultimate result. The blue eyes held Rory's incredulous stare and he heard Edward saying in a mock admonitory tone, "Rory, you have such a pleasant way of insulting your friends, but I accept the blame for trying to be funny and must apologise for my peculiar brand of Danish humour. I can see that you are prepared to forgive me; after all we would be poor friends indeed if we could not insult each other now and then without resorting to war."

The pressure subsided and as they withdrew their hands, Rory could not withhold the grin already spreading over his face, nor control the deep throaty gurgle building up inside him, finally exploding into a gale of laughter so loud and vibrant that the glasses on the table danced a merry jig. As the gale died down and the calm returned, all he could say as he looked at this little great Dane was, "Edward, you're a helluva man."

The palpable good humour and sheer cheek of this man was infectious and in spite of his mere sixty-eight inches, Rory felt that this man was as big as himself - not tall, but big.

Sven heaved a sigh of relief and decided that he also could afford to laugh. Conversation now developed around Edward's experience during his first week in Scotland.

"I arrived a week ago up in the Grange on board the S.S. Vestero. We were carrying timber from Finland and, after discharging the cargo, I decided I would look for something ashore. After a number of unsuccessful attempts looking for a job, I decided on a little private enterprise. I went back to the ship and contacted the Steward and Captain and they agreed to let me handle the victualling of the ship before setting off for the Baltic. Then I boarded a Norwegian whaler and told them I was agent for the local ship chandlers and provision merchants."

"But you said you were unsuccessful in getting a job," interjected Sven.

"You are not listening, Sven. I said I would try a little private enterprise and in this I succeeded and, believe me, the ship chandler, the butcher and others were very happy to know that I had made myself their agent, particularly when they saw the size of the orders they were given and, of course, I was very pleased to accept my commission on the deal."

"Now I remember," said Sven, "you mentioned a butcher this morning, Richards & Sons, I believe."

"That's correct," replied Edward, "and apart from acting as his agent, he wants me to help him in the butcher's shop."

"And what do you know about the butcher's trade?" asked Rory.

"I am not a Master Butcher," said Edward, "but I have enough experience to do all that he will want and, after all, if you can kill a pig and cut it up properly while you are being tossed about at sea on a square-rigger, surely it can be done more effectively on dry land and I should think the same will apply to cutting up sides of beef. Anyway, I think that most of my time will be taken up with the agency side of the business. There are two reasons for saying this, number one, I like talking to and making friends with seamen of different nationalities, and number two, I am sure it will prove more lucrative."

"So you say," said Rory. "I'm thinking that you will enjoy the drink just as much as the companionship."

Before Edward could reply, he placed a bottle of clear liquid on the table and asked him to help himself. There was no label on the bottle, but this did not stop Edward from lifting up the bottle to sample the contents, but the grin on Rory's face made him apprehensive. He decided that discretion was preferred to hasty decision. Rory laughed at Edward's discomfiture.

"Some Viking! Afraid of a wee bottle, you don't think I'd poison a friend, do you?"

Edward gingerly uncorked the mystery bottle and, on sniffing the contents, he smiled and, looking blissfully at Rory, he agreed that he had been foolish.

"A label is not required, Rory, you are indeed a true and compassionate companion. I smell the pure strong sweet aroma of Aalborg, a wonderful akvavit of high standard. Your contribution to civilised society will one day be recognised and suitably rewarded. Please accept my profound thanks for making my first day in Leith a happy and most memorable occasion."

"Don't mention it. You help yourself, Edward. I knew you would like the Danish drink, enjoy yourself and, who knows, after a wee while in Scotland, when you grow up you may even learn to appreciate the purest distillation known to man. We in the West call it Usquebaugh."

Chapter 3

It did not take Edward long to experience what happens when you abuse usquebaugh. A fine whisky is like a mature woman: both must be handled with loving care and a deep appreciation of their true value. To be rushed or raped is an offence never easily forgiven.

Not being an angel, he had rushed in and the akvavit and usquebaugh had been forced to struggle for supremacy and poor Edward, unwittingly, was the battleground,

"Usquebaugh!!" He was babbling now and it was no wonder, considering that he had accepted Rory's invitation to sample a whisky of the third generation and, having already had his fill of akvavit, the combination had proved disastrous. Rory had left the two friends and Sven was trying to ensure that Edward got back to his digs in reasonable shape.

Edward was confused and unco-operative. He could not fathom why, when he put his right foot forward, his body swung over to the left; and even he, in his state of alcoholic anaesthesia, realised that he was in a trough that would require expert seamanship and accurate navigation if he wanted to reach port in one piece.

"Stop your babbling," said Sven. "Thank providence that your friend is a Swede with a hard head."

"You mean a wooden head," replied Edward, an inane grin spreading over a very flushed face.

"You're hopeless, you'll never learn, but I will try and explain what happened to you. Usquebaugh is the name these Scots use for whisky."

"But it was a very fine liquor, not like anything I got from the bar," burbled the young Dane.

"Yes, and why not? It was Rory's own whisky. Don't you remember, he had a bottle filled with akvavit? Well, he also had a bottle of whisky sent to him by his father."

"Well, what about it?" murmured Edward.

"Well, you may know something about akvavit, but precious little about whisky. When a West Highland man talks about usquebaugh, he refers to a fine liquor distilled three times, which makes it much stronger than ordinary whisky and you had to mix them. It must have been like two rivers of fire water clashing together. Just imagine the concoction you swallowed tonight, the strong liquor of the Viking berserkers mixed with aqua vitae of the West Highland barbarians."

"Keep quiet, you romantic fool," lisped Edward. "Can't you see I'm walking on air."

"Yes, just walk another metre and you'll have to learn to walk on water. Another two steps and you're in the harbour."

"Christ!!"

"Yes, he could have, but you can't. Now turn round the other way and we will manage to get home somehow."

The shock had a sobering effect and he did as he was told. Ten minutes later they landed back at the Browns' residence in Sandport Street.

"Quiet, quiet, ssh - we don't want to waken anyone."

"I've got the key," whispered Edward. "You - you - open the door, p--put the key in my pocket, Sven, a-and then leave me, I'll be all right."

Sven made sure that Edward was safe inside before he beat a rather hasty, but silent, retreat.

Edward felt his way to his bedroom, sat down on a chair and removed his shoes and socks, telling himself all the while to be very quiet. He reckoned that bare feet would ensure silence, but he need hardly have bothered.

23

There was a brilliant eye-searing flash of lightning, followed by thunder that shook the building. Then the rains came and Edward felt sure that Sven would be cursing him now for preventing him reaching his lodgings before the deluge.

As if to invoke the gods to desist in their rain-making, he stretched out his arms in supplication, but the gods, they heard not, and the storm intensified. Making ready for bed, he looked out of the window and realised that his room was above a small ship-repairing yard and beyond its locked gates he could see across the water to the shore, but what he did not see was a Swede drenched to the skin plodding homewards, weary and angry that he had allowed a dumb Dane to compromise him thus.

Edward lay back in bed befuddled and more than a little conscience-stricken. As he watched the pyrotechnics of the elements and heard the rain lashing the window, he thought he felt the bed move, but realised that this was an alcoholic phenomenon. He gave a little smile as he thought of mariners at sea on a night such as this, but he had the humility to murmur, as he closed his eyes in a soporific stupor, 'Poor buggers!'

One way or another excesses have to be paid for. As far as Edward was concerned, he was all at sea. Dreams and nightmares are said to be of short duration; in the case of the young mariner cum salesman, his nautical manifestations seemed interminable.

Suffice it to say that in one night alone he sailed three times round the Cape despite horrific conditions, was summoned before the captain and 'keel hauled' for having danced a jig on a dead man's chest - this after only one small bottle of rum. He was ship-wrecked on several occasions and ended up ultimately on a tropical island as a castaway. An important redeeming feature was the miraculous appearance of Elsa to keep him company. Unfortunately, just as he was blissfully realising that two's company, they were rescued by old Captain Langstrom, who immediately imprisoned him for what he might have done. Confined to the ship's paint locker and dolefully contemplating the probability of hanging from the yard-arm at sunrise, he was not assuaged by the smell of raw linseed oil or Stockholm tar.

But of course in a dream anything is valid: the ship struck a reef and foundered, but not before Elsa had unlocked the door and freed her lover. They clung together as they descended into the deep, but for some reason she started pushing him away. In consternation he called out, "Elsa, Elsa," and then something struck him on the back of the head, leaving him impotent and distraught in an all-enveloping purple haze, from which there seemed no escape.

Gradually, however, the mist cleared and he saw the green eyes of a young woman, an appealing mouth and, as his gaze travelled downwards, the cleavage between two well formed breasts held tight in her cotton dress. He recollected that Elsa's eyes were brown, but this did not deter Edward; to miss an opportunity such as this would indeed be criminal and could be construed as a gross indifference to the womanly charm of the young lady. Acting his part, he pulled her closer and in an impassioned voice inquired, "Oh, Elsa, what happened?"

But the young woman reacted swiftly and pushed him away with such force that his head hit the wall for the second time. To say the least, he was disconcerted and prayed that the head-thumping would not prove habit-forming. Although dazed, he could see the soft red lips of the green eyed maiden moving, and in a tone of admonition, he heard her say, "It's too early for fun and games. I'm not Elsa and fine you know it. Maggie is my name and Ma says it's half an hour to breakfast time, so waken up sailor and get your clothes on."

It was a very contrite and abashed Scandinavian who completed his toilet and dressed for breakfast. He felt slightly humiliated, but was man enough to realise that he had brought this upon himself.

He had to admit that he had overplayed his hand. Thinking in his somnolent fantasy that he could play the king, he had instead played the knave and lost the game. Being a Dane with a sense of humour, he laughed at his stupidity, but forgave himself his trespasses and swore to be more selective in the future.

Passing the young lady as she rushed off to work, he apologised and asked her forgiveness. She smiled and replied, "Next time take more water with your whisky."

Edward was wide awake now and his rejoinder made her laugh merrily. "Never fear, Maggie, next time, if I may, I will take you with me. You'll do me a lot more good than whisky and, by the way, my name is Edward."

Just as she closed the door it was not her comely figure that registered in his mind, but the unmistakable smell of Stockholm tar. I must be crazy, he thought, an attractive woman passes in front of me and instead of appreciating her female charms, I think of a ship's paint locker - yes, I do need my head examined. Poor Edward, but then how was he to know that Maggie worked in the tarring section of the local ropery.

After breakfast he paid his respects to Mrs. Brown and then made preparations for setting out to Grangemouth. He first of all made certain that all his personal effects were duly accounted for and packed safely into a small bag and then strapped to the carrier at the back of the bicycle. He examined the machine with due care and attention to ensure that it would do the job it was designed for. After all it was a new Sunbeam he had borrowed and would obviously be considered a valuable piece of capital equipment by that canny Scot, Mr. Richards.

Then out onto the open road speculating on what the future might hold for a young Dane whose modest aspirations could be summed up as a desire for a modicum of fame, a little good fortune and the development of as many friendly relationships as possible.

He cast his mind back over the past week and wondered if in fact he had achieved anything of value. It was true he had met and made friends; whether transitory or long term, only time would tell. However, his limited experience in the business world had taught him something of value. Reading a business manual, it could be construed that, provided you followed the editor's advice, it was perfectly simple to make friends and achieve success without really trying; the operative word 'trying' is the stumbling block.

In reality, the business world is concerned with hard facts and hard cash and anyone trying to separate a businessman from his cash with only a pleasant smile and some so-called original line of patter, would find his behaviour was very trying indeed and the normal reaction 'close the door when you go out and do watch you don't fall downstairs'.

However, communication is necessary in all fields and Edward had an advantage in that he had progressed beyond the sign language and lingua franca used by sailors and small traders in dealing with other nationals. He was in fact a tolerable linguist in the Scandinavian, the Baltic, the German, French and English languages, but evidently more than this was required if he wished to matriculate in the world of business. He had thought that his English would be good enough to have made a favourable impression on the various employers he had contacted, but had found in practice that dealing with those people had been more difficult than he anticipated. He had not realised that more than proper usage of the English language was required, such as commercial terms, local slang, hybrid words used to describe some industrial process or other and the inevitable dialect from some odd corner, whose native sons laid claim as speakers of the perfect language.

He had learned his lesson quickly: it was not just a matter of language, but really a matter of salesmanship. After all, he had been asking for something and they had not been convinced that Edward would be able to give them the profit margin they required. On the other hand, he recollected that it had been different when he had supplied the shipping orders; then their conversion had been rapid when they realised that Edward had something to offer.

He had learned from this that if you wish to sell something, be it an idea, be it merchandise or what have you, first you have to make the prospect aware of the value to him or to her of what you have to offer; in essence, you have to give before you can expect to receive.

He was so engrossed in trying to analyse his experiences since setting foot in Scotland, that he completely forgot that when riding a machine whether power-assisted or self-propelled, it is incumbent on the driver at all times to keep his eyes on the road.

"Ring your bell, you bloody fool," he heard a man's voice bellow in his ear as he clipped the heels of an unsuspecting native of the small town of Boness. He felt ashamed and, as a Scotsman might have said, mortified that he had almost injured a fellow man because of his daydreaming and decided on the spot to make amends. To this end he parked the bike, ran back to the man and profoundly apologised for his misdemeanour. To say the least, the man was surprised, but responded in a friendly fashion and commented, "I'm all right, mac, dinna worry, but for Christ's sake watch out or you'll have the polis on your top."

He was relieved that the man had been so sensible about the incident, but could not suppress a smile as he walked away thinking that it was a coincidence that the Scots and the Swedes used the same word 'polis', but be it polis or police, it would not have been funny to fall into the clutches of these denizens of the law. He decided that it would be safer and probably more interesting to walk for a bit, after all a man on foot can assess the value of his surroundings far more effectively than a man travelling three times faster on some type of velocipede or other.

It was fortunate that he did this. He had only gone some fifty yards or so when on his left he spied a shop with a number of windows displaying drapery, soft goods and general merchandise. It was the centrepiece that attracted his attention.

This was surely the most magnificent physical specimen he had ever seen, more than six feet in height, broad shouldered, a powerful neck supporting a noble head, from which smiled two blue piercing eyes set in a strong weather-beaten face, resplendent with black moustache and neatly clipped beard. In his left hand he held binoculars and his right hand beckoned Edward into the shop. He had to go very close indeed before he realised that it was the most lifelike dummy he had ever seen.

Although taken aback, he could only feel admiration for the person responsible for such a convincing display. His eyes travelled upwards to find out who the proprietor might be and, to say the least, he was surprised to see the name Einer Wevling.

He wondered if it could possibly be? And decided that there was a simple way to find out. The first person he encountered was a pretty young girl who had obviously been well trained to create a favourable impression on sailors home from the sea.

"What would you like to see, sir?" she said.

"Not what," replied Edward. "But I would like to see Mr. Wevling. Please tell him that a Mr. Sorenson has come back from the East to see him."

Almost immediately a powerfully built Norseman came through what appeared to be a private door, to greet this man called Sorenson.

"I am Einer Wevling," he said. "What can I do for you?"

"I don't know that you can do much for me at present, but we might be able to do something for each other at a later date; but first I would like to ask you, have you a young brother at sea? To put you in the picture, about three years ago I was on the Aalborg Dutch East Indies run as Hovmester on the S.S. Danafoss when I came into contact with a young seaman who seemed anxious to learn all that he could about seamanship. I took him under my wing and sure enough he made rapid progress and in no time at all he rose to leading seaman and is probably a ship's officer by this time. His name was Eric Wevling and he was forever boasting about an older brother in Scotland whose name was Einer."

Einer grabbed Edward's hand in a vice-like grip and pumped his arm up and down. "I am pleased to meet the man who could do something for my young brother. He was certainly a young tearaway when we lived in Norway, but lately my letters from home declare that he has developed into a fine young man and at present is sailing as first mate with the Hansen line and will shortly sit his captain's ticket. You have achieved something I thought would never happen."

"You must give your brother the credit, Einer. I may have influenced him, but, nevertheless, his is the achievement."

"I know your name is Edward," said Einer. "Eric has mentioned you so often in his letters and now before we talk any more, come with me, Edward, and I will introduce you to my wife and two of my best friends."

On entering the inner sanctum, the all-pervading smell of percolating coffee and fine Danish cigars transposed Edward momentarily from Scotland to Scandinavia. He was introduced to Einer's wife - "Norma is a countrywoman of yours, Edward, and lived in the south of Denmark before we married." And then turning to a big man and a neatly dressed woman, he introduced them. "This is Herr and Fru Thorvaldson."

The big man, it appeared, was a director and main agent in Scotland for the Norsk Fiskeri & Whaling Company.

The fuss that Norma made over Edward, the rest might not have existed. She was completely uninhibited and as she brought him his coffee, she managed to lean over further than was necessary, revealing a panoramic view of female fulfilment designed to arouse any potential amorous activity.

Edward thought, 'What the hell is she playing at?' And the next moment, she ran her hands through his hair and shouted to her husband, "Hasn't he got lovely curls?" Edward was nonplussed at this unexpected behaviour and, considering that he had really entered the premises with a business proposition in mind, he was unsure how he should react. But this lasted only a few seconds and his rejoinder to Norma - "You are just like my mother, she also thought I had lovely curls," - evoked laughter all round, with the exception of Norma, who now felt that her little flirtatious fling had blown up prematurely.

Over coffee and cognac, Edward outlined his intentions while in Scotland. "I hope to establish myself as an agent for shipping supplies and think I could achieve this. I know what is required concerning the victualling of men at sea and I am confident that I will be able to persuade provision merchants, butchers and others that I have the qualifications to make a deal mutually profitable. Oh, incidentally, Einer, when I go aboard ship I will ensure that any sailors who feel like kitting out are made aware of that handsome mariner you have standing in your front window."

"So you have seen Handsome Harry," said Einer. "Yes, the man who fashioned that head is the finest in the business, in fact he is one of the top sculptors, an Edinburgh man who owed me a good turn. Actually I dragged him out of the 'drink' while we were doing a bit of fishing down at Berwick and that was how he repaid me."

Edward turned and spoke to Mr. Thorvaldson. "I wonder if I could in any way interest you in my endeavours?"

"You will have to prove yourself, Mr. Sorenson, but I am sure you will become established and, when you do, I have no doubt we will be able to do a little business; but please remember that most of our sea stock orders are handled centrally from Oslo. However, in the meantime, here is my card and I will be pleased to hear from you. If, as it appears, you are a friend to Einer Wevling, then you can assume that I will certainly value your friendship," and so saying, he shook Edward's hand and then departed with his wife.

Edward also was anxious to be on his way, he felt he was being unfair to Mr. Richards, the butcher at Grangemouth, and that he should really be discussing future developments with his new employer. Although in the main he would to some degree be a free agent, he felt he owed it to the butcher to achieve something tangible in the immediate future.

"I will have to go, Einer, as I have an appointment with a Mr. Tom Richards, butcher up at the 'Grange'. I am late and he will be wondering what has happened to me."

"That's a coincidence, Edward, I know Mr. Richards; in fact we are friends and I know him as Tam. Now don't you concern yourself. I will phone Tam and when he knows you have been with me the last hour or so, he will, I am sure, understand that you have not been wasting your time or his."

Half an hour later Edward reached the 'Grange' and almost immediately he started negotiations with the butcher, Tam Richards, concerning what his duties should be.

"I am sure that with your knowledge of languages and your pleasant personality, Edward, you should make a good Water Agent. Regarding your ability to operate as a butcher - that is another question. I have no doubt from what you have told me that you do know something of our trade, but I intend to ensure that you are not let loose in my shop until I am sure that you can handle that side of the business."

"That's fair enough," said Edward. "I think you will find that I can cut up meat effectively and properly and I will soon adjust to the cuts of meat you supply to your customers in the neighbourhood, but first I must get on with the job that I know I can do, and I don't intend to let anyone stop me getting these shipping orders."

"You may find that more difficult than you think," replied Mr. Richards. "Remember there are others in the field competing with you, in particular a rather nasty type who plays dirty. He is an American, I am not sure of his name, but I have heard him called Chancellor or Challenor and other names that we don't use in decent society."

Edward only smiled and gave a little chuckle. "Until I know this man I will call him the challenge, and never fear, Tam, I promise you that if I find he is devious, he will get what he deserves."

As he left the shop the butcher handed him a card. "Take this with you," he said. "I'm sure Mrs. McGregor will look after you."

Chapter 4

"Yes," said Mrs. McGregor, "your room is ready for you and should you find that there is anything you require, you have only to ask. Oh, and by the way, will you be in town for long?"

"A number of weeks, I should imagine, if not longer, the amount of business I do will determine how long I stay."

Mrs. McGregor looked approvingly at the young man and replied, "I wish you every success."

Edward smiled. "Thank you, Mrs. McGregor, I feel I will be with you for quite some time."

That evening, after luxuriating in a hot bath, Edward lay back in the big armchair in his bedroom and, puffing contentedly on his marcella, speculated on how long it would be before he contacted a Danish ship and replenished his particular brand of cigars. As the smoke spiralled upwards, he was in a state of near soliloquy, turning over in his mind the events which had so far influenced his life in Scotland.

As Edward cogitated, the Swedish motor ship 'Auric' was making heavy weather out in the Firth, and Chief Engineer Bjorn Bengtson was deploring the fact that the new fuel injection system had slowed his ship to a crawl and Ship's Steward Nils Thorenson was exhorting Bjorn to do something about the refrigeration system which had failed completely.

However, the speed of the ship suited Ignatius Lucius Chancitt, an American of dubious background who, as a self-professed businessman of impeccable character, had decided in the most magnanimous fashion that the ports of Leith and Grangemouth should be granted his unique talents as a water agent.

To this end, he had managed early the following morning to board the limping 'Auric' even before the officers of His Majesty's Customs and Excise. The skipper had allowed the American aboard, unwittingly thinking that he was some kind of Scottish maritime official. Fortunately for the American, the Captain did not speak English and the business card confused him even further. This, together with the trouble aboard ship and a strange man who talked through his nose, meant that he was only too pleased to pass him over to Nils.

Nils listened to Mr. Chancitt outline the type of business that he was involved in. It appeared that he was in a position to supply the best quality beef and other comestibles at prices which no-one could compete with and a special personal discount was available to anyone capable of ensuring that the sea stock order was left in his trust and care. Also, he could arrange purchase of ship-chandlers' dry goods, auxiliary ship's equipment and sailors' outfitting, if required.

Nils allowed the American full scope, realising that there was little point in interjecting; he knew the drill, he had heard it all before in various parts of the world. The proof of the pudding would be in the eating and sailors from Scandinavia always expected the best available.

"Even if everything you say is correct, Mr. Chancitt, I will not be interested in re-stocking until I am sure that the refrigeration system is working properly."

The tall cadaverous American seemed to rise a foot from his perch and, spreading his arms like the wings of some oversized vulture, pushed his beak-like nose within inches of Nils' face.

"Say, man," he drawled, "if I get your ice system fixed, do I get your sea stock order?"

Nils, although taken aback, soon asserted himself.

"You Yankees are all the same, always in too much of a hurry. However, if you can influence the engineer, Bjorn Bengtson, that his engineering problems can be solved and my refrigeration system restored to normal, then I will certainly look with favour on your tender for our sea stock order. But please remember this will not deter me from seeking the best value. If I think that you will give me value, then the order will be yours; if not, then the order will go to the agent who convinces me."

The Yankee kept pushing, but to no avail. He reckoned he had done enough to clinch a deal and thought the Scandinavian too dumb to recognise value when it was offered.

It was a very disgruntled Mr. Chancitt who descended the gangplank when the 'Auric' docked. As Edward walked up, they met halfway and the American tried to push rudely past, but Edward stepped back quickly and the man's own impetus almost put him over the side.

"Steady, old chap," said Edward.

"Go to hell," replied Mr. Chancitt.

Edward introduced himself to the Steward of the 'Auric'. Nils looked at Edward and, in a tone designed to deflate, he uttered in rather poor English a few choice expletives and ended with, "And if you think I'm going to listen to another bloody salesman this morning, then you are out of your tiny mind."

Edward, although taken aback, replied in similar vein. "Look, Herr Thorenson, I am also a seaman and can use seaman's language, but if we are going to continue insulting each other, let's at least do it in Swedish."

Thorenson was completely discomfited and felt that this man was either an extremely cool customer, or possessed the cheek of the devil. Either way, the smile on Edward's face did not dispel his embarrassment.

Edward took full advantage, "Look, my friend, I have a job to do and so have you. If someone has annoyed you, then give *them* hell." The barb struck home and Nils apologised for his bad behaviour.

"Forget it," said Edward. "There is obviously something worrying you - and speak your native Danish if you wish, your Swedish is almost as bad as your English."

Nils looked abashed and then suddenly laughed.

"How did you know I was a Dane?"

Edward's eyes twinkled and he replied, "Because I am also a Dane and when a man starts swearing he reverts often to the locality of his early manhood and, at a guess, I would say you come from Odense and your choice language from the ship yards in that area."

Edward had done it again. How could you be angry with a man such as this?

Nils burst out laughing, tears ran down his cheeks and as he wiped his eyes he felt a tug at his sleeve and, on looking up, there was Edward insisting that they call each other by their first names.

Then Nils started giving vent to his disappointment concerning his inability to conserve the ship's food supplies. Edward cut him short. "Stop worrying, Nils, I think I can solve your problem. This calls for the expertise of an engineer. I have a friend not too far away and I guarantee he will be able to help, and the ship's engineer will be pleased to know that the man is a fellow Swede. Although it is my job as a water agent to win your sea stock order, that can wait. Trust me, Nils, your problem will be solved."

An hour later Edward was seated in Sven's Edinburgh office trying his utmost to convince his friend that there was no engineer in Sweden as clever as Sven. But Sven told Edward that he was no dumb Swede, he felt he could not comply with the suggestion that his engineering experience would be invaluable in restoring the Auric's motive power and refrigeration systems. Edward was adamant that Sven was far too modest.

The conversation proceeded with Edward trying his utmost to convince his friend that his intervention was absolutely essential; and Sven declining to be involved on the basis that his engineering knowledge was limited and in any case he was employed by the Anglo-Swedish Trading Company, so his first loyalty was to them; and, of course, he was far too busy to concern himself with some hare-brained scheme that Edward might be hatching.

Edward shrugged his shoulders, shook his head in apparent resignation and as a parting shot, indicated that he was sorry that his friend was not prepared to consider increasing his earning power.

At that moment a young woman entered the office, smiled at Edward, acknowledged Sven and strode rapidly over to her desk and proceeded to deal with the day's business.

Sven introduced the young lady.

"This is my secretary, Miss Felicity Brown."

Edward was taken aback - the name Brown conjured up his erstwhile landlady and her three marriageable daughters. If this was one of them, then she was certainly worth looking at. A graceful figure, a head of flaming gold, soft hazel eyes and a face he seemed to recognise. He wondered ... if only her hair had been auburn and the eyes a clear sea green, then she could have been the young woman he had met in the house in Sandport Street.

"I am pleased to meet you," he said. "You remind me of another beautiful girl, her name is Maggie, is she a relative?"

She blushed slightly and turning to Sven she remarked, "Your friend is very observant, or could it be his usual line of patter, Sven?"

"Cut it out, Edward, I must inform you that Felicity is not only my secretary, she also happens to be my fiancée."

Edward was not in the least perturbed.

"I must congratulate you, Sven, you certainly have good taste."

And turning to Felicity, "I meant what I said."

Felicity smiled. "Yes, Maggie is my sister and as you seem to be a connoisseur of womanly charm, it might interest you to know that I have another sister, Jeannie."

"How interesting," said Edward, "but please do give my regards to Maggie when you see her."

"I will," replied Felicity, and her female curiosity prompted her to ask what Sven and Edward had been arguing about when she entered the office.

Edward deferred the answer to Sven, who was adamant that his friend was like that other Dane, Hans Anderson, and seemed to live perpetually in fairyland.

But Felicity had heard Edward mentioning earning power, and if, as she suspected, this was linked with the man she was grooming for marriage, then any propensity towards pecuniary gain must be considered seriously.

Edward seized the opportunity to outline his reasons why Sven should accept the challenge of solving the mechanical problems of the M.S. Auric, and further his reputation and earning power accordingly.

Once the woman understood the position, she agreed with Edward and their combined forces overcame the reluctance of Sven to comply.

"Well," said Edward, "after two hours trying to convince Sven, you appear and a few minutes later he agrees. It all happened so fast, Felicity, or is your name velocity?"

The young lady was not amused. "Call me that again and I'll thump you," she replied.

"And if she doesn't, I will," interrupted Sven. "I don't think you realise, Edward, that to imply a young lady is fast in Scotland is an indication that her virtue is in question."

Edward was taken aback; he knew he had blundered and apologised so profusely that Felicity could not help but forgive him. And then, advancing towards Sven, she asked him, "I hope you remembered to get the dance tickets for tonight?"

"Yes, I have the tickets, in fact the Seaman's Institute gave me some to sell."

With an alacrity which surprised Sven, Edward asked for two tickets.

That evening Felicity and Maggie Brown arrived at the dance accompanied by the two young Scandinavians. Sven's behaviour as usual was impeccable and Edward conducted himself in the correct and proper fashion of a young man who had determined that he would never again give Maggie cause to bang his head against the headboard. He tripped the light fantastic with consummate ease and so delighted Maggie that when the St. Bernard's Waltz was announced, she steered Edward through what to him must have seemed uncharted waters. Having a natural rhythm, he did not disgrace himself and reacted to Maggie's ministrations with such enthusiasm that she could not deny dancing with him for most of the evening. They would have danced all night had not Felicity and Sven succeeded in exhorting the dancers to accompany them in search of refreshment.

On leaving the dance hall, Felicity and Maggie lagged somewhat behind the two men, conducting an animated discussion as they walked. It seemed to centre mainly on the type of meal they should have and where their appointed escorts should take them.

"Sven usually takes me to the Elite," said Felicity. "The cuisine is the best in town and the people you meet there are so refined."

"Good for you," replied Maggie. "You can keep your posh nosh as far as I am concerned. I'd rather have something substantial in the company of real folk, so I'm going to ask my laddie to take me to Dagostini's Fish Restaurant."

"You're always the same," snapped Felicity. "It won't do your figure any good either."

The men exchanged smiles and agreed that the sisters would have to be steered in different directions if disaster was to be averted.

Just as the sisters were preparing for round two, Sven nudged Edward and then, smiling to Maggie, stepped forward and taking Felicity by the arm, led her away in the direction of the Elite. Edward, meanwhile, had linked arms with Maggie, assuring her as he did so that he too preferred a substantial fish dish.

"Now show me the way to Dagostini's, Maggie, and I will ensure that you get the type of supper you relish."

It had all happened so quickly and she wondered why she had allowed Edward to take her arm. Then, looking at his smiling face and feeling his jaunty step at her side - this, together with the obvious happiness he was experiencing in being with her, answered her question.

She laughed merrily when Edward assured her that Felicity's remarks should not be taken seriously and, as far as he was concerned, she had a lovely figure. After all, her work was hard and a working girl should be looked after properly. He wondered, however, why she was so fond of that fellow McCallum. She tore her arm free and almost spat out the words, "What did you say?"

Edward, still smiling, indicated that he was only reiterating what she had already said to her sister. "I heard you say that you have always liked McCallum."

Her anger subsided rapidly and gave way to laughter.

"Away you go, you daft Dane, a 'McCallum' is an ice cream dish very popular in Edinburgh."

Edward, in no way abashed, smiled serenely, and as he did so she caught a glimpse of mischief in his eyes.

"You must forgive me Maggie, my knowledge concerning things Scottish is very limited, but with you to help me I am sure I will learn fast, so let's not waste time, a working girl must be fed, do lead me to Dagostini's."

She thought, 'He is not as daft as he appears.'

But she said, "You are forgiven and, as I am starving, let's go."

They re-linked arms and, as they did so, Maggie intertwined her fingers through his and as they strolled happily along she looked into those mischievous eyes and said, "I think I like you."

Anyone reading the Evening News that night would have had their attention drawn to a prominent front page advertisement indicating that Dagostini's were equipped to supply what they so eloquently described as a 'Piscatorial Feast'. Edward and Maggie availed themselves of the offer and afterwards Maggie expressed the view that the supper was just fabulous, with Edward readily agreeing that Dagostini certainly knew how to cook and present fish.

Relaxing after supper, Edward caressed his Marcella and blew small smoke rings, while Maggie contentedly sipped her McCallum. The young couple exchanged knowing smiles, an indication of an experience that had brought them that bit closer together. From then on, like many young people attracted to each other, they recounted their lives in retrospect. They would have talked all evening had not Edward realised that they were the only ones remaining in the restaurant and that possibly he was failing in his duty as an escort in keeping the young lady out so late.

As they strolled down the 'Walk', Edward attempted to apologise for talking too much and keeping Maggie out later than he intended.

"Never fear, Edward, I'm enjoying myself. I like your company and, what's more, I could listen all night to you recounting your experiences in foreign parts and I would rather that you should spin yarns than I should have to think about spinning rope down at the factory tomorrow morning."

Edward understood how she felt, but being a realist, he knew he had over-elaborated his adventures and wondered if he had just gone too far. Still, on the other hand, if it amused Maggie and made her happy, then possibly he could forgive himself his tendency towards exaggeration.

"Tell me, Maggie, surely life in Leith must be interesting; to me the place looks a bustling prosperous sea port."

She smiled. "It is, Edward, but when you work at a monotonous job all day as I do, then you tend to forget how interesting life in Leith can be."

By this time the young couple had reached the foot of The Walk and, turning right, they entered the Links, a long tree-lined sward which led down to the Docks. It was dark now and, as Maggie held closer to Edward, she confessed to a feeling of unease as they made their way along the main path. Edward assured her that she was safe and that he would look after her. As they passed a dimly lit gaslight, she smiled to him and he caught a glimpse of Maggie in profile. He liked what he saw and felt that good fortune had indeed smiled on him. But what intrigued him was the strong jaw line of the young lady. To him it indicated character and he knew then that Maggie was no more afraid of the dark than he was, but if, as he suspected, she liked being close to him, then he would assist wholeheartedly in such a pleasant exercise. And if, as it seemed, walking was involved, then he was all for it, particularly when it entailed going hand in hand or arm in arm with such a delightful companion.

They had almost reached the end of the path when just ahead of them loomed what appeared to be a rather large stone building and, to the right and in the background, a number of shed-like structures were beginning to appear. Maggie gave a little shrug and pulled on Edward's arm.

"Let's go to the left, Edward, I don't want to see the Ropery tonight - time enough in the morning."

By this time it was quite dark and the stars were clearly visible.

"How right you are, Maggie. Forget the job, look up at the sky and let me tell you something about the stars."

Edward, although a young man, had amassed in his short life as a sailor many experiences both weird and wonderful which, allied to an exuberant spirit and an acute imagination, made him an accomplished storyteller. To the delight of his companion, he expanded on his adventures as a sailor, but this time he did dwell on how the stars assisted the mariner in his peregrinations. Whilst drawing attention to the heavenly bodies, he circumnavigated Maggie's waist and from time to time he gave her a gentle hug. By the time they reached the Shore, the young couple were exchanging confidences and had tacitly agreed that they were indeed good for each other.

As they crossed the bridge, they were so engrossed in mutual adoration that they almost bumped into the two men standing outside the Sailor's Rest.

"So we meet again, Edward!" a voice boomed out and looking up they saw Sven and Mr. McLeod smiling at their apparent discomfiture.

"You are late, Edward. I left Felicity more than an hour ago."

Edward, recovering rapidly, answered with his usual aplomb.

"Time stands still when I'm out with Maggie. As you can see, I have become quite attached to her."

Maggie gave his arm a gentle squeeze indicating her appreciation. He smiled to her and, turning to Mr.

McLeod, he attempted to introduce Maggie to the big man.

"You are too late, Edward," said McLeod. I've known Maggie since she was a bairn; she was bonny then, aye, and she is even bonnier now that she has reached womanhood."

Edward seemed bewildered and, as his brow furrowed, Maggie realised that the young Dane could not be expected to understand some of the Scottish terms that the Exciseman had used and hastened to explain what they meant. Once explained, he smiled broadly, turned and complimented Mr. McLeod on his acute perception.

"I agree, Rory, and I feel sure that beauty deserves her sleep and if you will excuse us, gentlemen, I will escort Maggie home without further delay."

As they parted company, Sven reminded Edward that he had an appointment the following morning.

"I will see you as arranged, Sven; nine o'clock tomorrow morning at the Imperial Dock."

As they passed the Commercial Hotel at the foot of Sandport Street, Maggie was prompted to ask Edward where he would be staying the night. When he told her he was lodging with Mrs. McGregor at Grangemouth, she left him in no doubt what she thought.

"The 'Grange' is more than twenty miles away and, if you intend to meet Sven tomorrow morning at nine, you won't have much time for sleep, and in any case, how are you going to get there at this time of night?"

When he explained that he intended to cycle, she immediately advised against it. Woman-like, Maggie had already decided that Edward must be safeguarded, even against himself. She impressed on him that to get to the 'Grange' and back would take far too long. She also felt that having treated her so well all evening, it was now time for her to reciprocate by looking after her partner. The spare bedroom was vacant and Maggie felt sure that her mother would be delighted if Edward made use of it for the night.

Edward, knowing full well that the essence of diplomacy is in keeping one's mouth shut, did just that, smiled and then acquiesced. After all, being with Maggie for the rest of the evening was most appealing.

As the cold east wind from the Firth swept up Sandport Street, Maggie clung closer to Edward. When they reached the stairway leading to Mrs. Brown's house, they swept up to the first flat, arms entwined, laughing and stamping their feet to keep out the cold. Momentarily Maggie's mood changed.

"We'll have to keep quiet, Edward, or we might waken the auld yins."

Although he did not fully understand what she meant by the 'auld yins', he realised that silence was paramount. He put his arm round her neck and shoulders, drew her close and whispered his apologies.

"I will be as quiet as a mice."

It required a great effort on Maggie's part not to laugh out loud. Singular or plural, it was hard to conceive anyone less mouse-like than Edward.

"You need a man to keep you warm, Maggie, in this cold weather."

She pushed him away. "I wouldn't see a man in my road and what is more I don't need a Scotch Muffler, let alone a Scandinavian one."

Edward, although bemused, smiled and contrived his most innocent look, trusting that his underlying natural charm would influence Maggie in his favour.

"If I have offended you, then I apologise, Maggie."

Her heart melted. "All right," she whispered, "it's as much my fault as yours, but let us keep it quiet."

Opening the door she ushered him in. As she lit the lobby gas, allowing just sufficient light to illuminate the parlour, Edward settled himself down in the low-down sofa. He was joined presently by Maggie, who nestled down beside him. They looked into each others' eyes, words were unnecessary, the auld yins would not be disturbed that night.

While Edward paid court, caressing, fondling and flattering, Maggie responded by encouraging, acquiescing or playing coy, according to the prevailing mood. They were happy in each others' company and Maggie thought of Edward and those who had preceded him. There was Jock Broadbent, the butcher, and Alec Mackay, an Edinburgh Compositor. Both had paid court to Maggie. Jock was the physical type, a footballer, an accomplished dancer, but awkward in the social graces. Whilst Alec could talk the hind legs off a donkey, but also danced like one. Edward, though, despite the very short time she had known him, was unique. He was kind, had an acute sense of humour, could dance divinely and was certainly accomplished in the social graces. Most important, she liked him and could see the potential happiness ahead in linking herself with such an exciting and enterprising young man.

Had Edward known what Maggie was thinking, he would no doubt have awarded her top marks for intelligent observation. Maggie, likewise, would have been pleased and flattered if she had known what Edward thought of her.

Although the young man had been engrossed in paying attention to Maggie, he had, for a few fleeting moments, thought of some of the women during his life as a young sailor. There had been Cilexia from Lithuania, a beautiful blonde who had welcomed Edward's attention, but in the final analysis lacked a sense of humour.

Also Nicola, the Hungarian spitfire with the oversized hips and ponderous breasts, full of fire, but too prone to promiscuity. Most recently, Balim, a dusky maiden from the Friendly Islands, full of eastern promise, but for Edward the promise was never fulfilled.

Yes, thought Edward, Maggie was indeed unique. She was, as McLeod had said, bonnie. But she was far more; she had a delightful sense of humour and most certainly a lovely figure, which he was in the process of discovering. Also, she was a woman of strong character and independent mind. Edward, realising this from the start, had accepted the challenge and without hesitation had set out to please his companion, and, happily, there had been a rapport between the two young people which had developed into real affection.

Making love with Maggie was an experience he would not forget and to think that, if he had been dumb enough, he would now be wearily cycling back to the 'Grange'.

Someone once said, 'We live and learn', or was it 'We love and learn'?

Chapter 5

The following morning the eastern seaboard from Aberdeen to Leith and beyond was shrouded in dense fog, visibility was almost nil. The low wailing of the sirens brought Edward to the bedroom window and what he saw made him frown, but almost immediately he felt a warm feeling and chuckled when he realised that if he had not spent the night with Maggie, he would now be attempting to cycle some twenty miles or so from Grangemouth to Leith in icy fog to keep his appointment with Sven at the Imperial Dock.

Having time to relax, he leisurely stropped his German razor, a gift from his father, and contemplated a possible programme for the day. Toilet finished and plans made, he thanked Mrs. Brown for her hospitality, descended the stairs, then lit the acetylene lamp on the front of Mr. Richard's elegant velocipede.

Cycling down Sandport Street, his attention was drawn to a shop sign that interested him. In the swirling mist, he could just make out the words 'John Blackwell - Butcher'. He dismounted, crossed the street and parked the bicycle outside the shop. After waiting until the shoppers had been served, he entered and was greeted by the owner.

John Blackwell could be described as a patriarchal type. He had white silvery hair, pale blue penetrating eyes and a smile which indicated his readiness to satisfy any potential customer.

"What can I do for you?" he asked.

Edward, although appreciative of the old man's attitude, left him in no doubt that it was not just a matter of what Mr. Blackwell could do for him, more important was what they could do for each other. A wonderful smile wreathed the character-lined face of the old man, his eyes seemed to sparkle as he surveyed Edward through his rimless spectacles. He liked the young man and listened attentively to what he had to say.

Edward expressed himself candidly and did not hide his association with Tam Richards, the Grangemouth butcher, but indicated that what he had already seen in Leith gave promise of a bright future for a go-ahead Water Agent. He stressed that although his immediate loyalty was to Tam, he was seriously considering transferring his attention to the Port of Leith and, if he did so, would Mr. Blackwell be interested in what he termed mutual aid?

The old man, although kind, was no fool, a shrewd businessman, President of the Butchers' Federation; he had lived long enough to feel that this man would be worthy of trust. After their conversation they shook hands and, as Edward left, Mr. Blackwell assured him that he would be pleased to see him again should he decide in the future to make Leith his base.

The fog forced Edward to cycle warily through the docks. On reaching the Imperial, he dismounted at the gangway leading up to the Auric. Having time to spare, he looked around, wondering how long it would be before his friend arrived. After a few minutes of peering through the swirling mist, he became restive, speculating on what could have happened to the usually punctilious Sven. Deciding to shelter from the cold wind, he ascended the gangway, whilst keeping a weather eye for any sign of the Swede. As he stepped onto the main deck, a big figure loomed in front of him. It was Sven.

"Where the hell did you come from?" exclaimed the startled Edward.

The big man smiled and gestured towards amidships. They entered an alleyway which led to the steward's pantry, and sitting inside was Nils Thorenson and a big powerful man in engineer's overalls.

"I know you have already met Nils," said Sven, "but let me introduce you to Bjorn Bengtson, Chief Engineer of the Auric."

Bjorn apologised to Edward for persuading Sven to board the ship while he was waiting for him at the dockside.

"You see, Edward, we both served our apprenticeships together in Gothenburg and, as we had not met for years, I'm afraid he succumbed to my insistence that he should come aboard."

"*Frucost*, Edward," interjected Nils, as he pointed to a table on which rested the essentials of a Danish breakfast. Edward shook his head, assuring his friend he had already breakfasted on good Scottish fare, including the redoubtable porridge. But Sven suggested he should still eat something after cycling more than twenty miles in icy cold weather. When Edward revealed he had spent the night with Maggie at Sandport Street, Sven grimaced as he turned to Nils and Bjorn.

"And to think I was worried about Edward. I should have known better."

Bjorn shrugged his powerful shoulders and indicated he was glad that Edward was a survivor; after all he had been instrumental in bringing them both together again. Edward addressed himself to Nils.

"While these two Swedes concern themselves with my ability to survive, don't you think it's about time that something was done for this dehydrated Dane."

Nils laughed heartily, disappeared into his pantry and returned almost immediately with drinks.

"*Varsigo*, Edward," he said, "here is your schnapps, the lager could have been colder if Bjorn had been able to fix the refrigeration system in time."

Bjorn shook his head, his usually impassive face crinkled at the eyes and the corners of his mouth rose, exposing strong white teeth in an admonitory smile; but he assured Nils, as he did so, that his 'ice box' would function once he had solved how to maintain power in the auxiliary system. Then, turning to Sven, he reiterated the difficulty he had been experiencing with the new fuel injection system. Sven assured Bjorn that he had just two years before supervised the installation of the same type of engines and auxiliary equipment in a ship similar to the Auric.

"Between the two of us, Bjorn, it will not be long before the Auric thrusts its way out to the North Sea."

On hearing Sven's remarks, Edward asked excitedly, "Are you telling us, Sven, that you are confident of success?"

"Yes, I'm confident," said Sven, rather testily.

"I am pleased," replied Edward, "that my trust in your ability to solve Bjorn's engineering problems has been fully justified."

Bjorn seemed perplexed, wondering if Edward, as well as being a salesman, was also an expert in marine engineering. Sven gave a wry smile and agreed that Edward was indeed an expert: he was an expert in dreaming up weird and wonderful ideas which in their execution had been a source of happiness to his associates; but some of his projects had, on occasion, proved abortive, causing feelings of anger, amazement or amusement, according to the circumstances in which the participants found themselves involved. One thing was certain, Edward was an expert optimist.

Sven had to agree, however, that on this occasion Edward had been right in persuading him to offer his services to the Chief Engineer of the Auric. After all Edward, in his persistence, had been responsible for reuniting the two Swedes.

Bjorn, now in a more forthcoming mood, had to agree that whatever the motive, the end result was such that Edward this time should be complimented. Edward agreed wholeheartedly with this observation and promised that his good services would always be available when required. Then, complimenting Nils on keeping a good establishment, he raised his glass and gave a skol to the Auric and her crew.

Having achieved the first part of his day's programme, Edward was elated, but realised that good fortune had played a bigger part than he had in the end result. If Sven and Bjorn had not known each other, his task would have been much more difficult, but he felt confident that he had been chosen as the appointed instrument of providence. As he descended the gangway of the Auric he found that the fog had almost lifted and decided that it was an opportune time to explore the docks and the immediate neighbourhood before returning to Grangemouth.

It took almost an hour to cover the area and acquaint himself with the names and position of the various docks. He smiled ruefully when reading the names above the dock sheds. Victoria, Albert, Imperial and suchlike, all names associated with an advanced imperial state. He recollected what his old fisherman father had said, that the English always had to be at war. He wondered how such a relatively small country through its naval power had been able to subjugate almost half the world and felt sad that such a powerful nation had advanced no further in the pursuance of peace and humanity than his Viking forebears who had pillaged these shores more than a millennium before.

But this was Scotland - surely this beautiful country, which had produced such men as Burns, Maxton and McLean, would sooner or later assert itself and ensure that need would ultimately replace the greed and imbalance of the present system.

As he passed through the dock gates which led to the shore, he was soon reminded that he was not the only one concerned with earning a living. From what he had seen, he reckoned that the people of Leith were fully occupied ensuring that their town could, with satisfaction, be called the busiest and most successful port on the eastern seaboard.

He stopped and watched the little world of Leith pass him by. Horse-drawn carts trundled through the gates, loaded with goods for export, cases of whisky, engines, boilers, engineering equipment and many other manufacturer products. While in the other direction came loads of timber, sacks of grain, fruit, butter, bacon and other comestibles. Crossing their path, both inside and outside the docks, were locomotive-drawn wagons filled with coal to fuel ships setting out to sea. The heavier lorries were drawn by powerful Clydesdales.

This was not the first time he had witnessed life in a busy port, but it was the first time he had seen such tremendous loads pulled by those famous horses. The Swedish dalarna and other Scandinavian horses, although powerful, were much smaller and could not match the Clydesdale for size and strength. These magnificent animals, in Edward's eyes, constituted the strength athletes of the world of horses. He could only stand and stare at those big beautiful beasts and admire their outstanding physical condition and the gleaming harness which reflected the pride and esteem in which they were held by the Carters of Leith.

Crossing over to the shore, he was stopped in his tracks as a motor horn blared in his ear and, to his left, a small petrol float almost ran him down. It was loaded with blocks of ice, presumably on its way to the local butchers. As it passed, a young man took his hands off the steering, placed them together at the sides of his head and, smiling, indicated that Edward would have to stop daydreaming if he wished to stay alive.

Edward raised his arms in a gesture accepting that he was at fault, but thought that if progress meant that there would be more of these noisy and smelly petrol-driven vehicles, then he was all for retention of the horse. He felt that to meander longer would accomplish little and set off quickly along the shore, noting as he walked the whereabouts of offices, shops and other establishments which might have to be contacted should he decide to reside in Leith some time in the future.

By the time he reached the swing bridge, the road had been closed to traffic to allow a small steamer clear passageway to a repair yard upstream. He knew that to make for Grangemouth he would have to cross the bridge and then straight on for almost two hours before he reached his destination. A few minutes later the bridge swung round and Edward crossed over. Reaching the other side he stopped to admire a rather imposing building, not because of an interest in architecture, more the artistry of the caption well above eye level. It read 'The Sailor's Rest'. Remembering the night out with Sven and Rory, he felt that this place would be as good as any for a little refreshment and sustenance.

When he entered he thought he was in a different place - the roof seemed higher and the bar much longer, but he soon realised that he was in what the Scots called the Public bar, whereas his friends had entertained him in the smaller lounge bar. The bar was filled to capacity, carters, dockers and shipyard workers drinking their pints and eating scotch pies or sandwiches. Despite the height of the roof, the room was filled with tobacco smoke emanating in the main from short-stemmed clay pipes. But this, it seemed, did not deter the workers from enjoying their pie and pint. Edward had never tasted a scotch pie before and wondered if it would prove a worthwhile experience. Arming himself with a pie and a pint, he elbowed his way gently through the madding crowd until he reached a small table in the far corner. From his vantage point he could see that, despite the pall of blue black smoke, some fifty or sixty hungry and thirsty men were refuelling for their next stint in the docks.

His attention was drawn to a docker who approached a brass plate on the counter filled with clay pipes, selected one, broke off a piece of the stem and dipped it into his beer before inserting the pipe in his mouth. The ritual puzzled Edward, but he noticed that some of the men were smoking pipes so short that the bowl seemed almost to rest in the mouth.

One old man, the focus of attention, was regaling his audience with jokes that had them in stitches. As he spoke, his toothless mouth contorted in such a way that the pipe seemed to disappear into his mouth and re-appear every few seconds. Edward could barely restrain himself from laughing outright and felt sure that the audience were enjoying his sleight of mouth more than the content of his stories.

Two Norwegian sailors seemed to be holding court at the far end of the bar, surrounded by sailors, dockers and company porters. They were in the main big men and appeared to be trying to resolve the question of who was the best hand wrestler amongst them. Having bought his pie and pint, Edward started to move towards them, but seeing a carter lifting a clay pipe from the tray, asked politely why the men smoked their pipes with such short stems.

He looked Edward up and down and then rather brusquely said, "I can see you are not from these pairts. Just you think what it is like to sit on a cairt wi' the auld horse ambling slowly along wi' a heavy load and the man sitting cauld and sair because he canna move and has tae suffer the cauld East wind blawin in his face. Then a pipe o' tobacco can be a solace and the closer ti yer moo the better and the warmer it is. To sum it up, we call it the 'jaw warmer'."

Edward thanked the carter, smiled and acknowledged that he understood. When he reached the hand wrestlers, he sat down at a small table where he could weigh up form and watch the final stages of the competition. It appeared that one of the Norwegians had been eliminated, despite his six foot and fourteen stone frame. The other Norwegian still in the contest was bigger and heavier than his compatriot by some four inches and four stones, and when he divested his seaman's jacket, his physique brought forth gasps of admiration from all around him.

Two of the other three men remaining in the contest agreed that he certainly looked the favourite, but the third man, a company porter, thought otherwise. He had, as he said, 'couped a bigger man not so long ago.'

"But you are not expected to coup him, Hector," said one wag. "The idea is to flatten his arm to the table before he flattens you."

But Hector, all nineteen stones of him, was not in the least impressed. After the tossing of a coin, the draw was made. Hector was drawn against a 'Bull-neck'ed German sailor with powerful shoulders, and the remaining competitor, a young warehouseman six feet in height and weighing barely thirteen stones, was drawn against the Scandinavian giant.

Although more than four stones lighter, he looked decidedly athletic, his strong arms and wrists indicating strength far in advance of his weight. But the young man had no illusions, he knew full well that his task would be formidable, if not impossible; but like a true Scot, he was determined to prove that at the least he was a competitor worthy of respect.

The penultimate stage having been reached, the atmosphere was now tense and as the two men sat down at the table next to Edward, the hubbub of voices ceased dramatically as men moved nearer to the two contestants. Edward, fortunately, had a good view as the referee ensured that there should be enough space between the competitors and spectators to guarantee a proper contest. The two men started in the approved fashion, left hand behind the back, elbows on the table with forearms as vertical as possible and hands clasped firmly together.

For the first minute the determined young Scot made headway and shifted his opponent's arm two or three inches from the vertical position, but by the end of the next minute, their arms were back to the start. From then on the young Scot's face took on an ever ruddier hue and his arm quivered progressively more and more as he strove to resist the inexorable strength of the big Scandinavian. As his arm was forced flat to the table, applause broke out, not so much for the victor, more for the young man who had tried so hard. They gathered round, clapping him on the back for a gallant effort and the big Norwegian smilingly acknowledged that his opponent had indeed performed with remarkable tenacity, and, as if to emphasise his feelings, he ruffled the young man's hair, shook his hand and congratulated him on his performance.

As the stage was being set for the second semi final, Edward drew the young man aside and asked if he could speak with him. The conversation which ensued centred on the sport of hand wrestling, Edward offering the opinion that although strength was a major factor, there was also an art involved which, if applied properly, could enhance the performance to such a degree that often the lighter man could win. As the young man listened attentively, Edward explained the more intricate mechanics of arm wrestling. It was not long before they realised that introductions were necessary and Edward found he had been speaking to Steve Allrock, a warehouseman in the bonded stores of the Highland Princess Distillery Company. Steve became increasingly enthusiastic as Edward developed his subject.

While Steve and Edward had been talking, Hector the company porter and the German sailor, already dubbed "huff and puff" by a discriminating audience, had finished their stint. Hector, it appeared, had, with one last grunt, vanquished the German as he emitted his final groan.

After a short refuelling interval, Hector drained his pint and stepped forward to prove that he would be capable of 'couping' the big Norwegian. However the big, strong, but rather overweight company porter was completely outclassed by the powerful Norwegian sailor. As the top harpooner in the whaling fleet, his strong chest, shoulders and arms were ideally designed for the sport of arm wrestling.

Watching the contest, Steve admitted that he would like to have been matched against Hector, but confessed that the company porter had beaten him every time they had met in the past. However, he felt that he might possibly have beaten him on this occasion. Although he could not have expected to win against the Norwegian, at least he would have been one of the final contenders. As the contest finished with Hector having been eliminated in about three minutes, Edward encouraged the young man to think in more positive terms.

"If you are prepared to trust me," said Edward, "and to do as I instruct you, I will not only arrange a match for you with Hector, I will wager that you will win."

Steve, after a little hesitation, smiled and agreed to Edward's proposal. After several minutes of teaching, followed by a short spell of mutual plotting and planning, Edward approached the bar and asked Hector if he would like to win a pound. Hector's brow furrowed and then he asked, "Depends what I have to do."

"Beat young Steve in an arm-wrestling match," Edward answered.

"Is that all?" was the big man's offhand rejoinder.

"Not quite," said Edward. "If he beats you then you give me a pound."

"It will be the easiest pound that's come my way for a long time," was the big man's reply.

Edward felt a tug at his shoulder. As he turned abruptly his forehead almost struck the beak-like nose of Mr. Chancitt, the American, who at that moment had entered the bar. The mouth of the American opened wide, displaying a prime example of advanced tooth decay, salvaged to some degree by the miracle of American dental technology. As he spoke from that gold-flecked labyrinth, his words were accompanied by gusts of stale alcohol, camouflaged by some obnoxious perfumed cachets.

"Bud, I've an English pound here that says Hector will flatten the kid."

Edward, although annoyed by the American's abrupt behaviour, felt he had to react without being too rude. With a disarming smile, he took the rather soiled note from Mr. Chancitt and, placing it on the counter, together with two pounds from his pocket, he turned to Hector and asked him to add his contribution if he still felt he could beat Steve. The big man's attitude was decisive.

"Let's no waste time, I've a couple o' pints to down before I start my shift at the docks."

Edward was pleased; so far his plan had worked.

"I see that the table is occupied. Have you any objection to risking your reputation right here at the bar?"

The big man did not deign to reply.

Both men were now at the bar, Edward having ensured that Steve was standing to the right of Hector. The referee was a man of medium height, neatly dressed, almost dapper, who had originally been second mate on a Finnish steamer carrying timber to

Grangemouth. Leaving his ship, he had secured employment in the timber yard and by a series of steps had ultimately become chief clerk of the biggest ship chandlers on the East coast. In his spare time he was the self-appointed chairman of social amenities in most of the pubs in Leith's dockland. He was known as Karl and, in his most professional manner, he saw to it that both men were so positioned that only the use of the right arm would determine the winner.

Hector was grinning now, he had always beaten Steve in the past and saw no reason why the pattern should not continue. The dockers and others around thought the same, but many felt that it would do no harm if only young Steve could deflate the pompous and belligerent porter.

With a grunt louder than usual, Hector moved Steve's hand some three inches from the starting position. Steve's expression was grim and determined and after two minutes he had managed to hold steady, much to the surprise of everyone, including Hector. His brow furrowed, a sure indication that everything was not going to plan.

At that moment, Edward caught the eye of Steve. The young warehouseman seemed more relaxed now and gave a ghost of a smile as Edward nodded. Steve knew then what he had to do. It was with some satisfaction that Edward saw Steve curl his wrist ever so slightly towards his chest. For a full minute Hector again tried to shift Steve's arm towards the counter, but with no success. The atmosphere was tense, the audience knew that something unusual was happening. An attentive observer would have noticed that the young man was more intent on holding his position and pulling his arm closer to his body than in trying to force the big man's arm downwards. Even Hector realised this, but rather late. By this time Hector's hand was very close to Steve's chest, which meant that he would have to exert far more pressure than Steve if he was determined to win. Edward had made sure that Steve understood that the nearer a weight or force is to the body, the easier it is to control and, conversely, as the hand travels further from the body, control and effort becomes progressively harder.

Added to this, Steve had the advantage of facing outwards, which meant that in addition to the strength of arm, his body weight could be added, whereas Hector, facing inwards, could rely only on the strength of his arm.

Two minutes later, the new-found skill of Steve had triumphed over the brute strength of Hector and, with one last despairing grunt, Hector felt his arm slap down on the bar counter.

It was all over and the pent-up emotions of the crowd erupted. They gathered round Steve, clapping him on the back and congratulating him on teaching big Hector a lesson he would never forget. Collecting his winnings from Karl Kaluka, Edward put two pounds back in his pocket, gave the pound he had won from Hector to Steve and gave the remaining pound to the barman, asking him to set up drinks for the competitors.

Steve, with a drink in his hand, approached and thanked him for the advice and support he had given. Edward smiled and, acknowledging Steve's thanks, advised that in the future should Hector challenge him, he should ensure that he took up position at the right side of the bar, with his forearm facing outwards.

"Remember what I said, Steve, all muscles pull and the closer your hand is to your body, the stronger you will be."

As Edward started towards the door he was halted in his tracks by the big Norwegian, who raised his glass in front of him and gave the salutary 'skol'. Edward looked at the man in a quizzical but friendly manner and asked "Norske?"

The big man smiled and nodded and within seconds the two Scandinavians were recounting their reactions to the Scottish scene. It appeared that the big Norwegian and his mate had arrived in Grangemouth in the whaling ship Odin to pick up some special equipment, prior to sailing to South Georgia. Edward's ears pricked up when he heard what had happened on the journey from Christiania. Leaving Norway, the weather had deteriorated rapidly and within two hours a force ten gale had hit that part of the North Sea and five members of the crew, including the second steward, had become violently sick. The old sailors aboard had felt that the young men were not tough enough, not realising that other factors had intervened with most unpleasant results. It was a very worried ship's doctor who, after intensive investigation, discovered that his patients were suffering from an insidious type of food poisoning. It was found that the young steward had drawn, contrary to instructions, food from sea stock designated for consumption between Scotland and the Antarctic. The doctor had struggled valiantly and had succeeded in saving the young sailors, but unfortunately the second steward had died just before the ship entered Grangemouth. When the ship berthed, the sailors had been rushed to Edinburgh Royal Infirmary where, after examination and treatment, they had been allowed to return to their ship, except Big Olaf, the second engineer, renowned as a trencherman extraordinaire. The infirmary had outlined their findings to the Department of Health and, after a threat of quarantine, the Norsk Fiskeri Company had destroyed all food stocks and ensured that all food containers and implements were rendered completely sterile, thus ensuring that the ship could be effectively cleared and allowed to proceed to the whaling grounds.

As the story unfolded, Edward became more and more interested. Although he deplored the death of the young steward, he realised that the ship would have to be re-stocked before setting out for South Georgia. Not being a devious man, Edward was frank enough to divulge his thoughts to the big Norwegian. He understood and, appreciating Edward's candour, replied, "If I were you, I would move very fast if you want to clinch the Odin sea stock order. There is already one man after it and he is not very far away."

He gave a wink and a nudge and as Edward slewed round on his stool, he came face to face with the American. He reacted quickly.

"Ah, the man who thought that Big Hector would beat the Kid."

The American was not amused.

"You Norskis think you've got it made," he said and, pointing to Edward, he gave vent to his feelings. "You've had it, you son of a bitch, I've already secured the order for the Odin."

Although perturbed, Edward responded in characteristic fashion and, smiling serenely, replied tersely, "I very much doubt it."

The American's arms moved out from his sides in a most dramatic fashion and as he rested his hands on his hips he resembled a gigantic crow, unable to fly but able to croak.

"Call me a liar? Do you know who I am? My name is Ignatius Lucius Chancitt, citizen of the U.S. of A. and at present the top Water Agent on the East Coast of Scotland."

Edward contrived a look of open-mouthed amazement and then, adopting a more serious expression, offered his condolences. "I am indeed sorry that such a brilliant fellow should have such an unfortunate name."

Before the American could respond, he continued in a most learned fashion. "Surely you realise that you will impress no-one if you say, 'Trust me, I. L. Chancitt'."

65

The American, realising rather belatedly that Edward was having fun at his expense, gave a loud squawk of rage and lunged towards him. As the claw-like hand reached out, Edward stepped clear and as he did so he saw the American's arm stiffen in mid air. When he turned, he saw the big Norwegian holding Chancitt's wrist in a vice-like grip. For the first few seconds he squealed and squirmed, his face becoming grey with pain as the powerful fingers bit deep into his flesh. The usually voluble Mr. Chancitt was now reduced to almost silent sufferance, but despairingly just managed to whimper, "Oh - for Chris-sake."

The Norwegian, his face impassive, released his grip, then waving an admonitory finger, delivered an ultimatum.

"You are a bad man, you go now - quick, or I get very angry."

As the big man released him, he lost no time in scuttling for the door, but found time to snarl at Edward. "I'll fix you, bloody Norski!"

Still sitting on his stool, the big Norwegian looked straight into Edward's eyes and seemed to contemplate what might have happened had he not intervened between him and the American. He then gave vent to his feelings in the Norwegian tongue, knowing that Edward would understand.

He described himself as a man who deplored violence and had seen too many tragedies where men, for one reason or another, were determined to assert what they thought was their superiority. He thought Edward could probably have handled the situation himself, but for the sake of peace, he did it his way to ensure that neither he nor the American suffered serious injury.

"Believe me," he said, "I know only too well what can happen. Even I, strong as I am, know that a knife or a bullet from some dark corner could finish my short sojourn on earth. I warn you that when that American is around do not leave your back exposed."

Edward assured his new-found friend that he understood perfectly.

"Such morbid thoughts, but I know that you mean well, my friend, and I will do as you bid," said Edward, "but let us not be so morose, let's give a skol to happiness and a brighter future."

They toasted each other, then Edward shook hands with the two Norwegians and made his way towards the door after bidding them farewell.

Mounting his bicycle, he made post haste for Grangemouth. Would he reach the 'Grange' in time, or had Chancitt really been telling the truth?

Chapter 6

The three women were enjoying themselves, their peals of laughter could even be heard in the front shop, although they were ensconced in the inner sanctum of Einer Wevling's Emporium.

The manageress nudged an assistant. "Sounds as if Norma is hitting the brandy bottle," she asserted rather unkindly.

However, although alcohol might in part have assisted in producing merriment, it was not an absolute essential, as the three women had decided some years before to meet once a week for the very special purpose of overcoming life's vicissitudes by ensuring that the funnier side of life was given precedence over the tragic or the mundane.

It had become almost a ritual that they should help each other banish stress and had placed a virtual taboo on sorrow. It was Norma's turn to entertain Mrs. Thorvaldson and Mrs. Mathieson and as usual she had achieved the level of jollity the occasion demanded. The room was clean and comfortable, it had a polished pine floor and from the wood-panelled walls hung a few of Einer's trophies and souvenirs of his sailing days. On a pedestal facing the door stood a gramophone, but instead of the usual amplifying horn, there rose a beautiful replica of a Viking *lur*.

In the centre of the room there was a large Nordic wood-burning stove with its smoke pipe rising straight up through the ceiling into the central flue system, which Einer had built into the rather old but substantial building.

The ladies appreciated the warmth of the room and relaxed in the low-slung cane armchairs positioned around the teak coffee table. As the coffee gurgled on the stove, the smell of freshly-ground beans percolated through the spicy aroma of Danish cheese, salami, anchovy and other savouries tastefully arranged on the table.

Norma addressed Mrs. Thorvaldson cheerily.

"Some more cognac, Greta?"

Greta smiled. "Mange tak," she said and poured the residue of her glass into her coffee before accepting.

"And what about you, Jessie?" asked Norma, looking at Mrs. Mathieson.

Jessie, a tall angular woman with a good complexion and a determined jaw-line, reminiscent of Highland women, the wife of Douglas, an Edinburgh surgeon of international fame, gave her companion a quizzical look and replied in her own inimitable fashion.

"As you know, Norma, I'm not one for the strong drink, but I will have a wee dram of your whisky, as my husband Dougie informs me that he prescribes whisky in small quantities for the patients who suffer from complaints of the heart and circulation. And as I want to circulate amongst you for some time yet, a wee tot o' the 'cratur' will suit me chust fine, but I would be grateful if you will also let me have some o' yon lemon water to tak awa some o' the sting o' the strong drink."

A glass of whisky and a small bottle of citron water was put in front of her so that she could mix the drink to her own satisfaction. To Norma, Jessie's behaviour, although predictable, was still a source of wonderment and amusement. For one who professed a dislike for strong drink, Jessie certainly had a propensity for absorbing alcohol with a composure which was truly remarkable.

As Jessie and Greta sipped their drinks, their conversation centred on their respective families, while Norma lit a long Danish cheroot, then, drawing out a footstool from under the coffee table and resting her bare legs on it, twiddled her toes and gave a sigh of delight as the hot air from the stove swept up her skirt.

This did not mean that she was insensitive to what her friends thought, but she was inordinately concerned with her legs and would brook no adverse comment on how she should behave with those shapely and substantial limbs. As a young girl she had worked hard on her father's farm in Denmark and had only covered her legs when winter days were well below zero. She had worn clogs outside, but indoors she never transferred to house shoes, preferring always to walk about in bare feet.

As the smoke from her cheroot travelled upwards, she gave a little sigh of contentment and smiled as she recollected the advice given her by her Finnish mother.

"Always walk in bare feet where circumstances permit, never stand too long in one position and, when you sit down, see to it that your feet are higher than your bum."

She felt relaxed now that her friends had been seen to in terms of liquid refreshment and Norwegian smorbrod, and could listen attentively to the experiences of her friends during the past week.

It appeared that young Hamish, Jessie's nephew in his last year at Heriots, had been selected as wing three-quarter for the school's first team.

"And as you may have heard," Jessie proudly announced, "they say he is so fast that he can run one hundred yards in chust under ten seconds."

Greta, recognising the achievement, applauded it and then told her companion that her son Axel had just passed his exams in Pathology and Physiology at Edinburgh University. She knew that Jessie's husband had indicated that if he worked hard, he could expect to have a good career in medicine.

Norma was at first content to allow her friends the opportunity of developing a self-congratulatory dialogue, but it was not long before she felt impelled to contribute towards the conversation. Having no member of her family passing exams at university or scoring tries on the rugby field, she felt a little out of the local picture, but then she remembered that Einer's young brother had written to say that he had become Master of one of the latest factory whaling ships which was at the present time heading for the South Antarctic. The excitement in her voice as she outlined what would be expected from a young man finding himself in such a responsible post in that cold and dangerous part of the world was such that Jessie and Greta could hardly wait for Norma to finish. After all, they were interested in one way or another in an event which also involved seamen.

Greta, although excited, was worried that her husband, as Scottish Director of the whaling company concerned, had the onerous task of re-establishing the credibility of the company after the tragedy of the whaling ship Odin, where one man had died and five had become seriously ill. Jessie, sympathising with Greta, outlined how her husband had been consulted in the case of one of the seamen who needed intensive care.

Norma felt a little guilty that she had inadvertently led the conversation into such a gloomy channel, but hastened to assure her friends that the seaman in question had now recovered fully and Einer had travelled up to Edinburgh to collect him and take him back to the Odin.

"It would not surprise me in the least if our husbands returned this afternoon in Einer's car," said Norma.

Feeling that a little light relief was just what was required, she pointed to a corner of the room where a spiral stair rose up to a small gallery where French windows looked out onto the Firth of Forth. Jessie and Greta smiled, they knew what was coming next. It was common knowledge that Einer spent much of his time up in the gallery making models of the ships he had sailed in before settling in Boness, and that Norma complained that he thought more of his model ships than he did of her.

"It's not up there, girls," said Norma. "Look under the stair and you will see the latest contraption made by that crazy man of mine."

On a dais adjoining the stair, there rested a long glass tank in which the model sailing ships floated.

"He's made that tank into what he calls an auxiliary cistern so that when anyone uses a hand basin or W.C. in this part of the house, the water flows in and the ships start sailing. Let me show you how it works."

Norma turned on a tap and, sure enough, the model ships started sailing like life-sized craft, and then, as she turned off the tap, they slowed to a leisurely pace, then stopped as they reached the doldrums.

Jessie was impressed and asked Norma if she could start the ships moving. Norma, giggling a little, nodded her head signifying her assent and Jessie strode over to demonstrate her prowess in nautical affairs. Had she known what was in store, she would not have been so enthusiastic. The tap turned, the water flowed and just as the ships started to sail, all hell broke loose. Lightning flashed through the French windows, almost blinding the three women, and the rolling thunder was so intense that it sounded as if the whole of the British Navy were firing off their salvoes in competition with each other from Rosyth Naval Base a short distance away.

Jessie was horrified and wondered what she had done wrong. Norma and Greta were momentarily transfixed with fear, but as the lightning and thunder became less intense, they calmed down and could not suppress a laugh when they saw Jessie standing aghast and shocked at what had been happening. Realising that she was not to blame for the display of pyrotechnics, she smiled to her companions and, walking sedately towards them, sat down and relaxed. The tap was still running and the ships were sailing merrily along in a storm of their own.

Jessie turned to Norma and asked diffidently if she should turn off the tap. Norma thought it was a good idea. Having regained her composure, Jessie duly obliged and, as she did so, the storm immediately abated. She smiled serenely, raised both thumbs in the air and looking directly at Norma, said, "I've always thought that your Einer was awful clever."

Twenty seconds later and some twenty miles away in the city of Edinburgh, Thor had resumed his handiwork, bouncing his thunder clouds around that rather small and unique mountain called Arthur's Seat. As they rolled around, the God of Thunder gave an almighty swipe, sending them crashing up the East coast.

The four men travelling towards Boness were awestruck by the enormity of Thor's display of light and sound. The driver of the car, Einer Wevling, normally phlegmatic, was so excited that he became quite romantic and, nudging his companion, Dr. Mathieson, in the ribs, he almost shouted, "Look at that sky, Douglas, those clouds, like enormous horses bumping and boring as they race along with shafts of light and sparks flashing from their hooves."

Einer's view of natural phenomena was rudely interrupted by a torrential downpour of hailstones that battered the roof of the car like machine gun fire.

Douglas, an eminent Edinburgh surgeon, dour but possessing that dry humour peculiar to the Scots, was not impressed by Einer's extra-terrestrial observation and sought to bring him down to earth.

"Forget about those phantom horses in the sky, Einer! Concentrate on handling this horseless carriage of yours before we come to grief."

His warning was timely, for, although the hailstones ceased, the rainstorm that followed was so intense that it fell as a continuous sheet of water almost completely cutting off visibility. With his credibility called into question, Einer returned rapidly to earth and asserted that determination and optimism had taken him successfully through many a storm at sea.

"Don't you worry, Douglas, I've never lost a ship yet."

"From what I remember, it was in weather like this that you ran aground in the Antipodes."

It was the voice of Mr. Thorvaldson, who had sailed with Einer on some of his voyages.

"Well," Einer reflected, "at least I never lost a man."

But Douglas was in no way comforted. He could see no parallel between navigating on the high seas and driving a vehicle through the busy streets of Edinburgh and made his views known in no uncertain manner.

Einer, in no way abashed by Douglas' remonstration or Thorvaldson's remarks, seemed ready for any emergency. He indicated in a cool, matter of fact voice that the flashes of lightning were acting in much the same way as storm or rescue lights at sea.

"The lightning is being reflected by the tram lines. All I need to do is follow them and I can't go wrong, but never fear, if I smell trouble I will soon drop anchor."

Some minutes later he wondered why the tram rails were veering to the left and he decided to slow down. Suddenly it all happened, a black hole seemed to swallow up the car. He slammed on the brakes and everyone in the car was thrown violently forward. As the car stopped, it lurched to the right and then an eerie silence prevailed; even the downpour had stopped. Peering through the gloom, he could see two yellow lights dancing towards him and to the left, not far away, a seemingly disembodied face accompanied the first light.

As the face moved nearer he could see it was attached to a dirty blue boiler suit and the man was giving vent to his feelings in a most unfriendly fashion. It was with a feeling of guilt and trepidation that Einer put his hand on the door handle, anxious to find out what had happened and hoping that he was not responsible for a tragic accident.

As the door opened, a stream of invective blasted his ears.

"Yi stupid bugger, what the hell di ye think yer doing?" and then in a tone to forestall further tragedy, "for Christ's sake, dinna step oot or you'll fa inta the bottom o the pit."

Einer felt a tug on his left arm and heard Douglas exhorting him to come out through the passenger door. When he stepped down, he found he was standing, together with his companions, on a cobbled path. The storm had stopped and they saw now that they were inside a large building. On either side there was a number of channels five or six feet deep and at some could be seen tramcars at various stages of maintenance and repair.

Storming down the path towards them came a tall portly man of florid complexion sporting a Kaiser Wilhelm moustache which seemed to bristle with rage, and perched precariously on his head was a bowler, signifying that he was the gaffer of this particular establishment.

Einer stepped anxiously forward ready to accept responsibility for any damage he had caused, but Douglas, feeling that he could handle this type of situation more effectively, persuaded Einer to let him do the talking.

It was a very angry Gaffer indeed who pointed to the entrance of the building, demanding to know why they had chosen to ignore the notice which clearly stated that no unauthorised person was allowed on the premises.

Douglas replied very coolly, "We never even saw the building until it was too late, let alone the notice, but first let me introduce myself. I am Doctor Mathieson, present address, The Royal Infirmary, Edinburgh."

The Gaffer seemed taken aback, he could only stand and stare. Mr. Macnab, for that was his name, had no respect for authority unless it was his own, but he was prepared to at least listen to a man of learning, be it the cloth, the wig or the scalpel. His deference was most definitely to the scalpel for after all, the joy of his life, his wife, had been saved by the skill of Dr. Douglas Mathieson at the Royal Infirmary.

When Douglas had finished explaining how they had lost their bearings and had landed in the tram depot, Mr. Macnab could contain himself no longer.

"Are you Doctor Mathieson, the surgeon?"

"I am," said Douglas. "Is that so important?"

"To me it is," said Mr. Macnab.

After explaining how his wife had suffered from a rather rare condition which would have ended in tragedy had not Douglas intervened with exceptional surgical skill, he asked Douglas if he could shake his hand. As they shook hands Douglas remembered the case and asked, "How is your wife faring now, Mr. Macnab?"

Mr. Macnab's reply was significant. "She's never been better, Doctor." Macnab at that moment only wanted to show respect and appreciation for the man who had done so much for his wife. He looked at the car which had arrived in the most dramatic fashion. It had tilted over dangerously to the right with the front wheel overhanging the pit and the front axle resting on a thick wooden batten, which fortunately had stopped the car sliding to disaster.

"We will soon get you back on the road," said Mr. Macnab.

Douglas thanked him, revealing as he did so that his task for the day was to ensure that his patient Olaf Bengtson, a sailor, was returned to his ship in the best of health. Olaf, the fourth member of the car party, was a fair-haired, blue-eyed genial giant of a man, who knew he probably owed his life to the Doctor and, feeling happy to be alive, was ready to do anything to assist Douglas. As Mr. Macnab sent for the foreman, Olaf drew Einer aside and pointed to the baulk of timber supporting the front axle and then walked over to the car. He bent down, feeling under the car for a grip that would hold, and, satisfied that his powerful hands were properly positioned, he pulled upwards steadily; keeping his back as straight as possible, he gradually took the weight on his legs.

Einer watched with bated breath, wondering if Olaf could possibly succeed in rescuing his beloved vehicle. As he watched, the axle did rise from the baulk of wood; he pounced on the timer and removed it, then jumped forward to assist Olaf. The genial giant smiled and, with a supreme effort, they lifted and levered the car away from the pit.

The onlookers were taken completely by surprise and for some seconds there was complete silence. Then Mr. Macnab, who had just learned that Olaf was a patient being transferred back to his ship, felt it necessary to express his incredulity. He took off his bowler, scratched his head and then, putting his hands on his hips, he looked at Douglas.

"The wonders of medicine will never cease! To think that only a few days ago your patient was as weak as a kitten and today he has become as strong as a lion."

The doctor appeared to ignore the compliment paid to his profession; he seemed more concerned with making his former patient aware of the enormity of his action in risking his health while lifting Einer's car to safety. He rebuked him angrily.

"Olaf, you are a convalescent, not an adolescent. I know you meant well, but remember there are machines for lifting cars. What is the point in saving your life if you are prepared to so readily put it at risk.

The big Norwegian looked crest-fallen. Although he did not fully understand what had been said, he realised he had offended Douglas. However, his composure returned almost immediately, a big smile lit up his face as he cradled the doctor lovingly in his powerful arm and excused his behaviour by indicating that he had felt it necessary to indulge in a little exercise.

Douglas shrugged himself free, shook his head and replied that in the future if he felt the need for action, he should exercise his brain instead of his brawn.

Meanwhile, as Douglas instructed Olaf in the art of post-operative survival, Einer had successfully manoeuvred the car into position for departure and called upon his companions to join him. As the car moved off, Mr. Macnab wished them well and insisted on shaking the doctor's hand.

They emerged from the repair depot into weather that had changed dramatically. No longer the lowering black sky, the oppressive atmosphere, the violent hail and rainstorms; instead an almost cloudless sky, brilliant sunshine and clear clean air.

Having survived a car accident which might well have been tragic, they were all in good spirit and felt fortunate to have escaped so lightly. Einer was overjoyed that everything had turned out so well. The car, an Argyle Supreme, a product of Scottish automotive engineering and his pride and joy, had emerged with barely a scratch and was now purring contentedly towards Boness.

Hr. Thorvaldson and Dr. Douglas Mathieson felt able to relax now and settled down comfortably in the back of the car, while Olaf sat beside Einer in the front. This arrangement suited the big man just fine, he had a rapport with Einer that he could not expect with Hr. Thorvaldson, who was after all his boss, and was considered rather stiff and formal with employees of the whaling section of Norske Fiskeri.

As they emerged from the city suburbs into the countryside, the aftermath of the storm became more marked. Whereas in the city, minor flooding had taken place and some windows had been broken, they were now confronted with roads that had been undermined by the erosive force of the storm. Hedges and small trees had been blown down, some of them on to the road itself.

As Einer drove the car cautiously over the debris and circumvented the longer trees, he felt disconcerted when he thought of the *faux pas* he had been responsible for at the tramway workshop.

Douglas, sensing the nervous state of his companion and recognising the potential hazards ahead, decided to encourage the driver.

"You are doing fine, Einer. We all know that we are safe in your hands."

The others agreed and Einer managed a wan smile. Although such loyalty comforted him, he hoped fervently that no further displays of nature's pyrotechnics would restart and make a hazardous task nigh on impossible.

After passing the village of Crammond, driving became much easier, the small trees and hedges gradually thinned out as they neared open country. It was with mixed feelings that the travellers greeted the improved road conditions, for they were now faced with a scene which could only be described as horrendous.

As far as the eye could see, everything growing had been flattened. It was as if some gigantic monster from outer space had descended and scythed great swaths through the Lothian and Fife countryside.

Rounding a bend in the Hawe's Brae near the descent to South Queensferry, Einer caught sight of a lone cyclist about two hundred yards ahead. He could see vapour rising from the man's clothes and realised that the unfortunate fellow had either fallen into a stream or been mad enough to persist in cycling during the storm.

As he drew abreast he had anticipated seeing a farm worker; instead this man wore a seaman's jacket and cap.

As he passed him he caught a glimpse of fair hair curling from the nape of the neck, almost covering the back of the cap and knew that he had seen this man somewhere not so long ago. Einer glanced back at Thorvaldson, gave a nod in the direction of the cyclist, expecting a positive reaction, but the Fiskeri director's response was negative, he shook his head and shrugged his shoulders.

The lone cyclist was soon forgotten as they entered Boness.

Chapter 7

Edward smiled grimly as the car disappeared from sight, wondering if it really had been Einer at the wheel and if so, had he been recognised. It was natural that he felt his dignity might be in question considering the state of his clothes and general disarray.

He traced his misfortune back to his attitude after leaving the Sailors' Rest. Although he had deflated Mr. Chancitt, he felt that the man was evil and could prove troublesome in the future. Edward had not believed his assertion that a deal had been made for Odin's sea stock order, but felt perturbed that he had begun to doubt his original judgement.

After travelling barely a mile he had reached the small fishing village of Newhaven, where something had caught his eye which made him stop. Voyaging around the world he had seen many small harbours similar in layout, but this one evoked just the slightest whiff of nostalgia. It was not the harbour, more the people and their movements that had interested him. Strolling along the quayside he had seen an old man emerge from a storage shed and make his way over to a pile of fish boxes; up-ending one, he sat down almost in Edward's path. He had little option but to hesitate before passing, but as their eyes met, he felt compelled to stop.

In his mind, it was as if in some delightful way he was transposed to the Danish island of Laeso. He felt he was looking at his father, the likeness was so outstanding.

The physical frame, colouring and clothing of the old man was almost identical; the strong hands and shoulders, the firm neck and bearded weather-beaten face of a man of the sea; all the qualities and features he associated with old Lars Villem. The eyes were the same; those grey laughing eyes and they were laughing to him now.

Realising that he had been staring rather long at the old man, he apologised, explaining that the uncanny resemblance between him and his father had caught him unawares.

"Aye," he replied, "there are guid folk the warld ower jist like yer faither and masel."

Although the old man had spoken in the vernacular, Edward soon learned that they both had a common heritage, the sea. While listening to the old man outline what life was like in the fishing community of Newhaven, his attention was drawn to a group of women mending nets, baiting lines, performing all the tasks essential in ensuring that the inshore and deep sea boats were properly equipped before setting sail.

The old man had followed his gaze and felt it worthwhile to impress upon Edward that these women were "Braw Lassies" who worked every bit as hard as their men folk, contributing a great deal to the prosperity of Newhaven. Not only did they work in the harbour, they accepted full responsibility for the selling of the fish caught by the men.

Edward smiled on hearing the women referred to as 'lassies'; he had the impression that lassies were girls or very young women. Certainly some were young, but in the main the women were mature in the full sense of the word, even more so when he considered how they were dressed. They wore striped skirts of good quality, mainly red and white or blue and white; covering a multitude of petticoats that would have been acceptable to any Edinburgh lady of society. The top was a short coat in black or dark blue resembling, in some respects, the naval pea jacket worn by sailors. The sleeves of the jacket were rolled up to the elbows and the skirts were hitched up in such a way that the haunches and posterior of the women were much larger than nature had intended. Some wore a kerchief as combined head gear and muffler, others the linen mutch, the close fitting qualities giving protection against the cold winds of the East coast.

Whilst talking, a woman had approached them carrying a creel of fish on her back, the broad canvas supporting belt attached to the sides of the basket pressed against her forehead; while the hitched up skirts provided a platform or support for her load. As she passed, the old man asked, "Whaur's it the day, Meg?"

"Trinity, faither," was her reply.

The old man explained that his daughter would be pleased as she would be selling in the Trinity district which was near enough the harbour, although he admitted that distance did not matter so much since the inception of the electric trams in Leith and Edinburgh.

At this point Edward had felt the urge to resume his journey and, thanking the old man, made to move off, but the old seaman warned him to take care and be prepared for a turn in the weather and had concluded, "I'm Sandy Baxter, any time you're passing through I'll be pleased to see you. I can always be found at the Auld Peacock Inn."

As Edward cycled towards Queensferry, bedraggled and sodden, he remembered this and thought he would have been better off in the bar of the Auld Peacock supping ale with old Sandy.

However, he had been given a second chance to slake his thirst. This was at the hamlet of Davidsons Mains where he found a small hostelry which seemed admirably suited to his purpose. He ordered a pint of the local brew and settled down in the corner of the big fireplace, or as the Scots would say, 'the Ingle nook'. A genial red-cheeked countryman, pint in hand, strolled over and asked if he could sit beside him. Edward readily agreed and, with potential business in mind, he asked questions concerning the social and industrial life of this community. His companion proved more garrulous than he had anticipated; within minutes he had dished out a historical *pot pourri* of his own neighbourhood, embracing the iron works on the River Almond which had all but disappeared in the time of his grandfather and up to his own time when agriculture had taken precedence. He had taken care to impress upon Edward that he was a shepherd and proud of the fact that his flock was probably one of the biggest in Scotland.

With a twinkle in his eye, he admitted that outsiders had christened the Mains 'Mutton Hole' because of the preponderance of sheep. Having assuaged his thirst, Edward excused himself and made for the door. He was ready to cycle off when a voice hailed him from the pub entrance. The shepherd was calling to him and pointing skywards. "Yon goat's beard up there means that a fell storm's brewin, ye'd be better back in the howff here wi another pint till it blaws ower."

Edward, however, feeling refreshed now, had ignored the warning, given a friendly wave and replied that he hoped to be in Grangemouth long before the weather broke.

After passing the village of Crammond, the weather changed and looking skywards he had wondered if the forecast might prove correct after all. The sky was now a deep purple and darkening by the second and in the background he could see small clouds moving towards him. They were joined together and looked like so many skeins of light yellow wool and, as they moved forwards, they appeared to vaporise, to be followed by similar formations.

Suddenly Edward remembered that Scandinavian sailors seeing such a sky knew that a storm of violent proportions was imminent. He remembered the name 'The hair of the mountain goat' and knew that if he did not find shelter, he was destined to suffer an almighty buffeting.

There was no sign of shelter, he was in open country now and he had either to back track to Crammond or make for Queensferry as quickly as possible. Always the optimist, he cycled furiously towards the 'Ferry', but Thor had already set in motion the atmospheric plan for that part of Scotland and paid scant attention to the rather insignificant latter-day Viking speeding hopefully towards sanctuary. Within seconds the storm had erupted with such ferocity that Edward was powerless to resist and had to suffer the ultimate consequences of his actions.

The storm that wreaked havoc in the East coast of Scotland had not only frightened the women in Boness and placed their menfolk in jeopardy in Edinburgh, but had also ensured that he be dealt with in summary fashion.

A sudden gust of wind had propelled him across the road and tossed him unceremoniously into an evil-smelling ditch. Lying there stunned and stupefied, he had cursed himself for not using his native intelligence and paying more attention to the wisdom of seamen and the shepherd.

The hailstones as big as golf balls had battered and bruised his body with such force that he had to draw his jacket over his head and embed himself deeper in the mire.

When the hailstorm ceased he felt his body stiff and sore and as he started to rise, there was a torrential downpour which washed away the mud from his body, but left him wet, weary and woebegone.

However, it had not taken Edward long to overcome his despondency, knowing that he would soon be dry, his vigour restored and his woe be gone. He had recovered his bicycle some yards away impaled on a hedge; surprisingly it had not been damaged. Having remounted, he had not travelled far before Einer and his friends had passed him in the car. He was still not sure that the driver had been Einer, but felt relieved that the people in the car had not witnessed his ignominious descent into that muddy ditch.

The weather had changed dramatically as he neared Queensferry, the sky was almost cloudless, the sun was shining and his clothes were drying; he was happy that it would not be long before he reached Grangemouth and satisfied his curiosity concerning the American's boast that he had secured the Odin sea stock order.

He travelled quickly down the Hawe's Brae and minutes later had left Queensferry behind, but it was not until he reached the open country that he fully realised the damage caused by the storm.

As far as he could see, all ground crops had been flattened, broken barley stems, hedgerows, tree branches and even trees had been blown across the highway, slowing up his progress.

It made him feel ashamed that he had been so preoccupied with his own discomfort that he had not realised many others had suffered real hardship. Looking at the devastation, he knew how he would have felt had his father in Denmark been faced with the croft flattened and his small fishing craft probably destroyed. He felt angry that the farming community had been subjected to such disaster.

As he approached Boness, he could see men not far off trudging slowly towards the town. As he drew abreast, he knew by their weary gait, the pallor of their skin and the coal grime on their clothes that they were miners returning from the local colliery.

He could see tiny white rivulets where the rain had run down their coal-blackened faces and he felt he could have cried knowing that these men from the bowels of the earth were in a state of exhaustion. It was indeed, for Edward, a humbling experience.

His mind flashed back to an incident during a storm in the South China seas, where a young German sailor had acquitted himself well in the performance of his tasks, even smiling when the hurricane threatened to blow him overboard.

Edward had asked him how he could smile in such dangerous conditions. He replied that as a youth he had worked in the mines, had to lie on his side in water in a space barely two feet high as he hacked out coal. The terrible conditions and claustrophobia had so affected him that one morning when the cage reached the top, he had run and kept on running till he reached the sea. "I will never go near another mine," he had said. "In a wind storm such as this, I can smile knowing that I am free."

On reflection, Edward could understand why the German sailor had smiled.

As he approached Einer's Emporium he could see the handsome captain in the window exhorting him to come in and he wondered if he should accept the invitation. He knew that Mrs. McGregor would be expecting him back in Grangemouth, but balked at the idea that the old lady would be worried when she saw the state of his clothes. Standing in the doorway, he speculated on whether he should or should not impose on Einer's hospitality.

"So it was you after all," the voice said.

On turning, he saw Einer smiling at him, offering his hand in friendship. Einer ushered him in and, seeing the state of his clothing, led him towards a welcome hot bath. As Edward relaxed in the bath, Einer returned with cigars and cognac and there they were, those men of the sea, smoking their cigars and toasting each other with cognac.

Lying back with his arms well clear of the water, Edward ensured that the prerequisites of blissful recovery were properly safeguarded, while Einer, sitting on a three-legged stool, leaned expectantly towards him. Happy in each other's company, they were soon swapping yarns and exchanging confidences.

When it came to a recap of the day's events, the atmosphere became increasingly convivial and what had appeared to them a short time before as a frightening and dangerous experience, had now become the subject of gentle leg-pulling.

"What I can't understand," said Einer, "is why you, an experienced mariner, so lightly dismissed the advice offered you by the old fisherman and the shepherd."

Edward smiled wryly and admitted that the intrusion of the American into his thoughts had clouded his judgement and landed him in trouble, weather-wise. Einer laughed, leaned forward and, slapping him on the back, reassured him that the sea stock order was still in the balance. Edward would have leapt out of the bath that instant had his friend not restrained him.

It was a lively and well-dressed Edward who entered Einer's inner sanctum, Einer having ensured that his friend made full use of his young brother's wardrobe.

Edward, resplendent in a blue serge suit, cream shirt and polka dot tie, looked good and felt even better. As his blithe spirit returned he felt the urge to share with others his contentment and happiness.

Smiling to the people in the room, he inclined his head in Norma's direction and gave her a barely perceptible nod. Although she appeared engrossed in conversation with the doctor and his wife, she still managed to see and beckon him over. Before he approached the trio, he asked Einer to facilitate a meeting between himself and Thorvaldson. Einer winked and whispered, "As arranged."

After introducing him to the doctor and his wife, Norma ushered her guests to a long table of pre-dinner drinks and Danish open sandwiches. When the doctor learned that the unfortunate cyclist he had seen near Hawe's Brae was Edward, he found it hard to believe that the young man in front of him had cycled from Leith to Boness under such atrocious conditions.

The doctor prescribed a 'wee dram o' the cratur' after such an exhausting effort, but Edward politely declined, knowing only too well from recent experience that the water of life had to be treated with respect. Wishing to negotiate a deal with Hr. Thorvaldson meant keeping a clear head and, having imbibed a surfeit of cognac, he knew he had to defer homage to the 'cratur' to a time and place more suitable than the present.

He did feel peckish, however, and sampled some of Norma's sandwiches, complimenting the hostess on her ability to supply the best variety of Danish cold table he had seen for a long time. Norma was delighted that her handiwork had been recognised and could have hugged him had he not stepped deftly aside.

The Mathiesons soon discovered that Edward could be a most interesting and entertaining young man; as a born story-teller it appeared that his material had been culled from many diverse sources. Edward was well into his stride telling a most unlikely story concerning two Danish sailors and two mermaids they had met in Greenland, when he saw Einer and Thorvaldson coming towards him. He thought this could be the opportune moment he was waiting for. He heard Einer persuade Thorvaldson to try Norma's latest speciality, a mixture of lobster and mayonnaise on rye bread.

Bringing his rather salty yarn to a quick and happy ending, he excused himself and turned to his friend. Einer immediately nodded and Edward saw the Fiskeri Director sitting alone on the other side of the room.

Although it was a careworn and worried man who faced Edward, he was kind enough to enquire how he felt after such an arduous cycle journey. Edward admitted that being forcibly tossed into a ditch had been rather frightening, the journey had not been too hazardous, but had been too wet for comfort.

However, he was dry now and feeling fit, his experience had been a triviality compared to those who had really suffered during the storm.

"I feel very fortunate," said Edward, "that I am speaking to you now. If it had not been for the storm I would probably be looking for you somewhere in Grangemouth."

Thorvaldson's eyebrows narrowed in cryptic fashion as he asked, "Oh, why?"

Edward recounted rapidly how he had learned of the Odin tragedy, expressing his sorrow that a young sailor had died, indicating that he understood how Hr. Thorvaldson would feel as the man in charge while the ship was stationed on the East coast. And then, with a candour that disturbed Thorvaldson, he added that he knew that the ship would have to be re-equipped for the Antarctic journey and he was offering his services for that very purpose.

The Fiskeri Director smiled wanly, but replied curtly, "You don't waste much time, Mr. Sorenson."

Edward apologised. "I'm sorry if you think I am pushing too hard, but I must be candid. I have been told by Mr. Chancitt, an American, that he was in possession of the sea stock order. I did not believe him, but if I am wrong I will apologise and withdraw."

A smile played around Thorvaldson's lips before he answered. "A point in your favour, Mr. Sorenson; the American is indeed a liar, he almost persuaded me, but I felt he could not be trusted."

Happy that he could still capture the order, Edward set about convincing the Director that he had the ability to conclude a deal that would be to their mutual advantage. His straightforward approach to business matters impressed the Director, but he had reservations regarding his competence in handling such an unusual situation. Edward seemed to have the uncanny talent of providing solutions before he even voiced them.

Edward asserted that the quicker the Odin reached the whaling grounds, the better it would be for the company. As it appeared that the ship would be cleared, surely the re-stocking of the ship was a priority, shopping around for the cheapest deal could prove time-consuming and represent a false economy when increased dock dues and sailing times interfered with the firm's original schedule.

"It is all a matter of trust, Hr. Thorvaldson. I know I can handle the provisioning of the Odin and guarantee that the quality will be good, the price competitive and, probably more important, I can do it immediately."

For a full minute Thorvaldson looked pensive, then his right hand came forward; Edward responded and the deal was made.

Pleased with his success, Edward felt the urge to consolidate and, excusing himself from the company, he thanked Norma and Einer for their hospitality and departed for Grangemouth with an authorisation in his pocket.

He was in cheerful mood as he cycled along, contemplating on how eventful the day had been and wondering what the future had in store, when a nasty pot-hole in the road decided to move into his path. For a split second the horror of the fall into the ditch was mirrored in his mind as the bike was severely jolted off course. He recovered his composure just in time to avoid crashing and decided there and then that if he desired to fulfil his schedule, he would have to relegate his somnolent behaviour to bed time when he could dream in comfort.

Reaching Grangemouth, he made immediately for the docks, but after fifteen minutes searching for the ship without success, he made straight for the Harbour

Master's office. On entering the building, a young man directed him.

"The Maister's office is on the second floor," he said.

Reaching the second floor, he saw straight in front of him a massive oak door with a sign indicating that this was the office of Alastair Ross, Harbour Master. He knocked on the door, a soft pleasant Highland voice bade him enter. He stepped inside and was greeted by a burly, jovial man of the sea, who levered himself laboriously from the depths of an enormous red leather armchair. Once out of his chair he advanced, arm outstretched, and addressed Edward in a somewhat extravagant fashion.

"I am Captain Roderick Ian Alastair Ross, Master of all harbour affairs in this lowly part of Scotland."

Edward, wondering if this pretentious attitude was for real or in fun, decided to respond in like fashion. Grasping his hand firmly, he replied, "I am Edward Sorenson, formerly a sailor in the Royal Danish Navy, latterly Chief Steward of many ships, both sail and steam, and hoping in the future to establish myself as the leading Water Agent in the Firth of Forth area."

The Highlandman, still holding Edward's hand, responded, "So it is Edward Sorenson himself, a Dane who speaks the perfect English of a learned gentleman."

That they were both kindred spirits was evident from their first handshake. Despite the banter, Mr. Ross sensed that Edward was anxious to make headway.

"Iss there anything I can do for you?" he asked.

When asked where the Odin was berthed, the jovial man gave a throaty chuckle and replied, "The ship Odin at present iss not berthed in Grangemouth."

Before a perplexed Edward could reply, Alastair ushered him over to a big bay window which looked out onto the Forth, handed him binoculars and asked him to survey. Almost immediately Edward focused the glasses on a very big ship almost two miles away. He could see quite clearly on the bow the word 'Odin'. He thanked the Harbour Master, but professed that he was curious and would appreciate being told why the ship had not been docked. As often happened with Edward, the relationship had within minutes reached the first name stage.

"Sit you down, Edward, it's a bit o' the cratur you'll surely be wanting while I unfold the story of the good ship Odin."

Accepting his dram, he felt a strange warmth and realised that it tasted and smelled the same as the old malt whisky dispensed to him not so long ago by Rory the Exciseman. He remembered his indiscretion and knew that usequeba, or 'the cratur' as Alastair called it, could destroy if treated with contempt, or be a warm and soothing friend when treated with due deference. He sat back, relaxed and deferred to the 'cratur'.

According to Alastair, a form of quarantine had been imposed on the Odin because a mysterious illness had struck down some of the crew; this had been resolved and the ship would berth in the morning. Edward confessed that he had hoped to board the vessel quickly and still saw no reason why he should delay.

"Oh, so it iss yourself that would be for going out to the big ship today," said Alastair.

Edward nodded and apologised if Alastair thought he was being rude in being impatient in his pursuance of a planned objective.

"No offence taken," said Alastair, "but if you would chust be taking your time, you will find that I can be helpful to a friend."

"You are right," replied Edward, "sometimes I speak when I should be listening."

Alastair smiled. "Havers, man, sit you back now and haff another wee drappie o' the cratur."

Alastair had taken an instant liking to Edward and wished to develop the association, but recognised that the young Dane might feel the West Highland tempo too slow, so he sought to reassure him.

"Never fear, Edward, it iss myself who will assure that you will get out to the big boatie in plenty of time." As he said so, he held out a box.

"Haff a cigar, Edward. They are Dutch and rather special."

Edward willingly obliged and both men settled down to a cigar-length conversation of mutual interest. A conversation serious in parts, but in the main controversial, with leg-pulling playing a major part.

"See you," said Alastair, "our families over many years haff travelled a similar path."

Edward agreed that their forefathers could be called small farmers and fishermen, but the Danes remained on their farms and resisted all attempts to remove them, be it fellow Dane or Swedish marauder.

"So it iss clever your kinsmen were, eh!" snorted Alastair, "and it iss lies you are telling me. If your folk had stayed at home tending the land and feeding the pigs instead of coming over in your longboats, murdering and plundering, we would still be living in the West Highlands."

He ended on a partly plaintive note, his face full of sorrow and just the slightest sign of resignation. Edward appreciated his histrionics and almost sang his reply.

"Who's telling lies? Who's heaving sighs? No more smiles. In those Western Isles."

Alastair laughed out loud. How could he retain a serious countenance when Edward looked at him with such a comical, quizzical look from those blue mischievous eyes?

"So, it's the songwriter you are now."

But Edward seemed serious. "Don't change the subject, Alastair. The Vikings may have been a murderous lot, but the Scots could have learned a lot if they had studied our creed."

"I think it iss myself that will be letting you know that we taught your berserker ancestors the true meaning of Christianity," retorted Alastair.

"With that I can agree," was Edward's reply, "but whereas we practised what you preached, your clan chiefs and lairds sold your kinsmen to the enemy, just like Judas, for pieces of silver." Edward was in full flow now.

"What surprises me, Alastair, is that the Scots, a highly intelligent race, professed experts in theology, should so mistakenly deify their clan chiefs to such a degree that those gentry in subservience to English businessmen were able to burn down your cottages and clear you from land to make way for English mutton. It was your own lairds that cleared your folk from home, not the Vikings. In Norse law, the land belonged to the Viking and he retained his land so long as he fought for and helped his community and they were wise enough to compensate and give succour to those who had suffered in the common fight against the foe. I think Christ himself would probably have thought more of the Danish pagans than those so-called Scottish Christians. How could your forefathers have been so stupid that they allowed themselves to be chased out of such a beautiful country."

"Chust a moment, Edward, chust a moment," Alastair broke in, the slightest twinkle in his eyes as he looked condescendingly at Edward. "It iss the clever man you are, to be having all the answers to the problems of my Scottish forefathers and suggesting that it would haff been more to their advantage to adopt your pagan creed."

After a pause for breath, Alastair continued. "However, you were correct in suggesting that we are highly intelligent, even clever, but we are also one of the most inventive races on earth. We may be considered dour, but behind that facade we are a sentimental, soft-hearted people who have allowed ourselves in our Christian faith to be fooled into believing that our leaders were God-ordained; foolish perhaps, but never stupid."

He eased himself back in his chair and looked at Edward as he replenished his drink. Edward acknowledged, but shook his head, and Alastair continued.

"Could there be anything more stupid, Edward, than a man sitting on a throne down at the sea's edge commanding the waves to go back, and him sitting there until the water washed over his hurdies?"

Edward appeared perplexed. "Oh, who did that?"

Alastair effected a sneer. "It's not fooling me you are, fine you know who it wass, it wass yon daft Danish king, Canute they called him."

And so the banter proceeded and the cigars burned shorter.

"Regarding matters serious, Alastair, how did you come by these cigars? This is one of the best I've had for a long time."

Alastair tapped his nose with his right forefinger in a most significant fashion and replied, "You are not the only Chief Steward that I haff had dealings with and I am not the one for telling stories."

Edward attempted to elicit more information, but Alastair merely smiled and said, "I am pleased that you enchoyed your cigar and I am not the one to be stopping you any longer from getting out to the Odin."

As they walked to the end of the quay he put a big arm around Edward's shoulders and confessed, "It iss happy I am that I haff met you."

Edward responded by shaking Alastair's hand with a vigour that astonished the West Highlandman. "We will meet again," he assured him.

Some minutes later he was on his way to the whaler and as the small craft putt-putted its way, his aversion to the petrol engine diminished gradually as he realised the commercial advantages of owning such a craft.

He rationalised his thoughts, logically of course, in the following fashion. The petrol engine, although an advantage in terms of road transport, was probably harmful to health, particularly in confined spaces, but at sea that was different: the wide open space would guarantee that noxious fumes would dissipate quickly. Also if he desired to contact ships lying in the Forth Estuary, it would be more efficient and far safer to use, as opposed to risking heart failure by using a rowing boat in an endeavour to beat a competitor. Yes, a craft such as this was the answer; it would make his task much easier and more profitable.

On the pleasure side, one could do a little fishing, or take Maggie for a cruise. He harboured naughty thoughts of a little innocent smuggling. After all it would harm no-one if Leith worthies could enjoy a really good cigar at a reasonable price and their women folk feel content that they could at last afford real French perfume.

Just as his mercantile horizon was widening, he felt a slight jolt as the small craft rubbed against the Odin.

A voice beckoned him. "Here yi are, Mr. Sorenson, mind yer step, Alastair says ave ti wait fur yi."

Edward needed no second bidding. Within seconds he had boarded the ship, contacted the Captain and Chief Steward and got down to business. The letter from Thorvaldson enabled him to speed up matters. A lading list issued prior to the ship leaving Christiania was produced and fortunately a separate provisioning column was included. This helped him settle with the Steward the level of the order and how it was to be delivered.

It was with a feeling of elation, the Odin order in his pocket, that Edward entered Tam Richard's butcher's shop just before closing time. Tam smiled, but Edward detected a touch of relief in the man's face and then the butcher's features hardened as he attempted to upbraid the young salesman.

"I hope you were not just visiting friends; I expect more than that, like maybe a wee order, eh?"

He uttered the last syllable through bared, clenched teeth, with such gusto that his Kaiser Bill moustache seemed to stand to attention. Always the gentleman, Edward deigned to effect his most benign smile in Tam's direction, shaking his head in a most tolerant fashion.

"Tam," he said serenely, "you are just like my father, always worried, always wondering."

"You could be right at that," snapped the butcher, getting ready to launch a short sharp lesson on ethics for Edward's benefit.

But the young man was too quick. He put his finger to his lips and mimicked Tam: "Hud your wheesht man and you'll learn something to your advantage."

The effect was dramatic, the butcher taken by surprise could only gawk. The look of stupefaction on Tam's face was such that Edward could have laughed outright had he not realised that to do so would have meant an immediate end to their friendship.

He felt constrained to apologise for the piece of mimicry, put his hand on Tam's shoulder and, hoping to mollify him, handed over the Odin sea stock order. Tam looked at it for fully a minute before he would comment.

"It's the biggest shipping order I've ever seen," he replied. "I hope it's awright," and then on a note of resignation, he added, "I don't know what to say."

"You could say thank you," said Edward.

It was an embarrassing moment, but Tam Richards rose to the occasion. His grey eyes appeared pensive and then he smiled as he shook Edward's hand and thanked him for what he had achieved. "But," he added, "I still think you are an awkward bugger."

Edward outlined the way the deal had been made between himself and Thorvaldson. "So you see, Tam," said Edward, "it is more a matter of trust than just salesmanship and if you will allow me to handle the order in my own way, I promise that you will not only make an immediate profit, but could well lay the foundation for similar orders in the future."

"Aye, aye, mmmmm, mmmm," he murmured, which is a variation of the maybe theme.

But Edward was well satisfied, after all Tam's head had been nodding up and down when he uttered his M-m-m-m-s and the note had been on the ascending scale, which obviously meant approval.

"That is something I admire about you," said Edward, and as Tam inclined his head expectantly, Edward concluded, "your ability to make a quick decision."

Before the butcher could answer, he outlined a proposal whereby if Tam gave him a letter of introduction to the meat contractor, he would take the first train in the morning to Edinburgh. Tam was nobody's fool; he had listened to Edward's plan and could see it was a good one; if anyone could sell the proposition, then that man was Edward.

What irked him was the speed at which Edward conducted business, but he did admire the cheek of the man.

"Yes, I agree, Edward," he said, "but could you no jist slow doon a wee bit."

Edward looked so innocent as he softly replied, "I will try, Tam."

Mrs. McGregor was pleased that her young lodger had returned and, on hearing about his experience during the storm, was adamant that he should take a hot bath immediately, before as she said "he caught his daith o' cauld."

Edward explained that he had already bathed away the rigours of the storm and did she not see he was wearing a new suit?

"Indeed I do," she said, after her attention had been drawn to it.

She complimented him on having quickly discovered such good Christian friends and then asked him about the meals he had taken during the day. Edward told her that he had breakfasted at Mrs. Brown's in Leith and thereafter had only been able, through pressure of business, to eat a couple of snacks. She smiled, shook her head in mock despair, and gave him his instructions.

"Away to your room, young man, make yourself comfortable and it won't be long before you are eating a proper meal."

When she called him forth she had already served up the mouth-blistering soup to cool. Edward enjoyed and appreciated the kale and the good Scottish fare that followed, but felt constrained to refuse a slice of Mrs. McGregor's 'clooty dumpling'. After the old lady had told him that it had been fried in butter and sweetened in some special way he surrendered and was delighted that she had insisted. He thanked the old lady for her ministrations on his behalf.

"An excellent meal, Mrs. McGregor," he said and, pushing his chair away from the table, he put his hands over his midriff and added, "I enjoyed it to the full."

Mrs. McGregor was well pleased. "Would you not like another slice?"

But before she could finish, Edward interjected, "Please don't think I'm rude, but I could not eat another bite, the meal was so appetising; I'm afraid I ate more than I should have and feel, as you might say, 'unco fu'."

The old lady was thrilled, not just because her young lodger had praised her culinary skill; it was even more rewarding that he had taken the trouble to highlight his appreciation in her own language.

"And who taught you the 'Scots', Mr. Sorenson?"

Edward explained that he had an aptitude for such things, but it would be presumptuous to claim that he could converse in the language of the Scots. He could speak a number of languages quite fluently, including English, and had been fortunate enough to acquire a book of poems and letters by Robert Burns.

Mrs. McGregor was delighted that the young Dane had shown an interest in the National Bard and proceeded to elicit the Scottish words and phrases that he knew. She was agreeably surprised that his vocabulary was more extensive than he had led her to believe.

The discussion with Edward was proving interesting and enjoyable. "Weel done," she said. "Oor Rabble wid hae been prood o ye."

Edward replied, "I would like to think so, but far more important, the world of the common man is proud of Burns and to use your language, Mrs. McGregor, Rabble is weel loo'ed the Warld ower."

Before she could reply, Edward, with the next day's journey in mind, asked to be excused. "I have enjoyed our talk, Mrs. McGregor, but you must forgive me for when I start I often don't know when to finish and as I have an early train in the morning, I would like you to excuse me."

As he looked at her pleadingly, he added, "Perhaps another wee blether in the not too distant future."

"Of course," she said, agreeing that he must not be late for his work, but she thought, 'Such an extraordinary young man!'

Chapter 8

Harry MacSween was a powerful man, well suited to his trade. Born and brought up on his father's farm in Angus, he had worked hard in caring for and rearing some of the best beef cattle in the country. Over some years he had, as a consequence, developed a physique reminiscent of some of his supreme champion bulls. He had progressed by stages from the arduous rearing of cattle to the easier and more profitable task of selling to the market and was now the leading butchers' contractor in Scotland.

He was a solid man in almost every sense of the word, his brain included, according to some unkind competitors who took great care not to mention their thoughts when the 'Sween' was around. Had they used the word stolid instead, it would have been more accurate, for his brain functioned very well indeed, but he rarely displayed any emotion. Acknowledged as a successful and astute business man, he was respected for his integrity and fair dealing.

Although low on the humility scale, he was capable of real love and affection and the hard lines of his face would soften from time to time as he thought of the good and happy days of his youth down on the farm.

He was reminiscing thus when the gruff voice of one of his butchers startled him.

"There's a man to see you, Mr. MacSween."

The 'Sween' scowled, he did not like being taken unawares.

"Well, show him in," he barked.

For almost a full minute MacSween looked impassively at the young man in front of him and then, referring to the card in his hand, remarked dourly, "Aye, so you're the new Water Agent, eh?"

"I am," said Edward, and then holding out his hand, he continued, "my name is Sorenson and you are Mr. MacSween, I presume."

But Mr. MacSween coolly ignored the proffered hand. Edward merely smiled and then stated his business; that he had been mandated by Tam Richards to handle the shipping order. The butcher looked for what seemed an inordinately long time at the order before he spoke. When he did, it was a sullen man indeed who, looking at Edward suspiciously, asked if the order was genuine.

Edward's affirmation was polite and precise and when MacSween was told that it was up to him to accept or refuse, he almost lost control, but realising that he might be forfeiting a lucrative order, he answered that the order was the biggest that he had seen for a long time and wished to ensure that everything listed could in fact be supplied.

From then on, Edward took the initiative and ensured that Mr. MacSween was made aware of the way he intended to conduct business.

If Tam Richards had been there he would have been proud of the way that the young agent had handled the 'Sween'. During negotiations, Edward drew attention to the fact that the order was far bigger than MacSween had come to expect from Tam Richards and therefore he expected an appreciably higher discount when delivery was effected and payment made.

MacSween feigned sorrow, but being a very patient man, he explained to Edward that times were bad and profit in the beef business was at an all-time low, but, he added, he had no intention of letting down his old friend Tam and would consider giving a discount, but not the ridiculous figure Edward had asked for. As he put his arm on Edward's shoulder in a fatherly way, he secretly cursed himself for being stupid enough to admit that the order was extraordinarily big.

Edward appreciated Mr. MacSween's desire to help his old friend Tam, but he was still concerned with facts and figures and had little time for fiction.

It was an angry and blustering man who informed Edward that there was not another contractor in the Lothians who could give him a better deal, not even in Lanark either.

Having reached stalemate, it was an extremely grave-looking young man who rose from his chair, thanked Mr. MacSween for having granted him so much of his valuable time, turned and, as he made for the door, took from his pocket, with a somewhat theatrical gesture, a book, declaring that it looked as if he would have to use it after all.

MacSween, perplexed and in a state of wonderment and unease, asked him what was so important about the book. Edward's demeanour was as bland as the statement that followed.

"It is an up-to-date railway timetable and will, I presume, tell me when the first train leaves for Lanark.

Feeling that it would be better to reduce his profit level rather than lose a potentially good deal, he decided to control his anger and almost politely asked Edward to come back and try once again to reach agreement.

Edward responded to the appeal and calmly returned to the table. Within minutes the prices had been agreed and MacSween impressed upon Edward that it was the kindness in his heart which had influenced him in agreeing to Edward's figures. Edward, being a well-brought-up young man, thanked Mr. MacSween for his kindness and said that now that the prices had been fixed, he would like to see the merchandise.

"Don't tell me you want to examine every carcass," the 'Sween' retorted.

"That I don't want to do," was the reply. "In any case the deal has been made and Tam Richards has impressed upon me that you can be trusted and that is good enough for me."

When Edward told him about the tragedy of the whaling ship Odin and how one man had died and others had been hospitalised due to laxity in meat examination, Mr. MacSween was truly shocked.

After being shown over the premises and his inspection invited, Edward shook hands with MacSween, who assured him that only the best Scotch would be delivered. Thanking him, Edward indicated that he hoped to be back in the near future with a similar order.

Leaving the meat market of Gorgie behind him, he set out towards the centre of the city of Edinburgh. As he walked along he felt happy that he had achieved his target, but wondered what he would have done if MacSween had called his bluff. He was relieved that everything had worked out and felt he could now indulge himself in a little sight-seeing.

He remembered Sven telling him that Edinburgh was one of the most beautiful capital cities in Europe. Having recently perused a short history of the Scottish capital, he had read that two hundred years before it had been a medieval town, built on a series of hills, with deep ravines in the most awkward places.

As the population increased to city proportions, the capital did not expand, but rose forever skywards, acquiring as it did so, the dubious distinction of having built Europe's first skyscrapers. To save space it became common practice to house families in buildings eight to twelve storeys high. The narrow closes and wynds could not, space-wise, absorb this type of building and because of the lack of air flow and sanitation, it was not long before the streets became canyons of dirt, disease and ultimately, decay.

It was true that there had been plans to widen streets and ventilate Edinburgh by building outwards beyond the old fortified walls, but the bourgeoisie were divided, with the majority too mean and conservative to risk capital on the construction of bridges and modern buildings which would be required to establish Edinburgh as a European capital.

While they procrastinated, dirt and sewage accumulated, the death rate rose dramatically and decaying buildings had to be pulled down for safety. One dark day, following a thunderstorm, the side of a tall building collapsed and several of the more affluent families were left stranded on the various floors.

The ridicule that followed and the realisation that they, together with their proletarian neighbours, were an endangered species, prompted the conservatives to accept, grudgingly, that a fundamental change was necessary.

For a long time the nobility, the landed gentry and rich merchants had forsaken their town houses in Edinburgh's Cannongate. Their sensitive nostrils could no longer thole the stench which emanated from the adjoining vennels and closes, or the close contact with those wretched common people. They by-passed Edinburgh and sought more salubrious quarters in London.

This prosperous and ever expanding metropolis drew them like a magnet. It offered them an opportunity to invest in a thriving centre that paid handsome dividends. How delightful to meet leading musicians, artists and members of the literati in the congenial company of their own class. As they travelled south, they talked of going 'up to London'. The more intelligent Scots ignored this geographic misnomer and vowed that it would not be long before travelling up to Edinburgh would be far more fashionable.

Scottish architects and engineers had acquired a reputation for excellence over the years. Unfortunately, their skills had been more in demand in England and the Continent than in their homeland. But this was an opportunity not to be missed, although they knew they faced a daunting task in planning, designing and constructing a new town which would compare favourably with their southern neighbour. The difficult topography of Edinburgh, as compared to London, was a factor that the Scots would have to overcome.

London and its environs were flat when compared to the hills, canyons and ravines which were a part of the Edinburgh scene. That they were able to overcome these difficulties, and even use them to advantage, is now a part of history.

It had been the start of the Edinburgh renaissance, when Scottish genius transformed Edinburgh in less than a century into an example of civic art, without equal anywhere on earth.

Armed with the knowledge he had acquired from his small booklet, 'Historic Scotland', Edward was looking forward to absorbing and enjoying the atmosphere and character of the great city.

Leaving Gorgie, he by-passed Tynecastle, then walking through Murrayfield, he arrived at the Coate's Estate. Looking through the massive iron gates he could only stand, stare and wonder at the creative genius of the man who had designed and built such a beautiful structure. He was looking at Donaldson's Hospital, designed by the architect Playfair and considered by many to be the most magnificent Tudor-like building in existence.

It was the tall delicate spires placed at each corner and above the main portico that caught his attention. In his imagination they appeared like golden propellers which might suddenly activate and draw the massive building skywards. For a full minute he looked heavenwards before realising that he could not expect such an ethereal experience or manifestation. He laughed, knowing that he had allowed his imagination too much scope, but gave credit to a man who had lived so long ago and now provided him with such enjoyment.

The effect was such that, as he walked blissfully through Drumsheugh, he failed to notice the solid splendour of city mansions and the ecclesiastical elegance of St. Mary's Cathedral.

His day-dreaming came to an end on reaching Charlotte Square. He entered the square through a narrow lane and his attention had been drawn immediately to the pleasing symmetry on either side. He lingered for a while, admiring the houses and reading the inscriptions on the stone walls, indicating that a number of famous Scots had made this place their home. He could well understand how pleasant it must have been to live in a house such as this, overlooking a beautiful tree-lined park.

Looking through the trees, he could just see what appeared to be a statue of a man on horseback and decided to investigate. He walked forward to the edge of the pavement, not realising that he was now on a raised carriage stone. Just as he was about to hop down into the roadway, a clattering of hooves warned him not to be hasty. A carriage and pair drew up directly in front of him, completely blocking his path. The coachman, top-hatted and wearing maroon and gold livery, scowled and muttered something unpleasant.

Edward retraced his path, but as he did so, he caught sight of an old lady, stick in hand, coming down steps towards the carriage. He decided to help and reached her just as she relinquished the railing at her side. He offered his arm, she smiled to him and gladly accepted his assistance.

It always happened to Edward - women were attracted to him and felt relaxed in his company or presence. Class played no significant part, whether young or old, it mattered little, Edward to them was the confidant to whom secrets could be told.

As she settled back in her carriage, she had a quizzical look and enquired if he was a visitor to Edinburgh. Edward's candour seemed to disturb her slightly, for within seconds he had told her that he was Edward Sorenson, a Danish sightseer who, having caught a glimpse of the statue, had made a rather clumsy attempt to satisfy his curiosity. His frankness was such that she felt constrained to be equally frank and told him she was Lady Margaret MacKaskill.

Edward leaned over, took her hand gently in his own, pledging friendship.

"It is my pleasure to have met you, Margaret MacKaskill," he said, "and now if you will excuse me, I will make the acquaintance of the man on the horse."

As he turned to go, he felt a tug at his sleeve. He gave her his attention and as she spoke, he could see a sparkle in the old eyes.

"Never mind Prince Albert, you can see him any time, he's not going anywhere. If you sit beside me, I will take you to a place where you will see most of Edinburgh, a breathtaking sight, I can assure you."

Accepting the offer graciously, he sat down facing the old lady, wondering what would happen next. Her remarks concerning Prince Albert had surprised him; he had not expected that someone so aristocratic could be so flippant about His Majesty, now deceased.

The nearer he drew to Princes Street, the more impressed he became. He had seen many castles before, but never one such as this. He visualised a gigantic rock plummeting to earth, burying most of its mass in the green meadow, with the castle on top forming an integral part, as if it had grown from the rock itself.

She seemed to read his thoughts. "Just wait till you see the view from the top," she said.

When they reached Princes Street, she bade the coachman to halt for a moment.

"If you look left, Mr. Sorenson, you will see almost the whole length of one of the most beautiful streets in Europe."

Edward readily agreed, but seemed curious concerning some structures a mile away at the east end of the famous street. Margaret MacKaskill informed him that they were pillars, part of a monument built in memory of soldiers killed in the Napoleonic wars and the adjoining column was a monument to Nelson, an English Admiral.

She felt compelled to add that the pillared structures were to have been a copy of the Pantheon in Rome, but were never completed because of the lack of funds and had become known as Edinburgh's Disgrace. In her opinion, the real disgrace was that the City Fathers had wasted money lauding an English Admiral.

Although amused at her scant respect for authority, he felt that the monuments were too far away for comment, but had become interested in a Gothic-like structure not so far off.

Following his gaze, she smiled approval and indicated that the fantastic edifice he was looking at was Sir Walter Scott's Monument. She was about to wax eloquent on the subject when the pumping of a motor horn and the rasping sound of a klaxon disturbed the peace of Edinburgh's famous thoroughfare. Unwittingly, Margaret MacKaskill had, by stopping her carriage, ensured that no vehicles could turn left into Princes Street.

The owner of the klaxon stepped down from his red and gold automobile and, leaving the engine running, advanced in the direction of the miscreant who had prevented him from being punctual for his rubber of bridge at the Officers' Club. Being the scion of a noble family, he was dressed in the appropriate motoring clobber. A deer-stalker cap, a red, white and blue silk scarf flapping around his neck, black leather jacket encasing an ample girth and tartan plus-fours, his legs terminating in ox blood brogues, designed especially for walking all over ordinary mortals.

The first person he encountered was Edward and in a stentorian voice he demanded, "Are you in charge of this carriage, sir?"

Edward smiled brightly before replying.

"I would like to be, but that honour belongs to the lady by my side."

Turning to Margaret, he snapped, "Get this carriage out of here, madam, and let people get about their business."

She gave him a withering look.

"Your manners are deplorable and who are you, may I ask?"

He reacted aggressively. "I am Major Marmaduke Macsporran."

She nodded her head before replying. "I can see that you are one of the Macsporrans, I must speak to your mother some time concerning your bad manners."

The Macsporran started spluttering, but before he could reply, a policeman had arrived, a fine figure of a man. The Sergeant held up his finger for silence.

"One at a time, please," he admonished.

Lady Margaret seized the initiative.

"Would you say, Sergeant, that leaving a vehicle unattended with the engine still running is a safe thing to do?"

The Sergeant's brow furrowed as he asked, "Which car?"

Margaret pointed. "That red and gold monster that looks more like a small fire engine, the engine is running and this man appears to be the driver."

"But ..." spluttered Macsporran, and he got no further.

"Is that your car, sir?"
"Yes, but - eh?"
"Come with me, sir, this is a serious business."

Then turning to the old lady, he instructed her, "Move your carriage away from here and ensure that you do not hold up traffic in the future."

"Certainly, Sergeant," she said cheerily.

As the carriage swung round and up to the castle, Edward was in a contented mood, looking forward to what seemed to be developing into an interesting experience. Having already achieved his work target, he was now enjoying his share of recreation. He had been fortunate in meeting Lady MacKaskill, finding her to be not only kind, but interesting and extremely resourceful. The way she had handled the obnoxious motorist, he wondered how he should address the old lady.

"You have been very kind to me, Margaret, or should I say Lady Margaret?"

She accepted his thanks gracefully and immediately put him at his ease. "Call me Margaret," she said. "All my friends do. To my intimate friends I am known as Meg, and to the policeman and so-called society I am known as Lady Margaret."

She had acquired the title when she had married Harry MacKaskill, the renowned Naval Commander, and she admitted that she had been 'all at sea' ever since.

Edward, unaware of the implication, was of the opinion that, as she had married a top naval man, then it seemed normal that she would accompany him on his travels. In an endeavour to stifle her laughter, she gave a throaty gurgle and with some difficulty managed to explain to the naive young man what she really meant.

"I should have said that I felt like a fish out of water."

Travelling around the world with Harry had been a happy and rewarding experience, but it had been the official ceremonies and discussions that had disenchanted her. Reared on a farm in Wester Ross, her attitude to life had been diametrically opposed to those she was expected to associate with. Being used to hard work and loving the fresh air and country life, she had found the overheated stale air and malicious gossip in the Edinburgh salons almost intolerable. Mixing with the ladies of high society was bad enough, but even more objectionable had been the behaviour of their husbands.

As Peers of the Realm, financiers and state dignitaries, they constantly peddled the idea that they were born to rule, and, to conserve this privilege, they submitted the poor to an indigestible diet of pompous patriotic pageantry and propaganda.

The old lady, having suffered the pantomime until the death of her husband, had decided to seek the company of students and radicals. Feeling free to express her thoughts, she did so and almost overnight she was ostracised by Scottish high society. It suited her fine, for she was now able, she said, to keep the company of real people. It was therefore natural that she would be attracted to Edward for both had one thing in common, the dignity of man and a healthy disregard for peremptory authority.

As the conversation developed, Edward felt at a disadvantage. Although he could not be expected to know much about the Edinburgh scene, he had not anticipated the old lady knowing so much about seamanship. Seeing his look of surprise, she confessed that her knowledge of the sea had been taught her by Harry and had been the happiest time of her life.

By the time they reached the Old Tolbooth, they were talking like two cronies who had known each other for years.

When the carriage drew up at the church, they parted company, but not before Margaret had made

Edward promise to visit her should he in his travels find himself near Charlotte Square.

"Now up that brae, Edward," exhorted Margaret, "and you will reach a wide esplanade, then through the gate and you will be in Edinburgh Castle."

He did not find it all that interesting, but the panoramic view from the battlements was something he would not readily forget.

Down in the immediate foreground he could see the beautiful gardens of Princes Street, stretching for almost a mile from the west end to the Waverley Market at the east end, a profusion of colour to delight the eye of the most fastidious flower lover. His eyes swung from left to right to encompass the fine buildings of the new town and the environs of the city stretching out to the sea, wondering, as he looked towards Leith, if he would settle there sometime in the future.

Edward, seaman-like, scanned the horizon and, looking coast wise, could see well beyond the Forth down to Berwickshire, and, swinging northwards, the Hills of Fife became visible. Having visited the coaling port of Methil some two years before, he tried to visualise where it might be and now felt he should have brought his binoculars.

"Step this way, please."

It was the authoritative voice of a castle guide conducting a group of keenly interested visitors. Edward, his eyes firmly fixed on the Fife coast, paid no attention to the people who filed past and they, in quest of historic information, seemed oblivious to his presence, except for a young man and woman who had tailed off from the group and quietly took up a position directly behind him.

Conscience is that indefinable quality that is supposed to influence man in making true moral judgements, but Edward had never been sure of this, particularly when he learned that no-one, so far, had yet discovered one within the human anatomy. He knew he had an inner voice, but had of late developed a habit of discussing with it when he was alone and had a problem to solve. It did not worry him unduly for he knew that some great men 'enjoy a little 'non'sense now and then'.

He called his inner voice "Little Eric" and had done so from childhood. This phenomenon had arisen during his formative years, an association with a young sea captain called Eric Sorenson being mainly responsible. For some months he had captained the ferry between the island of Laeso and Frederikshavn and had lodged with Edward's parents. During off-duty spells he had spent much time with Edward telling him stories of his adventures on the high seas and his experiences in foreign lands and how a man should react in difficult situations and how he should remain calm and never panic.

One day Edward had ignored his father's instruction and gone too far out on the sands. He had boarded a derelict rowing boat and had played for a long time in the boat, imagining himself as an early Viking exploring the world. He had paid scant attention to the incoming tide, knowing he could wade ashore when it suited him, but had become so engrossed that he had failed to recognise the turning tide and had been swept out to sea.

Cut off from the shore and in deep water, he almost panicked, but remembering what Eric had said, he calmed down. It was almost as if a small voice was giving him instructions concerning survival. As he was swept out to sea, a violent storm broke, threatening to toss him overboard. Realising the danger, he salvaged a piece of an old tow rope and tied himself to a thwart in the centre of the boat and tried to relax, ultimately falling asleep.

Fortunately, it was early autumn, he survived the ordeal, was rescued the following day and returned relatively unharmed to his parents. From that day onwards he called his inner voice, 'Little Eric' in honour of his hero.

Man does not always obey his inner voice and Edward was no exception, but the small voice was becoming impatient.

"How often have I to tell you, Methil can't be seen from up here."

Edward was not convinced. "I'm not so sure, I think I could see Methil if I had my binoculars."

Sven and Felicity, standing directly behind Edward, could contain themselves no longer and started to laugh. Hearing the laughter and hoping that no-one had heard him talking to himself, he turned round in a nonchalant fashion, but when he saw his friends, he knew that they had heard. He felt dismayed and wondered how to salvage his dignity.

But Sven, still laughing, asked him how he expected to see Methil, unless the binoculars could see round corners.

"Methil lies just beyond the headland you see out in the Forth," he said.

But Felicity felt she had a little score to settle.

"Who were you talking to, Edward?"

Edward, having recovered his composure, and knowing that the game was up, gave Felicity such a sweet smile and confessed.

"I was conversing with Little Eric."

Sven intervened, "Well, at least that sounds original."

Edward felt a little sad. "I thought you would believe me, Sven."

But Sven just smiled and shook his head.

Felicity was definitely quizzical. "We saw no-one, Sven, did we?"

Edward looked approvingly at his friends and asked them to listen carefully. "I must say that you are both very observant and I feel you are both due an explanation."

He told them the whole story concerning his dramatic experience when, as a young boy, he had found himself adrift in the Kattegat. He had drawn inspiration from Captain Eric, who was his hero. The voice of Eric had seemed to come from the depths of the ocean and from then on, when in trouble, the voice would return. He had christened it 'Little Eric'.

Edward thought it fit to clarify.

"Our conversations are, I think, of the telepathic kind and you would not hear him, nor see him, because he lives deep down in the Kattegat. Unfortunately, I started to argue and raised my voice. I can only hope that Little Eric will forgive me."

They laughed heartily at Edward's explanation, but he remained calm and unruffled.

"I am pleased that you are both happy, but do I detect just a slight hint of disbelief in my explanations?"

"Tell me, Edward," said Sven, "did Little Eric tell you that I have completed my engineering work on the motor vessel Auric?"

Edward's smile was one of indulgence, before he replied.

"Totally unnecessary. I know you, Sven, you would not be up here gallivanting, as the Scots would say, unless you had completed your task successfully."

Edward's hand shot up to his forehead.

"Hold on, Sven," he said - his voice, although not strident, had a note of urgency. "Keep quiet please, Little Eric is talking to me, I think it is something very important."

As he pontificated, he was surprised that his act had been taken seriously and could have laughed out loud when he saw the looks of wonder in the faces of his friends.

Sven, realising that Edward was probably fooling around, broke his silence.

"And what did the little bugger say, Edward?"

But Edward was concentrating. "Blasphemy does not suit you, Sven, please let me concentrate."

Then spreading his hands out towards the horizon, he invoked Little Eric to be patient and update him on future developments. He turned round, his blue eyes twinkling as he placed his hand on Sven's shoulder, and said, "This is a happy day, my friend! You will be offered contracts that could make you rich, all because of your engineering achievements aboard the Auric."

Felicity could not restrain herself.

"It's true, Sven? But how does he know?"

Sven's reply was interesting.

"I'm sure he does not know, but has made a calculated guess and it would not surprise me in the least that he knew we were standing behind him and decided on a little leg-pulling."

Edward was definitely relieved and smiled his appreciation.

Sven continued, "However, it is true that I have been offered another contract because of success on the Auric, but I have to admit that it was your salesmanship and Felicity's persistence that made me do it."

Chapter 9

Leaving his friends and the Castle, he strolled slowly down towards the High Street. As he passed the Old Tolbooth at the foot of Castlehill, a grin spread over his face as he visualised Lady Margaret inside invoking members of the Women's Guild to fight for their rights and support the fight to end class distinction and the greed and corruption associated with it. With the help of the true Lord, of course.

Edinburgh's Royal Mile extends from Castlehill to the Palace at Holyrood and, to many a foreigner, has proved to be a weird and wonderful place. It is steeped in history and has shaped, to a great degree, the law, religion and social structure of Scotland.

It has been the home of many outstanding Scots in the fields of medicine, engineering, architecture and the arts.

It also has the dubious reputation of being the scene of more mystery, melodrama, murky deeds and murder most foul than any comparable stretch of road in these Isles.

Felicity had persuaded Sven to follow in the wake of Edward and discover some of the romantic history of that regal thoroughfare. But Sven was more interested in the skill of the Scottish builders who had overcome the difficulty of penetrating deep into the rock to offset the declivity towards the Nor Loch and Princes Street. Felicity, meantime, had wandered into the various shops in the Lawnmarket, pricing and speculating, but hesitating to purchase any of the crystal, tartan or jewellery on display.

Sven emerged from one of the courts and joined his fiancée at Wardrop. They were about to pass Wardrop Court when an unearthly wailing of bagpipes broke the peace.

Together with a number of tourists, they passed through the narrow passage-way between the tall buildings into the courtyard beyond. There in the centre stood an extraordinary figure, surrounded by dozens of children from the immediate neighbourhood. He was clothed in such a ridiculous fashion that one could describe his appearance as the acme of incongruity.

His trousers were blue and his feet were encased in large white painted boots, he wore a bright red tunic with big brass buttons, surmounted by an ancient black cape and a tall green top hat balanced precariously on his head. The whole ensemble was made even more ludicrous by the Mackenzie kilt wrapped round his waist and a sporran, from which hung the three brass balls of the pawnbroker.

The wailing from the bagpipes gradually ceased and a modicum of good music emerged, sufficient for the music lovers in the crowd to hesitate and stay awhile. Coming to the end of a Highland air, the busker laid his pipes down on the front of a balloon-bedecked barrow, reached into a pocket in his coat tails, produced a flute and within seconds the children were dancing and cavorting around to jig time, while the adults tapped their feet to the rhythm.

As he stopped for a breather the crowd clapped and he acknowledged their plaudits with a graceful bow, allowing his hat to topple from his head, roll down his arm to his outstretched fingers. Then, summoning forth a sturdy urchin, he handed him his hat to collect contributions from the audience.

Satisfied that no further contributions were forthcoming, he addressed himself to the people, mainly women, who were enjoying the spectacle from their tenement windows. When the pennies from heaven had stopped, he declared his trade in a voice that would have done credit to Stentor himself.

"Balloons fur jeely jawrs and auld claes

balloons fur jeely jawrs and auld claes."

The children rapidly disappeared. Balloon Bobby, for that was his name, again produced his flute and started to play, while the urchin went round with the hat, hoping to separate some of the tourists from their small change.

As the crowd slowly melted, the children returned, carrying jam jars, bottles and bundles of old clothing. A brisk trade started, balloons were exchanged for the articles that the children had been able to extract from their parents and the children who had produced woollens were given a bonus in the form of various animals constructed on the spot by the deft fingers of Balloon Bobby.

As Sven and Felicity left Wardrop Court, Sven could contain himself no longer, he laughed all the way down to St. Giles. Felicity had heard of Balloon Bobby, but she had never seen him and although shocked by his appearance, she had enjoyed his performance and musical skill.

She chided Sven, "He wasn't as daft as all that, at least he knows his music."

But Sven seemed unconvinced.

"Come off it, Felicity, he was so funny, he was grotesque, it's the first time I've seen a Scotsman wearing a kilt and trousers at one and the same time."

Felicity gave a little shrug of resignation.

"At least the man is a good entertainer."

Sven readily agreed.

"He was an entertainer all right and I enjoyed his act despite his appearance, but what really intrigued me and made me laugh for so long, was the way he ended his show with that horrible war cry."

"You big daft Swede," retorted Felicity. "He was shouting to the women in the tenements that if they would send down jam jars and old clothes, he would give balloons to the children in exchange."

As they left the courtyard, they did not see Edward speaking to a young kilted soldier. The soldier, a Glaswegian, quartered at present in the Castle, had wandered down to enjoy, as he said, 'the antics' of Auld Bob. Interested in people's behaviour, Edward queried the young soldier regarding the bartering that was taking place.

Surely he can't make much from jars and old clothes?"

The young soldier put him in the picture.

"That's where you're wrong, mister - balloons ten a penny; jars a penny each, it's as simple as that."

Edward realised that money from jars and clothes, particularly woollens, could give an income augmented no doubt by his busking ventures, but surely this was seasonal - what about winter time?

The soldier chuckled and replied.

"Auld Bob's nae fule, he hires his'el oot as a gravedigger an wi oor climate the wey it is, ther's plenty auld yins waitin fur burial."

Edward sucked in his breath. What a macabre situation, to be an entertainer during the summer to the living and a gravedigger to the dead in winter, he could only equate Bobby with the quick and the dead.

Finishing his stint, the balloon man trundled his barrow quickly through one of the vennels, followed by a retinue of excited children, disciplined into some semblance of order by the urchin. As he headed down the Lawnmarket to his next pitch, Edward decided to join the procession. He drew level at St. Giles and was able to examine the balloon man at close quarters.

What he saw intrigued him, but made him sad. His attention was drawn to the fingers encircling the barrow shafts: they were long and strong, but gnarled, they were the fingers of a gravedigger, but with a vestige of a past gentility. He had the straight back of a hussar and the noble features of an aristocrat.

122

Edward determined that he was not a happy man: his eyes were pale blue, glazed, and had a faraway look. He marvelled that a man such as this, with toil-injured fingers and a sagging, turned-down wistful mouth, could coax such sweet music from a flute.

He was so engrossed that he failed to see Sven and Felicity disappear round the side of St. Giles and they in turn did not see Edward - they were too engrossed with each other.

The Tron Church is a rendezvous popular with the Scots and reaches its zenith at Hogmanay. Situated at the intersection between the High Street and the North Bridge, it is a bottleneck, but despite this large numbers of citizens often pack the area to capacity just before the Tron chimes the twelve strokes at midnight, on the last day of the year.

As the procession approached the Tron, he saw a cobbled square at the side of the church. His attention was drawn to a man and woman who seemed to be the centre of attraction: he recalled having seen the woman before. For a fleeting moment he was back in Newhaven listening to the old fisherman recounting the hazards of coastal fishing and then he remembered that the woman was the old man's daughter.

She was selling fish from a float and dispensing mussels to those fastidious people who prefer the smaller bi-valve to the oyster, claiming in their wisdom that the mussel is weight for weight tastier and, very important, cheaper.

They called her 'Mussel Meg' and, although she appeared to be the main attraction, the importance of the distinguished looking man sitting a few yards from her was in no way diminished. In a strange way, each was complementary to the other. Meg had sold her mussels at the Tron for some years now and the man was her best customer and stoutest advocate.

Danes like mussels and Edward was no exception. He moved forward when his turn came. She recognised him immediately.

"Ma faither says you're a Dane, so you'll ken your mussels. Efter ye taste them you'll be back for mair."

He looked at the mussels, licked his lips, gave Meg a smile and replied, "Probably."

She smiled in return. "You'll be back," was her response.

Edward was in a position to study the man now at close quarters. He was elderly and in good physical shape, his features were those of a man who was kind, strong and caring. He wore a perfectly tailored grey suit, with a fancy waistcoat of fine material, partially obscured by a napkin fastened at the neck. He sported a dark blue topper and an overcoat of the same colour draped his shoulders. He sat with his legs splayed out in front, his body reclining backwards and his coat tails almost touching the ground.

Edward was mystified, he could see no visible means of support. Turning to one of the locals, he enquired how the trick was performed. The man, a surly individual, gave him a queer look before answering,

"He has a pole stuck up his arse, of course."

As a member of the World Brotherhood of Sailors, Edward had heard just as lurid language at sea, but it was the malevolence in the voice of the man that angered him, making him feel that he should respond.

"I see you are a kind and considerate man, you must not worry unduly about the old gentleman's condition."

"Worry, to hell wi the auld bugger!" he snarled.

Edward, always the peacemaker, did his best.

"Now calm down, be thankful that you have at least an extensive vocabulary. Which University did you attend."

It was all too much for the man, his patience was exhausted.

"F-* off," he shouted and swung his fist towards Edward's chin.

Edward reacted quickly. Moving his head back fast, he brought up his left hand, pushed so hard on the assailant's elbow that the man spun into and scattered the crowd, largely by his own momentum. He scrambled to his feet, determined to do Edward an injury, but hesitated when he saw him standing there calm, unperturbed and smiling. Hurling obscenities as a preliminary preparation for battle, he peeled off his jacket, thrust it into the hands of a spectator and almost howled his intention.

"Haud ma jaiket, till a kill the bastard."

But it was to no avail, a strong voice full of authority stopped him in his tracks.

"Make one more move, shout one more obscenity, MacNab and I'll have you arrested."

It was the voice of the distinguished old gentleman.

The effect on MacNab was dramatic: he made as if to reply, but instead gnawed his lips rodent-fashion and slipped away through the crowd.

It was all a bit of an anticlimax from Edward's viewpoint, he had been ready for action, the excitement of preparing for an onslaught had gripped him, and now suddenly, peace. He felt disorientated.

He wondered at the power of the old man and why MacNab had disappeared from the scene so rapidly. He moved over towards Mussel Meg. "I thought you would be back," she said.

Edward smiled. "The mussels are good," he said, "but it is information about the old gentleman that brought me back. I can see that he is your friend and I would be grateful if you could tell me how he manages to wield such power."

125

Within a few minutes Meg had given him a potted history of the old man. It appeared that her mother had sold fish and mussels at the Tron many years before. One day a well-dressed young lawyer had wandered down from the law courts, had positioned a small folding chair a few yards from the stall, purchased his mussels, enjoyed the repast, thanked her mother and then departed. From that day on the procedure had never varied. The young lawyer's name was Cedric Simpson.

There was a short pause, she gave a little sigh and then continued.

"When ma mither died, I took over and Cedric still comes every day for his mussels, only now he is Judge Simpson."

Edward thanked Mussel Meg and as he walked slowly towards the judge he mused, no wonder the rogue disappeared so quickly.

"Excuse me, sir, could I speak with you?"

The old gentleman looked penetratingly at him and in a pleasant resonant voice, asked, "What can I do for you, my boy?"

Edward explained what had happened prior to MacNab's bad behaviour and offered the opinion that he was, to some degree, to blame. The judge's reply put Edward at ease.

"I saw what happened and, knowing MacNab, I am sure that the way he acted cannot be excused. I saw no sign of extenuating circumstances."

The old man put his hand forward, offering friendship. Edward responded and they shook hands.

It was not long before he recognised that Cedric Simpson had a most comprehensive and thorough knowledge of Edinburgh, its people and environs, invaluable for one who sits in judgement. He knew he had been fortunate in meeting a City Elder who was more concerned with the dignity of man than the vagary associated with the respectable, so-called upper class who put property and profit first and people last.

Listening to the old man he wondered why, with his views, he dressed in such extravagant fashion. The old man, sensing Edward's curiosity, smiled disarmingly.

"Say what you have to say, young man. Remember the truth will out sooner or later."

Edward accepted gracefully. "I was admiring your taste in clothes sir. Colourful I would say, but I did not expect a judge to be fashion conscious, having heard the expression 'sober as a judge', meaning, I suppose, that they transmit austerity in their demeanour and dress.

The old man chuckled at his description of how a judge looked and behaved in the eyes of the common man. During the course of conversation Judge Simpson had learned that he was a Dane; he complimented him on his grasp of the English language and his choice of words.

He confessed that many of his contemporaries were a dismal lot and he had decided during his struggle as a poor young lawyer that, should he succeed, he would bring a little joy into the profession. He had worked hard, had encountered and surmounted the difficulties that an ordinary worker could expect when attempting to establish himself in a post normally the province of the wealthier section of society. No wonder that many judges were sombre; they were expected to be fair and impartial, but how could they be? Many cases they dealt with were based on the State versus the Person and, as members of the ruling class, they tended to favour the establishment at the expense of the people.

The more altruistic person may have wanted to judge differently, but self-interest dictated otherwise. How difficult to be fair if you are a part of the wealthy five per cent of the population and know so little of, and possibly care less for, the other ninety five per cent.

Not a recipe for happiness when you wonder what will happen on your day of judgement, from whatever source.

But Cedric was his own man. Despite not being a part of the establishment, he had, through native wit and comprehensive study, managed to serve the people and relished the feeling of a task well done.

"I feel I have done a little for my fellow man," he said, "and as I wish to grow old gracefully and enjoy the process, I will indulge in the little vanities and appetites that bring me pleasure, such as wearing bright clothes, savouring Meg's mussels and conversing with intelligent people like your own good self."

Edward replied, "You may, or may not be a good judge, but you are most certainly a diplomat. I cannot see that you reached a verdict so readily concerning my ability to converse intelligently: after all you have done most of the talking; or could it be that your judgement is influenced by my extraordinary ability to listen, particularly when the person talking really has something to say."

The old man tilted his topper. "I raise my hat to you, young man, I've heard that the Danes have an acute sense of humour, but you are clever into the bargain."

Edward shook his head before replying. "Not so clever I'm afraid. For quite some time I have been trying to fathom out how you can sit at such an inclined angle without falling. Although partially covered by your coat, I can see a stick. Could it be that a back support is attached and hidden from view?"

"Nothing so elaborate or clumsy," said the judge, then standing up he withdrew the shaft he had been sitting on and handed it to Edward. Two elliptical wings were hinged at the top of the shaft and, when folded down, formed a seat almost a foot across.

Edward realised the appliance would be effective, but rather awkward to carry around. The look of wonder in his eyes and the way he gingerly handled the shaft seemed to amuse the judge. He took it from Edward and closed the wings together, thus forming a handle.

"You are now looking at a walking-cum-shooting stick, young man."

It appeared that a certain Lord Appletross had made a present of the stick to the judge when out grouse shooting on an estate in Perthshire. He nodded approval as the old man elucidated.

The leisured classes had found that grouse shooting was rapidly becoming an onerous task and were delighted when some ignorant peasant suggested and designed a stick with adjustable flaps. To this day, they still debate whether the word flaps refers to the wings on the stick or that vulgar word used to describe their noble posteriors.

"At least," said the old judge, "it is not as harsh sounding as the word 'arse'."

Edward was learning fast. "Ah, I understand, when their lordships see the birds coming, they prepare for action and cry 'get your flaps down'."

The old man was a little puzzled. Although he knew that the young man was capable of using a little blarney, he wondered if he was not also taking the 'Mick'. Even so, what did it matter? He had enjoyed his chat with the young Dane. They both agreed it was time to adjourn, but before departing, the old man thanked Meg for supplying the mussels.

"But they were a wee bit sour today, Meg."

Meg was ready for him. "Awa ye go, Cedric, it's yer mooth that's soor."

The judge laughed, looked at Edward in mock fear and replied, "We'd better go quickly before I'm sued for slander."

When they reached the opposite pavement, Edward asked if there was a place nearby for food and drink that the judge could recommend. They had only travelled a few yards down Cockburn Street when the judge pointed to a pub directly in front of them.

"I think this would suit you admirably."

Looking up he saw a quotation, probably from the Bard himself:

'Wi tippeny we fear nae evil.
Wi Usquebach we'll face the Devil.'

He turned to Cedric Simpson and thanked him for his company and added that it was too early in the day to face the Devil, but he might try some of their tippeny ale.

As he savoured the local brew, he felt quite happy and contented. It was just as he was ready for his final quaff that he heard the voices. He thought he knew the voice of the man, but as the voices of the women predominated, he could not be sure. Curiosity made him move in the direction of the serving hatch and as there appeared no way through, he made for the main door, glass in hand.

"You can't take your glass outside, sir," said the landlord.

Edward apologised and made him aware of his intentions. The landlord smiled, then took his glass and, transferring it to the serving hatch, advised him to go outside and enter the side door called 'Jug'. Opening the jug bar door, Edward saw three women sitting in the corner discussing in animated fashion their trials and tribulations.

It was the striking difference between the women that caught his attention and made him stand and stare. His eyes focused first on the eldest of them, an old craggy angular person whose rheumy red-rimmed eyes, full of woe, peered out at the world from a ghost-like face, with deep furrows running down from the eyes to the mouth as if years of weeping had eroded the skin.

On her immediate left sat a small, cheery, rosy-cheeked woman; her vitality and exuberance, like her rotundity, were bursting out all over. Their companion, a handsome young woman, well-dressed, listened patiently with limited interest to the conversation of her elders, while she fortified herself with sips from her glass of stout.

Edward had a strange but pleasant feeling he had seen her before. He walked to what remained of his pint on the serving hatch, leaned over apologetically and, as he salvaged his drink, realised that he was looking into the smiling eyes of Mussel Meg. The difference was astounding. Only a short time before he had seen her in the voluminous clothes of a fishwife with a mutch covering her head and now here she was clothed in an attractive costume that accentuated her charming figure, with no head covering hiding her vibrant chestnut hair. He stood dazed and dumbstruck, but happy, and then her lips moved.

"Weel, have you got your eyes filled?"

Having recovered his composure, Edward spoke his thoughts.

"You are ravishing, Meg, and I am delighted to have made your acquaintance, even though it has only been for a fleeting moment."

As Edward excused himself, Meg felt gratified that her female virtues had been expressed in such a frank and appreciative manner in the presence of her friends.

The little rosy-cheeked woman broke the spell and asked,

"Is that your chap, Meg?"

"Deed no, dinna be daft," retorted Meg.

But then the eyes of Meg and Edward met again and the vital message flashed between them: 'let's be friends,' it said. Edward stood, glass in hand, pondering his next move. Had she been alone it would have been simple; the charm of Meg aroused in him the desire to be friendly, very friendly, and she had acted in his favour, but the prospect of entertaining the older women simultaneously appeared somewhat daunting.

The impasse was resolved when a voice from the door greeted Edward.

"And where do you think you're going?"

Looking round, he saw Sven and Felicity, who had entered and seated themselves in the far corner. Times there are when one would wish that into the back of beyond friends would quietly and discreetly disappear.

He excused himself. "I'll see you again," he said.

She smiled and murmured, "Of course."

But Edward, being the forgiving type, walked over and sat down beside his friends. When seated he looked coyly in their direction and Felicity, feeling slightly bewildered, averted her eyes momentarily. As she did so, Edward pursed his lips and, looking straight at Sven, shook his head in mock despair.

His meaning received, the big Swede could only shrug his shoulders. Edward wished fervently that he could have spirited Meg away from the present company and have her all to himself. But being bereft of magical power, he unfortunately had to settle for the mundane. He knew he had to answer Sven's question.

"Having asked so kindly where I was going, I should inform you that after a hard day's work I was returning to Grangemouth when I heard a familiar voice and decided to investigate."

Sven nodded his head. He knew only too well that Edward was being slightly sarcastic, he understood why, but did feel guilty of unwittingly acting the part of 'gooseberry'.

"And," added Edward, "you no doubt noticed that I was paying my respects to a very dear friend."

Felicity, no longer bewildered, seemed interested.

"I'm curious, Edward, how long have you known her?"

His blue eyes twinkled as he answered, "I am sure you are, Felicity, and you have asked a very good question. Let me just say that I feel I have known her for a very long time."

As they strolled down Cockburn Street Felicity's curiosity increased, but it was to no avail. His serene expression and profound statement which contained no real information was, to say the least, exasperating.

"Meg and I are children of the sea and we have decided to swim together through the sea of life."

Sven could no longer contain himself, he laughed heartily before giving a verdict.

"Don't believe him, Felicity, he's the Danish sailor who failed his swimming test."

But Edward, nothing daunted, responded admirably, looking directly towards Felicity. "True, dear friends, true, but this is Scotland and for Meg I could swim till the seas gang dry."

When they reached the carriage entrance of the Waverley Station they parted company. By this time Edward had Felicity laughing, but although she had forgiven his nonsense, she could not resist a parting shot.

"Seeing that you are in the swim with Meg, I'll tell Maggie you won't be dancing tomorrow night."

Edward said nothing, smiled cheerily, knowing that some day she would learn the truth.

Mrs. McGregor, known as 'wee McGregor' to her friends, was in a happy mood. Mrs. Ferguson, a special friend, was paying her weekly visit and coming as she did from Leith, Mrs. McGregor, a former 'Leither', was very interested in local news or gossip. Her friend was bursting with information.

It appeared that the shipyards and engineers were very busy. The docks were operating to full capacity and despite rumours of war, everyone was optimistic because of increased trade and prosperity. And then a deathly hush as Mrs. Ferguson drew breath prior to divulging the next item.

"What I'm going to tell you is a secret."

She hesitated so long that her companion became restive.

"Weel, tell me," she interjected.

It appeared that Mrs. Simpson's daughter, Clarinda, had become pregnant and it was thought that a sailor from one of the Danish butter boats was the father.

Having unloaded her secret, she folded her arms over her ample bosom, sat back in the armchair and, looking very smug, she said, "What do you think of that then?"

Mrs. McGregor shook her head before replying.

"Not very much, at this very moment there are thousands of women pregnant and that hardly makes Clarinda a special case."

Mrs. Ferguson felt deflated, but was not finished.

"Aye, but you know what sailors are."

Mrs. McGregor reacted sharply - she might countenance a little gossip, but snide remarks and anything which ran counter to the dignity of man, she would not tolerate.

"As you seem to have acquired a great deal of knowledge of the behaviour of sailors, you tell me what they are."

Mrs. Ferguson appeared distraught, she sputtered a little, but said nothing.

The 'wee McGregor' continued.

"As far as I am concerned, sailors are men and, like women, are good and bad. My limited experience as far as sailors go is in the main a good one. In fact, my present boarder, Mr. Sorenson, was a sailor until quite recently and seems set to become a successful water agent. He is a sailor that I would trust."

Mrs. Ferguson knew this to be true; her brother, Tam Richards, had already told her quite a bit about Edward. True or not, she felt that Mrs. McGregor was far too fussy, but to keep the peace she decided to mollify her and admitted that she had been a little hasty in her judgement concerning sailors.

The McGregor relented, but could not miss the opportunity of delivering a little lecture.

"We've been friends for a long time, Lizzie. In the future you would be wise to form your opinions on facts and don't allow yourself to become the mouthpiece of newspapers and old wives, whose main hobby is to peddle scandal."

Lizzie breathed a sigh of relief and agreed with her friend that Edward Sorenson was truly a very upright young man.

They had just finished their meal, an event that Mrs. Ferguson always enjoyed, when a crunching of shoes on the garden path was heard. Mrs. McGregor opened the door and, as Edward entered, her face lit up as she welcomed him. It was as if a sailor son had just returned from a long voyage, a performance no doubt for Mrs. Ferguson's benefit.

Introductions were made, after which Mrs. Ferguson decided to leave. Paying compliments to her hostess, she turned to Edward.

"Mrs. McGregor has just been telling me about you. You seem to be a very interesting young man."

"That's too kind of her," he replied. "She's probably exaggerating. If I am being looked after by the best cook in these parts and wish to remain, then it is up to me to be always on my best behaviour."

She glanced at her friend and then turned to Edward, who smiled.

Mrs. McGregor smiled in return and said, "After all, Mrs. Ferguson, you know what sailors are."

Chapter 10

'Thar she blows!' Edward smiled ruefully as a nearby factory whistle blew for the morning start and wakened him from a deep and restful sleep. As he dressed, he thought of his advent into the life of the City the day before, the places he had seen, the people he had spoken to and the characters he had met. Yes, the characters were extraordinary, he would remember them for the rest of his life.

The whistle blew for a second time, as if summoning him into action. Today would be the day that the whaler's call would be answered. He had already arranged the terms of delivery and payment of the sea stock for the whaling ship Odin, but intended to be on the spot himself to ensure that everything went according to plan.

As he sat at breakfast Mrs. McGregor fussed around trying at the same time to elicit what had happened the day before, but Edward was not forthcoming and the old lady chided him in a friendly fashion. He excused himself.

"You may think I'm rude Mrs. McGregor, but having other things on my mind, I can assure you that your expostulation will achieve nothing. However, when I return tonight or tomorrow, I will be glad to give you a full report of what happened in Edinburgh."

She smiled and replied, "Are you the one for big words!"

He gave a little laugh and again apologised.

"I know I can be a bit of a bore and show-off at times, but I can promise you that what happened will take more than a little time in the telling and will be well worth waiting for."

The old lady was happy and satisfied.

"I'll look forward to that," she said.

When he left for the docks, she felt it necessary to advise him that all work and no play was not a recipe for happiness. Edward wholeheartedly agreed and made her aware of his intentions to go dancing in Leith in the evening.

Arriving at the dockside, he was pleased to find that ship loading was well on target and it was not long before the S.S. Odin was properly provisioned.

Edward bade the Chief Steward good sailing, settled accounts with the company agent and then asked Harry MacSween if he would care to accompany him to the local tavern.

As they sat drinking and talking, he witnessed a marked transformation in Harry. He was no longer the truculent bully he had dealt with the day before, but was now affable and friendly; even a sense of humour prevailed. Suddenly he became serious and, putting his hand on Edward's shoulder, told him that a suspicious looking character had been glancing in his direction for the last few minutes.

Edward thanked MacSween for being so observant and insisted that he should have his reward.

Harry's big red face beamed. "A dram will dae just fine," he said.

For a moment Edward wondered if it could be the American. He was about to dismiss the thought when Harry added, "He disnae seem particularly fond o' you, such an ugly bugger too, he looks like a big black craw."

Edward looked straight ahead and up at a large mirror advertising whisky, and there was the American lounging at the bar. He told Harry he knew who it was and was sure that he would be able to deal with him. But Harry was not so sure and advised extreme caution. Never one to waste time, Edward decided to act.

He went straight to the bar and ordered the drinks, then, turning abruptly, faced the American.

"You wish to speak to me," he said.

Although taken aback, the American reacted quickly.

"Yeah, sure. I wanna tell you that Ignatius Chancitt, an American citizen and southern gentleman, has no intention of allowing an insignificant Scandinavian sailor to stop him from becoming the one and only Water Agent in this neck of the woods."

Edward gave a little smile and nodded.

"I see you are what your countrymen would call 'a real go-getter'."

"Amen to that," said the Southern gentleman.

Edward seemed sympathetic. "I sincerely hope you get what you deserve."

Mr. Chancitt, who was not convinced that Edward meant him well, retorted angrily, "Ya bum, think you're clever?"

Edward informed the American that he did not think he was particularly clever, but clever enough to beat his competitor to the Odin sea stock order. His competitor was not amused.

"Listen, you Scandinavian scum, no one, but no one, will beat this American."

So saying, he poked Edward's chest with a talon-like finger.

Edward reacted sharply. As the offending finger travelled forward for a second poke, he gripped Chancitt's wrist as if in a vice, and, diverting the forward propulsion downwards, rapped the American's fingers with a resounding crack on the marble bar top. He yelped with pain, swung a fist at Edward's head, fell off his stool and landed in a bedraggled heap on the floor.

He struggled to his feet, cursing and swearing in a peculiar American idiom. Old salts sitting around paled visibly when they heard a torrent of invective that did an injustice to decent swear words.

But Edward appeared most solicitous.

"Be careful, old chap, you could fall again."

The American made an inexcusable mistake, he let go another mouthful, ending with the words 'son of a bitch'.

Edward's mood changed dramatically, from easy-going to one of cold menacing anger. His blue eyes seemed to flash as he transmitted a cautionary message. Those nearby only heard the words 'Listen, you miscreant'. The voice was not loud, but carried an authority that could not be ignored.

The American appeared transfixed as Edward's eyes bored into him, then, leaning forward, Edward said something which, although inaudible to those around, made Chancitt cringe against the bar.

It seemed almost incredible that such a blustering braggart could in a short time be reduced to a whimpering creature who, bereft of action, could only gaze at his enemy with a mixed look of fear and malevolence. Edward turned his back on him and, picking up the drinks, walked back to his table.

The look on MacSween's face intrigued him.

"Something worrying you, Harry?" he asked.

The big butcher smiled and replied, "Not really, but if you look to the left, you'll see what looks like an overgrown black craw slinkin oot the door."

Edward was not impressed and asked his companion to drink up.

"Enjoy your drink. I hope he has learned his lesson, it's about time the American disappeared and stopped interfering in the affairs of honest people."

Harry nudged Edward. "A competitor, lad?"

Edward shrugged.

"I suppose so, but his remarks, which were uncalled for, made me very angry."

Harry insisted that Edward should tell him what he had said that quietened the American so quickly. There was a mischievous light in Edward's eyes when he admitted telling the American that, as a direct descendent of Sorn Stig, the Viking Berserker, he had magical powers and if provoked too much, was quite capable of decapitating anyone.

Harry was suitably impressed. "You don't say?"

Edward appeared serious. "I do," he said. "Have you known me to tell lies, Harry?"

The big man replied appropriately.

"Of course not, perish the thought, but I do think you are a remarkably good storyteller."

Edward responded airily, "You are so understanding, Harry."

His constant flippancy seemed to annoy the butcher slightly.

"Don't act the daft laddie wi me," he growled. "Yon man is a dangerous cratur and turning your back on him was not very wise."

Knowing that he had treated the matter too lightly, he apologised to Harry, recognising that the butcher had been concerned for his safety, and assured him that he would be more cautious in the future. He did not relish a knife between the shoulder blades.

Harry, feeling that his advice had now been accepted seriously, knew he could be slightly magnanimous.

"I'll admit I was a wee bit concerned for your safety, but I was more concerned wi' the waste o' my drinking time."

It was agreed that such a waste was criminal and had to be rectified. For the next half hour they made up for lost time, drinking and chatting like two old cronies. Between drinks, Harry puffed contentedly on an old briar, while Edward sent smoke signals into the air from a 'marcella', envisaging, as he did so, prospects for the future.

Edward knew he had done well in clinching the Odin order, but realised that there was some urgency now in getting to Leith if he wished to prevent the American interfering with his plans.

Harry seemed to read his thoughts.

"Time and tide wait for no man, Edward, and Leith Docks is no exception."

Edward looked wonderingly at his companion and although he remembered making him aware of his plans earlier on, it was uncanny that the big man could be so accurate in penetrating his mind just at that moment.

Edward readily agreed that no time should be wasted. He preferred the bike for mobility in the docks, but might have to go by train to get there faster. Harry offered a solution.

"I'm off to Edinburgh shortly. Why not stick auld Tam's bike in the back of my van and I'll drop you off at Leith?"

To Edward, the journey to Leith was thought-provoking. As they passed through Boness he was reminded of the scene not so long ago of miners returning home, dirty, dishevelled and drenched by the teeming rain. Then on through the countryside beyond where the roads had been cleared of debris, but the ravages of the storm were still all too evident. The farm labourers were now busy redressing the damage, clearing away broken and felled trees, repairing drains and dykes and doing their best to restore the land.

At South Queensferry Harry had to exercise care in threading the van through the narrow main street of the small burgh.

As he did so, Edward caught glimpses from time to time of the Forth Bridge. It was not until they left the narrow street and travelled down towards the Ferry Wharf that he saw clearly that magnificent structure, its three spans towering sky-wards.

He sat back and looked with pleasure at the unfolding scene, recollecting that on the last occasion he had been blown down the Hawe's Brae at such a speed that survival had been, of necessity, far more important than scenery.

Harry spied the look on Edward's face and knew that here was something that would impress the rather self-assured Scandinavian. He stopped the van and beckoned Edward out and, pointing sky-ward, he said, with pride in his voice,

"Eh man, a wonderful sight, it's one o' the world's engineering marvels."

He gave a most graphic description of how the bridge had been built, its cost in terms of money, materials and men and, ultimately, how the Lothians and Fife had benefited from its construction.

Edward listened attentively, showing an enthusiastic interest in what had been achieved, but felt sad at the enormity of lost lives and human suffering during the building of the structure.

After finishing his mini-spiel on the Forth Bridge, Harry looked closely at Edward, hoping he had created an impression and, from Edward's reply, it appeared he had.

"I have listened intently to all you have told me about that fantastic structure and feel you should be rewarded. I would hazard a guess that you must be dry now; let me treat you to a drink at the Hawe's Inn."

Harry accepted graciously, but felt he would prefer to travel further ahead and take his refreshment at his favourite 'howf' in Davidsons Mains.

The Hawe's Brae is a long fearsome hill, steep enough to test the strongest Clydesdale, particularly when the carter has not the wit to moderate the load, or a van driver who might misjudge the efficiency of his petrol vehicle.

Having fallen unwittingly into the latter category, he had to suffer the consequences. The van, although now unloaded, was incapable of a creditable performance. After much mechanical grunting and groaning, interspersed with backfiring reminiscent of a machine gun, the van ultimately crawled to the crest of the hill.

During this lamentable performance, Harry had suffered the twin agonies of frustration and loss of dignity. His dignity had been sorely dented when he found that exhortation, threat or blasphemy made not the slightest difference to that soulless piece of ancient machinery. Added to this was the frustration of not having the necessary engineering knowledge to correct or discipline the brute.

The journey was now relatively smooth, but Harry felt an explanation was due to his companion.

"It was that bloody Magneto that caused the trouble."

Edward seemed in no way disturbed, but was sympathetic.

"Forget it, Harry. A few big sea stock orders and you'll be able to afford a new van."

Harry was relieved and smiled his appreciation.

Once more they were in open country and although the devastation was all too evident, the sun was shining, signalling a new hope for the future. Even the van ran smoothly, with only the slightest hiccup on the odd occasion.

Edward shuddered momentarily as they passed the place where he had been so unceremoniously ditched. Then over the River Almond and through the hamlet of Crammond and they arrived at Davidsons Mains and Harry's 'Howf'.

While Harry sought a comfortable seat, Edward purchased the drinks and brought them over to his companion, who was now seated at the big fireplace. Harry was speaking to an old man who sat in the 'ingle nook' as close to the spluttering fire as safety would allow. At the sight of the old man, Edward felt he had travelled back in time and suddenly he knew he was in the tavern where the same old man had prophesied so accurately the impending storm.

As he placed the drinks on the table, Harry excused himself to the old man, who responded with a nod and then smiled to Edward. The smile confused him, for it was not the smile of the man who had given the weather forecast. As he drank his beer, he studied the man closely. Although the physical resemblance was almost identical, there was a difference he could not evaluate or understand. He had not long to wait for an explanation.

Harry tapped him gently on the arm and then, cupping his hand over his mouth, he whispered that the man opposite was auld Bob Muir, the twin brother of the shepherd killed during the storm. It transpired that an hour after Edward had left the inn to travel to Grangemouth, the old shepherd had decided to go home. The storm having died down, he thought it safe to do so. Unfortunately, a belated gust had blown down a damaged tree on top of the old man only a few yards from his house, killing him instantly.

The news had a chastening effect on Edward. He had only known the old shepherd for a very short time and, having taken an instant liking to him, he felt in a peculiar but inexplicable way that he was, to some degree, responsible for what had happened. The irony of the situation impinged on him acutely and it saddened him to think that the wise shepherd had warned him, he had ignored the warning and had escaped virtually unharmed, yet the shepherd had perished.

He knew his thoughts were not rational, but he did feel that some token of sympathy was due the old man sitting in the 'ingle nook'.

He approached the old man and asked if he could speak with him. The old man nodded and Edward outlined briefly the conversation between himself and the old shepherd. The old man moved his head slowly from side to side and smiled wanly as Edward offered his condolences. For a minute there was silence and then Edward, feeling awkward, ended the hiatus by asking the old man if he would accept a drink.

"Thank yi kindly," he said. "A whisky wid be appreciated."

Edward always took particular care when treating others that the barman served the brand that would be acceptable. The barman must have dispensed powerful medicine, for in a matter of minutes the old man had become most loquacious; any inhibitions he might have had were dispersed and his arm was encircling Edward in a fatherly fashion. He started disclosing family secrets that soon had Edward in a state of embarrassment. Harry seemed highly amused at his friend's predicament.

However, when Edward signalled, he relented and came over to the ingle nook and informed the old man that pressure of business necessitated them leaving for Leith almost immediately.

They left shortly after, but not before the old man had extracted a promise from Edward that he would allow him to return the compliment the first time he visited the neighbourhood. As they departed, he saluted Edward with his drink.

"It's Auld Antiquary that keeps me gaun," he said.

As they headed for Leith, Edward was in pensive mood, then suddenly he spoke his thoughts.

"Making allowances, Harry, for my limited knowledge of the Scottish language, it appears that the old man believes that Auld Antiquary prolongs his life. Could you tell me, is this some ancient Pictish Deity that he gives homage to, or some apparition from the spirit world?"

Being unsure of Edward's tendency towards whimsicality, Harry gave an educated grunt and replied.

"That old man is not religious, has no time for ghosts, but is a firm believer in the spirit world and attributes his longevity to a happy association with one of the finest spirits in Scotland."

Edward smiled, appreciating the big man's potted eulogy of a particular Scottish beverage.

"Am I to assume, therefore, that Auld Antiquary is a fine whisky?"

"Aye, just so," was the answer. "And in future look at the label when ordering, it could save asking a lot of daft questions later."

Edward accepted the advice cheerfully.

As they passed through Granton, he was surprised to see what looked like a medium-sized marina, with small craft moving out to the Forth and others sailing into their allotted berths. He remembered that during his short stay in the Port of Leith, he had been made aware of the existence of Granton harbour, but no mention had been made of the marina.

Having set out in the morning on the business trail, it was natural that the sudden appearance of the marina should trigger off thoughts of adding yacht chandlering to his other activities. On reflection, however, he knew that the pursuance of additional business to the exclusion of developing a happy relationship with Maggie should not be tolerated. He was sure that Maggie would appreciate any spare time being spent in acquiring more skill in the terpsichorean arts.

Harry's voice broke in on his thoughts.

"Don't you think she's beautiful?"

Edward, in the middle of a daydream and looking sky-wards, replied mechanically, "I'll say she is."

Harry was not fooled, the vacuous expression on Edward's face was significant. He was annoyed and felt compelled to bring his companion down to earth. He stopped the van and, gripping Edward by the shoulders, turned him in the direction of the sea.

He pointed to an elegant yacht sailing towards Newhaven Harbour and spoke softly, "Forget the girl, Edward. I don't know who she is, but now that you are back in the land of the living, I would appreciate your opinion of that craft out there."

Although bemused, he readily agreed that the yacht was indeed a sight to behold, with its pleasing lines and the hull in light sea green, a thin band of gold separating the hull from the dazzling white upper structure. Regarding sea-worthiness, a closer scrutiny would obviously be required before an opinion could be given. He added as an afterthought that it looked as if the craft was Scandinavian-rigged.

"And why not?" interjected Harry. "That fifty footer out there is owned by Oskar Petterson, a countryman of yours."

It transpired that Oskar, a Danish sailor, had settled in Scotland and in five years had, through shrewd dealing, established a profitable import and export business.

Harry looked closely at Edward and offered the opinion that in some ways Oskar and Edward were very alike. Edward thought for a moment before replying.

"You mean that Oskar and I are polite, patient and persistent in all that we do?"

The big butcher looked quizzically at Edward and uttered the word 'umph-h-h', signifying neither agreement nor disagreement; then, hesitating for a moment indicating that pronouncement was imminent, gave his verdict.

"You are both the most polite, but persistent buggers I have ever met and as for you, Edward, you've a lot to learn. If you have the patience to substitute perseverance for persistence, then the folk in Leith will welcome you with open arms."

Edward knew that the advice was kindly meant.

From Granton, they passed through the rather select neighbourhood of Trinity. The look on Edward's face prompted Harry to explain that the big expensive-looking houses were owned by sea captains, active and retired. Speculating on the number of houses involved, Edward was compelled to add, "... and are also the homes of captains of industry and commerce, I would imagine."

"Aye just so," Harry conceded.

Approaching Newhaven, they were able to obtain a clear view of the yacht. Edward almost laughed when he saw the name. Who but a Dane would call a craft such as this 'Tivoli'?

It was a glorious day, the sea was calm, a breeze so gentle it barely filled the sails of the fifty-footer, a day for relaxation and pleasant thoughts.

Harry, anxious to see more of what he described as Oskar's pride and joy, stopped the van at the sea front, near the site of the old chain pier which had been swept away by a violent winter storm at the end of the century. From this vantage point, they could see the wide expanse of the Firth of Forth. The scene was one of small crafts, both pleasure and industrial, moving between the ports and small coves of Fife and the Lothians.

Harry, however, was oblivious to everything except the behaviour of the 'Tivoli'.

"She moves like a dream, Edward."

Edward readily agreed, but it was not a fifty-foot boat that intrigued him, it was a body movement not far away that left an indefinable feeling of an association with the immediate past. His bewilderment was short-lived, he could see now that it was indeed a swimmer, a woman and she was heading for the sea wall. She swam with a grace and elegance which belied the power and speed she achieved, and within a few minutes she reached a rocky ledge protruding from the base of the wall. Hoisting herself onto the ledge, she stood up straight, preparatory to drying off.

The wet bathing suit clung closely, showing clearly her physical attractions. He knew now he had seen her somewhere before, but where and when was the question. To obtain an answer would require careful examination and as she stood little more than fifty yards away, it should be a worthwhile and delightful experience. He could elicit very little from her head, for she faced in the direction of the Tivoli and her hair was encapsulated in a small tight-fitting bathing hat.

Her neck, a smooth firm column indicating vitality, flowed into exquisitely formed shoulders, her firm rounded breasts were a delight to behold. Her trim waist was greeted below by generous hips supported by beautiful thighs and shapely legs.

It was becoming an arousing experience in more ways than one. He knew he had to stop wandering and adjust to his original state of wondering who she could be. He had met and known a fair number of women during his travels, but was sure now that it was someone he had spoken to quite recently.

Suddenly it happened. She peeled off her bathing cap and tossed her hair free just as the sun emerged from a bank of cloud. As she turned towards the sun, her profile was clearly visible and the copper tints reflecting from her hair gave the final clue. It was Meg, the fisherman's daughter, the woman he had met at the Tron and later in the Cockburn Street tavern.

As he looked longingly in her direction, the Tivoli swung in towards the harbour and Harry, still determined to eulogise, felt compelled to proclaim: "See how she moves, Edward, look at her lines, have you ever seen anything so beautiful?"

Edward astounded his companion when he replied.

"I wholeheartedly agree, just look at her hair, such a glorious colour."

Harry was astounded. The look of bliss on his companion's face in no way pacified him, and seeing Meg, he realised that she was the cause of Edward's aberration. Harry felt that a little fatherly advice was called for.

"Well, all I can say, Edward, is that this time the dream has become a reality: yon's some woman. Too much for you to handle, I'd warrant."

Edward was quite serious when he replied, "I have already met the lady and I shall do all I can to further the relationship to our mutual advantage in the very near future."

"Harry, good man, was no gentleman and curtly replied, "Ye can save your fancy talk, young man, ye winna impress yon lassie."

Edward was in no way abashed.

"I think that Meg and I will get on just fine. I will do as you have already suggested, I will persevere."

And of course he did just that and, thanking Harry for his co-operation, he made arrangements for future business; then, mounting his bike, cycled the short distance to Newhaven harbour. As he walked casually round the harbour inspecting the various craft he was, in reality, hoping to catch a glimpse of Meg.

Ten minutes later and third time round, good fortune favoured him, for as he reached the kippering shed he came upon Meg's father sitting on an up-turned fishing box. He smiled; it was as if the old man had not moved from the time he had passed through on his way to Grangemouth.

The weather-beaten face of the fisherman crinkled into a smile when he saw him and, welcoming Edward back, he asked anxiously what had happened to him since they last met.

He had a story to tell concerning his misadventure on the road to Grangemouth, admitting that the old man had been correct regarding his weather forecast. The old man nodded and Edward continued his narrative, concentrating mainly on his experience in Edinburgh, but was careful to stress that the highlight had been when he met and talked with Meg at the Tron. When he told him how Meg had held her own in verbal exchanges with the old lawyer, he slapped his thigh, laughed and replied, "Aye, aye, that's Meg, she speaks her mind."

It was obvious that he was proud of his daughter and to ensure that full credit was given, he stressed she had been brought up to think for herself and act according to what she thought right. When the old man finished, Edward told him he had enjoyed speaking with Meg and hoped to have the opportunity of speaking to her again in the not too distant future.

The old man's eyes twinkled and before replying he gave a little cough.

"Well now, my lassie will be leaving shortly for Cockenzie to visit her aunt, so who knows wi' a wee bit patience, you could maybe see her."

There was a call from the kippering shed, the old man excused himself and Edward wondered if he should wait. He had an appointment with Nils in Leith and he was already running late. He knew the finalising of the S.S. Auric sea stock order was important, but the prospect of meeting Meg again was tempting. So he waited, and waited, and was rewarded.

Meg, dressed in the same clothes as the day before, came down to see her father prior to leaving for Cockenzie. On seeing Edward, she smiled to him encouragingly, then almost immediately a rapport showed signs of developing between the Scottish fisherman's daughter and the Danish fisherman's son.

It was not long before he realised that Meg was essentially the outdoor type. She admitted that she could trip the light fantastic and on the odd occasion liked watching theatre or a variety show, but was more interested in walking and swimming.

Always willing to learn, particularly from such an accomplished and attractive companion, Edward asked if he could accompany her on a hill walk, suggesting that at the end of the day they could dine at the Olde Peacock Hotel. She assented, but seemed highly amused at Edward's attitude and, giving a throaty chuckle, replied, "I think you are more concerned with the dinner than the walk."

He shook his head and assured her he was serious.

"Not so, Meg, I like you and I want to be with you doing something we could both enjoy."

She smiled her appreciation and the date was fixed.

It was a happy man who cycled to Leith, having upheld the motto of that Scottish sea port.

Chapter 11

The Chief Steward was edgy and apprehensive; looking at Sven he showed his displeasure and sought an assurance that Edward would not be too long. It was with some difficulty that Sven was able to placate him and if he had not diverted attention from Edward towards the ritual of testing the various proof strengths of Aalborg akvavit and Carlsberg, he would have had little success.

Although neither spoke their inner thoughts, they felt an obligation to try and be patient, for Edward in his own way had been helpful. Had it not been for him, Sven would not have felt compelled to solve the ship's engineering problems and the refrigeration system would not have become operative in time to salvage a considerable amount of the ship's food store. There could be little doubt that he was due his reward in the shape of supplying the sea stock order of the Auric, but where was he?

Two akvavits and three carlsbergs later, the steward felt relaxed, but it was not long before the anaesthetic wore off and he gave way to his real feelings.

"You said that your friend would be here by this time. If I don't see him shortly, I shall have to seek another source of supply. The Agent and the Captain have started asking questions and things are becoming just too awkward."

Sven, playing for time, raised his head and, looking fixedly at the Steward's drink, responded, "I think by the time you have finished your akvavit, Edward will have arrived."

The Steward seemed unconvinced and muttered something about procrastination being a major evil and as if to prove Sven wrong he picked up his glass, but hesitated when the cabin door swung open. As Edward breezed in, Sven was delighted and gave a sigh of relief. There was a moment of tension; the Steward seemed transfixed, his glass suspended halfway between the table and his mouth, while Edward, feeling responsible for the hiatus, decided to handle the situation in his own inimitable style.

"Relax Nils, relax, I am safe and I am here. Finish your drink, it's later than you think."

Nils, the glass now at his mouth, finished the contents in one spluttering swig and, looking menacingly at his countryman, slammed the glass back on the table, stressing as he did so, that had Edward been a minute later, he would have missed the deadline and lost the order. Edward countered that this was the first he had heard of a deadline, but there was no reason for anyone to worry unduly if the deadline had not been reached. He felt it prudent, however, to admit he had arrived a trifle late.

"I must apologise for the delay, gentlemen. I was unavoidably detained, but when I tell you that I met a beautiful young lady and that it took longer than I first expected to make a future appointment, I think you might understand."

Tension in the cabin subsided, even Nils started to smile while Sven, for reasons of his own, appeared serious and perplexed.

Edward took the opportunity to promise Nils that he would expedite the business on hand and would more than make up for any leeway.

Within the hour, the order was complete, the delivery arranged and Edward was on his way, leaving behind a happy and contented Steward.

As Sven and Edward walked along Leith shore, they shared their experiences over the last twenty-four hours. Big Sven, physically powerful, astute and normally cheerful, seemed miserable and despondent. Edward sensed from the conversation that his friend had allowed himself to be unduly influenced by his fiancée.

On the other hand, Edward felt that he had hit a lucky streak in business and social accomplishment. It was the latter accomplishment that worried Sven, feeling that it could affect his love life. He voiced the opinion that Felicity could be right in thinking that Edward was not a suitable companion for Maggie.

Edward laughed heartily, but the big Swede was not amused and replied that Felicity could well have a point; after all they had both seen him chatting up a woman in the pub the previous day and now this morning he had admitted to a liaison with another woman. Edward's reply was sharp and sarcastic.

"You surprise me, young Sven, I always considered you a man of the world, a very well-travelled one at that, yet here you are behaving like an over-sized Swedish bumpkin."

Before Sven could respond, Edward suggested that Felicity had based her opinion more on emotion than reason, which was probably natural, Maggie being her sister, but he was disappointed that Sven had apparently acquiesced without troubling to enquire further from his friend. Edward felt that he should expand.

"When I said I was talking with a beautiful woman this morning, I was referring to a fisherman's daughter I had met previously, the one you saw me with yesterday when you and Felicity were evidently anxiously considering my suitability as a companion for Maggie."

Sven felt uncomfortable and shuffled from foot to foot nervously, before advancing the reason for his statement. "I'm sorry I was inaccurate, but you did sleep with Maggie after the dance."

Edward's reply was scornful.

"Of course I did and so would you, unless you've decided to settle for sanctuary in a monastery. That we slept is the operative word and I found I was too fond of

Maggie to compromise her further. If it happens again, I'll have to think of marriage, but it's unlikely, I feel I'm too young to marry yet. So settle down, Sven, and enjoy your love with Felicity, but remember you have a loyalty to truth as well as love."

Sven was suspicious. "What do you mean?" he said.

Edward smiled in angelic fashion and spoke soothingly to his friend.

"I think we should be honest in our dealings with Felicity and Maggie. They should both be made aware of our behaviour with those dusky maidens we met in the Friendly Islands."

Sven was aghast and spluttered. "You wouldn't, you bastard?"

Edward laughed and pulled reassuringly on his arm. "Of course not, you bloody idiot, but give it some thought and in the future see to it that truth weighs a bit heavier than intuition."

The big Swede, bewildered, felt too puzzled to reply and Edward seized the opportunity to suggest that Sven had probably been bewitched at the time, but now that the spell had been broken, there was no reason for anyone to be concerned.

Sven wearily agreed and they both shook hands. When they reached the bridge at Commercial Street, Sven carried on to his lodgings and Edward crossed over to the Sailor's Rest.

As he entered the public bar, he thought he would order the traditional pie and pint, having acquired a taste for the small scotch pie and draught beer. It was unfortunate that he had arrived during the dockers' midday break. Several dozen thirsty stalwarts were clamouring to be served their quota of the drink that wets the 'whistle'. Feeling that time was of the essence, he decided on an out-flanking move towards the lounge.

He moved through to the relative quiet of the saloon bar. The pleasant little lady who attended him gave a wan smile when she informed him that she had strict instructions that only schooners of beer could be served in the saloon. Looking around, he noted that the bar stools and leather-covered chairs were adorned by members of an ascending social structure, probably small business men, potential entrepreneurs and a few sea captains. In the main, their tables were covered with small delicate glasses containing spirits of their choice and other accoutrements so necessary for graceful living.

He sympathised with the kind lady, observing that with so many small glasses absorbing space, the big pint tumblers could be a nuisance and a vulgar encumbrance. She smiled sweetly, appreciating his sarcasm and whispered that next time, if the bar was not too busy, she could possibly spirit him a pint from the public bar.

After settling down with his second schooner, his attention was drawn towards a trio at the far end of the saloon. As he pondered their identity, the man sitting with his back to him swung round, gave a friendly wave and beckoned him over to their table. He recognised the young warehouseman who had proven himself during the hand-wrestling contest.

Edward, however, with other things in mind, pulled out his watch and, pointing to it, indicated that he was in a hurry to depart.

After a hurried conversation, a man known as 'Cat's Eyes' approached him and invited him to join the company, if even for only a few minutes. Edward hesitated before accepting and the man reassured him that he meant what he had said. It was the man's appearance that intrigued him: he sported a long thin black moustache which seemed to lengthen as he spoke and move up and down like a large whisker on either side. His pupils were not round, but rectangular and appeared to expand latterly when he smiled. Little wonder he had been given the name 'Cat's eyes'.

When they reached the table, Edward realised that this was the first time he had met the third man. He certainly was a man of striking appearance, small and compact, he seemed self-assured and in a curious way, quite distinguished. Facially, although not handsome, his features were rugged and pleasing, eyes wide spread, an aquiline nose slightly out of alignment and a strong determined jaw, giving the impression of having lived in the time of the gladiator.

The warehouseman introduced him as Punchy Rush, formerly Stoker First Class and lightweight boxing champion of the Royal Navy, now retired and living precariously on his wits.

As they shook hands, Punchy smiled warmly and indicated that it was a pleasure meeting Edward. Edward was taken by surprise; Punchy's voice was so cultured and melodious; he was mystified and could not equate it with the tone and language one could expect from a Royal Navy stoker.

For several minutes there was a great deal of leg-pulling and good humoured banter, into which Edward himself was drawn. It was the friendliness of it all that impressed him, it was not long before he became completely involved and inspired by the music of laughter; the trio became a quartet.

An hour had passed before he realised that his itinerary had been severely dented. Still he would not have wanted to miss the experience of the last hour and would have liked to spend more time with his new companions.

That hour had been one of the happiest and most interesting since arriving in Scotland. Each one had felt uninhibited and contributed their share to the conversation and entertainment. Edward had discovered why the stoker spoke in such a cultured voice. Punchy, baptised Alister Rush, son of Angus and Morag, both school teachers in the Western Highlands, had moved to England where Angus had become Head English Teacher in a famous grammar school.

Two years later he had been sacked for openly expressing what the rather conservative board described as unwanted Socialist propaganda. After almost a year of victimisation, he had ultimately obtained the post of Headmaster on the South East coast - this through the good services of a retired Admiral turned landowner, who was progressive enough to recognise the value of having a talented teacher in the area.

It was from a background such as this that Punchy's style of speech had evolved. The pleasantness of his voice, Edward conjectured, could have been the influence of Morag, who was a music teacher. How Punchy had left a background such as this and become a stoker in the Royal Navy was a story he could look forward to in the not too distant future.

Wondering how he could overcome the hospitality of his new-found friends without offending them, he found his prayer suddenly answered. Punchy, alias Alister Rush, having finished his drink, rose from the table and addressed his companions.

"Well, gentlemen, there comes a time in the affairs of men when a move must be made if one's aspirations are to be fulfilled."

Edward half rose to facilitate Punchy's exit, but Steve Allrock, the young warehouseman, felt compelled to interject.

"Let the smooth-tongued rascal go. What he really means is that he is anxious to get on with what the police call 'nefarious activities'."

Punchy took no offence. Ruffling the young man's hair, he retorted, "I could wish now I had never encouraged you to try solving crossword puzzles. I'm afraid that your extensive vocabulary could now well land you in jail."

The repartee ended abruptly when they all discovered and declared that they had a deadline or appointment to keep, or a loved one to go home to. They shook hands, pledging that on the next occasion they would allow ample time for drinking and story-telling. Then off to their destinations they travelled, their speed determined by their ability and desire to succeed.

Having left his bicycle beside the police box at the dock gate, Edward walked back to retrieve it.

P.C. McIllwraithe sat in his small police box at the dock gate wondering if he would ever become a detective. Born on the Isle of Skye he had, as a young man, become attracted to the world of jurisprudence. It was natural, therefore, as a fan of Sherlock Holmes, that he would be drawn to Edinburgh, the home of Conan Doyle.

He would have liked to join the C.I.D., but settled gracefully for a truncheon-bearer's position in the Leith Police. Although a placid man, he was a wee bit annoyed with his Sergeant. He had hoped that the man with the three white stripes would have been more helpful in advancing his desire to become a detective. It was what happened the other day which had upset him. Being partial to a Crawford's Pie, he was about to swallow a piece when the Sergeant suddenly appeared on the scene, upsetting his timing completely. After coughing and spluttering, he ultimately managed to clear his throat and was duly complimented by the Sergeant for having the presence of mind to detect a piece of gristle hiding inside the pie.

"It shows," he said, "that you are making progress, your detection rate has improved dramatically. I remember it was only yesterday you said you intended to get your teeth into it."

The sarcasm of the Sergeant had bitten deeply, but was only transient for, on reflection, he appreciated the humour of the situation; after all the Sergeant was an intelligent Highlander like himself. He would have to be patient and persevere if he desired promotion; after all, he was a Leith policeman and 'Persevere' was the town's motto.

Walking towards the dock gate, Edward felt satisfied that he had achieved so much in a short time. He was so happy he felt like skipping for joy, but two steps, a stumble and a couple of whirls later, he stopped, knowing that if he continued he would come a cropper. Smiling wryly, he muttered 'usquebaugh' as he walked sedately, as he thought, trusting that no-one had seen his predicament.

But his gyrations had been observed and his every movement was now being detected by that aspiring criminologist, P.C. McIllwraithe. The constable reckoned that the man was a seaman, his rolling gait gave every indication. As Edward drew nearer, he noticed that the roll was becoming more pronounced and from time to time listed to starboard, probably an alcoholic inclination.

He knew that this was no ordinary seaman: although his cap was similar to that of a captain, his clothes were entirely different. There was no sign of a pea jacket or similar wear; instead he wore a well cut lounge suit of good cloth, styled in continental fashion. In the constable's estimation, he was probably a foreign businessman connected with shipping.

Edward's blue eyes twinkled as he addressed P.C. McIllwraithe.

"Good afternoon, constable, may I now be allowed to retrieve my means of transport?"

The constable was surprised; he had not expected the foreign man to speak such good English, certainly not the style of language Edward used. Taken aback, he felt he could only answer, "Certainly, sir," but wondered what his next step should be.

He recognised in Edward an eccentric character who could be a businessman of some influence and had to be handled tactfully.

Just across from the police box sat a royal blue limousine basking in the sun, its brass wheel trims unashamedly flashing the message that it was time for a little exercise. The message was received and partially understood, but the policeman, still apprehensive, turned to Edward enquiringly.

"It's a beautiful car, Mr. —?"

"Sorenson, officer," Edward replied.

P.C. McIllwraithe felt a little more relaxed now in the pursuance of his enquiries and gave a little cough before proceeding.

"I wonder, sir, are you thinking of driving that car? I noticed that you did not seem too well as you walked along the shore towards me."

Edward was amused at the polite interrogation and replied on the basis that when one is asked a question by someone in authority, it is wise to answer in as few words as possible and never over-elaborate. He smiled and replied, "I will not be driving that car today."

The constable seemed relieved and rejoined, "I suppose your chauffeur will be along later, sir?"

Edward shook his head, excused himself and walked to the side of the police box and returned with the bicycle. It was a sheepish policeman who looked at Edward, perplexed, crest-fallen and becoming ruddier by the second.

Edward began to feel sorry that he had given way to an impish impulse to mislead and then decided that he was duty bound to rescue the man from his ignominy.

"I'm sorry if I misled you, officer, but you assumed I was the owner of the car because I am well dressed, whereas it is the exact opposite, I am well dressed so that I can impress potential customers, become rich and own a car like that. So you see, you need not concern yourself too much, it was a natural assumption. I, like you, would have fallen for that one. Far more important was your concern for my safety. You thought I was a little drunk and could be a source of danger to myself and others. To sum it up, officer, you were very observant, kind and diplomatic."

Noticing a grin on the policeman's face becoming ever larger, he hesitated, but felt he had to finish.

"I would say, Police Constable —?" and he waved his hand towards him.

"P.C. McIllwraithe," the constable replied.

"I would say, P.C. McIllwraithe," Edward continued, "you are most definitely a credit to the Leith Police Force."

The Highlander could hold it back no longer; clasping his sides tightly as if to stave off a threatened hernia, he let go a gale of laughter so loud that Edward felt he had gone too far this time.

As if to compensate for his boisterous behaviour, the constable swept his long arm of the law round Edward's shoulders, as if for protection, then, giving him a pat on the back, admitted happily, "This must be the neatest way I've had my leg pulled." And before Edward could reply, he added, "I've laughed so much my ribs ache."

Edward was mystified. Not being conversant with the expression 'leg pulling', he could not understand how anyone could be happy having a leg pulled if the end result was aching ribs.

Feeling that idle speculation was now interfering with his timetable, he decided on a quick exit and replied accordingly.

"It has been a pleasant and interesting experience meeting you. I can only hope that when next we meet you will be kind enough to explain what is meant by leg pulling; it would appear that I have a lot to learn."

P.C. McIllwraithe could only gape as Edward mounted the bike for a quick getaway. After travelling a few yards, he knew there was something wrong and decided to dismount. His disorderly descent to terra firma brought a rather anxious policeman hurrying to his side.

"You will be for killing yourself, sir," he gasped.

Although befuddled, Edward knew he had been a source of worry to the man and felt he had a responsibility in dispelling his anxiety.

"Don't worry, P.C. McIllwraithe, from now on I will use the bicycle as a prop and will not remount until the fog clears."

"Yon's no fog, Mr. Sorenson, it's Scotch Mist that's bothering you," was the policeman's reply.

Edward understood and appreciated the humour of the situation and, after a few exchanges, was on his way to the meat market at Saughton. When he reached the bridge, he knew he had to turn left, but for a fleeting moment he looked across the bridge and pondered the potency of the Scotch Mist served up at the Sailor's Rest. The time factor was vital now, he knew he had to move and, as the earth showed signs of stabilising, he felt a little more secure. He even contemplated cycling, but dismissed the idea, knowing a faster and safer method of transport was essential.

Reaching the foot of Leith walk, he decided on the railway and, leaving his bike at the 'Central', travelled by train to his destination. The big butcher had not expected to see him quite so quickly, but when he learned that he had with him a large sea stock order, he welcomed him like a long lost son. Out came the bottle.

"You'll be having a dram, Edward?"

Edward acknowledged, but declined, having already consumed too much whisky and knowing he had reached the stage where he had to protect himself from the misdirected kindness of his friends.

Harry MacSween, realising a salvage operation was essential, opened his office door and, beckoning one of his butchers, gave instructions which were inaudible to Edward; then turning back to him he expressed his concern in a tone partly solicitous, but with a touch of sarcasm.

"Puir sowl, you've had a hard day. I'm thinking it's a big bowl of scotch broth you need."

Edward thanked Harry for suggesting a remedy for his malaise and quipped that he would prefer to miss the first course - felt he had been in the soup too long already.

Harry was not amused; he was curious and concerned in case his normally exuberant companion had in some way fallen foul of the law. He relaxed after Edward outlined the sequence of events since parting company at Newhaven and knew now that Edward had not been involved with the authorities.

Although Edward sensed Harry's concern, he dismissed it. There was something gnawing at him now, he was hungry, uncommonly hungry, affected with what the Scots call the 'whisky hunger' and it would continue to gnaw until satisfied. In desperation he asked, "Is there a place nearby, Harry, where a man can eat?"

There was a glint in Harry's eye when he replied, "Now that you are finished with soup, it will be a main course you are after."

Before Edward could respond, the office door opened and the butcher who had previously been given his instructions entered with a tray and set it down in front of him.

And Harry concluded, "That's your main course, Edward. Now get stuck into it, there is only one choice on the menu today."

Edward smiled his appreciation and Harry, forestalling any intervention, addressed the butcher.

"In case His Lordship is wondering what is being served, I think you should tell him, Peter."

Peter, a big grin spreading over his face, did as instructed.

"You will find in front of you a choice piece of Aberdeen Angus, baked Ayrshire potatoes, a large ringed and fried Spanish onion, with a special sauce prepared to my own specification. I trust you will enjoy your meal, sir."

Harry, a trencherman of the heavyweight division, looked on approvingly as the young Dane sliced with gusto through the tender steak, transferring mouthwards with obvious relish the Scottish fare so generously provided. Having finished his meal, he pushed back his chair, feeling replete, satisfied and happy.

He left for Leith shortly after, but not before thanking Harry for the most succulent steak he had ever tasted and commending Peter for his outstanding achievement in the culinary art.

As he travelled back on the train to the port, he took stock of the day's events and felt, on balance, that it had been a success. He eased himself back into the cushioned corner of the compartment and, oblivious to those around him, gave thought to matters personal.

Almost absentmindedly he pulled a letter from his inside pocket and started to read. For a few minutes he seemed almost asleep, then suddenly his body stiffened as he reached the ending, 'Glaedlig Jul, Din Mor.'

He cursed himself silently for not having replied to his mother's Christmas letter enquiring after his welfare. Due to travelling to various parts of the globe, the letter had not reached him till two months later, but it was summer now and he had still not replied. His father had already rebuked him for not answering letters from home and although sorry that he had annoyed his father, it was unforgivable that he had been a source of worry to his mother. A reply to his mother had to be his first priority.

There was a rueful expression on his face as he pushed the letter back into his pocket, but seconds later it changed to one of happiness as his fingers touched the pieces of pasteboard and he knew the tickets were safe, and hopefully it would not be long before he was escorting Maggie to the dance. This was something to look forward to, he liked Maggie and felt sure she liked him, but he wondered if the intervention by her sister would damage the relationship.

He had little time for speculation as the train drew into Leith Central a few minutes later.

On entering Sven's lodgings, the big Swede welcomed him with an enthusiasm that seemed strange, particularly after their disagreement earlier in the day. Pleased, but curious, Edward asked what had brought about the transformation. Sven seemed rather abashed, but smiled a little as he replied.

"After Felicity knew that you had been paying your respects to the daughter of an old friend you had met recently at Newhaven, she felt sorry that she had misjudged you."

Edward pondered the statement carefully and decided that justice had prevailed. After all, it was true that he had befriended the fisherman, the man was old and Meg was his daughter. He could therefore afford to be magnanimous.

"We all make mistakes, Sven. The important thing is that harmony has been restored."

It was a merry quartet of young people who crossed the bridge on their way to the dance at the Assembly Rooms. The two sisters walked a few yards ahead, discussing the type of perfume they had selected. The reason for the style of dress they were wearing and all the accessories thought necessary for such an important event were given full and proper appraisal.

The young men discussed what would be required to ensure that their ladies were suitably amused and entertained during and after the dance.

Reaching the appointed venue, Maggie and Felicity, assisted by Edward and Sven, removed their cloaks and after the essential preliminaries, the dancing started. Maggie and Edward were first on the floor and were soon into their stride, but Edward sensed an unusual urgency in his partner's movement. As the dance progressed, the natural rhythm returned and he felt happy to be with Maggie.

Hi-di-hi, ho-di-ho, change your partners, have a go.

He entered into the spirit of the occasion and danced with Felicity, but found her rather stiff and staid and was pleased to return to his original partner. As they danced, he knew that something was amiss. Maggie was becoming sluggish and faltering in her steps. The next dance was cause for real concern. Looking at Maggie, her face drawn and eyes lacklustre, he ventured a question.

"What's wrong, Maggie? Tell me, how do you feel?"

She summoned a weak smile and answered in a voice so soft that Edward could not hear her reply. From her expression he knew dancing and romancing were over for the night and that action was needed. As they reached a secluded part of the hall, he drew her from the floor over to a convenient seat, knowing that if he wished to help his partner, he would have to be imaginative in his approach; to appear to mollycoddle would be disastrous.

He looked earnestly at Maggie.

"I am Doctor Sorenson," he began. "I advise complete relaxation, accompanied by regular deep breathing, until such time as I return with some cool clear water."

She almost laughed, but did as he requested.

As Edward walked towards the cloakroom, his mind switched back to his youth in Laeso. He and his sister Anna had been playing around the various fishing vessels in the harbour. He had dared her to jump from one craft to another, something she had done many times before. But this time she refused and he had teased her. The outcome had been most unexpected: she had started to cry and insisted vehemently that she would find her own way home.

Edward had been scolded by his mother and then referred to his father, who had rebuked him for his lack of sensitivity. During the lecture, his father acknowledged that although, as teenagers, they had both been taught biology by Martin Svenson the Headmaster, there were however finer points which impinged on proper social behaviour and had to be recognised and considered seriously. He remembered his words.

'There are times, or should I say periods, when women are disadvantaged physically, but what is more important, they are vulnerable emotionally and should be treated with respect and tenderness.'

As he walked back to Maggie, he decided the least said regarding her state of health, the better it would be for both of them. While she sipped the water, he spoke of their surroundings and offered the opinion that it was difficult to enjoy good dancing on such an overcrowded dance floor, especially when the ventilation left something to be desired. The colour was returning to her cheeks, she felt more relaxed and agreed with Edward.

"You could be right," she ventured.

And he was a little guarded. "I was wondering if you would prefer a walk, or should I say a stroll and then supper?"

She agreed readily, and as they left the hall Maggie seemed almost happy as she waved to her sister; and Edward, always helpful, gave Felicity a reassuring wink.

Maggie was relieved she'd been given a choice; a brisk walk with Edward would normally have been enjoyable, but the way she felt, a stroll was more acceptable. As they strolled up Constitution Street, he asked her if she felt fit enough to circle Leith Links. But Maggie, not wishing to pass the Ropery and be reminded of work, opted for the road ahead and then back through the Kirkgate and home.

Having seen Maggie home safely, he set off for Grangemouth. As he cycled up Ferry Road the sky was darkening and the city lights in the distance seemed to creep gradually towards him. He dismounted and, after some fiddling around with the water valve on the acetylene lamp, he managed to achieve the white light in front, as required by the constabulary.

After remounting, he noticed the creeping lights coming nearer and was surprised when he saw what appeared to be a man with a long pole about two hundred yards away directing it upwards, when suddenly a light appeared.

Out of curiosity, he stopped and waited for the pole-carrier to approach him. He was a tall, bent-backed man; facial features were those of old Father Time, but instead of the scythe, he carried a long pole which rested against his shoulder. He stopped at a cast iron lamp standard and seeing the quizzical look on Edward's face, asked, "Can I help you, son?"

Edward smiled apologetically and responded, "Not being a native of these parts, I was wondering what you were doing with that long pole."

The old man gave a throaty chuckle. "I'll soon show you," he said.

Pointing the pole to a small glass flap on the lamp some ten feet up, he then in one continuous movement pressed open the flap, turning on the tap or valve, and lit the gas mantle by pulling down a small cylinder, exposing the light on the end of the pole. Result, 'gaslight'. Then, reversing the procedure on the way down, closed the flap and, pushing the cylinder up, enclosed the light at the end of the pole.

The old man smiled serenely as he spoke. "So now you know," he said.

Edward replied graciously, "Thank you for your demonstration: it was most enlightening."

The old man, although a little puzzled at Edward's style of speech, was quite capable of holding his own.

"Aye, laddie, as I've always said, science is a weird and wonderful subject."

And Edward, appreciative of the old man's wit and helpfulness, rejoined, "I appreciate your patience in tolerating the curiosity of an inquisitive Dane."

The old man laughed and replied, "Just tell your folks, when you get home that you met, in Leith, the man folk call Learie the Lamplichter."

Learie waved to Edward as he mounted his bike and re-started his journey. It was really dark now and he felt happy that Learie had at least made his task within city limits a little lighter.

After Cramond, there was no road lighting, but he was not concerned, the acetylene functioned well; he wondered if Learie would have approved.

From Cramond to Queensferry the road, though dark, proved no problem, but travelling down Hawe's Brae he had to be careful; to attempt to free-wheel with a back-pedalling brake could prove disastrous.

Having negotiated the notorious bend at the bottom of the brae, the rest was plain sailing and after passing through Boness, he reached Grangemouth, having completed the journey in just under two hours.

Mrs. McGregor sat musing in her chair; she hoped her young lodger would not be too late, she considered

Edward Sorenson to be a gentleman who deserved to be looked after. For a foreigner, he seemed to know the works of the Bard, surely a sign of intelligence. She was looking forward to his arrival, bearing in mind his promise to up-date her on his recent activities.

When he arrived, she ushered him to what she described as the best chair in the house and then, sitting back in her own chair, invited him to talk about his experiences in the big city.

Edward liked the old lady and, knowing that she was genuinely interested, was keen to give her a comprehensive account.

She appreciated Edward as a story teller and her eyes sparkled as he described the circumstances that brought him in to contact with various people. It was, of course, the names of the women he had met that interested her particularly. Although excited concerning any romantic trends which might surface, she restrained herself, allowing Edward to finish his story.

She settled further back in her chair, a smile on her face, then as she looked at Edward, her eyes moistened slightly when she revealed that she knew 'Meg' MacKaskill and Mussel Meg.

He was fortunate indeed, she said, that he had met and been befriended by two such well-known people on the Edinburgh scene. She respected 'Meg' MacKaskill and knew her as a vigorous and intelligent rebel, a source of embarrassment to the dignitaries of both church and state.

Mussel Meg she had known from the time she was a child up to the present time, she had developed into a handsome woman, entirely self-reliant, she had travelled like most fishwives to seek custom, but had found it more profitable and congenial to develop her own mussel stall and now had Edinburgh people flocking to consume her wares.

Edward's reaction was enthusiastic; he wanted to know more about Meg. Mrs. McGregor obliged. It was a pleasant experience for both of them, she reminiscing about Meg and her family and he showing a fond interest in anything connected with Meg.

The old lady was pleased that her young boarder had met Meg and recognised in both of them a spirit of independence and enterprise. Although Meg was outspoken, even blunt, she was nevertheless kind and compassionate. Her limited knowledge of Edward led her to believe that he was strong, but gentle, had a keen sense of humour and a ready wit, a combination she felt had possibilities. She wished them well.

Bidding Edward goodnight, she went off to bed, with marriage aforethought, her dreams would be pleasant indeed.

Edward remained sipping a nightcap his landlady had insisted would do him the world of good. He thought of the future and felt that prospects were good in his adopted land.

The Scots were kind, friendly and fair. For the short time he had been with them he had experienced a natural human warmth. It was sad that his main business rival had been an American of dubious background and behaviour. But was he really being fair? Having in the past sailed with Americans, he had found them, despite their tendency to exaggerate, to be progressive and good company: perhaps Mr. Chancitt was not so bad after all, time would tell.

Had he known that Lucius Chancitt was wanted by the Colombian Police for murder and drug smuggling, he would not have felt so comfortable.

Chapter 12

While Ignatius Lucius Chancitt was nursing his wrath, Edward Sorenson was sitting in his own special chair assigned to him by Mrs. McGregor. He had just finished writing a letter to his parents, something he had managed to accomplish after months of procrastination. His feeling of guilt to some degree dispelled, his thoughts now turned to how his lifestyle had changed these last two years. He exercised his mind in chronological fashion recalling the people he had met, the places he had visited and the wonderful moments he had experienced.

From time to time, he could hear Mrs. McGregor humming or singing Scottish airs as she flitted from place to place preparing the evening meal. He smiled at the musical intrusion, but felt it was most appropriate - after all, she was the first person he had been introduced to when he landed at Grangemouth.

When she reached 'Over the Sea to Skye', his thoughts flashed back some five years or so when he had fished on the Scottish West Coast. He had, out of curiosity, visited the misty island, but had been disappointed. As a Dane, from a country as flat as a pancake, he had been impressed by the rugged landscape, but as far as he was concerned the most beautiful scenery in the world was the sub-tropical vegetation and vista afforded by Glen Affric, a place he had stumbled upon by accident while awaiting repairs to a small craft which had been damaged in Loch Ness.

He sank further back into his chair, dreaming of the Highland scenes he had so far been privileged to see, and vowed that when time and circumstances permitted, he would explore the Scottish Highlands more extensively.

A noise in the kitchen startled him and hastened his return in space and time from the West Highlands back to Mrs. McGregor's living room. For some seconds he felt concerned and then relieved to hear the pleasant voice of his landlady singing 'Coming thru the rye'.

He was a lucky man indeed to have his needs catered for by such a pleasant, painstaking Scottish woman, and to think he would never have met her had it not been for the insistence of Tam Richards that she was the ideal landlady.

Tam had been the first person he had met after the Swedish timber-carrying ship berthed at Grangemouth. Being the ship's Steward, he had set out to replenish the daily stores and had ended up in Tam's butcher shop. By a happy coincidence, the meeting had benefited both men. Tam was on the look-out for a spare time butcher, Edward for an opportunity to leave the sea and develop a career in a country he was inordinately fond of.

Two days later he had become butcher-cum-salesman for Tam.

Ten days later, when the ship pulled away from Grangemouth, its sea stock had been replenished by Edward, who was now on course to becoming a Water Agent operating from Tam's shop.

Having been successful in launching his effort in Grangemouth, he was aware that economics would ultimately determine the spending of more and more time at the Port of Leith.

Almost immediately it reached the stage where he had to stay overnight in Leith and Mrs. Brown had been only too willing to oblige, and Maggie, her daughter, thought it was a rather good idea. At the beginning he was enthusiastic and inclined to agree, but as time passed, he became a little concerned. It was not that his fondness for Maggie was on the wane or that business was suffering; he had no fears that he could not absorb the workload while allowing time for social activities.

It seemed that, after a spell, the indoor social life lacked the spice and variety he desired. He enjoyed taking Maggie out, wining and dining her, and, if their stars were in the ascendancy, making love. However, there was more to life; he did not relish being a night hawk for too long a spell. Being a vigorous and vital young man, he also enjoyed outdoor recreation equally well and, for that matter, he was also fond of Meg.

Walking in the Pentlands, sailing or swimming on the East Coast, Meg was the ideal companion. Whether it was the desire for continuous change in the experiences in life, or the zest for life itself, or just disguised conceit, he felt he should share his time between Maggie and Meg.

To distribute his attention and talents equitably between the two women was easier contemplated than accomplished.

As business increased in the busy Port of Leith, he found himself more involved than he had anticipated in the dancing aspirations of Maggie. It was only natural that she should make full use of the close proximity of Edward. On the other hand Edward, seemingly happy to oblige, had difficulty arranging his outdoor activities with Meg. He knew he had to act and, having no intention of hurting Maggie emotionally or inhibiting her desire for dancing, he had to be careful in the way it was achieved.

It was about this time he met Ove Magnusson. Edward and Steve Allrock, the young warehouseman, were just concluding a deal when he walked into the Sailor's Rest. Steve had just acquired a case of whisky, for which Edward was prepared to exchange cigars and a few bottles of cognac. The serious business over, Steve was being flippant.

"Where did you get this stuff, Edward, off the back of a lorry?"

Edward, seemingly unaware of dockland lingo, replied, "No, not a lorry, probably from the back of a ship. All I can say is that I was out in the Firth in my small motor boat and I saw this wooden box floating around. I hauled it in and, lo and behold, it contained the merchandise you have now acquired. I should mention, however, that I have not informed the Customs Service and must warn you that Excise Duty may not have been paid on it."

Steve played along.

"I agree wholeheartedly, Edward. I believe that smuggling is illegal and could mean trouble for anyone found out."

Edward, his honour intact, was in appreciative mood.

"Thank you for your observations, my friend. As you know my knowledge of arm-wrestling is quite comprehensive, but smuggling, I feel, requires the application of someone with a criminal mind."

Steve could not suppress his mirth; he laughed aloud and, in a voice heard by many in the bar, exclaimed, "You may act the innocent, but I'll say this, you certainly know something about arm-wrestling."

Ove Magnusson, all ears, was very interested. A big beaming smile on his 'Icelandic' face, he approached the two friends.

"I could not help but overhear your remarks about arm-wrestling. It is a subject I have some knowledge of and I wondered if you would allow me to join you."

It appeared his father had been Scandinavian hand-wrestling champion, had proved his prowess in most of the world's major ports and had never been beaten. There followed some of the most outrageous and ridiculous assertions the two men had ever heard.

The impish look on the Icelander's face had them wondering what was coming next. He swivelled round in his chair, then, reaching down with his arm to floor level, he enclosed the leg of a heavy bar stool in a powerful fist and with consummate ease raised it above his head, then, replacing the chair, swung back to his original position and spoke his piece.

"Now, gentlemen, what you have just witnessed is a common exercise for strengthening the wrist, in the case of my father ..." and there he stopped, for the look of contrived astonishment on Edward's face unnerved him slightly, but Edward, always willing to help, urged him to continue.

Ove smiled his appreciation and obliged. "As I was saying, my father needed something much heavier, so he used the old fireside armchair."

Edward seemed incredulous and remarked, "You don't say."

The Icelander again hesitated, apparently enjoying himself, knowing that he was ready to deliver the punch line, but Edward beat him to it.

"And I suppose, on the basis of progression, he ended up lifting that chair while your mother was still sitting in it."

The look of deflation on Ove's face was a sight to behold. He rallied quickly, however, and was kind enough to say to Edward, "You might have told me that you knew my father."

Edward liked the man, but felt the play-acting had gone far enough.

"How could I possibly tell if I knew your father, when I don't even know you. You have not yet introduced yourself to our company. The story you told us is the same story that has been told in taverns throughout the world, before you or your father were born."

Whatever reservations the Icelander might have had, he still felt he wanted to belong.

"My name is Ove Magnusson, I am an Icelander and at the present time I am a rigger in Leith Docks and in my spare time I operate on a small scale as a ship chandler."

Introductions concluded, Edward saw to the honours of the occasion. As they absorbed their own particular beverages, they grew closer, trying, in their wisdom, to solve each other's problems in concert with an ever-changing world. Half an hour had gone and Steve became restive; excusing himself he departed, indicating that he had a distribution chore to perform. It suited Edward admirably, he could see the possibility of an arrangement taking place between himself and Ove Magnusson.

Like Edward, the Icelander had been attracted to Scotland; his mind already made up, he had remained in Leith when his ship departed. He had obtained work as a rigger in the shipyards and had acquired a small ship chandler's premises in Sandport Street. He was having difficulties, all his capital had been absorbed establishing the small business, he had no option but to remain as a rigger to balance his books.

To complicate matters further, he had promised his father that he would come home for the harvest. Within a few weeks he would leave for Iceland and he had still not decided what to do with the small shop in Sandport Street.

The Scandinavians accommodated each other. The Icelander would go home and the Dane would keep an eye on the shop. On reflection, Edward felt the bargain well struck. It allowed Ove to return home when the occasion demanded and gave him the use of the premises as a base for his activities in the port.

Whilst in Leith, he could bed down in the back shop instead of at Mrs. Brown's house. He could now take Maggie dancing when the feeling was mutual, without the inhibiting presence of Mrs. Brown. He could also take Meg sailing or walking when the weather favoured outdoor activities and Meg favoured him.

The deal proved successful: within two months Edward had sold more from stock than Ove had in the course of a year.

Yes, it had been a fortunate meeting and to think it had all hinged on the loud-voiced remark on hand wrestling by the young warehouseman.

On reflection, Edward considered he had been fortunate in his choice of friends. It was the other remark concerning smuggling that had made him think of Harry MacSween and his introduction to Oskar Petterson, the young Danish entrepreneur who had encouraged him to buy a small motor boat to assist him in his business as a water agent. Having overcome his revulsion for the evil smelling petrol engine, he had learned to use the small craft to good effect.

Arming himself with handbills advertising his services, he had been quite prepared to sail out towards incoming shipping and, using a megaphone or hammering the metal hull, to attract attention. He would then ask for a line, to which he attached his bill of fare.

If allowed, he had been quite prepared to clamber up a rope ladder and make a deal with the Steward concerning the immediate requirements of the ship.

Edward smiled when he thought of Steve's remark that the merchandise had fallen off the back of a lorry. What had really happened had made him realise that he would have to be far more astute in the future.

He had set out in the motor boat to collect the merchandise before the ship docked. An arrangement had already been made with the Steward to lower the container over the side of the ship. Unfortunately, there are such things as snags and one of these thought fit to interfere in the life of the ancient and inferior rope which gave up the ghost, relinquishing its grip on the valuable container.

As it plunged into the sea, the excitable steward had semaphored Edward that there was '-****- all' he could do about it.

Although a linguist, Edward was in no way interested, he had a salvage operation to attend to. For a full minute he wondered if the ship's propeller would send the contraband down to Davy Jones' locker. After some anxious moments, he managed to grasp the end of the broken rope and make it fast.

Reversing the direction of his small boat, he drew clear of the ship's wash and turned his attention to what might be a tricky and rather tedious rescue. Could he haul it aboard or should he be content to tow it along; that was the problem.

His mind was made up the instant he saw the sun reflecting someone's glasses about three miles distant. Instinctively, it was a case of cut and run. If he cut the rope the evidence would still be floating around when the Customs and Excise arrived on the scene. To destroy the evidence would mean knocking a hole in the box so that it sank to the bottom. But this seemed illogical; after all, he had just rescued the box from the thrashing propeller.

There was only one thing to do, run like hell. Looking back, he could see the glint of binoculars nearer now and what appeared to be the bows of a launch making towards him. Although no lover of the petrol engine, he knew the launch would probably travel twice as fast as his small motor boat.

Sanctuary in any of the Fife coves seemed out of the question; he felt he could never make it in time. He decided to head for Granton; although more open, he hoped to thread his way through the small craft in the marina and possibly jettison, temporarily, the box that was becoming a drag on his mind as well as the boat.

Providentially, another Dane was heading for Newhaven.

Oskar Petterson, after some relaxed fishing, was sailing back to his mooring in the yacht, Tivoli. Looking to port, he could see a small motor boat chugging towards him some three hundred yards away. Looking through his binoculars, he recognised Edward and wondered what the young devil was up to, why was he heading the small boat across the bow of the yacht.

Edward had seen Tivoli and knew that if he could cross in front instead of the stern, he would be outwith the view of the approaching launch for at least a few minutes. He managed to clear the bow and the container just scraped past. Oskar was annoyed and let it be known in no uncertain manner.

"What the hell are you up to, Edward? You should know better. Toy boats and steam must give way to sail."

Edward, meantime, had managed to swing round and shouted for a line to keep apace with the Tivoli. Giving his friend a sweet smile, he pointed vigorously at the oncoming launch; he almost shouted the word 'Control'. Oskar knew immediately that Edward's use of the Danish word 'Control' meant only one thing: Customs and Excise were moving in on a suspect.

"I can see them, Edward. What's your plan?"

Edward snapped back, "I have a valuable cargo at the end of the rope and I don't know whether to sink it or chance reaching Granton in time."

Oskar responded, "Let's heave it aboard, then on your way."

Edward knew that they would likely conduct a search of the Tivoli and he had no intention of landing Oskar in trouble, but there was a solution. Seeing a fish box lying amidships, he pointed to it and asked, "Empty?"

As Oskar nodded, Edward's voice conveyed the urgency of the situation.

"Then let's get this box hauled aboard, provided you attach the fish box to the end of the rope."

Preventative Officer McIntosh, the one with the binoculars who had been on the job from the beginning, knew that something out of the ordinary was taking place in the waters of His Majesty, particularly his patch. He had seen the motor boat cut cross the path of the yacht and it was now out of sight. Keeping a constant watch, he gave a curt command to his companion.

"Give her the gun, Bill, let's see what this bugger is up to."

It was no easy job getting the container aboard, but with Oskar pulling and Edward pushing they managed it in shorter time than they could have expected. Within another minute the fish box had been attached and the two friends were on course for their respective destinations.

As Edward's craft came into sight again, the ever vigilant Mr. McIntosh was able to inform his companion, "I can see him heading for Granton. It won't be long now, Bill."

Edward heaved a sigh of relief, knowing that 'Control' were definitely after him now and Oskar Petterson could expect to land at Newhaven with no questions asked. Edward adjusted the speed of the small boat to what one would expect from a perfectly respectable Water Agent.

A few minutes later the launch drew abreast of the motor boat. McIntosh very properly said his piece.

"Customs and Excise, sir. Would you tell me why you are pulling that fish box behind your boat in these waters?"

Edward gave a wry smile before replying. "I've been wondering that myself this last half hour, but when you see a box floating around with a rope attached, the natural reaction is to haul it aboard and examine the contents."

"I see," was the casual official response.

Edward continued. "My boat, being too small for such a manoeuvre, I decided to make for Granton and examine the box in the harbour."

Mr. McIntosh agreed. "Sounds reasonable, sir, I assume you will have no objections to us examining the box and its contents?"

Always willing to oblige, Edward replied, "Under the circumstances, I would expect you to; but could you inform me what the position is as far as salvage is concerned. If the box contains fish or, for that matter, treasure, do the contents belong to me?"

Mr. McIntosh was quite definite. "It would be up to the Authorities. Let's hope it isn't contraband."

Edward seemed unaware of the implications, but sought guidance.

"You mean that if it is what you call contraband, then my claim would be unsuccessful?"

There was no solace in the reply. "If we find contraband, Mr. Sorenson, you could be in real trouble."

The two officers conducted their search and found that the box contained, in the main, sea water. Mr. McIntosh, a kindly soul, tried to console him.

"I'm afraid your effort has been for nothing."

Edward was quite philosophical, at least the sun was shining. The two officers appeared friendly as they departed, but Edward was curious.

"You called me Mr. Sorenson. How did you know my name?"

Mr. McIntosh informed him that in the roads of the Firth there was a twenty-four hour surveillance by Customs and Excise and he had been seen on many occasions, also their Chief, Mr. McLeod, who was a friend of his, had told them his name.

Taken by surprise, all he could say was, "That's interesting."

Edward's reaction jogged Mr. McIntosh's memory.

"Oh, by the way, sir, Mr. Pringle at Customs and Excise would like to see you. I think it concerns something you could help us with."

Edward thanked them for their attention and promised he would call on Mr. Pringle in the near future. Feeling that Rory McLeod was in some mysterious way trying to protect him, he decided that an interview with Mr. Pringle was called for, and accepting the invitation, had gone down to the Customs House, slightly apprehensive and curious, wondering how much they knew and whether what they knew was to his advantage or otherwise.

Edward was agreeably surprised to find that Mr. Pringle was as human as himself. He relaxed, but remained alert to any development that might suddenly arise. Mr. Pringle, a friendly pleasant man, put Edward at his ease.

"I am pleased you decided to give us a visit, Mr. Sorenson."

Edward's reply was quite candid.

"Curiosity prompted the visit, Mr. Pringle. Whether I will be pleased or not will depend on the outcome of our discussion."

Mr. Pringle cleared his throat and made Edward aware that they were ever-watchful concerning the movements of men and ships on the East coast of Scotland.

"You must be the busiest Water Agent on the East Coast, Mr. Sorenson. Our men have seen you this past year in the areas of Leith, Grangemouth, also as far as Aberdeen and down as far as Berwick."

Edward knew he could relax now. "Nothing earth-shattering in that, Mr. Pringle. I would have been very disappointed if they had not seen me; after all my main function as a salesman is to make everyone aware of my presence."

As Mr. Pringle nodded, he told Edward he had already heard of his achievements from Mr. McLeod. Edward seemed almost blasé when he replied that he had found Rory to be honest and trustworthy, a person one could rely on. Mr. Pringle grinned a little and then suddenly became serious.

"Our department has a drug-trafficking problem to solve and I thought it possible you might be prepared to help us."

There was an uncanny silence for almost a minute before Edward, in a low soft voice, encouraged Mr. Pringle to carry on. Mr. Pringle outlined what he had in mind.

"We know that as a Water Agent you are constantly moving from ship to ship, and as a linguist you are readily accepted as a friend by sailors and, in particular, stewards, having been one yourself."

Edward moved his hand indicating that Mr. Pringle should continue.

"Extreme care has to be observed, Mr. Sorenson; we are dealing with people who have been known to eliminate any who stand in their way. There is a dual responsibility involved in this exercise. We have to ensure you know what you are being asked to do."

To Edward this was serious, he had to be frank. "You are asking me to spy and if it means bringing to justice those people who destroy others by peddling drugs, then I am more than willing to co-operate."

Regarding the dual responsibility Mr. Pringle had referred to, he was at pains to point out that Edward had been known to gain access to ships entering local waters before customs officials; this was contrary to the law and he hoped that he would be more careful in the future. Also, he recognised that water agents were often tempted to augment their earnings by smuggling spirits and tobacco. Anyone caught could be in real trouble and a water agent caught, however well-intentioned, would be of little value in a judicial enquiry where the department was attempting to put cocaine smugglers behind bars.

Edward was deeply introspective before he replied.

"I can appreciate your viewpoint as a government official, but I am primarily concerned with finishing off bastards who supply cocaine. I have seen too many shipmates suffer pain, degradation and ultimately death, to be very choosy regarding the way the object is achieved."

Mr. Pringle seemed slightly perturbed.

"Take it easy, Mr. Sorenson."

Edward smiled grimly before replying.

"Don't worry, I will. But you must realise that, if I'm to spy effectively, there could be the odd occasion when the timing regarding the boarding of a ship to collect vital information could conflict with the regulations; in which case I would trust that your department might come to the conclusion that a Danish seaman had possibly misconstrued what the regulations really required."

Mr. Pringle did not reply directly, but preferred to allude to the real danger involved. Drug-traffickers, he said, were a nasty lot; he could only hope that Edward would be extremely careful.

Edward assured him he knew what he was becoming involved in and he would safeguard the legal position by ensuring he was not caught smuggling.

Mr. Pringle seemed unsure that this was exactly the reply that he had expected, but he knew he was in no position to instruct.

"I am sure you know what is required, Mr. Sorenson, but I would suggest you contact Rory McLeod if you have any information to impart."

Edward left the Customs building feeling he should make a real contribution towards eliminating the cocaine smugglers, even though it meant modifying his own lifestyle. After all, Rory had put in a good word for him and it was only right that he should respond in a positive fashion. After all, what were friends for?

As he lay back conjuring up the events of the last two years, he relived those friendships, but did not realise how far down in the chair he had slipped. It was the word friend that terminated his reverie and so startled him that he almost knocked over his glass of Carlsberg.

Sitting up straight, he saw Mrs. McGregor standing in front of him, smiling.

"I thought you were asleep, Mr. Sorenson. Your eyes were closed and you had such a happy expression on your face."

"And why not, Mrs. McGregor? I was thinking how fortunate I have been in making friends since coming to Scotland."

Mrs. McGregor almost beamed at him. "Then you will be pleased to know that your friend Mr. Sjogren has arrived and wishes to see you."

It appeared that a Swedish timber ship had just managed to limp into Grangemouth and Sven had been sent as a trouble-shooter to find the fault and have it rectified. Having diagnosed the fault, he had set in motion the remedy required, and had decided that there was ample time to celebrate with his old shipmate. The two young Scandinavians set out on what Edward called a selective educational pub crawl.

It was after the second venue that Sven realised that his friend had become intensely interested in narcotics, but he failed to understand why he should be so attentive to some of the most disreputable characters he had ever seen. Edward attempted to put him in the picture and told him about his meeting with Mr. McIntosh.

"I've decided, Sven, to do my small bit in terminating their activities."

He explained that his reason for encouraging unsavoury characters to speak to him was in the hope that someone might slip in a little information. Sven was pessimistic and expressed the opinion that it was more likely someone in a dark alley would slip a knife between his shoulder blades. Edward tried to reassure his friend that he understood, but the risk was worthwhile if it meant a reduction in drug addiction.

By the end of the evening Sven had been converted and when he heard that Rory was leading the local drive, he became enthusiastic and decided to do what he could to help.

"You will be giving up your hobby now, Edward, I suppose?"

Edward laughed. "You must be joking," he replied. "It is not my intention to allow a gang of murderers who have defiled the honourable profession of smuggling to interfere with my lifestyle. However, as a conviction might affect Rory's credibility with his department, I will modify my requirements to essentials and be the soul of discretion."

Sven just shook his head in despair.

Feeling he had been too glib, Edward put his hand on Sven's arm, hoping to console him. "Not to worry, old friend, I'll be careful."

The change in Sven was almost dramatic: no longer serious, he was happy now and anxious to speak about something that had been on his mind all evening. It was his turn to put a hand on his friend's arm and, addressing him like one of the immediate family, told him that he was expecting a relative to arrive in Grangemouth for a fortnight and he hoped Edward would be able to help him entertain the guest.

Edward assented readily, but hoped fervently that it would not interfere unduly with his plan to spend a little time with Maggie and Meg. He wondered if he had been too quick in agreeing, envisaging having to escort an old aunt or uncle while Sven was enjoying himself with Felicity, but Sven soon dispelled his uncharitable thoughts.

"I think I have talked about her before, Edward - she is a young cousin called Amelia Sjogren and hails from Idala, a small farming area some forty kilometres from Gothenburg."

Suddenly Edward was interested. He remembered seeing a photograph of her shown to him by Sven, who at that time thought she was the most beautiful young woman he had ever seen. Whether this had been just family bias, or an objective opinion, he was unsure. Certainly from what he had seen of the photograph, she was good-looking. Edward was excited, but felt constrained, doubting his ability to entertain effectively a young woman from a farming background. Sven laughed at what he considered to be his companion's feigned discomfiture.

"I never thought Edward Sorenson would wonder how to conduct himself if found in the presence of a young country woman."

Edward appeared rather coy when he indicated his experience of farming had been confined to the small family holding in Laeso. He was concerned that he might let his friend down on any agricultural question which might arise - after all, the Swedes had a world reputation in that particular field.

Sven could barely contain himself. "You can stop your fooling, Edward, even if there is a vestige of doubt in your ability to entertain, I think it only fair to inform you that Amelia, or Emily as I call her, is the Stewardess on the S.S. Cecilia which docks in Leith within a week or so."

It was natural that Edward was curious and wanted to know a lot more about 'Emily' and Sven was only too willing to oblige.

Amelia Sjogren, a country girl from Idala, had left home and travelled to Gothenburg where she had obtained employment as a waitress in one of the big hotels. From there she had changed to a small family hotel, where she had been allowed to sleep on the premises, a definite advancement considering the expense involved in accommodation in a big city like Gothenburg.

One day a guest had influenced her towards accepting a position as shop assistant in a big delicatessen store which specialised in sea foods. It was there that a rich ship-owner, a partner in the business, befriended her and coaxed her to act as a nanny for his children while he and his wife enjoyed a cruising holiday through the Norwegian Fjords. She had accepted and, having proven her worth in handling children, had later joined the family on cruises.

The experience gained had given her the opportunity to apply for the position of governess to two small boys. She had held the position successfully for a year and then felt she should move on, seawards. Making use of contacts she had met during cruises, she ultimately secured a short-term contract to act as a stewardess on a Swedish cruise liner. From then on the sea became her life and she travelled the world as a stewardess. As Sven finished his story, he looked directly at Edward and, extending his arms, he said, "That's about all I can tell you about Emily."

Edward was enthusiastic and thanked his friend for re-adjusting the locale. He much preferred the sea to the land, he was sure now that he and Emily would be able to entertain each other regarding their experiences in the parts of the world they had visited.

Sven seemed almost paternalistic. "Look after her, Edward, she deserves special attention."

Edward's reply was almost predictable. "I will, Sven, surely you know that stewards and stewardesses are there to look after people. Emily and I will look after ourselves just fine."

His mission accomplished, Sven travelled back to his lodgings in Leith, but not before arranging a rendezvous with Edward at the Sailor's Rest.

Two days later, after a profitable day at the docks, Edward headed for the rendezvous with Sven. He was pleased with himself, having just landed a sea stock order for the big passenger cargo ship S.S. New World. The commission earned would be welcome, allowing him to spend more time entertaining the Swedish visitor. Fortunately, Ove Magnusson had decided to go back to Iceland for the next two months and this would allow him the scope to operate from the shop and cut down his travelling time.

It was a jaunty, breezy Edward who entered the Sailor's Rest, but his mood changed when he saw who was sitting beside Sven.

Lucius Chancitt was holding forth; gesticulating with his long spider-like arms, he proclaimed to Sven and anyone willing to listen what had to be done to ensure that the private enterprise of progressive entrepreneurs like himself should not be restricted by governments who did not understand market forces. After all, had it not been proved conclusively that free trade was the life blood of all the nations of the earth? No doubt he had in mind his inability to freely trade cocaine for hard currency because of the menacing presence of His Majesty's Customs and Excise.

Edward had no particular desire to meet the American, but it appeared he had no option. As he approached he knew he would have to be extremely patient and not be drawn into an unseemly argument that would place Sven in an invidious position. Sven introduced the American, who put out his hand, but Edward seemed unaware of it and replied with just a slight nod.

This did not disturb Mr. Chancitt, who was intent on finishing his spiel. "I was just saying to your friend..."

He got no further. Edward interjected, "I heard you telling all and sundry that you believe in free trade."

Lucius put forward his hand in a pacifying gesture. "Free trade makes the world go round," he said.

Edward was not accommodating as he replied. "A change of mind, Mr. Chancitt, or could it be that things have not worked out the way you wanted?"

The American shook his head and frowned as he said, "Ah sure don't know what you mean."

Edward told him that not so long ago he had said that it was his intention to be the one and only water agent in the area. Such an assertion signified monopoly, which was a contradiction of free trade. Lucius shuffled uncomfortably on his stool before replying, "Yeah, I was angry then and might have said foolish things."

Edward, however, was quite sanguine and congratulated him on learning from his mistakes. Not wishing to continue a desultory conversation with someone he could not trust, he turned to his friend. "I must apologise, Sven, it would appear that I have allowed myself to be side-tracked somewhat."

Sven, enjoying the rather enlightening conversation, assured him that no harm had been done and that he hoped the drink poured out for him would prove satisfactory. Edward toasted Sven and, so as not to appear rude, he asked Chancitt politely if in fact he had been successful. The American was not forthcoming and merely shrugged his shoulders, an indication that things were on the down slope.

Edward's reaction and reply, although conciliatory, had a peculiar bite to it. "Oh, what a pity, and to think that I have been rather fortunate in landing an order for seven or eight hundred pounds."

Lucius found it difficult to hide his chagrin. "Jeez, that's hard to believe."

Edward had no desire to prolong the conversation, but the imp in him made him do something that he would live to regret. With a flourish, he reached and drew from an inside pocket the order and handing it over to the American for scrutiny, proclaimed that there was no need for gloom - if he could obtain such an order, there was no reason why the American should not do likewise.

The American scanned the order and then handed it back, leering as he remarked, "Waal, you did it that time."

Edward carelessly stuffed the order into an outside pocket and, feeling he had done all that was socially required, turned his attention to Sven. It was just at this time that two characters entered and made straight for Mr. Chancitt. By ordinary standards they could be considered a rather peculiar couple. The woman, who led the way, was in her thirties, but, though her figure signified one more decade, her demeanour had all the verve and exuberance of a mature twenty year old, the flashy tight-fitting dress advertising the wares of her profession.

Her male companion was small and weasel-like, portraying what he was, a pimp. When they reached Lucius, he made great play of choosing and adjusting the position of a bar stool for his lady friend so that he could converse and look at her in comfort. Meanwhile, the pimp sat where he could take maximum advantage of any morsels of conversation thrown his way.

It suited Edward admirably, he was delighted that he could now spend a pleasant evening with his friend and hopefully be made aware of the date of arrival of Sven's cousin Emily.

An hour later, Sven drew Edward's attention to a young man who was signalling in their direction.

Edward swung round on his stool and there at a table on the far side of the room sat Steve Allrock with three friends. Steve introduced Edward to his friends and in the course of conversation he expressed surprise at the type of people Edward was prepared to associate with. Although Edward knew that the assertion was probably in jest, he was interested in why the statement had been made.

Steve admitted he knew that Sven, the Swedish engineer, was Edward's friend, but he was referring to the trio who had been sitting next to Edward at the bar. Edward laughed and indicated that although the trio were not friends, he would be very interested in knowing what Steve thought or knew about them.

Steve was forthright. "Yon big black spider you were talking to is an American by the name of Chancitt; well, the lads that have had any dealings call him the 'chancer'. The woman is Aggie Tyte, the local prostitute - at least she is honest and from what I've heard she gives value for money; and that wizened wee baukle that accompanies her goes by the name o' Wee Wullie Crockett, or Crookit, depending on whether you've had business dealings with him or not."

Although Edward was unsure of some of the Scottish terms used to describe the trio, he knew that they were most definitely 'persona non grata'.

He wondered how correct Steve was in his analysis; it was so easy not to be objective when you disliked someone. Looking at Lucius Chancitt he was inclined to agree, the American could not in any way be described as attractive. Sitting there on his perch, he resembled a vulture ready to sweep on a victim too weak to defend itself, or already dead.

He thought of the woman in a different light. After all was she not a member of the profession which had evolved on the basis of survival using the sexual desires of men to that end? She seemed a happy character, well suited to the job in hand, but, making allowances for her trade, he felt sorry that she had to entertain Lucius Chancitt. Steve interrupted his thoughts.

"You seem to be wondering if I was correct regarding the characters over at the bar."

Edward gave a wry smile. "You are probably correct, but I am still trying to figure out how the small man fits into the picture."

Steve was very accommodating and in a voice designed to protect the innocent, gave his version.

"Yon Wee Wullie is not only a pimp drumming up business for Aggie, he is also runner for the local bookie and runs the cutter and acts as an agent for Mr. Chancitt, if you please. I've no proof, but that wee bugger is probably supplying drugs to clients and the American is running the show."

The notion that Chancitt could be a drug trafficker startled him. It was strange that he had not thought of this before; after all being a Water Agent, he was in an ideal position to operate such a dirty business. From now on he would stick as close to the American as prudence would allow.

Having spent sufficient time with Steve and his friends, he returned to Sven and for the next hour they relived happy times, their eloquence of description being influenced by Carlsbergs and whiskies. It reached the stage where Edward felt it necessary to shed some ballast for relief. Returning from the toilet, he bumped into the American, who seemed in a happy loving mood and showed his desire to share a confidence.

"Say, bud, my lady friend just complimented me, she thinks I am like Sir Lancelot."

The stench of black cigar, brandy and some other adjunct from the breath of Lucius was certainly not endearing. But Edward was magnanimous. Having read the notices in the docks area concerning venereal disease and what to do, he thought it advisable to give a warning in the nicest possible way.

"Be careful, Lucius, she may have said 'Sir Chance a Lot'."

The American, although taken aback, was quick to react, his angry look was followed by a wicked smile as he replied, "So you are the clever guy! Well I know ma woman. It could pay you to give more attention to what you're drinking, man."

With that, he was gone, leaving Edward pondering the real meaning of the remark. As he made his way back to Sven, he dismissed the remark as trivial, but he was later to regret that he had not paid more attention to its significance. Reaching his bar stool, he could see Sven talking to Steve Allrock and his friends. He lifted his drink with the intention of joining them, but when Sven signalled he was returning, he sat still. For the next quarter of an hour he sipped his Carlsberg, considering whether this should be his last one. After all, he had passed his quota and this one seemed to have a more bitter taste than the others.

Suddenly a feeling of nausea gripped him, indicating he would have to move fast for sanctuary at Ove Magnusson's place or disgrace himself by being sick in front of Sven. He turned and spoke to his friend.

"Excuse me, Sven, I shall have to leave you. I'm very tired, I don't want you to have to carry me back to Ove's place."

As he rose to leave, Sven moved to restrain him, but Edward told him he would leave on his own.

"Don't worry, old friend," he said, "I will be all right," and before Sven could stop him, he was gone.

As he walked unsteadily along Commercial Street, he knew there was something seriously wrong. He had not gone beyond his normal capacity and thought the whisky or beer had in some way been adulterated. Within seconds he stopped contemplating the cause of his malaise and was considering what to do regarding the effects. The feeling of wanting to be sick was overpowering, his legs were leaden and there was virtually no feeling in his feet.

There was a pain in his chest now, big beads of sweat ran down his face and neck, his head was on fire, but he felt too weak to remove his hat, having to concentrate all his efforts in reaching Ove's place.

How he reached it he would never know, but once inside all his knowledge and cunning came into play, survival became paramount. Giving way to nature, he was violently sick, some of his senses of orientation were returning, but he knew by instinct that he had to prepare quickly for the siege.

By a supreme effort, he filled a pail with cold water, assembled all the towels available and placed them beside the bed. He felt his temperature rising rapidly, there was a tight band round his chest severely restricting his breathing, even removing his clothes required a superhuman effort. Even taking off his shoes posed a major problem: each time he bent forward, the floor seemed to come up and prevent him untying his laces.

He felt if he continued, the floor would surely come up quickly and knock him unconscious. He solved the problem ultimately by lying on the bed and bringing his feet up towards him, despite the pain in his chest, which was almost intolerable.

There was still a spark of humour in him: he felt that it would be most unseemly to be found dead in bed with his shoes on.

His body temperature was increasing rapidly, every joint and muscle ached and seemed to function in a sea of fire. He felt he was burning up and wondered how long he would be able to tolerate cremation whilst still alive.

Gradually the heat subsided in the body as a whole, but persisted in the neck, throat, ears and eyes, making him feel totally wretched. Physiologists would probably describe his condition as exquisite pain, but Edward, poor soul, could be excused for feeling that any second the top of his head would blow off. With great effort he managed to wring out a towel soaked in water, and wrap it round his head. Before he could consider his next move, he fell back onto the bed, unconscious.

Many hours later, when his senses returned, the fire in his body had died down, but his limbs ached intensely when he attempted movement. He was so weak he had to use one arm to help the other in establishing whether the top of his head still existed. It was with relief that he realised no dramatic change had taken place. He could see, he could hear and could lick his lips. With great difficulty he raised himself sufficiently to dip a glass into the pail and sip some water.

Within minutes he had been transported to Siberia, his limbs shaking and quivering so violently that he was sure the bed would collapse. He drew the bed clothes around him as best he could and mercifully an hour later he fell asleep.

For three days he had alternating dreams of the tropics and the polar regions, but the application of water and towelling saw him through.

Realising that he had survived, his first thoughts turned to business affairs. Suddenly, he remembered that the sea stock order for the S.S. New World should by this time have been delivered and was angry that he had missed a deadline.

His immediate reaction was to jump to it, which he did and failed miserably. Collecting his thoughts, he knew business as usual would take at least another day. To make himself acceptable to human society he felt he had to think back before he could move forward into the real world again.

What had happened that caused the malaise which at one time had made him feel he was dying and what to do to prevent such a catastrophe in the future?

Considering his behaviour over the last few days, the only variable factor that came to mind was his last drink with Sven. He could remember that the drink had tasted different. Checking his belongings, he found everything in order, with the exception of the sea stock order which should have been in the inside pocket of his jacket. Although missing, it did not disturb him, knowing it mattered little now; but suddenly he recollected transferring it to an outside pocket. On examination, he was disturbed to find it missing and conjectured on whether it was carelessness on his part, or had it been stolen?

He decided to dismiss it, but notched it in his mind for future consideration and then set about a regime of rehabilitation.

He sipped glasses of water, massaged his limbs and exercised his body to the stage where he could wash and dress himself in such a way that society might accept him as a normal person. He was hungry now, but still felt that liquids were essential, having heard from old sailors that water is vital for survival, even before food. Not wishing to advertise his subjective decadence in the Sailor's Rest, he sought the nearest pub.

After downing a pint of the local brew and working his way through a couple of Scotch pies, he was almost ready to meet the world. Another pie and a pint, he felt he probably could.

His first aim and desire was to re-establish himself as quickly as possible and what better place to start from than the security and comfort of Mrs. McGregor's home. Making himself as presentable as possible, he set out for Grangemouth, where Mrs. McGregor welcomed him like a son just back from a long voyage, and within two days of good food and care he was ready for anything.

Fortunately for his ego, his first day out proved very productive. Having landed an order from a Swedish ship and another from a Finnish timber carrier, he made straight for Tam's butcher shop.

He had barely concluded his business with Tam before Sven entered. His first greeting was straight to the point.

"Where the hell have you been all week?"

Edward smiled serenely, indicating he had no idea that it had been so long. Sven was still serious and concerned.

"Stop fooling around, Edward. What happened to you after you left the Sailor's Rest?"

Edward gave a detailed account of what had happened, but Sven, though sympathetic, told him not to worry about the shipping order. Edward could only stand and stare as his friend outlined what had transpired the following day.

It appeared that Mr. Chancitt had found the order late in the evening and in the morning had contacted Sven. They had both gone to Ove's place and knocked loudly on the door, but could get no answer. Sven looked searchingly at his friend.

"Either you did not hear, or were in no fit state to answer."

Edward mulled over the facts that were now emerging. The order he had stuffed into the outside pocket had been dislodged, either purposely or accidentally, and that Mr. Chancitt should find it and elect to return it seemed out of character. Edward was very curious.

"What happened after that, Sven?"

Sven was a little hesitant, feeling he was playing an intermediary part between his friend and the American.

"Chancitt said that you were expected to fulfil the order that day, and rather than letting it go by default, he would arrange delivery himself and see you in a weeks' time."

Edward smiled thinly before replying, "That's a likely story."

Sven frowned, but Edward was quick enough to reassure him.

"I know what you did was for the best, but I happen to know Chancitt and I shall be extremely surprised to see him if he sees me first."

Sven shrugged his shoulders before replying. "Well, anyway, I'm pleased I have found you, I have some news that may cheer you up. Emily will arrive in Leith in three days' time and I am relying on you to do your bit entertaining her."

Edward was once again his happy cheerful self. "I'm looking forward to that day, Sven, I won't let you down."

Emily, a stewardess on the S.S. Cecilia, had just finished duty and instead of retiring to her small cabin, had elected to go up on deck and watch while the ship ploughed through the Firth of Forth on its way to Leith docks.

Normally she would have stayed below, but this was a special occasion: she was looking forward to seeing her big cousin, Sven, and also see something of Scotland. Lately she had been homesick and wanted to see trees again, something to remind her of her Swedish homeland.

Chapter 13

As the ship neared the docks, she wondered and hoped that Scotland would live up to her expectations. Like all ships over five thousand tons, manoeuvring into position can take up more time than an excited and impatient stewardess can be expected to tolerate.

At last the S.S. Cecilia was safely berthed, and standing down on the quay side, opposite the point where the gangway would ultimately be lowered, was the tall figure of Sven. Standing beside him was a smartly dressed young man wearing a seaman's hat; even from where she was standing, he appeared to be smiling up to her. As she waved down to them, Sven shouted to her to remain on board as they were going to board the ship once the gangway was lowered.

As soon as Sven reached the deck Emily, normally a serene and serious young woman, rushed to him, flung her arms round his neck and gave him a resounding kiss.

Sven laughed heartily and chided her gently.

"Such un-ladylike behaviour from a young maiden, what would your Grandmother Sophia have said?"

Emily feigned petulance. "I don't care, I'm so happy to be with you, you big oaf."

After introductions, Edward asked if he could be accorded similar treatment. She replied, "I know too much about Danish sailors to risk it. Some day when I know you better, I may allow you to kiss my hand."

Edward's riposte had her laughing. "Such bravery, would you not be afraid that I would bite it?"

Sven intervened, telling them that he had an appointment with the Captain and Chief Engineer regarding some specialised equipment his company were hoping to install and he felt they would get to know each other better in the next half hour.

Emily smiled sweetly and invited Edward into the pantry. "Schnapps?" she asked.

Edward nodded his head in agreement and she poured out two measures of akvavit and, deferring to her guest, opened a Carlsberg. They clinked glasses. "Skol," she said quietly.

"*Skol Vackre Flicka,*" Edward replied.

Emily, or Amelia Sophia, as her passport indicated, was relieved that Edward intended to speak Swedish, but she felt from the start she should indicate to him that flattery would get him nowhere.

Sven's business stint stretched out for more than an hour, during which time Emily and Edward had covered much of their young lives spent in various parts of the globe. Emily had already confessed that she wanted to see as much of Scotland as was practicable while the ship was berthed in Leith and Edward had promised he would be pleased to make arrangements accordingly.

Sven had already made plans for the day and had decided to take his cousin up to Edinburgh to visit the castle and other places of interest, while Edward suggested she might like to visit the Botanic Gardens with him and view the trees and flowers.

Her eyes lit up as she smiled to him. "*Braw,*" she replied and from then on their friendship grew.

Within a few days they were always together and cousin Sven was happy; it left him more time to concentrate his attention in the direction of Felicity.

After a week they had become good friends and a fondness for each other was rapidly developing.

Sitting in the Royal Theatre during the interval of a variety show, Edward discreetly studied his companion and realised that the photograph did not do her justice - she was indeed a real beauty. It encouraged him to think that she was so happy in his company, particularly when he had come to understand that her intelligence was higher than he had expected from a woman raised in a Swedish farming community.

A week had passed and their friendship had grown into affection and was showing all the signs of maturing into something of a more permanent nature. Their relationship had reached the critical stage. Both knew full well that as shipping companies operate to a schedule, the ship could sail within the next day or two. Emily knew she had a decision to make, should she sail and keep in touch with a dear friend, or stay and risk her happiness in a foreign land?

Edward's dilemma was similar: had he the right to influence Emily to stay? The problem was held in abeyance when the company decided to dry-dock the ship for essential repairs, giving both of them a fortnight to make up their minds.

During this time, Edward worked and planned with only one thing in mind: the love and retention of Emily; while she knew the time for serious discussion was drawing ever nearer. It seemed to her that she had three options: she could sail with the ship when the repairs were finished, go home to Sweden, or stay in Scotland with Edward. Her first option was bedevilled by her love for the sea and her vocation as a stewardess. Any spare time she had was always spent above deck watching the ever-changing pattern of the waves, the antics of porpoises and the sheer mystery of flying fish, the glorious sunsets and their reflection on the water. Heavy weather and big seas in no way disturbed her, but she could not tolerate strong cold winds; even then she preferred above deck if she could find a wind-break for shelter.

It was life below deck that was becoming irksome, at the beginning it had been better, she liked people and performed her tasks cheerfully. As a stewardess on passenger and cargo ships, she had control over her own pantry and could normally satisfy the most fastidious passenger. Lately, however, she had worked on some of the larger passenger ships and had found that being one of many, her tasks were given her by the Chief Steward. On the passenger liners she rarely managed to get up on deck because of the extra duties that could arise, such as assisting women passengers, particularly those with children.

On the smaller cargo-passenger ships she rarely had trouble, the passengers were usually more seasoned travellers; but on the bigger vessels there were far more people to deal with, often their first time at sea. Looking after seasick passengers, tending them when they thought they were dying and cleaning up the subsequent mess became a little irksome; but when it cut into her off-duty time day after day, it became almost intolerable.

Still, she had tolerated it, always in the hope that her next ship might be another 'cargo-passenger', sailing to parts she had not yet explored.

Her next option was to head for home and see her family and try to adjust to life on the farm. She would dearly like to see her mother, but life on the farm was not for her; after all, she had struck out on her own as a teenager and had never regretted it. She had met people from all walks of life in the city of Gothenburg and, having enjoyed the experience, had determined that, as variety was the spice of life, the slow moving rural life was not for her.

Although excited by the changing scene as she travelled the world, her attitude towards men had been one of coolness and tranquillity; she liked and was liked by her shipmates, but romantic interludes had been rare.

The entrance of Edward had changed all that; this was no interlude, this was the real thing. She had thought at the beginning he was a rather brash, although likeable, young Dane and she had learned he was not foolhardy, but was an optimistic extrovert, physically and mentally equipped to achieve the targets he set himself. He was kind and considerate, indeed a man of character, and any controversial position which arose invariably evoked the words 'no problem' - and he meant it.

His gentle persuasion had left its mark. She recalled with delight how he had guided her through a waltz, which she normally avoided; but in his arms she felt safe and had been surprised to feel that success had been so natural.

She liked the man, she was very fond of the man, she thought she loved the man and hoped fervently that he loved her and that being together for the rest of their lives would be 'no problem'.

It was the intervention of Sven which influenced the 'to be or not to be' of popping the question. Having heard that the S.S. Cecilia would put to sea in four days time, he was anxious to ensure that his friend was aware of the latest news, particularly as his cousin was involved. Edward knew now he would have to move quickly and positively if he wanted to win Emily as a partner for life.

There was a remarkable rapport between them, despite their difference in nature. They found a common interest however in many subjects, particularly things nautical and any phenomenon associated with the seas through which they had sailed. There could be little doubt that they were very fond of each other - but could this alone guarantee they would sail safely through the sea of matrimony on a voyage into the unknown?

Edward smiled at the poetic trend of his imagination, but felt it worthy of further development. Would he be the Captain and Emily his First Mate on that fateful journey? Being a progressive young man, ahead of his time, he realised this could be construed as male chauvinism and felt he should influence his partner in accepting an equal share of the tiller. Hopefully, as they explored those uncharted waters, they would be blessed with a family in their search for the promised land.

Edward stopped his mental meandering and concentrated his attention on a problem that could arise immediately should they decide to marry. Would it be a church wedding, what were the religious implications, what would Emily want?

As far as he was concerned, a formal contract between two individuals should suffice, shake hands and then look after each other for the rest of their lives.

He knew he was deluding himself if he thought it would be just that simple. Civilised society exacts a price if you want to participate; the Minister, the Priest or Registrar has to be paid his fee before you can join the ranks of those deemed respectable, and enjoy the fruits of what has been peculiarly described as the Christian way of life. Although a man of principle, he was also a realist and was big enough to accept that the Minister and the Priest were doing their stint and should there be any truth that marriages are made in heaven, then at the very least he would have purchased an insurance policy.

The very next day Edward did Emily proud. In the morning they travelled from Leith by train to Inverkeithing on the Fife side of the Forth. He had determined they should both travel over the Forth Bridge, a structure he considered to be the most fantastic bridge he had ever seen. After a pleasant walk to North Queensferry, they crossed over to the south side and, after lunch at the Hawes Inn, they walked to Dalmeny and boarded the train to Edinburgh.

Disembarking at Haymarket station, they walked back to Donaldsons Hospital where Edward waxed lyrical concerning the architecture and what it portrayed, stressing that Edinburgh had many fine buildings. He wondered if he had gone too far in displaying enthusiasm for things inanimate, when his companion was probably more interested in the living planet.

She seemed to read his thoughts and gave him a dazzling smile as if to indicate her appreciation of his efforts at entertaining her, realising that he was selling the proposition that if she was interested in putting down roots, then Scotland had something unique for both of them.

She knew what he was up to and he knew that she knew what he had in mind and such moments are precious.

He felt that the programme he had in mind had reached the stage where his partner should be consulted.

"I know you love trees and flowers, Emily, and not far from here there is a place they call the Botanic Gardens. We can take a taxi and be there in a few minutes, or walk and reach the gardens in half an hour."

She looked at him, took his hand and, smiling encouragingly, said, "*Skal vi spasera.*"

Edward was delighted that she preferred walking, it gave him the opportunity to describe the Edinburgh scene in a more leisurely fashion. As they walked hand in hand the carefree young couple chatted merrily, reaching the gardens quicker than they expected. For an hour they wandered through the gardens, Emily constantly astonishing Edward concerning her seemingly comprehensive knowledge of trees and flowers.

Although more interested in fauna as opposed to flora, he knew he had to discipline himself and show that he was interested, he had to remember that this was to be Emily's day.

So Edward, apparently attentive, even engrossed, listened and tried to remember the names she mentioned so that he could prove later that he had been listening to her and might ultimately develop an interest akin to Emily's enthusiasm on the subject.

She knew he was doing his best, squeezed his fingers tightly, smiled to him and in a happy but slightly emotional voice thanked him for a wonderful day. As he thanked her for the compliment, he assured her there was much more to look forward to.

They could go up to the city and visit some of the famous buildings, see the Castle, or go to Corstorphine and visit the famous zoo.

As they made their way out through the gate, he ventured the question, "Possibly, you do not care to see animals in captivity?"

Smiling shyly, she respond, "If they are looked after properly, I do not mind in the least. In fact I am very interested in horses and, although I have only been here for two weeks, I have seen what I would describe as the noblest horses I have ever seen. They are bigger and more powerful than our horses in Sweden. They are, in my estimation, magnificent animals. I think they are called ..." and here she lapsed.

Edward came to the rescue. "Clydesdales," he said.

She beamed him a smile as she nodded her head.

Some twenty yards away from the main gate stood a carriage and pair. The young horses were restive and whinnying as if anxious to move. Emily spotted them and sought Edward's approval in approaching them before they departed. Edward, who always moved quickly when it was essential, dashed over to the man with the reins and asked if he would be kind enough to wait a few seconds and allow his young lady friend to look at the extremely well-groomed horses.

The man, appreciating the compliment, looked back enquiringly at the owner, an old lady flamboyantly dressed, wearing an enormous picture hat. Edward looked back hopefully, but could hear no audible sound.

The big hat moved up and down giving assent to the coachman, who in turn agreed.

Edward turned round sharply to wave Emily over and nearly knocked her down in the process, for she had decided to be as near as possible to the horses whether permission had been granted or not. He apologised, but Emily did not seem to hear, she was already stroking the nose of one of the horses, blowing and crooning in a husky voice towards the nostrils of the beast. She looked at Edward and in a happy excited voice she asked, "Aren't they elegant?"

Before he could reply, the voice from behind the hat enquired, "What did she say, Mr. Sorenson?"

Edward was truly flabbergasted and moved towards the back of the carriage to investigate. As the hat brim swept up to greet him, two old merry blue eyes twinkled and a voice he knew from the past repeated the question. For a few seconds he was dumbstruck, then suddenly the voice, the face, the horses and carriage all fell into place.

"How wonderful to see you, Margaret MacKaskill. I must apologise for not recognising you immediately, but you did catch me rather unawares."

The old woman smiled sweetly towards him.

"Yes, yes," she said, "I forgive you, but what was it your young friend said?"

Edward explained that Emily was a Swede and she had indicated in her own language that the horses were elegant.

The old lady gave a throaty laugh and offered the opinion that Emily was not only beautiful, but highly intelligent into the bargain. Margaret was enjoying herself.

"You say she is a friend of yours, Edward Sorenson. How friendly, may I ask?"

"Very friendly indeed," he replied. "I am very fond of Emily and I feel sure she is fond of me."

Edward made the introductions and when Emily knew she was in the presence of Lady Margaret MacKaskill she wondered, having in mind the Swedish trait of recognising protocol, whether she should curtsey or not. Edward laughed and Margaret, knowing that Emily's language was Swedish, was obviously curious.

When he explained that Emily was anxious to act correctly, she asked him to inform her that if she showed any signs of subservience to the aristocracy, she could expect a crack over the head with her parasol. Recognising Edward as a free spirit who, like herself, abhorred bigotry and privileges she felt she should at the least spend the afternoon with him and Emily, who patently appeared to be his fiancée. She invited them to tea and Edward, who liked the old woman, accepted on behalf of both of them.

Despite language difficulties, Emily felt living and enjoying life minute by minute was the best option available and she felt instinctively that Lady Margaret MacKaskill was a good person who wished them both well. From Edward's point of view, the meeting had been most opportune, for he had already planned to visit Princes Street. It could now be done in style through the kindness of the old lady.

The language barrier precluded any real dialogue between Emily and Margaret and, although Edward acted as interpreter and intermediary, it was natural that it would develop into a two-way conversation, with Emily the listener. It suited Emily fine, she settled back to enjoy the experience of travelling by carriage drawn by such elegant horses, whilst Margaret and Edward relived the first day they had met. Listening to the buzz of conversation, one might have thought that they had been friends for many years.

Whether it was her desire to spend as much time as possible with Edward, or to please Emily's love of horses, or that she wanted to ensure that the horses were not subjected to climbing the steeper braes of Edinburgh, Margaret decided, whatever the reason, to take the longer, easier road home.

The coachman nodded approvingly and headed the horses towards Fettes College; from there a canter at moderate speed took them down to Comley Bank and then, turning right, a gradual ascent was made through the sweet smelling area of Orchardhead. At the top of Orchardhead the coachman eased them round onto Queensferry Road and thence home to Charlotte Square at the West End.

Lady Margaret MacKaskill had a diary into which she entered only the important events in her life. It is to Edward's credit that she saw fit to enter that Amelia Sjogren, a young Swedish lady, and Mr. Edward Sorenson, a young Danish sailor, took tea with her and shortly after left to visit the famous gardens.

There could be little doubt that Margaret would have liked Edward to have stayed longer, but she recognised that Edward's almost undivided attention was directed towards Amelia Sjogren. And why not? That was as it should be. As they left, she wished them well, gave his hand a squeeze and, for him alone, a little 'wink'.

As they walked arm in arm towards Princes Street, Emily admitted to having been in the 'street' with Sven, but only for a short period. She hoped on this occasion to be able to take her time and explore the shops in a more comprehensive fashion.

Recognising a woman's prerogative to test the various values offered in the market place, Edward readily agreed and promised assistance should she require any. After examining woollens and tweeds, she disclosed a future interest, but contented herself with a few personal purchases for immediate use.

She looked appealingly at Edward, "Let's cross over to the other side," she said.

He was surprised, but delighted, that Emily had spent less than an hour in the shops; obviously the sight and smell of the flowers had been the main attraction. It suited his purposes admirably, he could now court Emily in comfort. Conditions could not have been better: a warm sultry day in July, flowers in their ascendancy and a brass band playing on the central bandstand.

As they reclined on a park bench listening to the music, he chose the intermission to advance his theories on the pursuit of happiness. He painted visual pictures that suited his purpose. How could anyone who had seen the Highlands and Islands of Scotland wish to live anywhere else? On occasion the weather might be particularly foul, but there was no such thing as perfection and after all experience could always guide one on holidaying elsewhere relative to the atmospheric variables likely to occur. Then there was the alternative of using their inherent skills, sailing to some remote tropical island and living an idyllic life, free from the constraints of civilisation.

By this time he had his arm around her waist and, drawing her closer, whispered sweet messages into her ear. She did not appear to restrain him, but her message, if not loud, was definitely clear. She warned him that if he gripped her any tighter, she would be physically unable to answer his questions. The look of consternation on Edward's face was such that she relented. As he released his grip, she caught hold of his hand and pulled his arm back round her waist and laughingly quipped, "I like your arm around my waist, but not too tight. Take it easy, we have a whole life ahead of us."

Edward heaved a sigh of relief. He knew he had blotted his copybook and deserved to be punished and replied accordingly.

"You are right Emily, I am too quick. A strange feeling seems to influence my behaviour and it's as if, if I don't grab happiness today, I might not be alive to enjoy it tomorrow."

Emily shook her head before chiding him.

"Don't grab, Edward, I will still be by your side tomorrow and I hope we shall be together for a long time to come."

She kissed him full on the mouth, they both laughed happily and from then on their hearts sang in unison. They were pals now and would do everything together, all inhibitions had disappeared as nature took its course. As they walked through the gardens to the west end, Emily absorbed to the full the floral beauty around her and from time to time she pointed upwards to what she called *Edinborg Schloss*.

Thorough as ever when planning a venture, Edward felt elated that everything had worked out even better than expected and looked forward eagerly now to a successful climax.

That evening they dined at the Caledonian and it was after dinner when they were sipping coffee and cognac that Edward took advantage of the convivial atmosphere to broach, once again, the subject of cohabitation or marriage. Emily agreed readily that she would like them to be together, but although the isolation on a tropical island might seem idyllic, she felt it would soon prove unrealistic. Can you imagine, she said, what life would be like living almost entirely on fish and coconuts? There would no civilised cuisine, no coffee or cognac, no akvavit, Carlsbergs or cigars. At that point he held up his hands and surrendered, agreeing that the tropical island idea was definitely a non-runner.

However, the Scottish option was attractive, but she felt uneasy concerning the language and admitted it could be a barrier. Edward tried to treat the matter lightly, assuring her he would soon teach her the language. She was sure he was a good teacher, but he might soon discover that she was not a very bright pupil.

He laughed and attempted to allay her fears and realised almost immediately that to try and flatter or cajole would prove ineffective. It was evidently a matter that required serious consideration, and, to allow time for thought, he switched the subject to religious beliefs and how it might affect them in a life together.

As a child, Emily had been brought up in the Protestant faith and had been taken every Sunday, religiously of course, to the village church. Learning about Christianity had been a mysterious affair, uncanny, and to her not a part of the real world. As she listened to stories from the Bible, she had built up a picture of the Deity and his son. Christ was a good man who lived according to the ten commandments, while God was an older man of gigantic proportions who, for reasons of his own, allowed Christ, his son, to be crucified. Years later as she grew older and bigger, God diminished in size until he barely existed in her mind, whereas Christ became ever more significant.

It was only after the ritual of confirmation that she gave the subject serious attention and, as far as she was concerned, it mattered little whether Christ had historically really existed or not, It was more important to know that someone of outstanding character and charisma had, by example and great fortitude, demonstrated to the world that the human race could only hope to survive if the evil forces of private greed were made to submit to the good of public need.

It was Edward's turn to bare his soul. He would have been taken to the Scandinavian church every Sunday had he been available and willing to attend. On hindsight, he had to admit that his father must have had the tolerance and patience of Christ to allow him to skip

Sunday observance on such specious excuses as temporary amnesia and a feeling of claustrophobia during a long sermon.

He felt he had attended often enough and long enough to form an opinion. His mind on religion had been influenced by a number of factors, such as the subject matter of the Preacher and the subsequent questionable behaviour of the leading Christians, so called, of the local church, together with the stories and observations of sailors down in the harbour, many of whom were engaged in the Baltic trade, including, on a few rare occasions, contact with Russian sailors, some of them Bolsheviks.

It was a story of dire poverty and oppression. Many millions of peasants and workers had perished in the first decade of the century. The Czarist police had been extremely cruel and in many cases the church had either ignored their flock or made excuses for the excesses of the establishment. It was the word of the rulers they accepted, not the word of God.

On hearing this, he had wondered why they called it Holy Russia. If the statements were true, then the Christian religion was surely flawed. These thoughts were in his mind when he was called before the pastor as a candidate for confirmation.

The Pastor, alarmed at Edward's attitude, hastened to explain that he should not believe everything he had been told. Edward agreed, indicating that although he was only a teenager, he had already learned to listen and observe before forming an opinion and then, if the evidence appeared irrefutable, possibly acquiring a belief.

He knew there were good people who really believed, but unfortunately there appeared to be too many Christians, so called, who used the word of God to suit their own selfish ends.

How often in history had Christian leaders, such as prophets, priests and adventurers, sent people to their deaths on the basis that they had received the divine word of God that his will be done?

The Pastor did his best, God bless him, but Edward was neither convinced nor confirmed.

As they left the Caledonian Hotel, Edward suggested they should drop into the second house of a variety show at the Theatre Royal. He signalled a taxi, but Emily would have none of it; she wanted the experience of travelling in an Edinburgh tramcar.

It was after the show, while they walked down to Leith docks, that Edward saw fit to re-open the conversation regarding the potential for a successful marriage. It was now clear that religion would not prove a barrier; it appeared that both were inclined to agnosticism.

On reaching the foot of Leith Walk, he steered his partner gently down through the links. It flashed through his mind that this was an action replay of an experience from the not too distant past. It was a most peculiar sensation, almost one of exhilaration, tinged with pathos; every movement was almost identical, it had been Maggie then, it was Emily now.

Edward could see the Ropery building now and knew the dramatic moment was nigh. He was happy and optimistic, but hoped that nothing would go wrong.

They sat on a park bench, he put his arm gently round her waist and asked: "The ship sails in two days' time. Will you stay with me, Emily, or sail away?"

She smiled and replied, "Maybe."

He looked anxiously at her. "What does that mean?"

She smiled again and shook her head slowly from side to side and answered, "It depends on you."

He looked at her longingly and did not reply immediately.

Then she gently scolded him. "For a man who usually acts so swiftly, on this occasion you are so very slow."

The transformation was dramatic, his serious face seemed to expand as a big beaming smiled sailed through. Then dropping down on one knee he extended his arms towards her and asked enthusiastically, "Emily, will you marry me?"

She nodded her head in a most definite fashion; only one word was uttered.

"Yes."

As they walked towards the ship, her bed for the night, he assured her he would always be at her side till she learned the language and should either of them feel the urge to return to the sea, then they would do so together. They would always be together, for the rest of their lives.

Chapter 14

The Caledonian Hotel at the west end of Princes Street is a rather large, posh establishment, where monarchs, celebrities and people like the Sorensons deign to spend the night before travelling on. Having agreed to marry, Edward busied himself organising the honeymoon, or what he termed the first holiday for his bride and himself.

Having sampled the fare and inspected the facilities of the good hotels, he had turned his attention to the cuisine and comfort of the hotels of distinction.

After some good food, some rather indifferent cuisine and taking a risk on the comfort as advertised, he had decided on the Caledonian; not because royalty had stayed there, although there could be little doubt it would be a reasonable hotel; it was the distinct advantage that they could, as the porter had said, drop out of the bedroom onto the railway platform below.

This had been the deciding factor in booking room 289 within this rather extraordinary monumental red pile.

He had set his heart on seeing the Western Highlands with Emily by his side and having a bedroom only a minute or two from the railway platform was extremely fortunate.

That morning they had been married by the local Registrar in front of their witnesses, Felicity and Sven, and then travelling by taxi they reached the Caledonian in time for a celebratory lunch.

After lunch they all retired to the privacy and comfort of room 289. Within minutes they were enjoying coffee and cognac and, while the men smoked their cigars, the women sampled some pastries and other little surprises, courtesy of a Danish baker and confectioner Edward had met in Leith some time before.

Edward had done his homework from the time that Emily nodded her head. In a little under two weeks, he had found Emily a temporary apartment in Grangemouth after the ship had sailed, had acquired a house and made it habitable, ensuring it was stocked with the essentials, not forgetting the re-stocking of his dwindling supplies of akvavit, cognac and cigars. His shipping contacts, friends and suppliers had been aware of what was expected of them. Being a popular man, they had responded magnificently and a little of the proceeds were now being appreciated by the company of four.

As could be expected, the bride was the centre of attraction, but what had not been taken account of was Emily's limited knowledge of the English language. After the initial adoration of the bride one could expect the women, God bless them, to discuss such important matters as dress, hairstyle and domestic plans for the future. While the men, God help them, would be expected to figure out the economics of life so that the aspirations of the family could be fulfilled.

Determined to make a success of what could be the most important event in his life, Edward noticed that his wife was showing signs of strain as she listened attentively, but without understanding what Felicity was saying. He intervened immediately in his usual frank and direct manner, offering a solution that would allow the party to roll merrily along.

"There are three of us who speak English, while Emily, who in my estimation is the most important member of the party, speaks only Swedish, her native language. I suggest, therefore, that she converses with Sven, her countryman, and I am accorded the privilege of addressing Felicity. In this way, we will learn more about each other and our particular interests and I promise you, Felicity, that if there are questions you wish to ask Emily that I cannot answer, then I will be more than pleased to act as interpreter."

From then on the party went with a swing, Emily serene and feeling safe, Felicity making full use of the interpreter and he in turn happy that he had intervened in time to make the small wedding party a success.

When they left, Sven gripped Edward's hand and, with just a trace of emotion, asked earnestly that he look after Emily with his life.

Felicity kissed Emily on the cheek, wished her eternal happiness and pointing towards Edward, she said without rancour, "Keep an eye on him, he's a terrible man."

Emily gave a little smile and nodded agreement, then just as Felicity passed her on the way out, she winked to her indicating she was learning fast and although some might consider her a country bumpkin, she knew she was no longer rusticating and, probably more to the point, she was no longer at sea.

The Scottish weather, although unpredictable, has one constant feature - there will always be plenty of it. It has an unending variety for such a small country, it can vary greatly from coast to coast. When the sun shines it can be warm and relaxing or humid and uncomfortable, dependent on location and wind factors.

When it rains, which is frequent, it can be soft or hard; if hard it dampens the spirit of holidaymakers and farmers whose crops have been flattened, and if soft, provides a bonus for the whisky trade. When it snows the children whoop with joy, while the transporters by road and rail bemoan the fact that the weather, once again, has left them too little time to reorganise.

For intrepid mountaineers from other countries, the smaller mountains of Scotland seem to reach Everest proportions when the chill factor intensifies alarmingly as the damp and dour gales sweep down through the glens.

Although all the atmospheric conditions outlined are obtained in one form or another in various parts of the world during different seasons, Scotland has the unique and macabre reputation of producing them all within an hour or so, but to do this in the middle of summer is unforgivable.

When Sven and Felicity left, the sun had been shining, but a sudden pit-a-pat on the windows changed the plans of the Sorensons. Within seconds the temperature dropped and the pit-a-pat had been replaced by the hammering of hailstones.

Originally it had been mooted that they should go for a walk in the gardens. As shepherds in the Lothians and fishermen on the East coast cursed the weather, the Sorensons changed their minds. Had they thought of those men at risk in the hills and at sea, their hearts and thoughts would no doubt have been with them, but this was their wedding night, a very special night and the sudden storm, which was increasing by the minute, channelled their thoughts instead to each other. Why walk in the storm when you can lie in the arms of a loved one.

Safely ensconced in room 289 with a service bell to hand, they had every reason to be happy. They took off their shoes, stretched out on the bed and, looking once more at the glowering sky, they hugged and embraced, acknowledging their good fortune. For a while they lay peacefully in each other's arms making love talk, but as the weather improved, their thoughts turned to the Scottish Highlands and their projected visit.

As the sun rose, they rose and dealt with things that would influence their holiday. As Edward consulted his diary and other relevant material, Emily examined her wardrobe to ensure that she had in her possession items which were essential and could prove invaluable while travelling, knowing that men often did not recognise the appropriate requisites.

When it came to the time for dinner, Edward became a little edgy; Emily seemed to be spending an inordinately long time in deciding what she should wear. Women seemed obsessed with colour, everything had to match and to ensure that proper comparisons were made, Emily had commandeered the bed, but possibly because of the Swedish fetish for cleanliness the shoes were still on the floor.

Edward, having resigned himself to a long wait, sat back in a chair and attempted to show a real interest in her choice of dress. At long last she was dressed and ready to meet the world.

"How do I look, Edward?" she asked.

"Gorgeous," he answered, "the dress looks excellent, but more to the point, it is your beauty that shines through, the dress is merely the frame."

She looked at him quizzically, but he assured her. "I mean it, Emily."

And he did, but his patience was wearing thin, his mind was no longer on dressing, more on undressing and looking forward to the ecstasy of ultimate fulfilment. He was happy that at last they were going down to dinner and Emily, quite radiant, remembered the words of her husband.

The dinner, the first evening meal since becoming man and wife, was excellent and quite literally gave food for thought; it was the precursor to meals much similar that they intended to prepare and enjoy in the near future. That they agreed in every respect and detail could obviously not be expected, but it was an appetising way of spending a part of the evening. Being at one time connected with the preparation and presentation of food, they both had an extensive knowledge of international dishes.

They vied with each other regarding the recipes they could remember and their ability to produce the best results. They had fun teasing each other: she seemed to favour the vegetables and sweets and he the fish and meats.

Emily's favourite was a special cauliflower soup made originally by her mother and Edward's preference was for a flounder or 'rod spotter' roasted in a certain way.

Edward teased her. "No wonder you chose cauliflower soup! Living on a farm you only needed to go into the backyard for your ingredients, not very adventurous, I must say."

Emily's reply was fast, if not furious, and delivered with just a touch of scorn.

"You poor fish, no wonder you're wet, always dangling your hook for a red spotted flounder."

Edward grinned and smacked his lips.

Emily proceeded. "Now that I know your preference, my task will be easy. Every day from now on when I ask you what you want —"

But Edward broke in, "I'll have red spots."

Emily smiled sweetly. "You could rue that remark, Edward Sorenson."

Having satisfied themselves that they had dealt adequately with food, they turned their attention to travel. After swapping stories of their adventures in weird and wonderful places, they returned to their new home, Scotland. Edward was just about to tell Emily what he had seen so far in Scotland when he noticed a waiter hovering near the table. On looking round, he noticed that they were the only guests in the dining room. He drew Emily's attention to the state of affairs. As he pointed upwards, she nodded and they left for the bedroom.

He suggested that they should have a nightcap and advised coffee and cognac. Although she agreed, she cautioned that coffee might keep them awake. Edward in a bright and breezy mood, expressed himself accordingly.

"Just the very thing we require, Emily, being our wedding night, I should think we will welcome the opportunity for a little extra time to get close and find out more about each other."

Emily acquiesced, but seemed rather diffident and Edward, recognising her shyness, cursed himself for being too hasty and tried to rectify the situation by apologising and assuring her that the speed of their love-making would be determined by her desire.

As they sipped their coffee and cognac, Emily put her hand on his arm and said softly, "I understand, Edward, I trust you."

As the coffee in their cups and the cognac in their glasses descended, so did their clothes, until they were standing facing each other, naked. Edward stretched out his arms in semi-invocation and asked earnestly, "Well, Emily, what do you think?"

She saw a muscular man of medium height, whose Scandinavian skin was lighter and finer than she had expected. She liked what she saw. She did not reply immediately, but seemed to be giving it consideration, her eyes mischievous, her lips moistening and turning gradually upwards, giving the impression that the verdict would be favourable. Edward was patient, he knew that a 'faux pas' could not be tolerated on the connubial threshold.

He took full advantage of the pause to look at and admire his wife. Her facial beauty he had become accustomed to - now was the time for the naked truth. Physical beauty is no guarantee for happiness, but to find that the woman you love has all the attributes associated with, what the pundits call, the perfect figure, was indeed heart-warming and exciting.

Emily gave her verdict. "You are better built and stronger looking than I anticipated; you have the finest skin I have seen on a man. I'm happy that you are my man."

It was with a feeling of exhilaration that Edward replied.

"I'm overjoyed and proud, Emily, that you, the most beautiful woman I have ever seen, should see fit in your gentle and patient manner to refer to me as your man. I am a fortunate man indeed to have such a wonderful wife."

There is no record of what took place during that glorious night, but it is safe to assume, from the look of serenity on their faces the following morning, that both had done what was required of them and had enjoyed it immensely.

After a substantial Scottish breakfast, they set out by train for Fort William. It was an interesting journey, particularly for Emily who, from imagining Scotland to be solely a land of mountains, rivers and valleys, was surprised and delighted to see so many trees. She was already feeling at home as they passed through dense forest land, there seemed even a greater variety of trees than in Sweden.

Arriving in Fort William, they deposited their luggage in the station and explored the Highland town and its environs. It was just outside the town, on the road leading to Corpach, that they caught sight of the summit of Ben Nevis.

Emily looked up at Scotland's highest mountain, then looked at Edward and he, in turn, repeated the performance, outlining the feasibility of the project. With proper walking shoes, they could probably reach the summit and be back in five hours.

She looked at her husband. "What do you think?" she asked.

Edward offered the opinion that they could do it, but not necessarily immediately. After all this was their first visit to the Highlands and, with only two weeks available for touring, it might be more rewarding to cover as much territory as possible and not spend too much time in any one place.

Emily looked wistful and Edward adjusted his stance. "We could do it now, but it might be useful to think of this as an exploratory visit. We can always come back for anything we consider rather special."

As Emily pondered, Edward recanted. "Come on then, Emily, we will visit 'Ben'."

She smiled, but looked puzzled. Should she or should she not accept his invitation? She took his arm and they started out towards the mountain, just as a veil of Scotch mist started descending.

Just before leaving the station, Edward had purchased a copy of The Times hoping to bring himself up-to-date sometime during the day. Had he looked at the left hand bottom on page one, he would have known there would be increasing precipitation in Western Scotland.

Being acquaint with the language of the weathermen, he would then have ensured that he and his wife were properly equipped.

As the mist turned to rain, he was annoyed, knowing their 'macs' were resting snugly inside their luggage at Fort William station. That the 'met men' had been correct in no way placated Edward; these were anxious moments. On his own he would have dismissed the possibility of saturation with a shrug, but he had the responsibility of ensuring the safety and comfort of his wife.

Emily, having had a special coiffure for her wedding day, was still wearing a rather petite Parisienne confection on her head. To face the probable ire of Emily with her hair dishevelled and the hat destroyed had to be avoided at all costs.

There was no sign of a taxi or similar conveyance in sight, but on the other side of the road he could see, about a hundred yards away, what appeared to be a stone cottage. He acted quickly: snatching The Times from his pocket, he opened it out fully and asking Emily to extend her arms, put the edges of the paper into her hands. He exhorted her to grip firmly, keeping the paper in tension.

She looked dismayed and questioning, but found she could manage it, and Edward tried a little encouragement.

"You're doing just fine, Emily. It may seem a strange umbrella, but it could keep your head dry until we reach that house down there."

Emily, dubious concerning the protective device, gave a sickly smile, but kept pace with her husband as they walked rapidly to the cottage. As it rained heavier, they increased their pace, hoping to reach safety before the deluge overtook them. Suddenly, a big wooden board stating B & B loomed up in front of them. Then a quick dash up the garden path, they reached a small porch adjoining the cottage and they were safe, at least for the time being.

Emily suddenly came to life. Discarding the sodden makeshift umbrella, she gingerly touched her hair and finding the condition acceptable, threw her arms round her husband's neck and gave him a resounding kiss. He laughed nervously, but was pleased that Emily was happy and wondered if she would approve of his next move.

Before he could speak, Emily intervened. "*Seng og Frokust*," she said and pointed to the door of the house.

Edward, although taken aback, felt relieved, but was surprised she had understood the big bed and breakfast sign. He had, as promised, started to teach her the language, but could not recollect making reference to what every tourist should know.

Again he attempted to speak, but she smiled in her gentle fashion, put a finger on her lips and, delving into her handbag, produced a translator and pointed to the relevant phrase. 'Seng og Frokust, equals bed and breakfast.'

He nodded acceptance of the interpretation and was ready to agree, but this time Emily took the initiative. She made use of the big brass knocker on the door and then, adjusting her clothes, brushing back wisps of hair which had strayed or had been whipped out of position by inconsiderate atmospherics, she felt ready to face the occupant of the house.

The door opened and a rather rotund and genial woman, whose complexion reflected a life spent in the country, smiled and asked, "Can I help you?"

Emily smiled back and graciously pointed to Edward.

And he responded, "I trust we have not inconvenienced you, we saw the sign."

Acknowledging that they were welcome, she ushered them into her house and asked them to make themselves comfortable. Within minutes an agreement had been made that they would stay the night and travel northwards in the morning.

Although Emily and the woman seemed to be relaxed in each other's company, despite the language problem, he felt uneasy knowing they could not travel far without their luggage. Emily, sensing his discomfort, looked questioningly at him and just as he was about to explain, the genial countrywoman entered carrying tea and scones.

All was forgotten as Emily commented on the delicious fragrance of the scones. As Edward hesitated, the woman entered yet again carrying photographs, maps and other materials advertising the benefits to be derived from holidaying on the west coast. She was sincere and enthusiastic about life in her corner of the world and seemed determined that all should recognise that there was no place quite like the West of Scotland. She addressed Edward.

"Your name is Sorenson. Forgive me for asking, would you be a Scandinavian?"

Edward felt accommodating. "You are right, it seems my English requires improving."

She blushed a little. "No, it was the name which interested me," she replied.

When she knew that he was Danish and Emily Swedish, she shuffled the photographs around and picked one out to show that they were not the first Scandinavians who had stayed with her.

She became quite excited and told them the man in the photograph was a Swedish timber merchant and the woman his wife. They had stayed with her on several occasions for periods of three or four week at a time. They had become good friends and she had even learned a little of the Swedish language.

Within minutes the two women were light-heartedly involved in establishing who knew more or less of their respective languages. Both admitted laughingly that they had a lot to learn. More important they were learning to understand each other and the end result was one of happiness in each other's company.

Meantime, Edward was able to relax and only intervened when asked to.

Suddenly the rainstorm stopped, the sun shone and peace returned at last to that part of the Western Highlands. He looked out of the window at the changing scene, then looked at the ladies, who in turn had followed his gaze, but seemed more interested in their discussion than the elements.

Edward, satisfied, acted promptly and preceded his exit by informing them that it would not be long before he would be back with the luggage. On his return, Emily told him about her conversation with Mrs. McCallum. As he showed surprise, she indicated that the name had come up in the course of conversation just after he had left. Remembering Maggie's preference for an ice cream topped with raspberry sauce, he felt guilty, but smiled and assured his loved one that he had heard the name before, but did not associate it with the Highlands.

Emily was quite excited and eager to tell him that Mrs. McCallum had said they should go to Mallaig before they journeyed too far north. He assured Emily the suggestion was a good one and that it was part of a plan he had been contemplating for a considerable time. Emily was pleased that she was making a contribution towards their holiday and, hoping to ensure its success, she produced a piece of paper on which was written a bed and breakfast address in Mallaig. As he looked up from the piece of paper, she smiled to him and, as if to be assured that she had acted properly, she uttered the words, "Seng og Frokust i Mallaig?"

He nodded agreement, adding that he was pleased she had been able to converse with and enjoy the company of Mrs. McCallum. They had been fortunate indeed in seeking sanctuary in Mrs. McCallum's house.

Having spent two hours on her own with a Scotswoman, Emily felt she had acquitted herself well, despite language differences, and looked forward to further progress. She looked appealingly at Edward and asked, "Would my husband learn me some more of the language?"

He was only too pleased and told her the difference between teaching and learning and then proceeded to teach her some useful phrases.

There would come a time when she would want to read as well as speak the language, in which case he warned her that English grammar could be difficult and phonetics played a significant part. For a little light relief, he gave an example of four words ending in 'ough' and thought it appropriate to set the scene against a farming background.

"The t-ough old farmer while working with the pl-ough, was soaked thr-ough to the skin and the following morning he was confined to bed with a sore c-ough."

It was imperative that the proper sounds were used relative to the preceding letters or the message would be nonsensical. He read out the message properly and when Emily indicated she understood, he asked her to listen to what could happen if read improperly.

"The t-oof old farmer while working with the pl-uff was soaked thr-off to the skin and the following morning, had to stay in bed with a sore c-ow."

Emily laughed at the illustration and realised she would have to be careful in the usage of the language, but added that the farmer concerned could not have been amused.

The following morning they set off for Mallaig, and Emily, pleased that she had been able to establish a rapport with Mrs. McCallum, who had given her an address for their next stopping place, felt she was making a worthwhile contribution to the holiday.

Her husband, happy that his wife was showing signs of wanting to play a major part in arranging their accommodation, sat back in his seat and planned ahead, while enjoying the scenery on the way to the West Highland sea port.

Having established base in Mallaig, they treated themselves to boat trips between the islands. It was a luxury indeed to have others looking after them.

Three days later, after a diet of Rhum and Eigg, and a final dinner of fish steaks, they moved northwards.

Boarding a small craft, they sailed to the small fishing port of Applecross where Emily, having done her homework, was cordially invited in by Mrs. Greig, the sister of their landlady of the night before.

To Edward's surprise, Emily had produced a letter and Mrs. Greig, a cheery buxom woman, had been delighted to receive it and was only too pleased to provide a bed for the Sorensons. She thanked Emily for coming and stressed, "If you hadn't, it would have been another three months before Mary put pen to paper. She's a great lass, but awfu slow in writing."

Her home was their home if they decided to stay and she informed them that her husband Anton was expected within the hour. The name Anton struck a cord; for Emily it conjured up a picture of her oldest brother who had emigrated to America. Tall, good looking, even distinguished, she wondered if this Anton would be like him.

Meanwhile, Edward speculated on the name Greig, it indicated a Scot or a Scandinavian, but a classic name like Anton seemed out of place.

The arrangement had barely been concluded when there was the crunch of solid feet on the pebbled path outside the house. The door opened and there he stood, Anton Greig, six feet and twenty stones of mighty muscle and merriment, his bearded face wreathed in an enormous smile. As he came towards them, Emily was amazed that such a big heavy man could move so swiftly and lightly.

Even more interesting was his perfect manners. Having introduced himself, he apologised for smelling of fish; after all that was his trade, but he assured her that after a bath he would smell like a rose. He then turned to Edward who, having heard the introduction, felt that a little nonsense might be tolerated, and asked, "I heard you tell my wife that after your bath you would smell like a rose. Being unaware of local habits, I wondered if you were referring the garden rose, or cod roes?"

Anton smiled wryly and appeared to look down despairingly at Edward.

"Mr. Sorenson, for a remark like that, I think you should be pun-ished."

Edward readily agreed. "My pun was a poor one. Could you suggest a place where my education might be improved?"

Anton Greig, born in the Arctic Circle, a product of a Norwegian fisherman and a Swedish country woman, knew what was required.

"I don't think your malaise is connected with education or the lack of it, but your ramblings suggest that you are suffering from severe dehydration and should undergo treatment without delay."

He turned to his wife and cheerily announced that he would be taking Mr. Sorenson down to see the doctor.

Emily immediately reacted, wondering what had happened to her husband, but Mrs. Greig placated her, indicating that her husband had his own peculiar way of suggesting that they adjourn for refreshments. She went through the motions of drinking and said 'Skol'. Emily, relieved, smiled tentatively, but Mrs. Greig was not amused and admonished her husband.

"Anton, Mrs. Sorenson is Swedish and that could make things difficult for both of us."

Anton, in no way abashed, replied that his wife had spent three months with his mother while he had been at sea and that had more than equipped her to make Mrs. Sorenson feel at home. Mrs. Greig looked at Emily, who smiled and appeared to give assent.

"All right, Anton, dinner an hour and a half from now, or a burnt offering can be expected," was her parting shot.

Edward, a willing patient, looked forward to seeing the 'doctor' and wondered if the brew would suit his palate. He already knew that when a Scot visits the doctor he is really stepping into his local pub and the prescription is his favourite tipple.

Before Edward could adjust himself to his new surroundings, he found himself in 'The Smuggler's Cave' with Anton ordering the first round.

After a little harmless fencing with no offence being taken, they were just establishing a happy relationship, when the hubbub around them suddenly ceased. It was this and the barman greeting a newcomer that made Edward look up. It was obvious that it was a person who merited special attention, for everyone in the bar smiled and accepted his vociferous greeting, "Evening lads."

He walked over to their table and, acknowledging Anton, looked questioningly at Edward, and Anton made the introductions.

"This is my very good friend, Doctor John Broad."

After introducing Edward, the trio took stock of each other before a meaningful conversation started and meantime Doctor John Broad had removed his deer stalker hat and started his pint, whilst weighing up the newcomer. It was natural that Edward was at the same time assessing the doctor. He saw a man of medium height, a rosy complexion indicating a life outdoors or a slight over indulgence in the national beverage, more probably a delightful combination of both. He had rather small hazel eyes, enquiring and mischievous, reflecting possibly a pre-disposition towards practical joking. He liked the man, but felt he would have to be wary.

Doctor Broad, formerly an Edinburgh surgeon, now retired, but active in local affairs, wondered why a Danish sailor should choose to holiday in Applecross.

"Well, what do you think of Applecross?" he asked.

Anton felt he had to intervene. "Steady on, John, Mr. Sorenson has just arrived. You could hardly expect an opinion in such a short time."

Anxious to engender an atmosphere of democratic equilibrium, Edward put a restraining hand on Anton's arm and suggested that from now on they save time and advance the fraternal spirit by using first names only. The doctor's eyes were twinkling as he spoke.

"Good for you, Edward, but the question still is, what do you think of Applecross?"

Edward was willing to comply and told his new-found companions how he and Emily had travelled by boat through the Sound of Sleat and Kyle of Lochalsh and thence to Applecross. His knowledge of Applecross was, therefore, limited to what he had observed from the boat as it berthed at the small harbour.

He had seen considerable stretches of fine sand to the north of where he had landed, similar to the sandy beaches in Jutland and the island of Laeso where he was born. He had not seen signs of coastal roads during the trip, but this could have been that trees, shrubs and the rocky shore line obscured them. Even local seamen might have difficulty in pin-pointing any roads against a landscape of such precipitous cliffs and small fjords, that were ultimately absorbed into the mountainous background.

He felt that the experience had been well worthwhile and, if Applecross was as beautiful as the places they had seen, then he would be more than satisfied. Even the apparent inaccessibility by land was not all-important.

Dr. Broad showed his pleasure.

"I am pleased, Mr. Sorenson that you think our west coast is so attractive. What intrigues me is that you, a Danish sailor, should give praise in such exotic terms. You could be an asset as an agent for the Scottish tourist trade."

Edward's reply baffled the doctor somewhat.

"Dr. Broad, let's be mundane and enjoy ourselves - surely first names are essential. Your assertion, John, that my description was exotic is incorrect. The Western Highlands viewed from the sea has a unique beauty all of its own, no transplant is required. Had you mentioned Glen Affric or a similar spot, I would have agreed, for that glen reminds me of the verdant growth one can expect in some parts of sub-tropical America."

The doctor nudged Anton in the ribs.

"You might have warned me that Edward was a Scandinavian intellectual."

Anton was quite happy to allow Edward to reply.

"I am a Danish seaman with an aptitude for languages and sometimes I am too serious regarding usage. The word intellectual sounds rather pompous, I would rather be known as an intelligent Dane."

The doctor nodded approval, but asked why Edward did not consider accessibility to be all-important and Edward replied that the sea villages probably felt that their requirements were met adequately by marine transport; if not, he was sure they would have ensured that proper road communication with the interior was established. As the doctor hesitated, Edward decided to continue.

"You made a remark in jest that I would be an asset in the Scottish tourist industry and I see no reason why the Scots, who are skilled engineers and ship builders, should not build small tourist ships which could transport passengers through the fjords and sea lochs."

To approach the beautiful West Highlands in this fashion was, in his estimation, a glorious experience.

"Just imagine," he said, "a foreign tourist sailing through one of your craggy canyons into a sea loch with a majestic mountain in the background and the captain, a Highlander, standing up on the bridge exalting the beauty of the Highlands in his soft lilting Highland voice."

Doctor Broad, who had been sucking his pipe while listening pensively, suddenly came alive. He shook his head from side to side and replied, "Edward you are a romantic."

Unabashed, Edward smiled sweetly and asked, "Be patient with me. Remember, I am on my honeymoon."

Before the doctor could reply, Anton suggested the quicker he and Edward left for home the better, he had no intention of risking the ire of his wife. Doctor John Broad, an old confirmed bachelor, looked despairingly at his companions and admonished them.

"Aye, away you go, laddies. Fine I ken the power o' petticoat government."

The two men need not have concerned themselves, for the two women had done very well together, thank you.

"Dinner will be a little late, gentlemen. Mrs. Sorenson and myself have had a fair crack the-gither."

Early the following morning, Doctor Broad called to enquire after the health of the newcomers and suggested that Edward might like to accompany him on a wee hill climb. Edward agreed and Emily insisted that she also would like to come along.

An hour later and a thousand feet up, Applecross was no longer visible. They were standing on a grass covered plateau looking down into the valley below. Edward, willing and anxious to learn, saw that despite the enveloping mist there was, some fifty yards away, what appeared to be the hard surface of a narrow road. Thinking of the previous night's conversation, he drew the doctor's attention to a seeming phenomenon.

John, a patient man when circumstances warranted, slapped Edward on the shoulder and congratulated him on a most singular observation.

"Yes, Edward, you are right, what you see is a part of the road, if you could call it that, leading up from the valley below. So you see, there is access from the interior over the mountain pass and down into Applecross, but to be fair, I should mention that motorists think it is probably the most hazardous road in Britain."

Edward seemed intent on tracing the path of the road in the swirling mist, but Emily's interest had been aroused by the sudden appearance of a mountain peak to the east of where they were standing.

She tugged at John's sleeve and when he turned, she walked her finger across the palm of her hand and pointed. He laughed at her method of communication and informed her that the peak was known as Ben Eighe, but to get to it could be long and dangerous under present conditions. She nodded her appreciation of his desire for her safety and then pointed in the direction of Applecross forest. Following his wife's gaze, Edward addressed the doctor.

"Put Emily in the direction of trees, John, and she will walk for miles."

For the rest of the day they explored, despite intermittent mist, the various forest trails and beauty spots, ultimately ending their walk opposite the Smuggler's Cave.

After dinner, Mrs. Greig asked Emily if she would like to accompany her on a visit to her friend, a Norwegian lady who had married a Scottish fisherman, a friend of Anton's. Emily responded enthusiastically, knowing the presence of another Scandinavian could assist her in learning the language and habits of the Scottish people.

Where three married women are gathered together, it is inevitable that the shape of things as they are and as they should be becomes the central issue in their conversation. Since the beginning of time, women have been only too aware that the dominant male, so called, has managed the affairs of humans in a somewhat questionable fashion and women, as bearers of future generations, have had no option but to react and plan on the basis of human survival.

For centuries men, in the guise of witch doctor, minister, priest or Pope, have indoctrinated women in the hope that they would assimilate their propaganda that women, as child bearers, had a special place in life and could not, therefore, live on the same level as man. But they had their place in the scheme of things, like staying at the back of the cave or kitchen cooking the produce of the weary hunter, caring for his children, even those of his concubines. Woe betide any female who, during her duties, attempted to brew herbs in an endeavour to cure man's ailments; she could expect to be dubbed a witch and burned at the stake.

Despite such little Christian inconveniences, the various Popes have referred to 'mulieris dignitatem' or the dignity of women. Having the privilege of conveying God's message to women, they proclaimed the Almighty considered women ideally suited for such tasks as water carrying, cooking, the caring of offspring, the wiping of bottoms and the drudgery to which they were ideally suited. However, there is a price to pay for such dignity. Women were expected to be silent in church, their heads covered, and dressed in such a fashion that the innocent male would not be over-excited.

The three women, Emily, Mary Greig and Gretha, her friend, would not have tolerated any man dictating to them when to be silent or how they should dress, irrespective of his social standing. But despite the incantations and exhortation of false prophets, clerics and other representatives of a male hegemony, they achieved a real dignity, the dignity of good motherhood.

Mary and Gretha both had children, it was natural therefore they should have a common interest in the care and training of children and although their conversation embraced such subjects as local politics and gossip, the major part usually focused attention on the family.

Emily was finding it difficult to follow the conversation until Gretha realised that the Swedish woman would be experiencing the same problem with the language that she had when first arriving from Norway.

From then on, Gretha translated from Scottish or English to Swedish, often via Norwegian. Conversant with the Norwegian language, Emily was grateful and it was not long before she was playing her part in the affairs of women.

Gradually the subject matter became confined to children and the disciplining thereof. Emily, newly married, could only sit and listen; not being a member of the Mother's Fellowship, her views would carry little authority, but, as a likely aspirant, she kept her ears open.

Some time later her thoughts turned to Edward and she asked Mary if the men would be joining them. Her reply was very much to the point.

"Bairns and men are better out of the way when women are having a serious discussion, but never fear, they will be enjoying themselves in their own way."

It was a sheer coincidence that Edward should ask Anton at that particular moment:

"Will the women be joining us?"

Anton grinned broadly as he replied. "I should hope not. We are free men for the next two hours at least and believe me, the women would not want it any other way."

Although a kindly man, Doctor Broad was intolerant of anything which suggested procrastination.

"If you laddies would stop nattering about your marital affairs, we could get down to the serious business of drinking and conversing amongst friends."

Edward responded immediately, pleading guilty to the offence, but asked that mitigating circumstances could be considered on the basis that he was unaware of the rules applicable in the Smuggler's Cave. Anton burst out laughing, offering an opinion.

"That should teach that pompous old bachelor, but I fear you were far too polite to him."

John ignored Anton and, looking straight at Edward, smiled and offered the opinion that, for a Scandinavian, his English was rather exceptional. It was this incident which put Edward's contribution on the agenda. He warned his friends that although he had an aptitude for learning languages, the telling of that tale could be boring, but John and Anton thought otherwise and encouraged him.

As a boy he had become fascinated by the glamour of yacht and schooner racing and the people who owned and sailed them. Those beautiful luxury craft were owned by Swedes and Germans and were normally berthed in the relatively safe Eastern bay of the island. Edward lived in Vestero near the working harbour and travelled over to the east side whenever the opportunity arose and involved himself in the nautical activities of the tourists. By the time he was seventeen he could speak Swedish and German fluently.

It was about this time he met Karl Koenic, the owner of a small merchant fleet which plied between the Baltic ports. While his yacht had been berthed at Laeso for minor repairs, he had impressed Koenic with his rope splicing skill and, when he asked if he could sail in one of his ships, the ship owner readily agreed.

Starting as a deck-hand, he was detailed to assist the ship's carpenter when required. Igor Petrofski, the carpenter, was a most unusual man, his face was that of a poet or revolutionary, his heavy body that of the peasant and his hands, powerful and dextrous, gave a true indication of what he was, an extremely accomplished and efficient carpenter.

He was a Russian and, like the carpenter who trod the earth two thousand years before, he preached his version of the Sermon on the Mount. The Holy Russian Empire could not be expected to countenance a young

Bolshevik expressing the view vehemently that Christ's Sermon on the Mount and true Communism were one and the same thing.

No Christian empire, so called, could tolerate such private enterprise based on real Christian ethics. After three years of torture and tedium, he escaped from Siberia and reached Finland. Ever watchful of the Czarist police, he managed one day to sign on as a crew member of a ship owned by Karl Koenic.

It was this man who taught Edward the Russian language and he, a willing pupil, learned quickly. Igor, anxious to pass on his knowledge and philosophy to the younger man, taught him to play chess and the finer points of survival in what he lamentably called 'this society of greed'.

For almost two years Edward sailed between the Baltic states and Scandinavia. It was from Copenhagen that his adventures into the bigger world outside started.

Esme, a petite vivacious young Italian woman, viewed Copenhagen from the bow of the 'Bella Napoli', a two thousand ton cruise and cargo steamer of modern design. Although known as Esme, her full name was Esmeralda Cala, the first child of Guiseppe and Maria Cala. Maria insisted that the girl be named Esmeralda, in memory of the honeymoon spent near a cove in one of the Spanish islands.

Edward, remembering the incident as told to him by Esme, laughed involuntarily as he recounted his version. His companions wondered, but said nothing and Edward continued.

The Bella Napoli was short of a crew member and the captain was having difficulty filling the gap. The Danish sailors available were not keen, knowing that the conditions on the Italian ship would not measure up to Scandinavian standards.

But Edward had not quite made up his mind; he knew he could tolerate the conditions; more importantly, the explorer in him was curious to know where in the world the ship was heading.

He had seen Esme silhouetted against the skyline, he liked what he saw and followed her movements as she walked along the deck and gradually descended the gangway to the quayside. Noting her Latin features, he mustered a little French, mixed with Spanish.

"Por favor," he said.

"Si," she answered, smiling sweetly.

Having heard of the vacancy, he danced a jig on the quay and pointed to the bridge. Her laugh was warm and infectious, he liked it. She seemed to understand his pantomime, for again she answered, "Si."

He made the motions of drinking and she responded with a throaty laugh, but shook her head from side to side. He put his hands over his heart and made a gallant attempt at 'O sole mio', his mischievous eyes fluttering in mock love.

She burst out laughing. "Si," she said, and the two young people departed to the nearest tavern.

Although Esme was Italian, much of her childhood had been spent in Spain and it was in this language that their friendship developed. Man meets woman, they both desire to know more about each other, solution simple, stay close together. Edward joined the Bella Napoli as a deck hand and having convinced the powers that be of his other skills, he was delegated to assist the Ship's Steward when required.

Esme, as personal maid to the Captain's wife, found access to the steward's working quarters relatively simple. When the Captain's wife, Louisa Garabaldi, realised that her young maid had a certain attachment to the young Danish sailor, she proved very accommodating. She relived her young life as a romantic girl in love with the dashing Captain

Garabaldi. Edward taught Esme Danish, while she taught him Italian, albeit with Spanish words intertwined.

A year later, the Bella Napoli was dry-docked in an Italian port and Esme was summoned to attend a funeral in Milan.

For a fortnight Edward kicked his heels in the port waiting for Esme to return. About this time an English sailing ship was leaving for the East to pick up a cargo of spices. The ship's steward had been rushed to hospital and a replacement had to be found.

Edward's credentials from the Bella Napoli, facilitated to some degree by the romantic Louisa Garabaldi, proved that he had been a useful member of the steward's staff. Captain Bullock viewed the document with some suspicion, but felt obliged to take the risk. Steward Sorenson and Bosun Jeffery from West Hartlepool struck up an immediate friendship.

Any steward who has the ability to negotiate and order up, economically, good nourishing food to feed hungry hardworking seamen is always a great asset.

The captain seemed pleased, the bosun happy and the new steward delighted at his success.

When the bosun realised that he was keen to learn the English language, he was only too pleased to help. It had been a matter of reciprocity, Edward giving lessons in Danish, while the bosun gave lessons in English.

Edward felt that he had held the centre stage long enough and apologised if he had bored them and finished by admitting that he had found English the most difficult language to learn and this had made him more determined to learn it properly and paid a compliment to the man who had assisted him. From his pocket he drew a small Danish-English phrase book.

"This, gentlemen," he said, "is the book the bosun gave me when we parted company."

Edward handed the book to John, who opened it and made a point of reading out the name of the bosun.

It read, Albert V. Jeffery. 2 Archer St. West Hartlepool.

There was a lull in the proceedings, then John commented.

"I'm surprised that you carry that small book about with you; your English is rather exceptional for a Dane. Surely the book is of little use now?"

Edward smiled shyly, before replying.

"It may just be sailor's superstition, but Albert Jeffery helped me so much in learning English, I feel I owe him something, and, when it is in my pocket, I imagine I am safe where English is spoken."

The doctor was still curious.

"What do you consider to be the most important factor in learning languages, Edward?"

For a full minute he sat looking at John, as if the statement, when it came, should reflect an honest considered analysis. As his head moved slowly from side to side, he admitted the doctor had posed an extremely difficult question and John, as a surgeon, would expect an answer based on science.

John nodded his head as he spoke. "We all have a lot to learn, but I would still value your opinion."

Edward felt relieved and gave his answer.

"There are thousands of languages and until we learn that there is no one language more important than any other, we cannot expect the harmony and peace we all crave for. I have always wanted to understand the language of others; therein may lie at least part of the secret in learning other tongues. It would appear that the prime factor is the desire to try and understand and be friendly towards the other person."

John smiled his approval and, raising his glass, toasted Edward, wishing him success in all his endeavours.

After a short interval and the re-charging of glasses, it was Anton's turn. He recounted how in his youth he had started as a young herring fisherman and then fished for tuna in warmer waters; returning later to colder climes in search of the giant whale.

Later he had returned to herring fishing on the West Coast and had met Mary. His love of the Scottish woman had spurred him to own his own boat and seek their livelihood in the Western Isles.

He had been moderately successful in fishing for herring in Northern waters and had more than made up for any seasonal shortfall by fishing down south for mackerel. But he had experienced a little trouble with his own countrymen from time to time, particularly when he strayed off course near the Norwegian coast. The English authorities had also impeded his progress when fishing for mackerel.

Life in the main, however, had been very good, but could have been better if the 'Englishers' had not interfered with his mackerel fishing target. His final comment as he looked at Edward was significant.

"The sooner we adopt your policy of all speaking the same language, the better for all of us."

John, who had just re-charged his pipe, was looking benevolently at his two young friends and felt the urge to speak.

"I suppose you are both anxious to hear my contribution."

Anton, who was probably John's best friend, could afford to say, "Not particularly."

The doctor, who was unmoved, advised, "Sit back, relax and I will tell you a story."

For Edward's benefit, he started the narrative from the time he had qualified from Edinburgh University, Anton having already heard of his exploits as a young medical student on many occasions.

After qualifying, he had spent much of his time in Edinburgh, but later, having become one of Europe's finest chest surgeons and being in great demand, had travelled extensively, but always gravitated back towards the Scottish capital.

After years of wielding the scalpel, he became disenchanted with the scheme of things. He found that patients he had treated some time before, were returning in a worse condition than previous. Being a conscientious man, he was most concerned and sought the reason why.

He discovered that many of his patients were miners and industrial workers exposed to the deadly danger of coal dust, asbestos and chemical fumes, and after treatment they had returned to their previous occupations. He blamed them for their ineptitude, but when he knew better, he cursed a system where men rearing a family felt duty bound to return to intolerable conditions so that their family might survive.

That working men should have to make such a choice incensed John, the surgeon. It did not assuage his feelings when some idiot from his own profession, posing as a democrat, said that they were free to work elsewhere. Although cynical to some degree, he had carried on as a surgeon, helping where he could, but feeling that wielding the pen might have more effect.

He wrote to the newspapers, politicians and others he thought might listen, but was given little support. He became an advocate of Socialist Medicine in the belief that the scientific prevention of disease was infinitely more acceptable than having to look continually for a cure.

He pestered the British Medical Association to mount a campaign to force the government of the day to legislate conditions in industry to outlaw the practices that injured or shortened the life of the working class.

It was natural that he would get support from the overworked and underpaid medical practitioners in the deprived and poverty stricken areas, but the hierarchy did not want to know of his existence. A former colleague, who had by stages crawled to the Harley Street level, put forward the position as kindly as he could.

"You must remember, John, that if it were not for the contributions of the mine owners and other enterprises, our hospitals would be in a parlous state."

John had lost his temper and pointed out that if those entrepreneurs had used some of their profits in ensuring proper standards in ventilation and other progressive measures, there would not now be the need to massage their consciences by belatedly providing funds to ameliorate the plight of their victims. John had been rather caustic.

"Your chums in Harlot Street have done very little to advance progressive medicine."

The colleague had been rather prim. "Surely you mean Harley Street, John?"

But John, still angry, had terminated the conversation.

"You know what I said and I'm sure that as an ear specialist, you heard it. Your chums prostitute their skill by conserving a system that gives them more for one operation than a hardworking miner is paid in a year, they are more concerned with the health of their bank book than the Hippocratic Oath."

Suddenly John banged the table with his empty beer glass.

"Enough of my blethers, gentlemen. I see your glasses are empty, this must be remedied at once."

Anton responded immediately.

"I should think so too! While we have both been unburdening our souls, Edward, whose contribution was the most constructive, has had to sit there smiling at an empty glass."

But Edward, good scout, was prepared. "Not so," was his reply. "Everything is under control."

Before his companions could reply, the barman had replaced their drinks. They both looked fixedly at Edward, who continued to smile.

"I never heard you order," said Anton.

"I didn't," was the reply, "I merely nodded my head as the barman passed and, like all good barmen the world over, he knew what was expected."

Anton raised his glass. "Skol to that, Edward," he said, and turning to John, he expressed the opinion that they both had been rather negative in the proceedings; it was about time they talked about things that made them happy to be alive.

John agreed and suggested that they talk about the hill walks in the area, hoping that Edward might be interested. The Norwegian did not seem unduly impressed.

"Well maybe, John, but to liven the proceedings, why not tell us about some of your climbing experiences where you only survived by the skin of your teeth?"

The doctor addressed Edward directly.

"You will have to forgive Anton's lack of maturity, he suffers from a form of schizophrenia, but normally he is a very nice fellow."

Anton laughed and raised his hands in surrender. "You win, John, let's stick to hill walking."

For the rest of the night, John and Anton vied with each other in describing the best local hill walks. Edward thanked them for their indulgence and promised he would bear in mind what they had said, but would not be hill walking this time round; however, he looked forward to it in the not too distant future. He asked Anton about the sea lochs and the precipitous cliffs around the coast. Did they bear any resemblance to the Fjords of Norway. Anton pursed his lips as he gave thought to the question.

"There is a similarity, Edward, but remember when looking up from the sea, the walls of the fjords are much higher. However the Scottish lochs have a charm all of their own and are unique; if you are very interested, I will show you a few in the next two days."

Chapter 15

It was a very pleasant day when the Sorensons set sail from Applecross in Anton's fishing boat to explore the sea lochs. From the start Anton proved to be not only a skilled sailor, but an interesting and enjoyable guide. Having married a Scottish woman, he had made a point of learning all that he could of Scottish history, particularly of the Western Highlands and how the Scandinavians had influenced the way of life.

As they weaved their way up the indented coast northwards, the indefatigable Anton kept up a commentary in his own inimitable fashion, describing the history and geography of the area in a most amusing style, adding, when he thought fit, bits of folklore interwoven with Viking mythology, hoping to prove to his Scandinavian passengers that the berserkers had not been naughty, but nice.

It mattered little to Emily and Edward whether the propaganda of the previous millennium was true or otherwise, it was far more important that the amiable Norwegian was doing his best to entertain them amidst such wonderful scenery.

Towards the end of the second day, whilst exploring Loch Torridon, Edward noticed Emily's look of fascination as she studied the red coloured mountains. He knew that her curiosity had to be satisfied; having already agreed with Anton that a two or three day trip could be terminated whenever they felt the urge to examine the countryside in more detail.

When he asked him if he could suggest a place where they could obtain a bed for the night, the big jovial Norwegian indicated that he would be pleased to take them to the Fergusons: they were friends of his and he had not visited them for quite some time, he was sure they would be made welcome. That this would prove to be their introduction to Gaeldom was hardly what they had planned for.

Anton found a safe berth and walked up to a cottage a short distance from the boat, returning some minutes later to inform them that Mrs. Ferguson would be delighted to look after them for the evening, or longer if they so desired.

It was an emotional experience for the two women and two men standing outside the cottage looking out beyond Loch Torridon to the Atlantic. Mrs. Ferguson, a sixty-year-old woman, was kind and considerate and Emily, a young good-looking woman, excited and wondering what the future had in store.

Edward, an optimistic young man whose immediate aims had been achieved, mainly through Anton, felt that this was the time to show his appreciation. And Anton, born in Norway, but now a man of the Isles, stood there serene, knowing he had done something to help his fellow man. He had known Edward for only five days, but in that short time they had become friends, and he now speculated, would this blithe spirit return some time in the future?

It was a dilemma for Edward; he knew that to in any way overstate the kindness shown to him and Emily would embarrass his friend, but something had to be done. He threw his arms around Anton, hugging him firmly, then seized his hand and proceeded to pump it up and down, hesitating only momentarily to thank Anton in a voice charged with emotion and in his native Danish.

"*Tak, Anton, Mange, Mange Tak.*"

Anton smiled broadly and replied in a language that sounded strange and mysterious. Edward's bewilderment seemed to tickle Anton's sense of humour.

"I thought you were a linguist, Edward. It appears there is a language you still have to learn."

Edward smiled feebly and replied, "I have a lot to learn."

Mrs. Ferguson, a compassionate woman, restored stability.

"Anton replied to you in the Gaelic, Mr. Sorenson, our local language. He expressed his thanks in recognition of the little he had done for his guests and hopes that in the not too distant future you will return."

Before Edward could reply, Anton kissed Emily on the cheek, slapped Edward on the back and jogged down to his boat. Edward was completely taken by surprise and by the time he had decided what he should do Anton had cast off from the small jetty and was some hundred yards away. He could only, along with Mrs. Ferguson and Emily, wave farewell until Anton was well on his way homewards.

As Mrs. Ferguson disappeared to prepare supper, the Sorensons gathered their luggage together and prepared to settle down in the home of their hostess.

After supper they were introduced to the family. Mr. Ferguson was a patriarchal figure, serious, very correct and courteous, but with that slight glint in his eye that indicated a canny humour. The two sons of whom Mrs. Ferguson seemed inordinately proud, Donald and Jamie, were both constables of the Glasgow Police Force.

It was during the night or early morning that Edward was disturbed by low voices outside the bedroom window; he was later to learn that the two young men were starting off for their stint of duty after a short rest at home.

In the morning, after breakfast, Mrs. Ferguson was curious and asked their intentions.

"And what would you and Mrs. Sorenson be doing today?"

His linguistic propensity somewhat restored, Edward replied, "My wife seemed particularly attracted to the beauty of the red mountains in this area and I feel that a little walking around Loch Torridon would do for a start; in which case, I would like to stay for two more nights, if this is possible."

Mrs. Ferguson was pleased and agreed they should do just that and stay longer if they so desired.

Just prior to starting their walk, she invited him into the kitchen and gave him a parcel of sandwiches and a bottle of milk; to have, as she said, 'a wee bite' when they needed it. As Edward accepted the mini feast of truly Highland proportions, Mrs. Ferguson drew his attention to a seven-pound salmon in the prime of death, lying glistening and inviting on the kitchen table.

"When I came in this morning, it was lying on the table, as you see it now."

Edward, ever helpful, offered an explanation.

"Your fishmonger has been on the job earlier than you expected."

She smiled sweetly.

"We haff no fishmonger here, but the good Lord, knowing that the Fergusons haff visitors, has looked upon us with favour."

Temporarily at a loss for words, Edward looked earnestly at his hostess, speculating on what was coming next.

"I was wondering, Mr. Sorenson, if you and your wife would like some poached salmon when you return?"

As he seemed to hesitate, she explained that after cleaning the fish, she cooked it slowly in water, to which vinegar and cloves had been added, and when ready it was served with potatoes and a sauce of her own which was, of course, a family secret. Edward was still hesitant, the word 'poached' was controversial and ambiguous, but he had enough sense to assure Mrs. Ferguson, "My wife Emily and myself will look forward to your poached salmon this evening."

Walking as near to the shore line of Loch Torridon as was feasible, they had almost reached Shieldaig before Edward called a halt. It had been an overcast day, the sun having difficulty in penetrating the clouds, but it had suited the Sorensons who welcomed the cool atmosphere while walking.

Looking across the loch he thought he could see the Ferguson house some three miles away, but the clarity disturbed him somewhat, particularly the sharp outline of the mountains in the background, which to him, as a mariner, indicated an impending storm. Although on this occasion equipped for an emergency, he hoped Thor would behave himself. Knowing that the sanctuary of the Ferguson base was some ten miles away, Edward suggested they return.

There was no rain, not even a mini peal of thunder and Edward heaved a sigh of relief. They were barely five miles from base when the sun burst through like a gigantic fireball. The mountains still outlined against the backcloth of the sky looked as if on fire, the incandescent light throwing into relief through the heart of the mass, nooks, crags, rivulets and passageways of man. For a full minute they stood enthralled by the awesome fiery spectacle, then gripping his arm Emily looked into his eyes and asked, "Have you ever seen anything so wonderful, Edward?"

Edward replied in English. "You are right, Emily, it is an awesome sight."

Emily did not comprehend. They had been speaking in Swedish, Edward having deferred to his wife during the walk. She frowned feeling that the magic moment might escape, then let fly in Swedish superlatives that almost took his breath away. He apologised for not replying in Swedish and agreed, in his wife's language, that it was a most outstanding experience to witness such a thrilling natural phenomenon. It made one feel very humble, it was something that would never be forgotten.

She looked at him with great affection, tears were not far away. He cursed himself for being stuffy when obviously Emily had expected a romantic answer in her own language.

He had managed to salvage the situation, but was extremely sorry that he had made Emily vulnerable. He took her in his arms and whispered in her ear, "*Emily, min feloved.*"

They clung close together, it was a glorious feeling, everything was forgiven and love reigned supreme.

From that point on they strolled serenely, hand in hand, down the glen, keeping as close as they could to the loch, ultimately reaching the house of the Fergusons.

Having been out in the Highland air all day, they had acquired an appetite commensurate with their activity; they were hungry and Mrs. Ferguson did them proud that evening.

After the nicety of a good sherry for the lady and a dram of the local whisky, with a carafe of pure spring water to adjust to taste, for the 'chentleman', the first course was served.

It was venison soup, made to a recipe jealously guarded by Highland Scots and still a mystery to French compatriots who tried to copy it. Rumour has it that Scottish seamen sailing into Marseilles in the eighteenth century had seen a placard obviously designed to attract their trade. The tavern, well known to seamen, advertised a dish called 'deer et moi!' It did not live up to expectations and from then on, Highland Scots have dubbed the dish 'oh deerie me'. Be that as it may, the Sorensons appreciated to the full the real venison soup and the sweet which followed the main course.

But the highlight of the evening meal was the main course; they would in the future remember it as 'Mrs. Ferguson's Salmon'. There the lovely salmon steaks lay nestling in a mysterious but delectable sauce, surrounded by thin cut potatoes fried to a crisp brown, each mouthful to be savoured.

As the succulent fish seemed to melt in his mouth, he had strange intriguing thoughts. He remembered the early morning voices and now knew that the two sons had been out on some ploy or other. There was the fish, obviously fresh and probably taken from the loch and, knowing that the word poached was not necessarily confined to cooking, he speculated airily as he relished his salmon supreme, feeling that he was not being charitable in suspecting the young policemen of having done anything presumed to have been illegal.

As they relaxed after a most enjoyable meal, Mrs. Ferguson entered and enquired, "Did you enchoy your dinner then?"

Edward replied frankly. "Speaking on behalf of my wife and myself, it is the best poached salmon we have ever tasted."

She smiled benignly at him as she spoke. "I am so pleased, Mr. Sorenson, I must ask Jamie where he got the salmon. He goes my messages, you know."

Edward could not resist complimenting Jamie on his choice.

Next morning, before setting out to explore the foothills of Torridon, Edward outlined his intentions to Mrs. Ferguson, indicating his desire to travel to Dingwall or even Inverness the following day and ultimately, if possible, down Loch Ness to Fort William.

It was a beautiful day and the Sorensons took full advantage to discover the red rock grandeur of Torridon and its immediate environs.

That evening during supper their hostess gave a gentle warning that she and her husband, together with two of their immediate neighbours, would be having a ceilidh in the back kitchen, an event which alternated between the two houses once each week. It would not be too noisy and she was sure it would not disturb their sleep.

Before Edward could reply, she added that her two sons were departing for Glasgow to take up duty early next morning and if the Sorensons were interested, there was room in the car for them as far as Fort William.

Edward's reply was in the affirmative, knowing that Glen Affric was on the road to Fort William and he had in mind showing Emily what he considered to be the most beautiful glen he had seen in Scotland.

Before the Fergusons retired to the ceilidh, it was arranged that Jamie would serve breakfast at seven the following morning and almost immediately after they would take to the road.

As they lay in bed the Sorensons could hear the voices of the old people; they sounded friendly, but being in the Gaelic were unintelligible to the honeymooners. Then the fiddle started sweet and low, the voices became slightly louder and more musical until they were all singing, keeping appreciable time and tone.

For most of the time it was a merry party, but interspersed with serious and mournful mouth music, which fortunately did not last long. Although the party could not be described as loud, there was an exception, a strident voice interfered in the scheme of things announcing that 'Jamie's awa' tae the fishin'.

Edward speculated that this was probably a member of the family who had crashed the party and was more concerned with gossip than the good conduct of the ceilidh. Curiosity got the better of Edward; he left the room and stepped into the lobby. He felt uneasy knowing he was wrong to prowl in the home of Mrs. Ferguson.

He was about to step back into the bedroom when he heard the voice again, it came not from the kitchen, but from behind a curtain covering a recess only a few feet away. It occurred to him that the merrymakers would not hear the voice and possibly a drunk intruder had managed to closet himself behind the curtain.

He tiptoed along, unsure of what to expect. Reaching the recess, he stood stock still and as moonlight filtered through the inner glass door, he wondered 'what next?' With a swift movement he pulled the curtain aside hoping he could hold the initiative or, if necessary, frighten a besotted but potential burglar or possibly a bemused but misguided relative in a similar state.

He was totally unprepared for what he saw - there was an animal element, but certainly not human. At first glance it looked like an eagle, but Edward was no ornithologist. Whether it was that he was thinking in terms Scottish, or that Scotch was the main influence in his thinking, he had certainly misjudged the size and character of the bird.

On close scrutiny he felt foolish, for instead of the powerful beak and gimlet eyes, he now saw in the dim light a rather hook-nosed bill and eyes that were closed as if in sleep. It seemed to be wearing a small ridiculous cap, or was it a crest, its features were multi-coloured. He could have laughed, but restrained himself, realising he was looking at a rather over-sized bird from the Tropics, either an exceptionally large parrot or cockatoo. It swivelled its head lazily from side to side, then, opening its eyes, stared for a few seconds directly at Edward and informed him in a voice almost human, "Jamie's awa' tae the fishin."

Edward was astounded. Taken completely by surprise, he stood staring at the bird, and it, as if realising that the stupid human did not understand, repeated the message.

This was just too much. Closing the curtain, he darted back to the bedroom and once inside he released the laughter he'd been bottling up. That night the Sorensons laughed themselves to sleep.

The following morning, they set out for Loch Ness. As arranged they accompanied Jamie and his brother. Their first stop was Dingwall, where Jamie gathered together food and materials required by his sister and her husband down on the farm. Just after leaving Dingwall, Jamie turned round and indicated it would not be long before they reached a part of the road where, if they kept straight on, they would reach Inverness and if they turned right, Fort William would be the target.

Edward, obsessed with one location in mind, replied, "We are grateful indeed to be travelling with you and, if it is convenient, any stop that brings us near Glen Affric would be most welcome."

Jamie smiled and nodded his head in approval, telling Edward that the farm was on the Fort William road.

It was a glorious day, one to enjoy to the full and the driver of the car seemed in tune with the atmosphere as he reduced speed to twenty miles per hour.

Suddenly, the car left the road as Jamie steered it down on to a stretch of shingle at the loch side, which Edward and Emily had failed to see. Jamie had obviously been there before. Turning in his seat he looked back at his passengers and cheerily announced, "I was thinking this could be a good place for a picnic."

As Emily and Edward looked around admiring the Highland scene, Jamie informed them that Donald and himself would be foraging a wee bit further afield to find something that would make the picnic more interesting.

While the two Scandinavians lay back on a grassy knoll, the two Scots set out to explore and exploit their habitat, in such fashion that four humans would enjoy a repast in keeping with a healthy balance of the environment.

Shortly after, Donald returned with the kindling and between a few stones soon established a cook-house. Having recognised that picnic equipment was available, Edward brought out four camp stools and a big box from the car-cum-van vehicle and set up the dining quarters, to which he added beer and whisky purchased in Dingwall - a bottle of sherry for the lady, of course.

Half an hour having passed, Edward was becoming a little restive and looked at Donald. The policeman merely pointed in the direction of a hollow partially obscured by overhanging trees and assured him that Jamie had a wonderful way with animals and fish.

A minute later Jamie appeared, walking jauntily and whistling a Highland air. He carried in his hand a long slender branch, speared on the end of which were two gleaming members of the trout family.

After an enjoyable picnic, the party of four set out for Glen Urquhart, Jamie explaining that he and Donald would be stopping at his brother-in-law's farm and would then take Roderick Ross to Fort William with them. They would then board the Glasgow train and Roderick, after making some purchases, would drive the family car back to the farm.

Edward notched the information in his mind, but was inquisitive, wondering how Jamie had caught the fish; he had seen no signs of fishing tackle. He questioned him diplomatically.

"I must congratulate you on the way you prepared the fish, but how you managed to catch them without tackle is a mystery to me."

Jamie, although driving, half turned in his seat and grinned.

"It wass chust hielen luck, Mr. Sorenson," was the modest reply.

But Edward was persistent and told him he knew that he was often away at the fishing. He looked at

Edward through the car mirror and, still grinning, asked, "And who would be telling you that?"

Edward smiled back and replied, "As you Scots would say, a wee bird told me."

Jamie said nothing. Being a good policeman, recognising that he had passengers to look after, he concentrated on driving safely.

As they neared Glen Urquhart, Edward quizzed him concerning prospective bed and breakfast houses. Jamie stopped the car to give him full attention; he knew of a place where they could be looked after. It was an ideal holiday spot, particularly for walkers; it was quiet and peaceful and there was no wee bird to disturb their sleep.

Edward, appreciative of the policeman's wit, asked if he would be kind enough to take them there, provided of course it was convenient.

Half an hour later, introductions had been made and Jessie Ross, Jamie's sister, was considering whether she could accommodate the Sorensons or not. Being a rather meticulous landlady and expecting visitors from Inverness in three days' time, she felt she might not be able to look after the Sorensons the way she would like to.

After a little persuasion from Jamie she agreed, and arrangements were made that Emily and Edward would be her lodgers for the next two days.

That evening they took a stroll to adjust themselves to their new surroundings and the following day was spent in exploring as much of Glen Urquhart as time allowed.

Edward was excited now the time had arrived when he would take Emily to see the beautiful glen that had captured his heart that day some years before when he had occasion to lodge at Drumnadrochit.

Jessie, like her mother Mrs. Ferguson, ensured that the Scandinavian couple would not be short of rations and Edward, as usual, had made sure that liquid refreshment would be to hand when required. The weather was ideal and the scenes from the lochside made walking a pleasure.

As they entered Glen Affric, Edward was a trifle nervous and kept marking in his mind certain reference spots to ensure they would be back at the Ross residence before sunset. Emily was enjoying herself; relaxed and enthusiastic, she veered to the right choosing a narrow path leading to higher ground. Edward was happier now, not just because of the interest displayed by his wife, but because of the knowledge that he was now recognising parts of the glen he had seen on his first visit.

Now sure of his surroundings, he realised the path would give a good panoramic view of the glen. He caught Emily up and taking her hand, asked, "May I join you?"

For the next hour they walked hand in hand through the heather until they reached a small plateau that gave a view for miles around. It was time for relaxation and lunch. Mrs. Ross had done a good job, providing them with venison sandwiches, sufficient in quantity and quality to properly 'meat' the occasion, with a selection of fruit for their sweet course.

After lunch, they settled back to admire, assess and form their opinions of the beauty and grandeur of the glen. Fortunately, they had chosen a spot where the panoramic view embraced most of the valley.

Low cloud had diffused the sun's rays, giving a golden backcloth to the distant mountains accentuated against the skyline, exposing their true colours from black and brown to almost red. Then rolling back towards them, the pale green of distant pastures to the luxurious deep green of sub-tropical vegetation, in which they were standing, they could view the trees, the mountain flowers and that unique Scottish experience, the glorious purple heather. Threaded through this tapestry of nature, the silver and gleaming white of the river flowed merrily through the glen.

Edward, meantime, had been watching his wife and knew she was undergoing an unusually pleasant experience. When she aired her views he was delighted that the long walk to the glen had been well worthwhile.

Emily was in sparkling form and gave vent to her feelings, thanking Edward for having made her day. In her exuberance she admitted she felt like singing, if she could sing, but of course there was always another outlet.

Pointing to a small heather knoll some fifty yards away, she challenged her husband. "I'll race you."

It was, of course, the old story of man chasing woman until she catches him. Within seconds, Emily was on her way and Edward knew he had a race on his hands, he had to move fast to keep up.

Just as they reached the knoll, Emily managed to stumble and Edward, gallant as ever, caught her in his arms. Mother nature had provided the ideal shock absorber and they rolled breathlessly, but safely, intertwined, down into the heather. They lay laughing in each other's arms for a few moments and would have lain longer had not the elements interrupted their joyful capers.

A darkening sky, a rumble of thunder and spots of rain alerted and spurred them into action, knowing that they had left their coats at the lunch site.

Racing back they were able to don their waterproofs before the storm enveloped them. They were still laughing, albeit nervously, but they were happy they had achieved their objective and the rain had not dampened their spirits. As they made their way down to the floor of the glen, the storm gradually abated and the sun shone through. They felt warm and contented as they made their way back to the farm.

In the morning Mr. Ross, having business to transact in Inverness, offered them a lift in the family car, which they gratefully accepted.

That evening, having made a short tour of the Highland capital, they settled back to relax and reminisce over the holiday so far and, having touched on the highlights, they turned their attention to plans for the future, knowing that in a few days they would be back in Grangemouth.

Emily was excited and hoped the house which Edward had acquired and equipped would meet the requirements she had in mind. She had never seen the house and although having confidence in Edward's ability to establish a base suitable for a home, she wondered in her woman's mind how much reorganisation might be needed.

It was later that Emily confessed to having been tardy concerning certain aspects of her wardrobe and as she intended to do a little sewing, would Edward like to take a little walk for an hour or so? Edward readily obliged and took a little walk downstairs to the lounge bar.

He had just settled back with his drink and lit his marcella when he felt a slap on the back and a deep voice boomed out.

"So it's yourself, Edward. What brings you up to the Hielands?"

Although startled, Edward knew the voice well and did not react until the big bulk of Rory McLeod, the Leith Customs Officer, was facing him, and then welcomed him lovingly.

"Ah, so it is Rory, the wee son of Mrs. McLeod."

The big man laughed, but did not seem unduly happy; he smiled wryly before replying. "You will be finding me poor company, I'll be thinking."

Edward was concerned, he could see Rory was beset with a serious problem. After seeing to the drinks, he encouraged Rory to off load his worries. Before he would tell his story, he asked that Edward should treat in confidence anything he might say, adding that Edward himself might be involved in the near future.

It was an intriguing thought, but Edward agreed to respect the confidence of his friend.

Rory had been sent by Leith Customs and Excise to liaise with the police in Inverness. It appeared that three cocaine addicts had died in the Leith area. One of them being treated in Edinburgh Royal Infirmary had confessed to being supplied by a pusher known to the Leith police and the local customs officials. He had, however, received his last and lethal dose from a man in Inverness and Rory had been assigned to investigate.

He confided that within the next half an hour he would, along with a plain clothes policeman, be engaged in a bit of pub crawling and hopefully catch the culprit. He seemed sure he would succeed in his mission, if not that night, then in a day or two, but what rankled was that he would have liked a free hand to track down the real criminals, the bosses as he called them, particularly one man known as Snowy by the hardened criminals.

His solution was based more on emotion than on reason; having seen the suffering of the man who had died, he had deduced that the best procedure was to cut off the head of the serpent and ignore the coils. He summed up his view quite succinctly.

"If I could trace the head, Edward, I would bring him to justice and in transit I would ensure that he had a fatal accident."

Edward put a restraining hand on Rory's arm.

"Easy, Rory, easy. I know how you feel, I am sure I would feel the same way, but that course of action would be self-destructive. To use hate as a fuel in a drive for justice, although successful, would be self-defeating - you would end up a very unhappy man."

The tension eased and both men for the short time left talked about things more mundane. However, Edward drew his attention to the statement he had made concerning Edward's involvement and assured Rory he had not forgotten the promise he had made to Mr. Pringle that he would, while canvassing shipping orders, keep his eyes open for any evidence of cocaine smuggling.

Rory smiled; he was more relaxed now. "So you still remember, despite being on your honeymoon."

Edward assured him he had given his word and intended to keep it. Within a week he would be back at work, economic circumstances dictated it; after all the setting up of a house, the wedding and the Highland holiday had brought his assets too near the thin red line for comfort. He asked his friend if he would like to meet Emily before leaving, but he declined saying that he was no fit company for a lady in his present mood, he had too little time to spare, but would be delighted to meet Mrs. Sorenson in the near future.

Next day, Inverness and its environs, including Loch Ness, were explored by the Sorensons. The loch, although beautiful in its natural surroundings, did not encourage the mythological to give a gala performance. The sight-seeing bus on which they travelled was small and comfortable and gave a good all-round vision. The driver of the bus was also the guide and had, like many of his kind, a natural wit which, with his comprehensive knowledge of the locality, contributed largely to what was an interesting and amusing experience.

It was only natural that queries were made concerning the absence of the Loch Ness monster.

The driver stopped the bus and, facing his audience, started with the words, 'Well, candidly ...' which always creates suspicion, but this was such a nice man so they all waited expectantly.

His opinion was that although there was no scientific proof of the existence of a monster, it was apparent from the sightings of many sober and respected people that a phenomenon of animal or marine content, or both, existed in the loch.

Over the past five years, he himself had seen strange happenings on three occasions. Twice at dusk and once during bright sunlight. The first sighting had been during the early evening after a heavy rainfall. It had been a hot day and a mist started rising from the surface of the loch, but despite the conditions he had seen a dragon-like animal with enormous fins rise up and then just as suddenly disappear, leaving a trail of white water.

The second time he had seen what appeared to him to be a snub-nosed whale with a hump on its back break the surface, but had to admit he might have been fooled by navy experts experimenting with what was now known as submarine craft. Like all good entertainers, he kept the best and most controversial episode to the end.

"It was a beautiful sunny day, ladies and chentlemen, and I wass wearing smoked spectacles given me by my boss, Mr. Mackenzie, to protect my eyes, as he said, from the effects of the eclipse of the sun that wass expected. Being a clever man trained at Aberdeen University, I believed him. I wass standing at the side of the loch when the moon covered the sun. I waited until the sun shone through and then as I wass ready to go back to the bus, this great big thing looking like some gigantic sea serpent broke through the water, rising hundreds of yards from the surface and seeming suspended in space. I wass transfixed, or should I say it wass myself that wass suspended in space. Then chust as suddenly it dived back into the loch and as I took off my specs all I could see wass a ripple of water about half a mile long."

"Could I haff been dreaming, I asked Mr. Mackenzie, and he said it wass chust my imagination and the ripple had probably been caused by a submarine under the surface of the water, but I'm thinking there could haff been another explanation. It iss well known that poachers use a torch to attract fish in the dark and it iss possible that chust after the eclipse, the sun shone through the water like a torch and that enormous beastie made for the surface of the water."

He hesitated and, looking benignly at his passengers, he posed the question.

"And what do you think?"

He paused again for full dramatic effect and before anyone could answer he beamed a big smile at his audience and agreed.

"You are right, ladies and chentlemen, if you believe that story, you would believe anything."

There were cheers all round for first class entertainment.

As the train left Inverness and sped on towards Aberdeen, Emily and Edward sat back in their seats watching the changing scene. They spoke very little, but both gave a great deal of thought to the change in tempo and character of the holiday.

From the day that Emily had met Edward, her life had changed dramatically; the speed with which he had wooed her had at the beginning been almost unnerving, rapidly followed by an awe which turned almost to ecstasy when she felt that Edward, a man of such marked humanity, had grown extremely fond of her.

Before she met him, she had vowed that her lifestyle had to change if she was not to become bored and unhappy.

It was true she had visited many parts of the world as a stewardess and, although healthy and active, had been given insufficient time off duty to appreciate the changing scene or the company of people in foreign parts. She had needed a holiday, an opportunity to escape from the duty of ship chores and enjoy for a reasonable time the social life on terra-firma.

Her wish had been answered, but initially the 'Edward' experience had been overwhelming. Fortunately it had all been well worthwhile. From the minute they decided to marry, Edward had operated with speed, precision and, surprisingly from her point of view, with decorum. He had acquired a rented house she was still to see, had made the necessary arrangements in such a way that the marriage had been conducted without the ostentation and religious fervour she had little time for.

Although recognising what appeared to be the tribal view of marital union in the presence of unrecognisable people, she was happy Edward had been able to organise a peaceful and relaxing wedding with only Sven and Felicity in attendance.

After a sumptuous lunch, she had been cosseted and cared for in a quality hotel and the following day the pleasure of leisurely walking downstairs and boarding a steam train to holiday in the beautiful Scottish Highlands was an experience she would treasure forever.

Her association with Highland people had been joyful and rewarding despite language difficulties and she had felt happy and safe in the time cycle of the Western Highlands. She was still happy, but everything seemed to be going just that bit quicker now. The people were still warm and hospitable, but she sensed a tenseness in the atmosphere, as if any task had to be done immediately, whereas in the West, if man's dignity or comfort was unduly stretched, then tomorrow would do just fine, thank you.

She felt the holiday was coming to an end too fast and wished she could slow down the train to suit the speed of her thoughts.

Edward, by comparison, was quite philosophical concerning the train's progress, but his mind had now left the tranquil West far behind and was already concentrating on what had to be done when they returned home to Grangemouth.

They stayed in Aberdeen that evening and, before joining the train in the afternoon for Dundee, Edward ensured that a morning tour of Aberdeen was undertaken so that in the future they could say that they had seen the enormous quarry where the tons of stone had been hewn to build the 'Granite City'.

Edward had felt like pushing for Grangemouth, but realised he was being unfair to his wife who was now sending signals that he was winding up the holiday just too fast and should take it easy.

As he slowed down, she relaxed. As he did all the nice little things that a dutiful husband could be expected to do, she settled back in their hotel bedroom and thought once more of the quiet and pleasant holiday, whilst Edward, duty bound, sought a telephone in the lounge bar. Having satisfied himself that his line of communication would be available, he mulled over the message he should send to Tam Richards at Grangemouth.

Whether it was the effect of his beer or a whisky he had never heard of, or merely a fault in the telecommunication system, he would never know, for Tam seemed to be speaking from another planet. Suddenly the atmospherics or whatever cleared and the message came through loud and clear.

"All right, Edward, I will do what I can."

Satisfied that his message would facilitate a rapid start to his canvassing the docks on his return, he decided to risk another whisky before joining his wife.

He found Emily in an enthusiastic mood, eager to know more about the house they would soon occupy. It appeared that one week before setting out on their holiday, Edward had managed to obtain possession of a house in Basin Street consisting of a main room, a kitchen and a bedroom.

Emily laughed when she heard the word 'basin' and Edward felt compelled to explain. As a part of a canal system, the basin was a huge catchment area with water flowing in from rivers and the Atlantic and then emptying out to the North Sea or it can be reversed, according to tidal movements. She had no option but to accept his theory and only hoped that the basin would not overflow and flood their home.

They arrived home in the early afternoon. Emily's first reaction was one of wonder and joy. For a woman who, as a Stewardess, had to live in the restricted space of ship's kitchens and pantries, this was just ideal for their first home.

She felt her man had done a good job and with just a little female know-how and effort the house could be all that she had hoped for, and she expressed herself accordingly.

As Edward stood smiling, awaiting her verdict, she suddenly threw her arms around his neck and, kissing him full on the mouth, said softly, "Thank you for a wonderful holiday - the house is grand, just what we need."

Chapter 16

Tam Richards looked fondly at the young Water Agent, so well he might, for the two weeks the young man had been away had seen his profit from shipping sales plummet alarmingly and now in front of him stood the man who could solve his financial problems.

Edward examined the list he had asked for over the telephone and patted Tam on his arm.

"From what I can see, Tam, there is a definite sea stock for the Danish ship coming in to Grangemouth this morning and two big probables in Leith docks tomorrow."

Tam beamed, but sought reassurance. "Do you think so, Edward?"

Sharp as ever and raring to go, Edward replied, "Yes, just make up the sausage meat and I will provide the links in the afternoon."

Having already dealt with the steward and the captain of the Danish ship S.S. Eventyr, he was confident and was able to keep his word. When Tam examined the sea stock order he was extremely happy and relieved, trusting that with Edward back it would now be business as usual.

A week and five shipping orders later, as Edward was walking through Leith docks, he met Sven. It was the first time he had seen his friend since the marriage, it was natural that Sven would want to know and it also followed that the best place to tell of the holiday was the Sailor's Rest. They had just settled down when the exciseman appeared.

Rory McLeod was certainly happier than the time he had seen him at Inverness and Edward hoped this was a sign that he had been successful in his assignment.

As could be expected, the conversation centred on the marriage, with Sven and Rory ribbing him concerning his newly acquired marital state. Edward, with patience and forbearance, tolerated their good-natured taunting until he felt it was his turn to give his final reply.

"I have listened and hope I have successfully replied to your inquisition regarding my pre-marital, marital and immediate post-marital experiences and trust that the initiation tests just concluded will now allow me to return to the world of the so-called dominant male."

Sven seemed surprised, but Rory could not restrain his belly laughter. When the storm died down, he looked at what he considered to be a very well-read Scandinavian and voiced in a deep bass his opinion.

"I've said it before, you're a helluva man, but I didna expect you to plead your case like an Edinburgh lawyer."

Edward grinned widely before replying. "I don't know if that is meant to be a compliment or an insult, so I shall rest my case and put on record that though I believe in sex equality, I have no intention of succumbing to the blandishments of any potential petticoat government."

As he finished he looked at Sven and gave him a wink. It was shortly after that that Sven looked at his watch and admitted, reluctantly, that he had a date with Felicity and would have to leave almost immediately. As he left, Edward comforted him.

"Quite right, Sven, you must never be late for an appointment with a lady. My felicitations to Felicity and, should you unfortunately be a little late, she will understand when she knows you have been in such good company."

Sven did not seem unduly amused as he left.

The conversation between the two men now turned to matters that Rory had decided not to mention in the presence of Sven. It had little to do with friendship, more with diplomacy, safety and predominantly with loyalty to his profession.

His trip to Inverness had brought meagre results, but enough information had been laid to help in the fight against the cocaine barons. It seemed almost conspiratorial the way he mentioned that an American was involved in the main distribution of cocaine on the East coast of Scotland and once again the name Mr. White, or 'Snowy', had been divulged by a street hawker caught in the act.

Rory admitted his chief had asked him to cultivate Edward in the hope that he, in the course of his activities, might hear or see something that could help the department put the cocaine smugglers behind bars, hopefully for life.

Having heard from his chief, Mr. Pringle, about Edward's alleged smuggling activities, Rory felt that his friend had been pressured into playing a dangerous part and had decided to say nothing. He now felt that cocaine smuggling had reached a stage where a decision had to be made. He felt a cautious approach was essential, knowing the potential quicksilver reactions of his friend. He transmitted his message as delicately as he could.

"I know you want to do something about dope smuggling, Edward, and I am sure you will do all you can, but for my peace of mind, go easy. I don't want a friend killed by these bastards."

Edward was quite moved by his friend's obvious concern for his safety and felt it necessary to inform him that he had no intention of approaching the problem in a flippant manner. He knew only too well that criminals of that type would be unconcerned in taking human life. But still he could not resist smiling and telling Rory, "After all, I'm a married man now and must act more responsibly and, who knows, it might not be too long before I become a father."

Rory just shook his head, but wished him well.

For almost a fortnight Edward commuted between Grangemouth and Leith. Although he had been extremely successful in a business sense, he felt as a detective he had been a bit of a failure.

He was happy that over a short period he had averaged one order per day, half of which had been substantial sea stock, but felt he was letting Rory down in not uncovering some plot hatched by the cocaine smugglers.

Now that he had re-established his commercial base, he knew he had to give more thought to matters beneficial to society. For probably the first time in his life, he had the uneasy feeling of being out of his depth. So far he had not even been able to flush out from the undergrowth the most insignificant cocaine pedlar and wondered why not. It was true he had not been over-zealous and he knew if he really wanted to contribute it would require a serious and determined effort on his part.

He pondered the problem as he cycled from the Imperial Dock up to Sandport Street and, after leaving the bike at Ove's place, walked down to the Sailor's Rest. After ordering his drink, he settled back in a comfortable seat in an atmosphere he felt might be conducive to the solution of the drug problems of Scottish society.

He recalled the time when Mr. Pringle had asked him to keep his eyes and ears open - he should have laid far greater stress on the latter sense. He had certainly used his eyes as he moved from ship to ship, whether in the docks or in the firth and had seen little which might have indicated the smuggling of drugs. After all, in his capacity as Water Agent he did not have the power of search of customs officials and had therefore been confined in the main to exercising his hearing potential.

This had left him with a rather limited scenario consisting of shipping agents, stewards and captains, who were most unlikely to unload information in an ex-gratia manner that could land them in jail for a considerable stretch.

As he cogitated, the corners of his mouth twitched slightly upwards until a smile developed, ending in a grin, a very wide grin, when he realised he was sitting in the right place to use his ears.

Everything has a beginning and an end and Edward knew that cocaine started in South America, leaves from the coca shrub being immersed in tubs of weak sulphuric solution; after almost a week chemicals were added and after refining and processing, a fine white powder emerged called 'snow' by both criminal and law enforcer.

Having seen the effects of cocaine on several shipmates, he knew he would not rest till he had achieved something of significance.

It seemed to him now that the coastal pubs were the stock exchanges where cocaine was concerned. Being cynically-minded, Edward felt that probably the only real difference was that the wheeling and dealing and throat-cutting of the normal stock exchange was much noisier than the murmuring of the dope peddler as he off-loaded his poison on his miserable captive.

Surely someone with acute hearing hiding behind a newspaper could sooner or later hear something that would put behind bars those pedlars of misery.

He knew a great deal of pub crawling might be required and speculated whether he would have the stamina and time to pursue his objective to a successful conclusion.

As he sat back and weighed up the procedure he would adopt, he wondered if he was just too far ahead of his time. He could expect little support from the general public: it would be some years before the selling of opium, morphine and cocaine without special licence would be a criminal offence. The only legislation curbing the activities of drug traffickers was the smuggling of narcotics and this was of little interest to the public, other than the relatives of some miserable addict who had died in agony.

Should he or should he not become prematurely involved ... and as he hesitated, Little Eric intervened.

"Stop dodging the issue, Edward. By all means think, but prepare for action."

Lighting his marcella, he started to think as he puffed smoke rings towards the ceiling. One ring, going slightly askew, widened and seemed to settle and dissipate around a group of men sitting at a table just too far away for eavesdropping.

Recharging his drink at the bar, he returned to a table just behind them. The conversation was desultory and would have been boring had he not heard the voice of someone he knew. It was that of Steve Allrock who, having seen him replenishing his drink, was itching to speak to him. Steve waited until Edward had settled in his chair and then swung round to surprise him.

"So, you don't speak to your friends these days."

Edward, more intent on listening than seeing, was caught out, but recovered quickly.

"Your voice is familiar. If you would be kind enough to come over to my table and I discover you are indeed a friend, I will be pleased to order a drink for you."

Steve, laughingly, not only accepted, but toasted Edward graciously with his reward. They had much to talk about and for the next half an hour they did just that. Edward was disturbed, but inquisitive when Steve told him the last time he had seen him was in the company of Sven, with the American hovering in the background.

Some days later, he had heard that Edward had been confined to bed suffering from the effects of a particularly virulent type of 'flu. Edward admitted he had been in bad shape and could offer no explanation. When Edward reached the part where Sven had told him the American had found a shipping order lost by Edward and had delivered it, Steve intervened in sarcastic fashion.

"And Mr. Chancer sought out Mr. Sorenson and said to him 'Look, I have found your order, I have delivered it and here is the commission, all I ask is that you pay me back the expenses involved'."

Edward shrugged and smiled before replying, "The American's name is Chancitt and I have not seen him since that night."

Steve gave a grunt before replying, "If you ever see him again, Edward, you can bet that his bottom dollar disappeared long ago."

Although Steve Allrock seemed bitterly biased, Edward listened with interest to what he had to say. Edward remembered leaving the bar for several minutes and recollected the American smoking one of his obnoxious cigarillos and stretching carelessly over drinks to flick ash into a tray.

Steve gripped Edward's arm tightly as he sought to convey his message.

"I'll bet that bastard dropped something into your drink, maybe not then, but when it suited him."

But Edward, wanting to be objective, asked him why he should want to do such a thing.

Steve looked despairingly at Edward and riposted, "Because he is a real bad yin and he knows, as the Yanks say, that you are queering his pitch and interfering wi' his other wee games."

Edward pursed his lips, but Steve was adamant.

"I've seen that bastard sitting in a corner, half-pissed, taking snuff, only it wisna snuff, it was white, mair like cocaine or other dope and yon wee scoundrel that accompanies him isnae just a bookie's runner."

Edward, feeling justified in his assumption that listening in pubs could give results, encouraged his friend to develop the theme. Yes, Mr. Chancitt was definitely a blackguard, both Steve and Punchy Rush had seen him in the company of known criminals.

Money and small parcels were exchanged and from time to time, at the behest of the American, the runner would vanish and shortly after, return.

At this point Steve gave an involuntary cough, laughed a little and then explained it had just crossed his mind that Punchy Rush had referred to the runner in the old fashioned term 'cut purse', signifying that he was also a pickpocket.

Steve, feeling Edward was slow in the uptake, gave his verdict.

"You didnae lose the paper, Edward, that wee bugger picked your pocket and handed it over to his maister."

Edward was excited now: the story and conclusion seemed laudable, he wanted to know more, much more.

"How long since you saw Chancitt and his associates?"

Steve laughed. That Edward should use the word associates when talking about what he considered to be a murderous gang was, to him, comical and dangerously naive.

Steve felt trapped. He knew from experience that Edward was a resourceful and intelligent man who would sooner or later track down Chancitt and in his own way balance the books, but at what cost?

"Relax, Steve," Edward advised. "I appreciate your concern for my safety, but surely you know me well enough to understand that I have no option but to bring such a person to justice."

But Steve did not understand why Edward should risk his neck for ten or twenty pounds. When Edward explained that he had official information that an American, probably Chancitt, was involved in a big way in the smuggling and distribution of cocaine, he realised that his friend was crusading, in his own way, against the drug pedlars who were a blight on the social scene.

Under such circumstances, he felt he had to give his friend all the support he required, despite any danger that might be involved.

It transpired that Edward's friends had on several occasions seen the American in the company of some desperate looking characters in a small pub in the Citadel area.

Edward felt he could now channel the conversation to spheres that might interest Steve and Punchy and hopefully build a camaraderie which might influence them to understand the vital importance of preventing the purveyors of misery pursuing their evil trade.

He left feeling reasonably successful. Steve, having agreed they should meet again in the Melodian Bar. It was Steve's final remark that interested him.

"Who knows Edward, the American might be there with your commission and an apology and, of course, pigs might fly."

That evening he travelled back by train, he liked the train, it gave him time to sit back, to think and dream and plan for the future. Normally a gregarious person, he seemed, this time, oblivious to an old lady sitting in the coach and settled down in his own little capsule of contentment.

The old lady, watching his behaviour, was interested and amused. He sat opposite her looking into space, his fingers tapping out some message or other, then produced from his pocket a small pad and a pencil. She wondered what and to whom he might be writing and was surprised when instead of writing, he reverted to his original position and started tapping the pencil rhythmically on the pad. Being musical, she smiled, realising he was attempting to tap out a rhythm attuned to the wheels of the train on the track and marry them to the sounds of steam which varied according to the speed of the train.

She spoke to him, but there was no response, and a minute later repeated the process, slapping him on the knee with her newspaper.

He looked at her in a dazed fashion, as if he was just returning from a cataleptic fit and apologised for not having heard what she had said. She smiled sweetly to him.

"I was asking you if you would like a wee train set for your Christmas?"

Edward, having just returned from Never-Never land, knew he had to concentrate. He looked closely at the old woman and then exploded into laughter.

"Excuse my laughter Mrs. McGregor, it's only a cover for my stupid behaviour. I am really sorry, I did not recognise you when I entered the carriage."

She smiled, accepted his apology and they both laughed at a rather comical incident.

She chastised him for working too hard, reminding him of what she had said to him not so long ago. Admitting she had been correct, he asked for credit to be given for having followed her advice over the past few months. He had, as advised, decreased his work load considerably and had used most of the time left in paying his respects to the ladies.

"During this last year, Mrs. McGregor, I have dated, danced and dined with more ladies than might have been good for me, but I think you might agree I reached the pinnacle when Emily and I were married."

The old lady smiled sweetly at him, then reaching over, patted his arm.

"Yes I know, Edward, and I'm sure you will both be very happy."

He was pleased and ready to respond, but Mrs. McGregor had more to say, informing him that there was a lot more to life than just earning money for material things. She liked Edward and felt she understood him, she was sure he would look after Emily who, in her estimation, was a guid and bonnie lassie, but a word of motherly warning would not go wrong, knowing that Edward would accept it in the spirit in which it was given.

"I know you work hard in providing the needs for Emily and yourself, but you would be wise to ease up a wee bit and use up some time entertaining Emily the way that you did before you were married."

Edward looked at her pensively, as if weighing up the most appropriate reply. But Mrs. McGregor still had something to say.

"Men think that when they have won a woman's heart, they can sit back and put their feet up. True happiness is knowing that he must court his partner to the end of life."

Edward sat dazed for a full minute before replying.

"You are a very wise woman, Mrs. McGregor. Your advice will be followed to the letter."

The old woman smiled acknowledgement, but before she could reply, a strident voice shouted, "Falkirk, all change for Grangemouth."

As Edward made for the connection, Mrs. McGregor hesitated and, as he turned to assist, the old lady suddenly changed her mind.

"You catch your train, Edward, I'll get the next one. I've an old friend I'd like to see just down the road, next time in Falkirk might be just too late, time travels quickly the older you get."

It was a serious man who sat in the train travelling homewards. The journey only took a few minutes, but he had made up his mind before stepping from the train.

That evening Emily served up crisp fried red spotted flounders and Edward acted appropriately.

"*Mange tak*," he said with enthusiasm and then suggested she might enjoy a trip to Edinburgh the following morning. She gave a little gurgle of joy, blushed slightly and then, kissing her husband, murmured, "Thank you, Edward, I look forward to it."

Edward was a very proud and happy man, his wife's English was certainly improving.

The little booklet issued by the Edinburgh Tourist Office confirmed that anyone travelling south towards the capital by train would find it more convenient to alight at Haymarket, should their immediate destination happen to be the west end of Princes Street.

For the rugby enthusiast, it stressed that be they Welsh, English, Irish or Scottish, they could all be assured of a welcome and after the event, if the referee had been ill-disposed to their particular side, what of it? The finest Scotch and Scottish beer would always be available to drown their sorrows.

He brought the booklet with him, thinking it could prove useful once Emily had decided what she wanted to do. She had already seen the Castle and Princes Street Gardens and although loving trees, she seemed to be seeking something new.

Suddenly she pointed excitedly to a hoarding high above the side of the track. Fortunately, the train had slowed to walking pace and Edward was able to read an advertisement urging everyone to visit the Edinburgh Zoological Gardens. He in turn pointed.

"So that's it," he said.

She nodded her head vigorously and Edward acted swiftly. They disembarked at Haymarket and travelled by tram to the Zoo at Corstorphine.

Famous zoos, like great circuses, have a remarkable effect on most of the population, irrespective of age. A visit to the zoo for many can be an extraordinary event, an experience that is thrilling, exciting, amusing and even educational. To a child, a zoo is like an enormous animal circus or playground; they hope and trust with some trepidation that the animals will view them favourably as playmates.

Men invariably agree that the most interesting aspects in zoology, as in other spheres, is what constitutes the fastest, the strongest and the most powerful. In the first category, it would appear the cheetah wins hands down, but as it is difficult to imagine a zoo with the space to develop a speed of seventy miles an hour, one has to be content to look and marvel at the long strong musculature of an animal that can accomplish such a feat.

The second category is always controversial. Many from the north prefer the bear, but many seem to favour the gorilla with its big chest and the phenomenal contractile power of these enormous arms. But in sheer power, all agree that the gentle giant, the elephant, ambles serenely forward for first prize.

Emily, however, had her own opinion and judged the animals in her own particular fashion. While her husband might aver that the lion was the king of beasts, she thought he was a bit of a show-off and overweight at that; there could be little doubt the lioness was most definitely the queen of the animals. Not only did she look a lot better, the loving attention she gave her delightful cubs as his majesty remained aloof, knocked his credit marks down to almost zero.

Her next preference was for the deer family and close relatives: their grace, speed and agility when required to move was truly amazing.

But it was the big bundle of white fur that brought forth her laughter. The polar bear seemed to take a great delight in flopping into the water, then swimming and turning somersaults majestically, he would suddenly ascend to a promontory high enough to ensure that he thoroughly drenched his curious visitors as he shook off water surplus to his requirements.

After the zoo, Emily opted for a little shopping, having, as she said, decided that as they were in Edinburgh, this was the time to update certain requirements.

Every young man has to undergo, sooner or later, what is known as the shopping experience. Had he known what to expect, he would have taken a crash course in the art and practice of fastidious shopping. He soon realised he was expected to be an expert in colour matching, to be a judge of style and size and, if unsure, to be very diplomatic.

To questions from his spouse such as 'And what do you think?', if he replied 'good', she would invariably retort, 'I think you're just saying that'.

Vanity plays a big part in the family of homo sapiens, with women probably making their mark more acutely in the sphere of dress and personal appearance. Had Edward known what to expect, he would have used his skills as a salesman in cajolery, blandishments, possibly even descending to the politician's economic use of 'truth', but although he might have emerged with flying colours, the thought of a tarnished conscience dissuaded him.

Instead, he behaved as a husband doing his best, but finding his patience wearing thin as Emily tried on dress after dress and persisted in asking questions that baffled and bored him.

What amazed and, to some degree disconcerted him, was the ease with which Emily appeared to make herself understood to the salesgirls, despite her limited knowledge of the English language. Although she turned to him, as he thought for guidance, she paid scant attention to his reactions and carried on a giggling relationship with the girls, interspersed with a shaking of heads as they gave a furtive glance in his direction. He felt he was rapidly becoming a victim of a female conspiracy.

By the time they reach Jenners at the east end of Princes Street, his patience, although not exhausted, was in a parlous state. Being loaded with parcels was a mere detail to Edward. If Emily wanted the stuff, then that was good enough for him. It was the seemingly interminable negotiating that took place before a sale was made that gave him a feeling of impotence.

As a student of English, Edward had been aware of an expression, 'They also serve who stand and wait' or something like that, and now he knew that it referred to husbands who had enough character and stamina to accompany their wives on what has so often been described by the female of the species as a 'shopping spree'.

As he staggered through the door laden with parcels, he saw a sign in big letters 'Wednesday open half day only'. Exultation was too grand a word to describe his feelings, but the more devious elements of his persona dictated that the next shopping event would be channelled into Wednesday - the afternoon, of course.

Edward must have felt that the Viking gods were on his side, after all Wednesday is Odin's day. Evil thoughts beget evil deeds, but he in a way felt more fortunate than the normal mortal insofar that he had an in-built warning system that, if obeyed, obviated the danger of self-destruction.

Where the average person might seek guidance or absolution from a minister, priest, witch doctor or psychologist, Edward was more fortunate in that he had a 'do it yourself' mechanism, an implant dating back to childhood that always warned him if he neared the line of no return.

On this occasion, 'Little Eric' decided that a moderate signal would do the trick, but Edward was not amused, the bell that rang deep in his head did not assure him, but he had to listen. The voice, although moderate, to Edward seemed like thunder.

"The woman Emily is your wife and must be protected at all time. Put aside all your childish prejudices, comfort her and do it quickly."

As he hesitated, Little Eric spoke again.

"Move quickly, you ill-begotten son of a Viking, the Lord God Odin is incensed that you should use his name in your ill-conceived plan and demands an apology."

Edward, knowing he had little time to negotiate and that he was too young to enter Valhalla as a persona non grata, decided to accept Little Eric's directive.

"I apologise, I apologise." He said it twice, just in case the Viking Gods were too busy to hear him the first time.

Emily looked concernedly at her man and asked him what was wrong; she had heard him say something, but couldn't understand. He smiled to her and told her that, feeling the parcels were slipping, he had involuntarily apologised for being a nuisance.

Emily's reaction was a caring one. She led him to a seat not far from the Waverly Steps and, taking some parcels from him, placed them on an adjacent seat and insisted that they both sit down and rest. She placed her hand in his and expressed her gratitude and joy for a lovely day out. He smiled acknowledgement, said nothing, but felt mean. There was still a lump in his throat as they boarded the train for Grangemouth.

For the rest of the week, Edward obeyed his conscience implicitly and ensured that Eric had no cause to ring him up. He kept close to Emily, visiting the Wevlings in Boness and others Edward knew would welcome his wife and make her feel safe in her new environment. He felt instinctively that certain dangers might arise in the near future and wished to ensure that Emily could rely on the support of friends.

It troubled Edward that innate capacity, or was it instinct, added to what he now regarded as fact, could only mean danger in the not too distant future. Had he known what was happening in room 116 in the North British Hotel at the east end of Princes Street, he would have been extremely anxious.

In room 116, two men faced each other, both were engaged in an animated and angry discussion concerning a water clerk called Edward Sorenson who, in some inexplicable way, appeared to be interfering in their dope peddling activities.

At least Pierre Blanc, known usually as Mr. White, Snowy or Snow White by other drug barons, thought that Lucius Chancitt's excuses for a drop in trade were mysterious and inconclusive. Snowy, known as Monsieur Blanc in Berwick, Newcastle and Carlisle, was the owner of well known restaurants, night clubs and an extremely profitable first class brothel which catered for the highest in the land.

He was extremely angry that he had felt forced to leave his profitable and comfortable lair to journey north for the purpose of investigating the affairs of Lucius Chancitt, who was now rapidly becoming a liability in the drug part of the business.

Having listened impatiently to Chancitt, he had formed the opinion that reference to the man Sorenson was more an excuse than a reason for diminishing returns in his cocaine trade.

Snowy put his hand forward imperiously and, demanding a hesitation in the American's babbling, asked pointedly, "If what you are saying is true, I would have thought you would have rid yourself of Sorenson by this time."

Lucius, feeling he might still gain credibility, seized the opportunity to tell how he had cleverly spiked Sorenson's drink. Unfortunately he had been unsuccessful, Sorenson was still very much alive.

The French Canadian, a powerful man, leaned across and, taking Lucius by his jacket lapel, pulled him down violently, almost slapping his head on the table, released him and in a voice controlled, but full of venom, spat out, "You did what?"

The American gave a whining summary of what he had done and why. Snowy waited until he finished his abject performance before berating him, analysing where he had failed and offering him advice concerning his future behaviour should he wish to survive.

"In our trade, only an idiot would try to poison a victim. If this mysterious man that you refer to had died, the police forensic squad would have been alerted and for us that is just bad business."

Looking aloof and contemplative, like a banker considering the request for a big loan, he continued, "It is unlikely, Lucius, that you are suffering from a form of cretinism, but I have to save the organisation from the actions of an imbecile who may not have learned his lesson. If your problem still persists, then arrange an accident, like the victim drowning in a dock."

The American had that sinking feeling, but just summoned up enough courage to murmur, "O.K."

Snowy smiled sarcastically before issuing his instructions.

"I'm sure you have learned your lesson, Lucius, but I am leaving two of my heavy gang with you in case action is required."

Lucius smiled vacantly in the direction of the French Canadian and prayed that he would not be the victim.

As Snowy left to join his train in the station down below, he turned and gave a last minute instruction.

"In the future when we are together in public, address me as Monsieur Blanc, never as Snowy. Remember I am a highly respected restaurateur now, you can forget we were once associates in Colombia."

For the next hour it was a disenchanted American who sat, still attempting to weigh up his immediate position. He realised it was extremely tenuous and knew he had only himself to blame.

It had all started with Sorenson beating him decisively in the rush for shipping orders. His income had been severely dented from that source and in an abortive attempt to square the account, his concentration had suffered and led to losses in his cocaine smuggling activities. It had been the close proximity of Sorenson as they competed for business that had bedevilled him, making him feel he was being watched; his imagination had done the rest.

Whatever the truth of the matter, he cursed the day that Sorenson had crossed his path.

Not far away, on the Scottish East Coast, sat the subject of his mental malaise, his arm lovingly encircled the waist of his wife Emily, as they listened to light opera on their newly acquired gramophone. Edward had been fortunate in having friends in the import and export business who could fulfil orders for certain Scandinavian articles he wanted in order that Emily would be able to settle down quickly and feel at home.

Although Edward had not lived long in the area, he was already well known and popular, having reached a status where his neighbours recognised him as a 'a weel kent face'. In a way the Sorensons were fortunate. It had started with Edward becoming a lodger in the house of Mrs. McGregor, a well loved figure in the community, who was considered to be kind and definitely very intelligent. It followed therefore that Edward would be thought of as someone rather special, for they knew she would not have accepted him as a lodger unless his credentials were of the highest.

Emily, being the wife of the popular Danish gentleman, was accorded the friendship that could be expected, particularly from the women in the neighbourhood, when they observed that Emily and Mrs. McGregor had become attached to each other.

The record had run its course, Edward rose and switched off the machine. Then turning to Emily ready to do her bidding, he was forestalled by a knock at the door. There she was, herself, the McGregor resplendent in her clan tartan, smiling and waiting to be welcomed in.

She started to speak, but he stopped her and pointed to the newly acquired sideboard. She smiled and nodded her head and Edward ensured that she got herself around a substantial gin. After a generous sip she coughed and Edward felt he had to apologise for the cigar smoke and the smell of strong coffee.

"I know how you must feel - the Scots are such delicate and genteel people."

Knowing Edward, she laughed and put a finger to her mouth as she riposted, "Haud your wheesht you daft Dane, have more respect for your elders. After all I'm here to deliver a message, but you will just have to wait now while I enjoy this gin, which just suits my gab."

"Skol to that," Edward replied as he toasted the old lady with a rather large akvavit. Drinking socially, although not an exact science, has a protocol all its own. It also has many national variants, one of which is that the guest's glass must never be empty. Legend has it that if a guest's glass remains empty for a period of time in excess of the time required for a sober person to recite the ten commandments, then any liquor poured to that glass will become contaminated.

As Edward tried to interest Mrs. McGregor in a refill, he recounted the legend, but the old lady was adamant.

"No thanks," she said, "I am not superstitious, neither do I believe your blethers, but I am prepared to risk the coffee you always boast about."

He had an evil grin as he replied, "Coffee will be served immediately after supper, a rule of the house, you know."

Mrs. McGregor laughed at the young man's antics, but was prepared to go along with the spirit of the exercise. She smiled to Emily as she agreed that a house, or more importantly, a home must have rules or a certain procedure to be run efficiently and harmoniously.

Turning to Edward, she accepted his invitation.

"I would be pleased to have supper with you and Emily, even coffee."

He laughed and replied, "My illustrious landlady of yesterday obviously spied me making homewards with lobster."

Mrs. McGregor ignored the assertion, but agreed that a wee bit of lobster would be acceptable, it would do just fine.

It transpired that the supper was more than just fine, Mrs. McGregor remarking that it was the best lobster dish she had ever tasted, the sauce alone was a wee miracle.

"I don't know how you do it, Emily."

Emily smiled shyly, but pointed to Edward, who shrugged his shoulders and affirmed modestly, "We do our best."

For the rest of the evening the Sorensons listened to Mrs. McGregor recounting, in her own inimitable style, the local history of Grangemouth over the past half century. She became so absorbed in the telling of her story, that it was not until she was ready to depart that she suddenly realised she had still not transmitted the message. It appeared that Tam Richards had been in the process of closing his shop when the telephone had rung.

Sven had asked him to inform Edward that a Scandinavian ship was due to arrive in Leith the following morning and he, Sven, had been assigned an inspection job and as the ship was of considerable size, he thought Edward should be informed; there could well be a big provisioning order going abegging.

Thanking the old lady, he assured her he would certainly do his best to ensure that the sailors aboard the vessel would sail from Leith provisioned by the best of Scottish.

After Mrs. McGregor departed, Edward restarted the gramophone and while Emily listened to music, he reflected on the tranquillity and happiness of the past month, wondering what the future held in store.

Edward felt good knowing he had done his bit for Emily and the message he had received showed potential for increased business, while at the back of his mind he thought of Lucius Chancitt and the portent, albeit rather nebulous, that he might find himself in a position where he could contribute in his own small way towards damaging the designs of the drug dealers.

'Tis well known that vanity plays a big part in the life of man and Edward, thinking in the lofty terms of the dignity of man, had to confess to himself that it was really his vanity or ego that had suffered a dent. He tried to be objective in his thinking and felt that Steve Allrock was probably correct and that the American could have been responsible for the malaise which had endangered his life. Whether it be dignity or just vanity, one thing was certain, given the opportunity, he would confront Chancitt and solve the problem.

The following morning he travelled to Leith, after assuring Emily that he would telephone Tam Richards so that she would know what was happening. He expected to be gone for two days and would sleep at Ove's place so that he would be at the right place at the right time to clinch a shipping order or two.

Chapter 17

Sven had just come up on deck after a cursory examination of the auxiliary engines of the S.S. Finlandia and was enjoying a mug of coffee, when he saw a figure a hundred yards away strolling, sailor fashion, towards the ship. Although having prepared himself, he was nevertheless caught unawares when the approaching figure shouted, "And one for me as well."

As they drank their coffee and sipped schnapps, the two friends exchanged their experiences over the past month. It was natural that Sven should enquire regarding the welfare of his cousin Emily and was satisfied that little Emily had been properly cared for when Edward recounted their happy experiences in the Scottish Highlands.

He was quite impressed when he learned that not only had the holiday been a joyful one, but as an added bonus Emily had acquired a working knowledge of the local language and since returning to Grangemouth they had increased their Scandinavian contacts, allowing Emily to settle down in the sure knowledge that she was not completely cut off from the country of her birth.

It was a happy time for both of them, Sven assured of his young cousin's life being in safe hands, and Edward feeling all aglow sipping his schnapps courtesy of the Chief Steward, a man from his own native Jutland. As the two Danes settled down to a nice cosy chat about their own local patch, Sven restarted his inspection of the S.S. Finlandia, returning from time to time for liquid refreshment to offset the pernicious effects of dehydration. By noon, the three men had achieved their respective targets.

Sven, when examining, had discovered that the steering gear was in need of urgent attention and had already arranged that a local firm, renowned worldwide, had been contacted to put things to right.

Other adjustments had been done on the spot, whilst Edward had been extremely fortunate in achieving the sea stock order in his pocket, without really trying and his fellow Dane, the chief steward, was satisfied that at least the ship's refrigeration system would operate.

As Sven and Edward made ready to depart, a lurid and lowering sky swept down on the Forth, the blue black backcloth throwing into relief the coves of the Fife coast, a sure indication to local seafarers that a nasty weather spell was in store.

As they hesitated atop the gangway, Sven turned and looked enquiringly at Edward, who gave him a gentle push, reassuring his companion.

"We will be there and dry in the Sailor's Rest if you move."

Sven laughed and pointed downwards. "Better let this man up first, only room for one at a time on this gangway."

As Edward looked down, he could only see a big broad-brimmed hat ascending, the hat tilted back exposing a face of yellowed parchment, a nose like the beak of some predatory bird and a mouth turned down at the corners, an indication that whatever lived beyond the face felt the world owed its body the right to do what was required to ensure that its appetites were served without question.

Alerted to thoughts of clarification, Edward reacted quickly and, asking Sven to step aside, he called down,

"Hullo, Mr. Chancitt, could I have a word with you?"

The mouth opened and curled to a snarl, exposing blackened teeth reminiscent of some dilapidated cemetery, then closed clap-trap fashion. The figure below turned abruptly and left the gangway, disappearing like an enormous bat through an opening in the dock shed below. Sven looked at Edward and asked, "What's wrong with the man?"

Edward ushered his friend down the gangway, telling him to forget the incident, he would explain later.

They were fortunate Edward had judged the weather well: the hailstones did not descend until they had crossed the Bernard Street bridge, just a few yards away from the Sailor's Rest. It was natural that, having reached sanctuary, they should rest awhile. Over a pie and a pint they discussed the weather in relative comfort, while outside hail splattered the windows like grapeshot. When seafarers gather together in conditions such as these, it is to be expected that rather tall yarns will be knitted together in a fabric of fairy tale dimensions.

But Sven would not have agreed when he re-told the story of how, in the South China seas, a hailstorm had erupted, and the stones of ice in some cases had exceeded a half pound in weight, confirmed later by the South China news. The storm had been so horrific that more than two hundred people had been killed and many thousands had been badly injured.

As if to qualify the story as genuine, he referred to an article in the Scientific American some years later confirming his story. Edward, knowing how serious and accurate his Swedish friend liked to be, felt that the story was probably correct; nevertheless he felt his contribution had in some way to edge slightly in front.

Edward decided that one of his more elaborate stories should be given precedence and chose the time he had paid a visit to relatives who had emigrated and ultimately settled in America, in the state of Arizona. Bjorn Sorenson had been unsuccessful in marketing a food-dispensing machine he had invented. Sven smiled indulgently before intervening.

"Nothing earth-shattering about that, Edward. They had machines dispensing fruit and pies at the end of the nineteenth century and it would not surprise me if the Chinese had not done something similar a few thousand years ago."

Edward, in no way abashed, continued. "Bjorn was the inventor of our tribe, but unfortunately he was a bad business man. I am sure that his invention or something similar will be used world-wide in the very near future."

Sven was not impressed, but Edward was determined. "Look, Sven, imagine you are standing in Waverley station, you are hungry and the fish and chip shops are shut, you are waiting for the London train, what do you do?"

Sven looked sympathetically at his friend. "Well, like a good Swede, I wait until my appetite can be assuaged."

Edward shook his head at such a negative attitude. "If Bjorn's invention is universally adopted, you will put a sixpence in a machine slot, pull a lever and hey presto, a hot succulent supper will appear with a separate condiment of your choice."

Sven thought for a moment before replying. "I thought you said that Bjorn had named his device Automat."

Edward was quick to reply. "Yes, Automat, remember the word 'mat' means hot food as far as a Dane is concerned and therefore, it was his intention that people should enjoy hot food at the press of a button, automatically."

Sven gave in, but not before indicating that they had started discussing the weather and somehow or other Edward's relative had intervened. Edward apologised for going off at a tangent, but told his friend it was really a lead to the original topic.

Bjorn had evidently spied a dust storm on the horizon and had informed the family and Edward that there was trouble ahead. Almost immediately, the sky had darkened ominously, lightning flashed and seconds later terrifying thunder engulfed them, then a deathly uneasy silence before the cannon balls of ice sped earthwards.

Edward paused, looked at Sven, and suggested that the hailstones were much bigger than the ones Sven had experienced in the China Seas. Sven, relaxed and seemingly enjoying himself, placed his arm lovingly round his friend, before replying.

"It must have been a terrible experience, but please remember I can confirm my story from reliable scientific sources."

Edward, seeming unconcerned regarding scientific back up, replied, "I may not have positive proof concerning the size of the hailstones, but I would venture to predict on the basis of probability that the American hailstones were much bigger. Surely you would agree, American is always much bigger."

Like many Swedes, Sven was a serious student of social behaviour, but was ready to join in the banter. "I can only assume, Edward, that you are a victim of American propaganda which propounds that anything American is always bigger than anything on earth; in a sense they certainly have the biggest and loudest mouths. What intrigues me is why they handicap themselves by speaking through their noses."

Edward could hardly contain himself before responding, "Knowing your reputation for factual analysis, I must concede you victory on this occasion and allow you to claim your prize in the accepted fashion."

"A small cognac and a Carlsberg will do just fine," was Sven's reply.

They sat chatting amiably for a short time, then Sven suddenly became curious.

"We were talking about America a few minutes ago; what's to do with you and Chancitt? He scurried away as soon as he saw your head at the top of the gangway."

Edward admitted that from the first time he had met the American he had found his social behaviour unacceptable. He referred to the evening they had all been together, how he had just managed to get back to Ove's place and had experienced for a night and a day a feeling so diabolical that he thought he would surely die.

He referred to Steve Allrock's information and opinion of the American and Rory's opinion that an American was probably in charge of cocaine smuggling on the east coast.

He knew he was prejudiced concerning Chancitt's mode of life, but felt he might have been amateurish when asking questions aboard ship which would possibly alert the American and force him to remain in the background. Sven was sympathetic, but thought his friend was possibly romanticising a little.

Edward agreed that his friend could be right, but Chancitt had acquired his sea stock order, had commissioned it and had kept the proceeds. Why had he scurried away when he saw him at the top of the gangway? Sven knew now that there was something serious to consider, but felt it necessary to cool things down. But before he could advise, Edward continued.

"Whether he is involved in drugs or not, I intend to search him out and make him pay the money he has stolen."

This in no way reassured Sven, who knew that Edward was always one for action and unlikely to sit still for any length of time; but on the other hand he knew a plan of action was required, if only to protect his friend from the physical danger he would be exposed to.

Although agreeing with Edward that the question of the commission should be resolved, he warned that it should not be attempted while the American was in the company of some of his disreputable cronies. Edward was still adamant, he knew the danger and would choose the proper moment to square the account. Sven offered his services.

"At least let me know when the moment is likely to occur."

Edward was light-hearted and cheery, assuring his companion that the services of a Swedish heavyweight would probably not be required. He poked Sven in the ribs as he reminded him of a past incident.

"Remember the brawl in Hamburg when you knocked the Latvian bosun stone cold and while you stood astride him apologising for using too much force, I had to knock away the legs of the man's mate before he crowned you with a chair."

Sven was serious. "All right, Edward, have your fun, but remember the offer is still there."

From then on the two companions relegated the seamier side of life to the background as they concerned themselves with family and local business affairs. It was about this time that Punchy Rush, known as the working man's entrepreneur, burst upon the scene and spying Edward made straight towards him. Reaching the table, came to attention in proper Navy style and addressed Edward.

"Permission to come aboard, sir."

Edward responded. "Welcome aboard. This is Sven Sjogren, ship's engineer and, Sven, this is Pugnacious Rush, stoker first class and agitator for vastly improved conditions on the ships of his Imperial Majesty."

Punchy laughed and corrected him. "Wrong, Edward, the name is Punchy and you missed out the word Britannic."

But Edward was enjoying himself. "Sorry, Rush, I was thinking that was an insurance company.

However, first things first. A rum Punchy would seem appropriate?"

The navy man appreciated the play on words, but felt a large rum, unadulterated, would be just fine.

Sven left shortly after and Edward and Punchy settled down to discuss the intricacy of local business, who to trust and who to avoid within the Port.

It was natural that the name of one Ignatius Lucius Chancitt should fit into the latter category. What surprised him was the interest that Punchy had shown in the American's behaviour and background.

Punchy had been fortunate in acquiring an education well in advance of his working class associates, but circumstances outwith his control and his own independent nature had combined in a peculiar fashion and channelled him into the navy where his mental agility had made him the darling of the lower deck, but a menace in the eyes of the conservative section of the officer class. He felt it was important that Edward should know the reason for the way he felt about the American.

"For a number of years I was thrown into conflict with officers of the British Navy. Some like myself were intelligent human beings, unfortunately too many were middle class discards whose parents, wishing to be rid of them, sent them packing to the colonies as remittance men, or used their influence in arranging commissions for them in the army and navy, relieving them of all responsibility."

For a moment he hesitated, sipped his drink and then developed his theme. The outcasts from the so-called elite, unable to adjust to normal society, reacted in an irrational and criminal fashion against those they considered to be their inferiors.

Although he understood the way they felt had been conditioned by their sires abandoning them, he was not prepared to forgive them for the misery and deaths of his companions because of their lack of courage and intelligence.

Edward said little, leaving it to Punchy who, although calm in delivery, was showing more than just a touch of emotion. Another sip and he continued.

"You know, Edward, someone once said, I think it was wee Napoleon, that 'the British soldiers were like lions led by asses'."

Edward listened patiently, knowing that the American would now appear somewhere in the picture.

Punchy confessed that he had tolerated the company of Chancitt more from a curiosity viewpoint than one of friendship, indeed his interest had been aroused when the American had claimed descent from the English aristocracy, similar to the misfits who had made life so miserable for him and his mates on the lower deck.

He had tolerated the man as he recounted how he had been cheated out of his inheritance by the criminal elements of his own family. He had quite enjoyed what he considered a fairy story, but had become disenchanted when Lucius had offered what he termed as 'snuff', particularly when the colour was white.

Punchy looked earnestly at Edward for his reaction, but Edward merely moved his hand indicating that he should carry on. Punchy shrugged his shoulders and obliged.

"From what I know of the man, I am sure he is a dope addict, whether he is a dealer or not is open to question and if it is cocaine, he will most definitely come to a sticky end."

Edward thought it was time to intervene, but Punchy thought otherwise. He informed Edward that having been in touch with Steve on that fateful night when Edward had struggled back to Ove's place thinking he was only suffering from alcoholic over-indulgence, they in hindsight both felt now that the American had attempted to poison him.

Edward agreed with Punchy that the American could not be trusted and his first move was to make him pay up what he had stolen and if in the process he uncovered proof of cocaine smuggling, he would, as rapidly as possible, seek to eliminate him from decent society.

Punchy smiled wryly at his companion's apparent naivety and asked that he should proceed with care and not confront Chancitt while his heavy minders were in the background. Edward sighed, indicating that life at times could be difficult, then, looking at Punchy, he asked if he had any idea where Chancitt might be.

Punchy hesitated, then grinned and admitted that if he kept to the timetable observed by Steve and himself, the American could be in the Melodian Bar that evening. Realising that he had still to contact Harry with the sea stock order, Edward asked if he and Steve were in the Melodian Bar, could he join them, say at seven p.m.

Punchy assured Edward that it would be a pleasure and hoped it would be an enjoyable and interesting evening.

It suddenly dawned on Edward that the evening could be an eventful one and he should prepare for it in serious fashion. After finalising his business for the day, he returned to Sandport Street.

Although an extrovert, he was essentially fastidious in preparing for an event he considered important, but unfortunately had forgotten that Ove's place lacked the essentials for toileting in a civilised fashion. Had he known that the conditions in the back room were so spartan, he could have done what Ove did when bath time was due, just toddle along to the local baths and soak himself in a big man-sized bath of hot salt water, but Edward, sometimes too quick for his own good, had opted for a 'do it yourself' job before he realised what it entailed.

The gas stove, a big kitchen kettle, the kitchen sink and an enormous jug unearthed from miscellaneous junk for the purpose of final douching, were the tools used to produce a thoroughly cleansed Scandinavian smelling of carbolic.

After dressing, he next gave thought to feeding the inner man and, having received from Harry MacSween a succulent fillet steak for services rendered, nothing would have suited him better than to grill the tender piece of Aberdeen Angus, add the necessary accompaniments and enjoy a very personal feast. But it was not to be, the tools were not available and time was running out, but there was always the 'Commercial'.

After dining at the hotel, his inner man assuaged, he relaxed with a cognac and as he smoked his marcella he dreamed of what the future might hold.

As he walked to the venue he was in philosophical mood, knowing that if the American did not appear, then a night of enjoyment with his friends was something to look forward to. If Chancitt did materialise, he was ready for a showdown.

A few minutes later he entered the Melodian Bar, ordered his drink and then glanced around hoping to see his friends. He was surprised at the size of the establishment, it was much larger than he expected. Viewed from the outside it looked impressive, not so much the size, more the solidity of the structure and Edward remembered Steve Allrock telling him that the pub had for a time been known as the Citadel.

In his mind this had conjured up a fortress-like structure and further examination of the locality had unearthed a place called North Fort Street, indicating that the area in the dim past had been fortified against sea invaders. The outside was certainly solid, though squat, but the inside was spacious and inviting and, more important, the inside vibrated with life.

Drink in hand, he enjoyed the unfolding scene, but was surprised to see it almost filled to capacity so early in the evening.

Suddenly he realised that certain circumstances influenced the size and temper of the assembled community. In the main they were a mixture of lively seafarers, dockers and shipyard workers. He had anticipated that the merry throng he now witnessed would have quaffed their quotas between five and six o'clock and then found their way home, but now understood that the vagaries of international trade had so influenced their work plan, that they were now obliged to work overtime or extra shifts to meet increased export and defence commitments.

Edward sighed when he thought of the word defence and knew, as an intelligent political observer, that the over-stress of the word defence meant the armaments manufacturers were licking their lips in anticipation. Rumours of war are often rife in an imperialist country and workers whose basic skills are required seem unconcerned. After all, they earn more, they drink more and declare vociferously that they are enjoying themselves and they probably are, and why not?

Who was he to question their thoughts and motives? After all, as a Dane, he was seeking naturalisation in Britain, hoping to ensure he and his wife could live in security and happiness.

This made him think of Emily when he had tried to influence her in applying for a similar status. He had considered himself knowledgeable in such things, but had been unable to convince her. She had been adamant, being born a Swede she would remain a Swede. After all it was recognised internationally that Sweden's efforts for World peace were second to none.

Why should she seek a British passport from a country that always seemed to be at war? She had been quite scornful and had terminated the discussion with the words *'altid krig'*, always war.

He stood still, glass in hand, oblivious to the merrymakers jostling around him, and thought about Emily and her attitude towards naturalisation.

He was no lover of British Imperialism, but loved the Scottish country scene and liked the people. He felt he had to be practical, but in a way he was proud of Emily.

He was almost in dreamland when a hand waved backwards and forwards across his eyes and the voice of Punchy Rush brought him back to reality.

"Stop staring into space, Edward. It looks as if the American has decided not to 'chance it'."

Edward, although appreciative of the play on words, did not reply, allowing Punchy to lead him to a table in a corner near the door and there a smiling and amused Steve Allrock welcomed him.

During the next hour they drank together with Edward still in introspective mood, saying little and the two Scots dominating the conversation. According to Steve Allrock, an American millionaire owner of the Bourbon Burden Whisky Company had attempted to buy out the Highland Princess, but had been sent packing with a flea in his ear, the Princess being definitely not interested in his advances.

Another piece of local news Steve rather proudly released for Edward's benefit was that he had won the East Coast hand wrestling championship while on holiday in Aberdeen.

Punchy's unstinting work on behalf of the arts and restoration of antique furniture had been duly rewarded. During a house clearance in Bridge Street, he offered to take the rather decrepit furniture, pictures and bric-a-brac at what he termed a nominal price. He had lovingly restored one of the pictures, thus saving it for posterity. A London dealer had given him £300 for the picture.

He was quite philosophical. "I paid £3 for the clearance and restored a picture I thought the world should see. The dealer no doubt will sell it for £3,000 and future generations will look at the picture that cost their national gallery £3 million to acquire for the nation."

Punchy looked towards Edward seeking his reaction and Edward, looking thoughtful, admitted that nothing so extraordinary had happened to him, but there was still time for something to happen. His companions looked at him meaningfully, knowing what was really on his mind, but made no comment.

As the babble around them gradually decreased, the sound of pint tumblers being gathered in increased, a sure sign that the happy hour was over and the workers were now wandering homewards.

Small groups still hugged the bar, but the floor space was clearing rapidly. It was at this point that Edward caught sight of the American. As two small groups moved, he could see Chancitt surrounded by four very rough-looking characters. His companions also having seen the group were concerned in case he would jump up and make straight for the American. But Edward seemed unduly calm.

"It would seem, gentlemen, that something rather extraordinary could still happen before the day is out."

It was obvious that the five men constituted a gang with the American probably their leader or paymaster, and from where they were sitting, they had a good view of all of them. The first was big, 'Bull-neck'ed and arrogant looking and the man facing him was of medium height and build, his hair a fiery red. Steve recognised him immediately.

"It's the rid yin," he said, digging Punchy in the ribs.

Punchy acknowledged the message but looked perplexed and Steve, seeing his expression, explained that the 'rid yin' was a local expression meaning the 'red one' and he had originally worked in the shipyards, had been jailed for stealing and was a dangerous and bad character.

It was the man standing behind Chancitt that particularly interested Edward. He was tall and looked athletic, but his sardonic expression indicated a man of ill intent.

The man standing opposite him with his back to the bar was a local man known as 'Tinker Tam', who it appeared had developed the bad habit of tinkering with bank safety deposit boxes in the dead of night.

These were the men gathered around the American and he held sway sitting on his bar stool dishing out drinks, just like the scion of a noble English family distributing largesse to his obedient retainers.

It was Mr. Chancitt's appearance that inspired Steve to compare him with what he imagined a hysterical anarchist would look like. He was dressed in a long black cloak and wore a cone-shaped hat flattened at the top. He smoked a cigar and his hand extended at such an angle that the cigar smoke, to Steve, might well have been a bomb primed and ready to throw.

Punchy had a different view; he reckoned that the American was dressed more like Guy Fawkes, a historical figure, who in one way could be associated with hysteria.

Knowing that his friends were engaged in a well meaning exercise in procrastination, Edward gave his version.

"I do not associate Mr. Chancitt with history or hysteria, I only know that he can answer my question regarding the sea stock order that mysteriously went missing."

Steve put a restraining hand on his arm, advising that he forget his quest, at least until Chancitt was left on his own. But Edward's mind was made up and he left his companions in no doubt that they should not intervene, indicating that he would be able to handle things in his own way. He left the table before they could stop him, but, when nearing the American, he found the 'Bull-neck'ed man barring his way.

Tapping him on the shoulder, he asked him politely to step aside so that he could converse with the gentleman sitting on the stool. Taken by surprise, he grunted his displeasure, but allowed him through. He was now virtually trapped between 'Bull-neck' and the 'rid yin' on the one side and the tall man and 'Tinker Tam' on the other. They all seemed apprehensive, except Edward, who was relaxed and smiling radiantly to his audience. He came straight to the point and addressed the American.

"I believe I have to thank you for finding the shipping order I lost and you commissioned on my behalf."

The American was taken aback, but managed to grunt, "What d'ya mean?"

Edward's reply was ambiguous.

"It is my intention to see that you are given what you deserve."

The American, feeling at a disadvantage sitting on the bar stool, decided to stand with his back to the bar counter, knowing now that Edward, being hemmed in, would not use physical force if that was his intention. He leered at Edward and was ready to take the initiative when Edward made his proposal.

"The commission you received would be at least ten pounds, I suggest you keep half for yourself and give me the remaining five pounds."

Chancitt almost snarled, but Edward, good soul, was quick to react.

"Don't upset yourself, Mr. Chancitt. I can well understand you feel a reward is unnecessary, but I insist that you keep half."

The American felt foolish and the guttural sounds and elbow-jabbing of his gang at his expense was the last straw. He knew he had to act. There was a sinister smile on his face as he replied, "I know what I will give you."

Almost immediately, a clenched fist shot towards Edward's chin, but, anticipating such an eventuality, he managed to avoid it and grasping the American's arm as it passed over him, he held it firmly, then turning and dipping low, he pulled hard. The American shot up and over his shoulder into a perfect Flying Mare.

Chancitt landed flat on his back, breathless and rather bedraggled. Punchy and Steve, witnessing the incident, were already on their feet fearing the worst, while Edward seemed unperturbed as he asked the American kindly if he was feeling all right.

Lucius Chancitt was not amused and although still breathless, he managed to croak to his gang of four:

"Get that son of a bitch."

Bull-neck reacted quickly, his arms encircled Edward from behind. With his arms pinned to his sides, he felt momentarily impotent, but knew it was vital that he should free himself quickly. He took his feet off the ground and tried to sway forwards, but his opponent merely laughed, swinging him backwards between his extended legs. 'Tinker Tam', intent on a little embroidery, whipped out a knife and advanced.

Edward, intent on survival, had little time to think and as 'Tinker Tam' struck downwards with his knife, Edward, on an upward swing kicked as hard as he could into the groin of his assailant. There was an ear-splitting howl of anguish as he scored a direct hit on the man's most vulnerable parts.

Fortunately for Edward, there was a slight deviation, the knife cutting his collar instead of his throat. 'Bull-neck' reacted by grunting and intensifying the pressure until he felt his chest would surely burst.

Suddenly the big man's knees buckled and he seized the opportunity to slam his heels down as hard as he could on his enemy's toes. The big man snorted as he released his grip and as Edward fell heavily, he caught a glimpse of Steve Allrock swinging a crunching blow to the chin of 'Bull-neck' and, despite the thick neck, the jaw swung round and the big man collapsed as if pole-axed.

Edward was to learn later that Steve had kicked into the big man's knees so as to bring him down to the right size for a knockout.

Punchy had gone straight for 'Tinker Tam' and was in the process of eliminating him, when the 'rid yin' jumped on his back. As Edward scrambled to his feet, he realised that if he attempted to pull the 'rid yin' off Punchy, the added weight might well bring his mate down to the floor and place him at a disadvantage.

Something unorthodox was called for. He kicked straight into the back of the thighs of the 'rid yin' who, yelping with pain, let go at once and as his feet touched the floor, he fell immediately and lay prostrate, his legs apparently paralysed.

Finishing 'Tinker Tam' with a solid blow to the solar plexus, Punchy turned to Edward and almost shouted that he should get out quick and head for home. A general brawl was now developing quickly, Steve was fighting with two strangers, Punchy was set to even things and on the floor the 'rid yin' was lying massaging his legs and was still squirming and looking around. Punchy pushed Edward doorwards and, pointing to 'Tinker Tam', his message was clear.

"Run for it, Edward, it's you they want, clear off before the 'knife' recovers."

Then Punchy was back into the fray and a few seconds later Edward made for the door just as the 'Tinker Tam' struggled to his feet.

Before passing through, he looked back and saw 'Tinker Tam', or 'the knife' as Punchy called him, hobbling, followed by a rather dazed looking 'rid yin'. The look of venom on their faces was fearsome.

"I'll get you, you bastard," 'Tinker Tam' shouted and, with the knife in his hand, made for the door.

Edward felt he was running away from a fight he had started, but knew that Punchy was correct in assuming that, as he was the main target, the fight would tend to stop if he disappeared from the scene.

Walking fast he cut diagonally right towards Sandport Street. Looking back he could see 'Tinker Tam' starting to jog and gaining on him. He wondered if he should stop and deal with him, but when he saw the 'rid yin' following up, he decided to run for it.

They were all running fast now and Edward was surprised that the Tinker was narrowing the gap. When they reached the top of Sandport Street, the enemy was some fifty yards behind; he knew now that he would have to sprint as hard as he could if he wanted to reach the sanctuary of Ove's place in time.

He drew away some yards, knowing he would need time to unlock the door and get safely inside. As he turned the key, he could already hear the heavy breathing and cursing of his enemy, who was now only a few yards away.

Pulling the door open, he stepped smartly inside and as he closed it he caught a glimpse of a hand attempting to forestall him. He turned his back and threw himself against the door and gave a sigh of relief as he heard it slam shut.

For added insurance, he leaned his full weight against the door, but was startled by the howl of rage and a horrendous shriek of pain of such intensity that he would never forget it for the rest of his life.

Fortunately there was a stout wire mesh covering the windows or they would most surely have been smashed. For a full minute the banging and howling continued and when it died down Edward lit the gas jet to examine any damage that had been inflicted on his person or clothes. He was completely relaxed now and, laying down the piece of steel piping he had unearthed in case of emergency, he walked over to the mirror at the wash basin.

His clothes appeared in good shape, with the exception of a torn collar which had been cut by the Tinker's knife. He had felt a slight scrape on his neck at the time and although he had discounted it, he was anxious to ensure it was not bleeding.

What he saw shocked him: there was a cut some three inches long which had been bleeding badly and it appeared that a flap of skin almost an inch thick had been forced out. He could not understand how such a gash could be painless, but knew that immediate examination was essential.

Having boiled water and soaked some strips of linen, he gingerly wiped away the blood from either side of the sausage-like skin flap, wondering as he did so why he still felt no pain. Suddenly the flap of skin fell to the floor and he knew he had to face up to the critical period of the blood from his neck.

Almost immediately he realised his neck had not been injured in any way, but where had the bloody skin flap come from lying on the floor?

He picked it up almost lovingly, cleaned it thoroughly and placed it on a white piece of linen. The object seemed to respond, curling up slightly as if beckoning. On close examination, he realised it was a human finger, but how it had attached itself to his neck was indeed a mystery.

Not being an expert in haematology, he was unsure of the time factor, but felt it must have happened just before entering the house or immediately afterwards. On reflection, it might have happened when he slammed the door on 'Tinker Tam'.

Taking a torch from Ove's desk, he examined the door and as he reached it he could see a similar bloodstained object lying at the base. The second finger and blood stains on the door confirmed that he had indeed slammed the door shut and severed two fingers from the hand of the Tinker.

He felt sorry that it had happened that way. Still, from the point of view of human economy, it was surely better that two fingers be sacrificed if this meant saving one life.

He could hear police whistles and the sound of running feet and wondered if his two pursuers had left the street. For safety, he picked up a piece of piping and approached the door and, just as he was about to unlatch, he heard the voice, a familiar voice.

"Are you all right, Mr. Sorenson? This is the police."

He opened the door and welcomed him in his own idiom.

"I see it's yourself, Constable McIllwraithe."

The young West Highlandman smiled and pointed to his three stripes.

"Sergeant McIllwraithe now," he said.

Edward congratulated him on his promotion and at the behest of the young Sergeant he gave his version of events from the time of meeting the American to the slamming of the door on two potential assailants. The young Sergeant, anxious to prove himself, was extremely meticulous in making out his report and congratulated Edward on his sagacity in preserving, in pristine condition, the fingers which might well prove important in any future proceedings.

"Haff you a container, Mr. Sorenson, in which I could place the fingers?"

He said it was his intention to take them to 'forensic'. They could be crucial in establishing by finger-printing if a known criminal was involved.

As he departed, he told Edward that two villains had been apprehended running across the bridge at Commercial Street, one of them a local called Magregor, alias the 'rid yin', had been arrested and taken to Leith Police Station and the other, in great distress and minus two fingers, had been taken under guard to Leith Hospital.

Shortly after, Edward left Ove's place and made his way to the Citadel, hoping and trusting that his friends had emerged from the fracas in good shape and uninjured. He was about to enter the Melodian Pub when he was stopped by a man professing to be a friend of Steve Allrock. It appeared that the police had been summoned and 'Bull-neck', 'Tinker Tam', Punchy and Steve had been taken to what he had described as, 'the jile'.

If they had indeed been taken to the jail, then Leith Police Station was, of necessity, his next stop. It was his intention to give an account of what really happened.

As he crossed the bridge, fog was blowing up the Forth making for poor visibility, but despite this he could make out two familiar figures advancing up the shore. The rolling gait of the shorter one and the more precise forward movements of the taller person led him to believe that Punchy and Steve were making for the Sailor's Rest.

Now that he could hear the voices, he was even more convinced and halted on the bridge, hoping to surprise them as they crossed over.

As they passed the King's Wark, a pub on the corner, they turned right instead of left, going deeper into the confines of Bernard Street and as they crossed the tram lines he knew he had to move quickly or he would lose them in the swirling fog.

He was just in time to see them disappear into what he thought could be described as an 'old warlde inn'.

They were standing at the bar awaiting their drinks when he intervened and insisted that, as they had been the victims of his precipitate action or folly, they should retire to the small table in the corner, while he paid and served the beverages of their choice.

As they sat down to drink and discuss what had happened at the Melodian and afterwards, Edward was curious to know why they had not gone to the Sailor's Rest.

Punchy stressed that as they had been absolved from the crime of disturbing the peace, he had decided it called for a special celebration and, as the Olde Warlde served the type of malt he liked, he had no option.

The point being taken, Edward ensured that his friend was adequately supplied for the rest of the evening. It was a joyful occasion, the evening had started in a controversial and lethargic fashion, but highlighted when Edward in his own inimitable style challenged the American to come clean. Chancitt, feeling secure in the presence of his gang, had lashed out and had suffered the ignominy of being flattened to the floor and from that moment on all hell had broke loose until the sound of police whistles.

What had started as a private affair had developed into a 'free for all', with gladiators, trained on their own type of spirit, joining in the feast of fisticuffs. On hearing the whistles, the semi-besotted heroes had broken ranks and left the field to the four main contenders. The police had arrested Punchy, Steve,

'Bull-neck' and 'Tinker Tam' and had taken them to Leith Police Station.

Edward, intent on ensuring his friends should in no way be victimised for what they had done on his behalf, was anxious to know how and why they had been released so quickly. Punchy touched his nose significantly and mentioned the name of a Sergeant who had an interest in sport, particularly boxing, and was, as he said, as straight as they come.

He had asked to be questioned privately and had informed the Sergeant that it could be worthwhile to search thoroughly the persons of 'Bull-neck' and 'Tinker Tam'. All four of the gang had been searched and a considerable quantity of cocaine had been discovered on their persons. Steve and Punchy had been congratulated for their consideration of the public good, but offered the gratuitous advice that it would have been better to inform the police first instead of taking the law into their own hands.

One way or another, the three of them had managed to put the gang of four behind bars, but what of their boss, the American, what had happened to him?

Steve and Punchy were not unduly concerned, being of the opinion that he would bob up again in some sea port other than Leith or make it back to 'God's own country', but Edward was sure the U.S.A. would not welcome back a national who was a drug pedlar with South American connections.

He remembered Sven telling him that Chancitt, in his effort to impress, had told of his exploits in Colombia as a soil analyst where, despite his endeavours to help the people produce excellent crops, he had been shot at by bandits. He could well imagine now that the crops referred to had a definite coca plant connection.

Still, such niggling thoughts should not be allowed to interfere with the legitimate enjoyment of three free souls.

For a full two hours the friends celebrated and would have continued well into the night had not mine host intervened in the traditional fashion.

"Time, gentlemen, please," he advised in a gently persuasive voice, followed twice in five minute intervals by the same message, the last one being stern and mandatory. The three looked at him in benevolent fashion, wondering if he was indeed addressing them and were caught completely unawares when he swept towards them and enquired despairingly, "Gentlemen, please, have you no beds to go home to?"

Looking around, they responded immediately. Punchy, who knew the landlord very well, made his apologies on behalf of the trio, adding that they were sorry they were also keeping an honest man from retiring to his own bed.

As they made for the bridge, Steve suddenly decided to go left along the shore towards the Kirkgate. He was off, he said, to the 'jiggin'. As he left for his favourite dance hall, his friends bade him a pleasant evening and walked homewards.

Reaching the foot of Sandport Street, they parted. Punchy set out for his small house in Newhaven, giving a deal of thought to Edward's macabre experience concerning the two fingers chopped off as "Tinker Tam" had reached out just too far. As a writer in a small way, he felt this was material for a thriller that was already taking shape in his mind.

Meantime, Edward walked slowly up Sandport Street in serious mien, knowing that "Tinker Tam" could well have killed him if he had not been alert. He had been foolish and far too hasty. His vanity and excuse that he was operating on behalf of the community was surely unreal. After all, he was a married man now and had a responsibility to act with care on behalf of his wife and himself.

On reflection, he knew he should have put Emily more in the picture and ensured she had more to say in their plans for the future. He had noticed the wistful expression lately as he told her breezily that he was intent on securing a shipping order and hoped to be home that evening.

Realising that he was leaving his wife in the invidious position where she was liable to worry unduly about his safety and also feel neglected, he decided that sharing and caring were one and the same thing. However, it did please him to know that Mrs. McGregor was near at hand in case of an emergency.

Mrs. McGregor's visits to the Sorenson house had become more frequent recently and Emily was happy the stately, but very human, old lady was paying her such kind attention; they had liked each other from the beginning and were quickly developing a close friendship. It was generally recognised that the old lady was rather fastidious, but, whatever the truth, the old lady saw in Emily the virtues of cleanliness and an organised way of living.

As the coffee percolated, the old lady would sit back in her chair enjoying the aroma and leisurely impart pearls of wisdom to her protégé, while Emily, a constant smile playing from her lips and eyes, would interject only when clarification was sought, usually with reference to language.

Mrs. McGregor would respond immediately, explaining and often amplifying in her own humorous way. There could be little doubt she played a significant part in Emily learning sufficient of the English language to equip her for the market place and do her shopping without feeling unduly inhibited.

She had difficulty with some words, but one in particular was more troublesome than all the other. It concerned the word 'the' and any words starting or finishing with the letters 'th'. For some reason, at the time of delivery, her tongue did not protrude far enough to make proper contact with her upper teeth and the end result was a rather weak 'ti', manifesting itself as 'taut' instead of thought and 'true' instead of through. Leith and length became Leeds and lengt.

It was during this exercise that Emily recalled the plight of a Swedish woman who, having arrived in London, had decided to join her husband in Leith. She had booked a seat for Leith, as she thought, and landed in great distress in Leeds, a victim of improper language. All the more reason, Mrs. McGregor stressed, to form the words correctly.

"Watch my tongue and teeth, Emily," she said.

Taking her time, she demonstrated clearly. "The Leith Police dismisseth us."

Emily tried really hard, she really tried and the old lady tried to keep her composure, but it was impossible and within a few minutes the exercise was abandoned and they were both laughing so heartily it hurt.

Even so, they would have continued laughing had not the coffee pot shown signs of boiling over. As she sipped her coffee, Mrs. McGregor conceded that the tongue-twister had stumped many of the local people, so it was in no way a disgrace that Emily had not succeeded. There was no necessity to feel in any way inferior because of difficulty in the usage of certain words. After all she was free to choose other words to suit her purpose; for that matter Scottish words were also available, such as braw instead of good.

Mrs. McGregor seemed quite cynical as she made reference to certain politicians and others who had amassed personal fortunes looking after what they called the 'common good'. Yes, the word good could be abused, but the word braw was not easy to manipulate and sounded better anyway.

Emily smiled and tentatively suggested that braw was a Swedish word and the old lady conceded that the word was from a Scandinavian or Germanic source.

For a while the conversation changed from matters educational to those of a domestic nature.

It was natural that Edward should come into the picture, the old lady having tried to influence the young man to spend a little more time with his wife. Of late she felt satisfied that he had heeded her advice and deserved a little recognition and linked it to what had already been discussed.

"You are coming along very well with the language, Emily, and I must say that Edward is a braw lad."

Emily nodded her head in acknowledgement, but insisted on her version.

"Edward is a man, a braw man and he is my man."

Mrs. McGregor was surprised that Emily was so adamant and so sparky, it showed that despite her usual placid manner, she was prepared to speak up when she felt that the issue was too important or personal to be ignored.

For some minutes the conversation lapsed and Emily, seeing Mrs. McGregor in deep thought, asked what was on her mind. The old lady looked dreamily in her direction, sighed softly and then told her she had been thinking of life when she was first married, how she had been considered good looking, but wanted Emily to know that she thought of her as an exceptionally beautiful woman. Feeling it necessary to overcome the shyness of the young woman, she reiterated the message in terms Scottish.

"You are a very bonnie lassie, Emily."

Emily coloured slightly, her mouth softened and tears were not far away as she replied, "Thank you, I hope Edvard tinks di same."

The old lady smiled, put her hand on Emily's arm, assuring her that Edward would certainly think the same. Acknowledging the compliment and assurance, Emily added she was fortunate in the life she had chosen with Edward, but had reservations concerning his appetite for work. He was working too hard, too often he would return tired and sometimes soaked to the skin, having stayed too long in the docks or out in the Firth in his small motor boat, chasing business.

Mrs. McGregor was quite forthright in her questioning and asked if Emily had told her husband of her concern. She did not reply, she appeared diffident and uneasy. The old lady felt obliged to inform her of what could and should be expected in a long, successful and happy marriage.

The first essentials were loyalty, trust and caring for each other; without the first there was no chance of real happiness; regarding the third part, it was obvious that they both cared for each other, but without trust everything could be undermined.

Emily would do well to make Edward aware of how she felt and ensure that all important issues were discussed openly; if not, then trust could be affected if Edward found out that she had been unhappy unnecessarily, when a few words could have solved the problem.

"Tell the man," she said. "I'm sure he will understand."

After all, there were so many things they were bound to discuss, such as house alterations, holidays, the bringing up of children and many other subjects of mutual interest. Looking affectionately at the young woman, she gave a little laugh as she finished her spiel.

"When the wee bairns arrive, you'll have plenty to talk about."

At the mention of bairns, Emily sat bolt upright and the old lady was alerted to the probable cause of her reticence. Never one to waste time, Mrs. McGregor went straight to the point.

"Are you pregnant, Emily?"

Emily, taken aback, seemed bemused, sighed rather loudly and, managing a little smile, expressed herself as best she could.

"I tink so," she said.

Mrs. McGregor was pleased to be privy to such sensational news at such an early stage. It was something she could savour; she hoped it was true, but was wise enough to know she had to be careful."

"Whether you are pregnant or not, the first person you must confide in is your husband."

As Emily nodded her head, the old lady gave her a wink as she added, "if you know what I mean."

This, she told Emily, was the ideal moment to influence Edward's tendency to take risks. She was sure that an intelligent man like Edward would be only too pleased to slow down and accept his role as a caring husband who looked forward to the added responsibility and pleasure of fatherhood.

~

The Sorensons had just finished breakfast, Emily was clearing away and Edward a little restive, was disciplining himself to sit down and do nothing for a change. Taking his final cup of coffee with him, he settled back in what had now become his favourite chair.

Deciding to be good to himself, he reached for the cognac and poured a dash into his cup. He felt justified in being good to himself. After all, had he not been on good behaviour since that eventful and perilous night a fortnight ago when he was in danger of losing his life. He had vowed then that in the future he would be more selective in the way he countered the plans of the drug traffickers.

Although determined to do his bit, he knew his immediate plans should be in caring for his partner and making her happy. It was a beautiful day, a day of peace and harmony that should not be sullied by thoughts of mercenary gain, a day that could and would be used for caring and companionship.

Finishing his drink, he walked through to the kitchen where Emily, finished with her chores, was standing silhouetted at the window. Having just finished her arm-circling exercises, she had stopped with her arms fully extended upwards, as if invoking the sun to restore her energy and warm her body.

To Edward she was a picture of beauty and desire, her excellent figure thrown into relief by the bright shafts of sunlight. He tiptoed towards her and just as she was drawing breath he gripped her firmly at the waist. She gave a gasp and, turning with astonishing speed, threw her arms around his neck and, lifting her feet from the floor, clung close to him.

Taken unawares, he stumbled forward a step, but having received the message, he acted manfully. Gripping her buttocks, he drew her closer and she responded, kissing him full on the mouth, and he reciprocated, gathering her tightly in his arms.

Some minutes later, when they surfaced for breath, Edward volunteered advice that was neither romantic or diplomatic.

"You know, love, when I had to take your full weight without warning, we might have fallen."

Emily burst out laughing and seemed almost unable to control herself, and Edward, the innocent married young man, waited patiently.

When her laughter subsided, she indicated that his warning was too late, she felt she had already fallen.

Consternation ruled his mind before he realised what was expected of him.

"You mean we will soon have a child, Emily?"

She gave him a loving smile, nodded her head and replied, "Maybe."

Chapter 18

Edward was excited at what he had heard and hastened to assure his wife that the probability itself was enough to warrant a celebration. The medical man could be brought into the picture if or when desired; it was enough that they were together and as it was a glorious day, it should not be wasted.

Over the past few months Emily had become quite fond of Grangemouth, particularly the waterway that ran not far from their house. The smell of good wood piled high in the area imported from Sweden and Finland reminded her of her birthplace. Even the regular traffic of ships gave her a link with the past and reassured her that Scotland could rapidly become her new home.

There was a quizzical look on Edward's face as he extended his arms with palms facing forwards. Emily smiled as she put forward the palm of her left hand and walked her fingers across the right hand and then pointed towards the canal.

They looked a handsome, friendly couple as they strolled arm in arm along the Forth and Clyde Canal.

As they walked, their thoughts at this stage centred on the probability becoming a certainty within months. Although both would-be parents were agnostics, there was the inexplicable feeling that baptism might be considered. Always willing to speed up any accepted proposal, Edward suggested that their son should be called Lars Wilhelm, after his father. Emily smiled patiently, but insisted the child be called Christina Sophia after her mother.

Edward was scornful and insisted that the boy could not be saddled with such a name and Emily, still smiling, was adamant that as she was the one directly involved in conception, the name Christina Sophia would be appropriate for their daughter. However should his son, like his father, barge his way in front, then she would agree to the name, but with one exception, instead of Lars substitute the name Johan, the first name of her father.

Edward, surprised and delighted at the rapport between them, seized Emily round the waist and, lifting her off the ground, almost shouted, "Agreed."

Happy and breathless, she put a restraining hand on his shoulder and advised him gently, "Put me down, Edward. I think you have just wakened up Sophia."

Edward appeared rather contrite, but Emily assured him that Sophia would probably be prepared to forgive.

Regarding first names, he assured her that her wish would be granted, but he reserved the right to register the child at Leith Academy for educational purposes.

Seeing the disturbed look in her eyes, he felt he had to explain that, as most of the business transacted now was in the Port of Leith, they would ultimately have to move.

He felt it was a time for reassurance. "Don't worry, Emily, we won't leave Grangemouth until you are ready; and remember, if we do, I will be with you more than I am at present."

They had just passed a series of timber yards and were approaching a shrub-lined avenue, when Emily decided to test his desire to satisfy a sudden whim. She pointed to a newsagent and confectioners shop some fifty yards away on the main road, indicating in sign language what she would like.

Making a circle with a finger in her palm, she continued inwards to a final dot in the centre, then placing an imaginary sweetmeat on the apex, she raised the confection to her mouth, bit off the top and relaxed in ecstasy.

As Edward hesitated, Emily frowned, feeling that he could be difficult at times, and he, realising belatedly that he had to adjust to pre-natal notions, laughed and sprinted towards the shop, shouting as he did so, "One walnut whirl coming up."

Edward always thought fast. Unfortunately this time his legs moved faster than his brain and, if it had not been for a screeching of brakes, he would have been under the approaching car that had been screened from view by the narrow alleyway.

It was his lightning reaction to danger that triggered a leap which landed him atop the bonnet of the advancing vehicle, instead of under the wheels.

Fortunately for him the driver of the car was an extremely careful man who, having seen his feet travelling rapidly below the screen of shrubs, put his foot on the brake, slowed the car and prepared for an emergency stop, just in case.

He now cursed himself for not having slammed down his hand on the klaxon horn; it might have saved him the inconvenience of dealing with the bedraggled idiot now lying prostrate on the bonnet of his car.

Edward raised his head and smiled at the man whom he now considered his saviour and gave what he hoped would be accepted as an appropriate apology.

"I do hope I have not damaged your car."

The car owner reacted angrily, he almost bellowed his reply.

"What kind of idiot are you?"

Lowering himself from the bonnet, Edward signalled the driver to open his door. As he did so, Edward quite frankly admitted:

"I'm a Danish idiot."

It was a shock when both men realised that they were friends. Einer Wevling, a Norwegian Ship Chandler, had been travelling back to his shop in Boness when the incident took place. He scowled and gave vent to his feelings.

"I know now, Edward, that you are a Danish idiot, but, good Christ almighty, man, you could have been killed."

Edward was sorry he had treated flippantly what could have been a nightmare to the big man, had he really lost his life. He felt now, looking at his friend's distraught face, that he had been far too facetious and uncaring.

He took his friend's hand in his own and apologised sincerely for the stress and trouble he had caused and hoped Einer would forgive him. Einer examined Edward closely and smilingly he admitted that he was more concerned with the possible damage to his brother's suit than to the man who was wearing it.

Edward laughed heartily before replying.

"Yes, lightning struck that day, Einer. I must have looked a soggy mess when I entered your shop. I will be forever grateful that you dried me off, clothed me in your brother's suit and sent me on my way refreshed and warm."

Einer was more serious now.

"And that is the way it should be between men."

As he dusted himself down and straightened his tie, Edward declared that the suit was just as presentable as the day he had been given it.

Seeing Emily approaching, he asked his friend not to mention the incident. Einer hesitated, then grinning widely, he said, "I'll think about it."

Although apprehensive and perturbed by Einer's attitude, he hesitated, but then decided to make a quick exit.

"I'll leave you to think, Einer. I'm off to the shop, I've been given my instructions."

Einer pulled on his arm and warned him. "Remember your road drill, look left, then right, before you cross the road."

When he returned he found Emily and Einer in a seemingly happy Scandinavian tête à tête. Turning to her husband, she pointed to the two small bags in his hand and asked if he had been successful. How could he fail. He was prepared to risk his life in providing the small luxuries so essential in the mind and life of a broody woman.

Einer intervened. "I was telling your wife that it was fortunate the way we bumped into each other. If I had been travelling any faster, I would probably not have seen you."

Edward looked at Emily and when she smiled, he knew his friend had realised the need for diplomatic language. Having given Emily her small paper bag, he turned to Einer and, giving him the other bag, he stressed it was a small present for his wife.

"I know that, like Emily, she is fond of a dark chocolate walnut whip."

Einer suggested they should accompany him in the car to Boness where other Scandinavian families were expected later and that the evening could well be one that all would remember.

It was barely noon as they travelled to Boness, Einer assuring them that Norma's smorgasbord selection would be sufficient to fill the gap before dinner in the evening.

As the car rolled slowly towards Boness, Emily wondered what to expect at the Wevlings. She liked the big Norwegian, she had also met Norma and although having found her friendly, she felt that her brash and unladylike behaviour could be a little disturbing. Still, there would be guests at the party and probably Norma, being the hostess, would behave in a more responsible manner.

Passing through Skinflats, Einer informed them that among the guests were Mr. and Mrs. Mathieson and the Thorvaldsons. Emily felt relieved, knowing that at least two of the guests would be Scandinavians and hopefully she would not have to flounder around in her new language.

That Hr. Thorvaldson would be there interested Edward. Having already made up his mind to enjoy the socialising, it would also give him the opportunity to sound out the ship-owner concerning the possibility of future trading.

When they reached Einer's emporium, the big man led them through the main shop into what he called the inner sanctum. Immediately they entered the private quarters there was a squeal of delight and a bare-footed figure bounded from the far end of the big room towards them.

Throwing her arms around Edward, Norma hugged him close and in her own inimitable fashion addressed him.

"Welcome, Edward, my favourite countryman."

Noticing the look of bewilderment on Emily's face, Einer assured her that Norma gave the same greeting to any Dane who crossed the threshold. Norma, mischievous and as exuberant as ever, retorted that it was not true; after all, she greeted Jessie Mathieson the same way and she was Scottish. Einer laughed and gave his view.

"Yes that could be true, but then I know you are determined to wrest Jessie's shortbread recipe from her."

Norma seemed undisturbed and flounced away, indicating that any more insinuations from her husband would mean no lunch for him.

After a lunch of Danish open sandwiches and carlsbergs, followed by cognac and liqueurs, Einer suggested that a motor trip along the coast could fit in nicely before all the guests assembled in the early evening.

Setting off down the main thoroughfare, Einer kept as close to the coast as the road would allow. Having lived in Boness for the last ten years, he had acquired a considerable knowledge of the geography and history of the town and its environs.

It was the smell of wood that attracted Emily. Looking down towards the sea, she could see what appeared to be a forest that had been flattened by an unremitting storm. As they drew near, she realised she had been looking at a big timber yard, but could not understand why the logs, as she thought, should be smaller in circumference, but longer, than the logs they burned in Sweden.

Knowing that most Scottish homes relied on coal for heating, she leaned forward and asked Edward if he knew what the logs were used for.

Einer stopped the car and answered her question, while Edward was still wondering what to say. Einer explained that what she called logs were in fact pit props, used, as the name suggested, to prop up the roof of a mine as the miners cut out coal and the length of the prop was determined by the thickness of the coal seam.

Emily's reply was, to Einer, just a little too ingenuous.

"And here was I wondering if Scottish firesides would be big enough to accommodate such long logs."

But Einer, as a host, played his part. "Well, now you know, Emily, that in a way, they do play an essential part in heating the homes of Scotland."

The big Norwegian was a good guide. Being a fisherman and having served in the Norwegian Navy, it was natural that he would be able to talk about the types of fish that could be caught locally and the activities of the British Navy.

Looking at Edward, he told him that just across the river was the Rosyth Naval Base and drew attention to a battleship which had just emerged from the base and was now cruising towards the Forth Bridge.

"As a Navy man yourself, Edward, I think you must agree it's a magnificent sight."

Edward, although unmoved, felt a reply was called for.

"I know how you feel, Einer, but just think how many fishing vessels could have been built for the price of that powerful war machine."

Just for a moment Einer seemed deflated, then, looking at Edward enquiringly, he asked, "Don't you think we could forget the reality of power politics meantime and enjoy the scene unfolding before us?"

Edward laughed and agreed.

"I'm sorry for being a spoil-sport, but I would suggest that we concentrate more on the yachts and fishing vessels emerging just now from the Marina at South Queensferry."

Einer felt free to explain the functions of the various colourful craft out in the Forth and those berthed at South Queensferry.

Some minutes later he stopped the car and invited his guests out so that they might admire, what he considered to be, the world's greatest man-made structure. There could be little doubt that he had taken a great deal of trouble to study his subject in some depth.

He had first seen the bridge twelve years after its construction and had marvelled at it ever since. Although he quoted figures, he seemed intent that the human and artistic values should be given precedence. Imagine, he said, the arduous and dangerous feat of laying the foundations, the caissons, in the middle of what could be a stormy and sometimes treacherous outlet to the sea, the handling of many tons of steel to form the three spans and all the interconnecting and auxiliary steel work.

He spoke with a slight degree of emotion when he referred to much of the work being carried out during bad weather and often inconsiderate tides. He told them he had made a point of seeking out some of the local men who had been employed on building the bridge. A number of these men had been riveters from nearby shipyards, some had complained of impaired or complete loss of hearing. Little wonder when the stitching of all the pieces of steel together probably absorbed more than six million rivets.

He pointed to the immense structure and, telling them the height, explained the engineering principles involved in ensuring that the perfectly aligned bridge would last for a thousand years.

Edward clapped Einer on the back and congratulated him.

"You did a good job there, Einer. I would agree with you, it is a world-first in engineering and I would say it is an extremely beautiful man-made structure - but a thousand years, very doubtful."

Einer grinned, appreciating Edward's remarks, knowing that he was really being supportive.

"Let's amend that to at least a couple of centuries," he said.

Norma was restive, having heard it all before. She felt it was going to rain and what made it worse was that she had been to the hairdresser that morning. Never one to be patient when she felt entitled to be naughty, she faced up to the two men, giving them a piece of her mind.

"Is this a mutual admiration society in the making, two grown men admiring each other, admiring a bridge that will be here after we are all gone?"

Acutely aware of what was required, Einer reacted at once. Looking at Edward, he acknowledged, "Norma is right, rain is imminent and the destruction of a 'hair do' is something we dare not risk."

"You can say that again," Norma snapped back.

The weather forecast proved correct, there was a rumble of thunder not far away, dark clouds rolled over the sky, blotting out the sun. A sudden chill wind sprang up and the sea, which had been blue and peaceful, had now a gunmetal hue, showing all the signs of becoming unpleasantly boisterous.

As the swell developed, the small boats in the Forth made for their moorings, but one caught Norma's attention. It was a trim fast-looking yacht coloured green and white and, as far as she was concerned, it was going the wrong way, out to sea. Norma was anxious and made sure her anxiety was conveyed.

"When you two sea dogs stop looking at that bridge, you might pay attention to what is happening in the river."

Einer seemed quite affable and recognised that, as a local storm was on the agenda, it was natural that the small boats would make for home. It was, however, a matter of concern for Norma.

"There is a green and white yacht down there, I think it might be going the wrong way."

Edward looked in the direction she had pointed and knew at once it was the 'Tivoli', Oskar Petterson's boat. Einer had also spotted it and looked to his friend for confirmation.

Edward responded, "Yes, it's Oskar's and he's heading for the Fife coast."

There was a look of triumph as Norma made ready to bring the two sea dogs to heel. However, natural forces intervened, ear-splitting and earth-shattering peals of thunder erupted too close for social niceties.

Big spots of rain heralding the storm sent the two men scampering to the car. After erecting and clamping the hood in position, all four were able to isolate themselves inside before the storm broke. The water cascaded with such force on the canvas roof that the

Scandinavians must have felt that Thor was using the rooftop for drum-roll practice.

For a few minutes the incessant noise unnerved them, then, realising the car was indeed waterproof, they were able to relax and enjoy a life of normality. Norma, who had been so rudely interrupted by the storm, thought it fair and equitable that her voice should now be heard.

"Why was Oskar sailing towards Fife, Einer?"

Einer shrugged his shoulders and replied, "Ask him when you see him tonight, Norma."

Einer's attitude in no way consoled Norma, who felt Oskar was rather reckless at times and could be in danger; more to the point, he might not turn up in time with the lobsters she required to ensure the success of the evening meal she had planned.

Edward, hoping to pour oil on troubled waters, suggested Oskar had taken a calculated risk; it could be he had a date with a lady on the Fife side and could not contemplate standing her up.

Norma gave a half smile: that was not the answer. She knew for certain that Oskar's affections were not on the Fife side - his present lady friend hailed from Newcastle.

Einer chuckled and, patting Edward on the arm, thanked him for a good try, but an explanation was still required.

"Every time there is a storm, Norma becomes a broody hen wondering where her chickens are."

Edward could not hide a smile, but to visualise Oskar as a chicken required a vivid imagination, considering he was over six feet tall and weighed in excess of eighteen stones.

Norma intervened angrily. "Of course I'm concerned for Oskar's safety, but that also applies to all who are at sea during a storm, particularly the North

Sea, which I happen to know something about, having had to sail over it to and fro for almost five years."

As Edward glanced at Einer, the big man confirmed his wife's remarks; she had been a stewardess on passenger ships between Gothenburg and Newcastle.

Emily, sitting silently in the back of the car, asked Norma if what had been said was true and Norma smiled as she nodded her head. Any inhibitions Emily might have had concerning Norma evaporated at once. From then on the two former stewardesses forgot about the men and, ignoring the storm, enjoyed immensely recounting their experiences at sea. Twenty minutes later they were still talking, but in a more intimate fashion, unaware that the storm had blown itself out and the men had fastened back the hood of the car and were ready to restart the journey.

At the behest of Norma, Einer drove the car inland along quiet country lanes. After passing Dalmeny village, they reached a fork in the road: to the right the surface was in reasonable shape, but to the left it was little more than a cart track.

Norma was enthusiastic about the road to the left: the wild flowers looked so pretty and she knew Mrs. Mackenzie, a member of the Women's Guild, lived a mile along the road and this was a glorious chance to see what the house looked like.

Before they had travelled a hundred yards, Einer knew he had made a mistake - he should never have allowed his wife to influence him.

From the photographic or artistic viewpoint, the narrow path could be considered ideal, with its grass verges overgrown with wild flowers, hedges tall and dense enough to allow twittering birds to plunder nearby fields and orchards and return to a secure base, not to mention busy bees who could do a quick 'kiss me quick' among their voluptuous floral partners.

To add to the picture, there was the small wood to the middle left, with the copper beeches demanding an audience and, beyond, a rolling pasture luxuriously green, inviting the parish bull to stay awhile till the cows came home.

Romance was the last thought in Einer's mind, realising it would be foolish to travel more than jogging pace along the narrow rutted and pot-holed road. As the car jolted up and down and lurched alarmingly from side to side, the three passengers showed little sign of stress. The women started to giggle as they remembered their teenage exploits on the cake-walks of the local fairgrounds, while Edward smiled contentedly in the knowledge that the ladies were enjoying themselves. But Einer, feeling responsible for his passengers, was unhappy and cursed the road that was behaving so unkindly to the car's suspension,

The road was narrowing and he was speculating what to do if he met another vehicle coming in the opposite direction. When Norma scolded him for decapitating a row of bluebells, he felt inclined to blast off, but he knew he had to be diplomatic, keep his mouth shut and hope fervently that the road and his horizon would widen a little.

His prayers were partially answered: the road improved, no doubt due to the farmers and nursery men having effected repairs for their own local benefit. He was able to relax a little and felt that conditions might improve, when the road suddenly broadened, bringing at last a smile to his face.

The smile turned to one of bewilderment when passing the entrance of an orchard, they came upon a scene which could only be described as extremely unusual or grotesque. Among the trees there was a clearing, it was littered with fallen leaves and rotting apples, but the strangest sight of all was the presence of half of dozen cows, lying apparently contented amongst the litter.

As it obviously merited a closer examination, the four of them left the car, curious and eager to discover why the cows seemed so content in an environment which normally would be foreign to their requirements.

Einer was of the opinion that someone had left a garden gate open and the cows had just wandered in and, being tired, had decided that a midday snooze was just the thing. But Edward was not so sure it was quite so simple; he noticed that crows were sitting atop of some of the cows, pecking away and the animals were not responding in any way to their tormentors.

Although he felt he should be serious, he had to smile when he saw one cow had slipped down into a gully and was lying with four feet stuck up in the air, exposing itself in a most unseemly manner.

He picked up two stones and threw them at the birds - they croaked ravenously before flying off. The stones landed heavily on the cows, but there was still no response, confirming his suspicion that they were either dead or in serious trouble.

Norma knew immediately that the poor animals were dead and was sure that they had been struck by lightning. Emily seemed concerned and suggested that they should examine the poor beasts. However to jump over the high stone dyke seemed to her impracticable, but why not walk back to the front entrance of the orchard?

As they entered, there was evidence aplenty that the cows had been there before them; but it was not the cow pats that polluted the atmosphere; in Emily's estimation rotting apples were now rapidly becoming the cardinal factor in the bovine mystery.

Einer was the first to approach, feeling it was incumbent upon him as the leader of the expedition to be the first to examine the cows. He poked and prodded at their flanks and admitted there was no response. He felt a mirror could establish if they were still alive.

It was too much to expect Edward to be completely serious. He had read a book, he said, by a person called Baden Powell who had stressed that 'nostril slime' was essential for proper breathing and they should examine the nostrils of the cows and, if anyone had a watch handy, they could also take their pulses.

But Emily, who had managed cows from infancy on her father's farm asked the men to step aside, while she examined them.

She looked very closely at their nostrils, examined their mouths so intently that her friends expected at any second to see her attempt mouth-to-mouth resuscitation. She gave one cow special attention - it lay on its side in a shaded part at the base of a tree. Placing her hand on the cow's udder, she held it for a full minute, then standing up, indicated she now knew what was wrong.

Edward was at her side at once, wondering if he could help in any way. She winked to him before turning to Einer and Norma.

"The cows are dead," she said, as if it was quite normal to have dead cows lying at peace in an apple orchard.

For a moment Einer thought her callous and Norma cursed a God that could have done such a thing. But Emily seemed quite relaxed and gave them a little smile, before informing them that she should have added they were 'dead drunk'. It was her theory that the cows had escaped from their own pasture and had been lured to the orchard by the smell of rotting apples, had gorged themselves until they collapsed from apple poisoning, or acute alcoholism.

Emily was serious now. They must contact the farmer immediately and ensure an animal doctor was brought swiftly to the scene. Within minutes they reached the Mackenzie farm and informed the farmer that six of his cows were in poor shape in the nearby orchard.

Norma had achieved what she had set out to do. She had seen the Mackenzie's house from the outside and a strange set of circumstances had afforded her an opportunity to examine the inside at her leisure, for Mrs. Mackenzie had, in her own charming way, asked them to stay for tea, while the men attended to the plight of the animals.

Angus Mackenzie, a son of the soil, looked at his animals, then spoke to Edward.

"I hope your missus is right, but the craturs look deid ti me."

He looked so woebegone as he approached the cow lying with its legs up in the air. As he stood shaking his head and wondering what to do, an explosion reverberated along the gully, accompanied by a most horrific smell. There was almost a smile on the farmer's face as he gave his view with some vehemence.

"Auld Nellie's fart shows we might be able to save some o the coos."

Turning to Einer, as the car owner, he asked him if he would be kind enough to fetch the vet as quickly as possible.

As Einer left, the farmer asked Edward if he would be willing to help in digging a path out for the cow trapped in the gully.

By the time Einer returned with the vet, Edward had cut out a broad strip of land down to the base level of the gully.

Mr. Mackenzie looked fixedly at the vet during the examination and wondered why it should take so long to confirm whether the animal would live or die. At last the vet stood up and gave a guarded opinion.

"Nellie is in poor shape, Angus, but could respond with a wee bit of encouragement. If she shows signs and we get her upright on her feet, I think she could survive."

Angus responded positively. "I'll see tae that doctor while you gie the ithers a wee bit look."

The vet agreed and promised to do his best. Turning to Edward, the farmer thanked him for what he had done and then, handing him back the spade, asked if he would be kind enough to tackle another task, while he departed for ropes and stakes.

Edward readily agreed and started tunnelling under the beast, in line with the inner sides of its legs. While Edward dug carefully and apprehensively, Einer assisted and obeyed the instructions of the animal doctor as best he could.

On his return, the farmer drove two wooden stakes into the ground and anchored ropes on them about six feet apart, then fed the ropes through the earth tunnels, brought them over the cow and back to the anchor point ready for action, in holding the animal upright, should it show signs of recovery from its alcoholic stupor.

Fortunately, they had not too long to wait. The vet had been successful in his ministrations, two had managed to stagger to their feet and were looking blearily at big Nellie, feeling she had let the side down exposing herself in such an undignified fashion in front of strangers.

Another two were contemplating rising, but still seemed drugged and were looking vacuously at their more successful comrades. The remaining animal was still in dreamland, grunting and whinnying like a horse - it was probably a nightmare.

Suddenly, all attention was focused on Nellie as she bellowed loudly, threshed her legs in the air and came down heavily on her side.

Einer and the vet rushed to help Edward and Angus, who had already pulled on the ropes in an endeavour to help Nellie back on her feet. As the animal lay building up strength for her next attempt, Edward shivered slightly as he thought of what might have happened had the animal rolled over while he was digging the two small tunnels underneath her fore and aft quarters.

She threshed again and as her feet dug the ground, the men heaved on the ropes and this time the ton weight animal temporarily gained the upright position, but the front legs crumpled, bringing the animal to its knees.

To Angus Mackenzie it was so near and yet so far. Normally a stolid man, he was excited now and felt a supreme effort was called for. Asking his companions to hold the strain, he rushed forward to the animal's head, put his right arm around the beast's neck, then, pushing his shoulder into Nellie's chest, anchored his feet into the earth, knowing that it was now or never.

He seemed calm now, his voice was soft as he talked to the animal. Gradually his voice grew louder as he exhorted Nellie to make the supreme effort. He felt her tremble and knew the time was near, he could hear the air being sucked in and held ready for the expulsion.

It was as if the animal sighed, then came the rush of hot air, followed by a desperate bellow as she made her effort. As she moved, Angus moved, thrusting upwards until his legs were straight. Momentarily the weight came off his shoulders as she was upright, but almost immediately he felt the downward pressure and knew she had not been able to lock her legs.

He knew he had no option but to remain rock steady. If he could keep his legs straight and locked, he could hold the position and give Nellie another chance.

He held on and prayed; the weight on his shoulders was immense. The beast rested prior to what could be her last effort, then suddenly his prayer was answered: the weight disappeared and he knew she had been successful.

For a moment he rested, his arm still round the animal's neck. He felt something moist and warm rasping his cheek, it was Nellie's tongue and she was thanking the maister. Angus was quite overcome as he stroked the animal, all he could say was, "Good auld Nellie, good auld Nellie."

The status quo now existed as far as all six cows were concerned, even the cow that had dreamt she was a horse had joined the others in the corral.

The dour Scot, Angus Mackenzie, seemed a little emotional when he thanked Edward and Einer for their help and was particularly concerned with Edward's contribution and apologised for having asked him to dig out the tunnels under Nellie.

"You know, Mr. Sorenson, I realise now if Nellie had fallen further into the gully, she could have flattened you."

As usual, Edward was quite dismissive.

"No problem," he said. "All in a day's work."

Leaving Farmer Mackenzie and the vet to make a full appraisal, Einer and Edward left for the farm to collect the ladies.

Mrs. Mackenzie was adamant that people who had helped them would surely stay long enough to 'tak a wee bite'.

Edward enjoyed his plate of scotch broth and hoped that Einer did likewise, but the ladies did not join in, having already taken tea with Mrs. Mackenzie. Norma's curiosity having been satisfied, she was now considering her next objective.

Thanking Mrs. Mackenzie for her kindness, she expressed the hope that the animals would recover completely and said she would have liked to stay longer, but as she had a meal to prepare for a special occasion, she knew Mrs. Mackenzie would understand why they would shortly leave for home.

As she wished them bon voyage, Mrs. Mackenzie turned to the men and thanked them for the service they had rendered and, looking directly at Edward, she added, "It would appear that you played a risky part in helping my husband put big Nellie back on her feet."

Edward said nothing, but shrugged his shoulders, indicating what he had done was just normal. She laughed gaily, took hold of his wrist and concluded, "Mind you, I sometimes feel he thinks mair o' the auld coo than his wife."

Einer was relieved when he knew they would soon be on their way. He had not been looking forward to driving along the narrow road, but now that the time had come he felt more relaxed: it was a case of the sooner the task was completed, the better. For some inexplicable reason he felt the journey back was much easier.

As the two women busied themselves in the kitchen, the men departed to the sanctuary, so as not to become a nuisance in the cooking quarters. Having served Edward with an akvavit and carlsberg, Einer poured himself a large brandy and settled back, feeling he deserved it, knowing that he was finished driving for the day.

Having no immediate plans, they discussed the day's events, wondering if Farmer Mackenzie's cows were back to chewing the cud and what about the lightning? Was it not an unforgettable sight, the Forth Bridge silhouetted against the pitch black sky?

Edward broached the subject of Oskar Petterson sailing towards the Fife coast - where was he now? Einer seemed sure and suggested that Oskar would now be on his way back to Boness. Edward was curious and asked his friend how he could be so sure. Einer smiled and explained.

"I know that Norma expects to see him at least an hour before dinner and if he turns up late he will wish he had been shipwrecked."

A voice seemed to materialise from nowhere. It was not loud, but it had a certain resonance and timbre which indicated a man who was self-assured and patient, with just a touch of sarcasm.

"Is that so, Einer?"

Einer swung round in his seat and there confronting him was Oskar. He winked to Edward as he came round from the back of Einer's chair to the centre of the room. He was a very presentable man, tall, handsome and well groomed, with a jovial grin on his face, an indication that he was looking forward to an enjoyable evening.

Einer, taken aback by his sudden appearance, had still not replied, but Edward broke the silence.

"We saw you near the Forth Bridge heading towards Fife. Did you make it or return to base?"

Einer having recovered, gave his opinion.

"He made for home, Edward, tarted himself up and now hopes that Norma will forgive him."

Oskar walked over to Einer and, placing his hand on the shoulder, told him that if he poured out a large brandy, he would not tell Norma what he had said. The reply was quick and succinct.

"Go to hell."

Oskar waved an admonitory finger.

"Careful, Einer," he said, "there are ladies present."

Standing centre stage, Oskar had seen Norma entering the sanctuary and was well prepared. Edward settled back to witness the event, comedy or otherwise; he had experienced Norma's flirtatious tendencies not so long ago.

She threw her arms around Oskar's neck and, giving him a resounding kiss, expressed her relief that he had survived the storm, then, stepping back to admire him, she invited his reply.

He thanked her for the concern she had shown for his welfare. It had been a rather boring day, apart from a little rough weather. He had sailed to Crail and now he was standing in front of her hoping he had arrived at a time that suited.

She nodded her approval and, with her mind on the smorbord preparation, but not wishing to look anxious, she enquired if he had been successful. Oskar was in no great hurry to reply, he was too engrossed in his admiration of Norma.

There was a pause before he admitted that he had been quite successful, he had judged it perfectly. Just as she was about to make another probe, he decided to put her mind at rest.

"Oh, by the way Norma, I think Einer has something you require for the evening meal."

She strode over to her husband and asked crossly where it was. The poor man was mystified and before he could reply, Oskar pointed to a canvas bag behind Einer's chair.

Norma gave a gurgle of delight as she spotted a lobster crawling on the carpet, seized it expertly and put it back among its companions, then turning to Einer, scolded him for not telling her they were there. Did he not realise she had a meal to prepare and there was no time to waste?

As she left, there was an ominous silence, she had smiled her gratitude to Oskar, but poor Einer was in the dog house. He had kept silent knowing, as a shopkeeper, the customer and his wife were always right. No sooner had Norma disappeared into the kitchen, than Einer asserted his manhood.

"What the hell are you playing at, Oskar? You've landed me in the soup."

Oskar was unrepentant and quite flippant, informing his friend that as soon as Norma had cooked the lobster for her culinary creations, everything else would be forgotten.

Before the disgruntled Einer could reply, Oskar told him how fortunate he was that he had not made Norma aware of what he had said concerning the choice of either bringing the lobster or being shipwrecked. After all, was he not the one who ate more than a fair share of Norma's lobster mayonnaise.

Einer knew his position was untenable, but felt he should not admit total defeat. He asked Oskar if he was finished speaking. Oskar grinned, nodded his head and Einer said his piece.

"Some of the things you said might be true, but I hesitate to ask you not to repeat them, knowing you, as an example of moral rectitude, would scorn a bribe."

Oskar laughed and replied, "I would, however, appreciate a double brandy."

Einer, feeling that his dignity had, to some degree, been salvaged, waved his hand and told him to help himself.

The dinner was a resounding success, Norma felt her efforts had been well worthwhile, even a slight hiccup had been more comical than serious. It had happened when Mr. and Mrs. Mathieson and Hr. and Fru. Thorvaldson arrived. She had run rather hastily to greet Mrs. Mathieson whom she particularly liked. Unfortunately, as she ran over the polished wooden floor, her big toe had caught one of the Persian rugs and had precipitated her into the arms of her friend.

Jessie Mathieson, although taken by surprise and feeling critical, knew she had to be supportive, and placated Norma.

"It's awright having a Danish floor, but thae brussels often cause accidents."

After dinner the ladies retired with their coffees into the lounge, while the men departed to the far end of the sanctuary so they would not pollute the atmosphere unduly with tobacco smoke.

As the women played cards and spoke of the way things were at the moment and how it affected their families, the men set out to solve the world's problems.

Amongst the ladies, the gentle Emily was the heroine. According to Norma her new-found Swedish friend had known what to do for the stricken cows. If it had not been for her, the poor creatures would certainly have perished.

Meanwhile, the men had decided that the first subject on the agenda should be tobacco and its function in civilised society.

Dr. Douglas Mathieson admitted the smoking of tobacco gave indications that cancer could arise, but the smoking of cigars was relatively safe. In his opinion much of the carcinogenic properties condensed on the broad layers of tobacco leaf and were not absorbed into the lungs.

There were reservations, but after such a professional assertion they decided to continue smoking and ensure that the stubs were emptied into the dustbin immediately they were finished.

Edward gave thought to the drug scene, particularly cocaine, having in mind the machinations of Chancitt and company, but decided against mentioning it, realising that Einer or Oskar, knowing about his recent experience, might unintentionally mention it and land him in trouble with Emily and that would never do.

Instead he switched the conversation to the car run in the afternoon and concentrated on the near catastrophe of the cows in the orchard and outlined the method of salvage of animals who were deemed to have collapsed into a drunken sleep.

Oskar and Hr. Thorvaldson laughed heartily, but the doctor was singularly interested in how Emily diagnosed a state of drunken stupor. Edward admitted to having no knowledge of the behaviour pattern of cows, but was sure his wife Emily would be only too pleased to give a professional opinion. The good doctor said he would request just that and was sure Edward would not object if he approached the Royal Dick Veterinary College in Edinburgh for a second opinion.

Edward's reply was tentative. "I agree."

Of the five men in the group, four had at one time or another spent a considerable time at sea. It was natural, therefore, that a great deal of the conversation was salty in character.

All four, it appeared, had sailed single-handed in tempestuous seas and survived, conveniently of course in different parts of the globe, thus ensuring that no mariner present could dispute the veracity of their claim to have battled the elements and won in such heroic fashion.

It was now the doctor's turn for the telling of tales; his demeanour was thoughtful as he spoke.

"I have enjoyed your fantastic stories, gentlemen. They reminded me of my young student days. I was deeply engrossed in serious medical studies and turned to what was known as blood and thunder novels for relaxation. You have all thundered your way around this mortal coil of ours. Being a surgeon, you might expect me to provide the blood - if so I'm afraid you are in for a disappointment."

He hesitated, then looking closely at the four enquiring faces, continued.

"You are all Scandinavians who, during your young days, sailed the high seas. You have now retired from the thunder and can relax. Surely you would not wish that I should talk of blood and pain; remember I have not yet retired from the surgical scene and tomorrow, whether I like it or not, I will have to go back to my bloody work."

For a full minute there was silence, then Einer, as the host, felt it was incumbent upon him to reply.

"I'm sure we know how you feel, Douglas, but we still await your contribution, which need not necessarily have anything to do with your work as a surgeon."

Doctor Douglas Mathieson smiled his appreciation, decanted the 'Glenmorangie' to his own safety level and, after adding water, addressed his friends.

"My contribution will probably be dull when measured against your exciting adventures, but it is an example of how even the humblest person can play a vital part in the saving of human life. The story might be a wee bit long, but I think you might appreciate the telling of it.

"In the past two centuries we have heard much of the rights of man, how all men are equal in the sight of God; this is the assertion of those who consider themselves Christians. There are those of us, as atheists or agnostics, who would disagree that this is inspired by a deity.

"However, it appears that the concept of equality is accepted by civilised men. The Scandinavian word for God is Gud, pronounced 'good'. Whether one is Christian or Atheist, they all believe in the common good of mankind. The equality of man is enshrined in the concept that every human being is important and that no one individual is more important than another.

"All men are equal when judged by good law. Neither the intelligence of the scholar, the skill of the orator, or the power of the wealthy must be allowed to tip the balance of equality in need, in the direction of damnation in greed."

The doctor stopped for a breather, refreshed himself from his 'Glenmorangie' and then continued.

"You must excuse me, gentlemen, if you find me long-winded; if so, you have Einer to blame, but to illustrate my point, I will tell you a wee story. It concerned a young doctor in a rural practice. Having received a call from a distraught husband that his wife was dying, he had set out by car, but unfortunately about halfway there the right rear wheel had parted company with the car.

"He had stopped in time only to see the wheel disappear over a precipice. Rummaging in the back of the car, he was slightly relieved that a spare wheel was available, but it turned quickly to despair when he realised that the four nuts required to fix it to the axle were missing.

"His heart sank, knowing his patient could well be dead before he summoned help from the nearest garage. Looking across the rolling meadows to his right, he could see a beautifully proportioned building and recognised it as a renowned mental hospital and wondered, could he expect help from the hospital maintenance staff?

"He was about to jump over the dyke, when a powerfully built man with a vacuous grin stopped him in his tracks.

"'You're no allowed in here, mister, unless you're a patient.'

"Although he knew he had been challenged by a man of limited intelligence, he felt that help of any description was better than nothing. The doctor pointed to his vehicle, indicating what was wrong, and to his surprise the man clambered over the dyke and made, surprisingly to the doctor, an intelligent assessment of what had happened and what was required.

"There was a big beaming smile as he asserted, 'I can help you, mister.'

"The doctor was not too sure, but accepted the help offered, stressing that speed was essential as it was a matter of life or death that he should reach the patient within the next half hour.

"Within a few precious minutes, the big genial man had jacked the car up to the appropriate level and pushed the wheel back on the studs. In desperation the doctor asked what could be done about the missing nuts. The man grinned widely indicating that three nuts would have to do. Before the doctor could reply, the big man asked him to hold the wheel steady while he looked for nuts.

"Within a minute he returned with three and another minute later they had been screwed firmly home. Turning to the doctor, he asked him to examine his car. Having unscrewed a nut from each of the sound wheels, each wheel had now three nuts screwed firmly in position. Putting his hands on the doctor's shoulders, as if to pacify him, he had said, 'On your way doctor, save your patient, you can aye buy anither fowr nuts when it suits.' Twenty minutes later the patient was given the vital injection required and her life saved."

Doctor Mathieson took another sip and concluded.

"I told you that wee story against the background of the equality of man. On a material basis men are not equal, some are weak, others strong, some are clever, others simple. Many are meek and some are brave, but no man on a moral basis is inferior to another.

"The doctor might not have saved the life of his patient, but for the intervention of a simple man; in a way you could say he proved equal to his task as a human being during a critical period. I was that doctor, gentlemen, and from that day on I have recognised that no man is superior, but he can be equal to the good of mankind."

His audience had seemed interested but said little, finding difficulty in analysing the implications of his avowed philosophy. After all something so serious required mental concentration and surely the spirit of the gathering was to tell tall yarns and entertain each other.

Still Douglas had made his contribution and his friends, good fellows, had nodded sagely.

The men joined the women, coffee was served and, as could be expected, a casual conversation developed concerning subjects that had interested both groups. It appeared that among the men there had been no star performer, but the women claimed their new member Emily was indeed a heroine. Jessie Mathieson made what might be termed a 'sarcaustic' remark.

"What would you expect from the men? They're aye boastin, just like wee laddies that have never grown up; but when it comes to things serious, it's a woman every time! If it hadn't been for Emily, thae puir coos would have perished."

Momentarily the men were stymied, but the good doctor rallied to the cause.

"I'm afraid you're mistaken, Jessie, there is no superiority between the sexes, both complement each other. Emily, as a farm girl, had the knowledge and was able to make a proper assessment of what had happened to the cows that strayed into the orchard. She should be complimented for using her knowledge in such a constructive fashion."

Before Jessie could reply, the doctor turned to Emily, congratulated her and asked if she would be kind enough to explain how apples could cause intoxication in cows.

Emily smiled timidly and indicated that she could, but it would have to be in Swedish. Edward intervened, suggesting that he could act as the interpreter. So while Jessie glared at her husband, the Scandinavians listened intently, gathering some pre-knowledge before the English translation.

Edward, primed by his wife, spoke with authority, using his skills as a salesman to sell the product.

Emily had been interested in cows from a very early age, before she reached her teens her father had delegated enough responsibility to make her feel that the cows were her very own. They lived in the rural area of Rostorp and one day the whole family had travelled to the city of Gothenburg. On their return they had found the cows in the same condition as the cows seen at Dalmeny.

Emily had run about two miles to fetch the local vet and had helped him in his resuscitation of the drunken cows. She had badgered the vet to explain what had happened and, recognising her concern, he had told her that they had been intoxicated by apple fermentation.

But Emily, dissatisfied, had asked how it was that humans who consumed too many apples developed stomach pains, while cows were rendered drunk and incapable.

According to the vet, the cow, unlike the human, had several stomachs and a process of distillation took place during digestion, which produced a gas capable of intoxicating the animals.

Doctor Mathieson, having listened intently, agreed that the theory seemed laudable and again complimented Emily on the part she had played.

Edward, intent on a final flourish, harkened back to the doctor's theory of equality and the rights of man and asked, "Would you say, Douglas, that Emily proved equal to the task?"

Without hesitation, the doctor replied, "Yes, very much so, a laudable contribution to mankind and the bovine species."

Edward smiled and promised he would look up the word laudable: it certainly sounded good.

There could be little doubt among the women that Emily had now joined the trio, making it effectively an interesting quartet.

As the Thorvaldsons and the Mathiesons were contemplating their journey back to Edinburgh, the Sorensons and Oskar Petterson were in a mild state of deja-vu. Oskar had been offered a lift by the doctor, but declined, having made up his mind suddenly to go back to his yacht and sleep aboard.

This, although his home was above his delicatessen shop in Bruntsfield, not far from the Mathiesons. He had in mind a few days of fishing and other activities that would facilitate an expansion of his import-export business.

Einer had offered Emily and Edward a lift back home, but Norma had been adamant that they should stay overnight. She saw no point in Emily risking a chill travelling back, while the cold evening wind swept down the Firth of Forth.

As she settled back in the comfortable bed, Emily felt at peace with the world; happy and relaxed, she gave thought to what had happened in such a short time. It had started with a beautiful morning, the sun shining, the birds singing, yet she had been reluctant to confide in her husband.

Edward's cheerfulness had encouraged her to tell her secret and from then on, all through the day, he had been loving, and attentive, assuring her he would remain by her side for as long as he could, promising to be hale and hearty when the great day arrived.

There had been the excitement of the thunderstorm, followed by the tragi-comic episode of the poor drunken cows, which had boosted her ego and had helped in the blossoming of friendship with Norma and her acceptance as a good friend of Jessie Mathieson and Greta Thorvaldson. She smiled as she remembered Edward's interpretation of Jessie's opinion of Emily.

"She was," she said, "an unco clever and sensible lassie and guid lookin tae."

And Edward, lying by her side, was similarly engaged in reminiscence. He felt that everything had worked out rather well. He was sure Emily would feel more secure now and happy that making friends in a new country was not so difficult after all.

Little did he know that his fellow compatriot had made plans and was already on his way.

Oskar whistled cheerily as he strolled towards Einer's Emporium; he had slept soundly, he always did when his bed was suspended over salt water. In his mind he was formulating the best way to spend his day out in the Firth.

Oskar made his mind up as they sat at breakfast; he asked Emily if a little sail around the Forth appealed to her. She thought awhile and then agreed excitedly that it would be very interesting to see what the seaboard around her home looked like.

On explaining the route he intended to take, both Einer and Edward responded in a most positive fashion and Norma also thought it a good idea. Since Viking times, Scandinavians have relished mucking about in boats. Even in a city like Stockholm, many Swedes have 'ferries' at the bottom of their gardens.

After breakfast they walked down to the jetty and boarded the 'Tivoli'. Norma and Emily had ensured no-one would starve during the mini-voyage; they had, at short notice, assembled a mouth-watering selection of Danish and Swedish smorgass, even citron vand and akvavit, despite the protests of Oskar who assured them it was really unnecessary, as the Tivoli was well stocked and had all the facilities for modern cruising.

Within a few minutes they were out in the Forth and heading for the famous bridge. There could be little doubt that the powerful Swedish auxiliary engine was just the job for a quick getaway, but Einer and Edward were not impressed, they felt they should be sailing, not just cruising by motor yacht.

Oskar smiled and replied, "I will leave the decision to the ladies."

The ladies shrugged their shoulders, indicating that boys will be boys and left the decision to them.

Oskar admitted that the nostalgia of the old sailing ship days had won and gave his command.

"As Captain of this ship, I will remain at the wheel and you, Mr. Sorenson and Mr. Wevling, will trim ship for the voyage, so hoist sail, me hearties."

As Edward and Einer did as they were told, the ferry boat set out from South Queensferry fully loaded with carts, cars and people, including a vociferous party of youngsters determined to enjoy a picnic on the Fife side of the Forth.

There must have been at least three dozen of them; they were aged twixt seven and ten and were accompanied by teachers or minders who, apart from looking after the comestibles and tea making equipment, were saddled with the onerous task of maintaining a modicum of civilised behaviour. A difficult task at any time, but when you have youngsters of that age group seaborne and heading for the coves and caves of Fife, they become pirates and buccaneers, even the tin tea mugs tied by string around their necks become rum tankards.

They had spotted the Tivoli sailing towards them and had taken up their gun positions on the port side, determined to capture the yacht for themselves and imprison the crew, probably on the May Island.

'Boom!', 'boom!', 'boom!', they shouted, scoring hit after hit, but still the Tivoli survived the ordeal. As the shouting reached a crescendo, the teachers gave up any attempt to quell the mutinous crew.

As the yacht drew nearer, the shouting died down as the young pirates made plans for capturing the vessel and incarcerating the crew. Suddenly the battle was over as the yacht swung round and crossed the bow of the ferry with only thirty feet to spare. The young pirates ran over to the starboard side and spontaneously cheered the valour of a gallant foe.

The five occupants of the yacht stood up and reacted enthusiastically. They waved vigorously to the children, who waved back and continued to wave until the yacht passed under the bridge.

Einer voiced his concern. "That was a narrow squeak, Oskar."

Oskar seemed unconcerned and replied flippantly, "Law of the sea, old boy, sail before steam."

Einer was not amused and retorted, "Regarding the legal position, I doubt if the Forth could be considered a part of the North Sea. In any case, the ferry would have smashed us to pieces had you misjudged."

Oskar replied that he was sorry if anyone had been frightened, but felt confident that the Tivoli could sail past the ferry without undue hazard, adding that he could have used the auxiliary engine had he thought otherwise - but then that would have been cruising, not sailing.

Edward could see a little diplomacy was required.

"As the Captain you make the decisions, but I am sure the crew will not object to the engine being used if you feel it is required."

Oskar could not resist a wide grin as he thanked him for the vote of confidence.

As they sailed out in the Forth there was a gentle breeze, the sea was lazy and the Tivoli sailed like a dream. Emily in particular was interested in the coast line and asked Edward to keep her informed concerning important places. Edward obliged and after an initiation into the use of the ship's binoculars, gave a running commentary as she scanned the coastline. By the time they reached the Bass Rock, she had learned quite a bit about the Lothians.

As the rock and the screeching birds were left behind, Edward informed her that they were now leaving Berwickshire and were homeward bound. But Oskar felt the ladies should at least see the island of Inchkeith.

As Oskar circled the island, Einer gave a short history of the island and the immediate coastline. The sandwiches and titbits the women had brought aboard had been consumed and, although the Tivoli was well provisioned, Oskar felt the ladies should be dined in relative comfort somewhere on terra firma.

He set course for Newhaven, but when Edward and Einer realised he was bypassing Leith, they tried to influence him to turn into Leith Shore where they could take the opportunity of conducting a little business.

However, Oskar was adamant that his next stop would be Newhaven; he had no intention of seeking a berth when he had his own berth at the fishing village and, in any case, it would do his shipmates no harm to walk back to Leith docks; it was his intention to invite the ladies to accompany him for a meal at the Peacock Hotel.

The ladies were delighted and accepted readily, while Einer and Edward declined graciously and set out for Leith.

On their return, their wives spared no praise for their host and seemed unduly happy when they informed their spouses that it was indeed a shame that they had not been available to enjoy the very special fish course. The men seemed happy enough and thanked Oskar for his kind attention to their wives.

Whether they had primarily been engaged on business was questionable, they appeared too merry to have been engaged in anything so serious. They did admit, however, that business had been minimal; fortunately they met friends they had not seen for quite some time. It had been a joyful occasion, there had been a great deal to talk about and, of course, drinks had circulated rather frequently to ensure that their throats were properly lubricated.

Norma and Emily smiled indulgently, recognising that their menfolk were indeed 'well oiled'. So what? Fair enough! They had enjoyed their meal at the Peacock and the men had enjoyed their pub crawl.

Everyone was happy, but it was not long before Einer and Edward confessed to feeling rather hungry; they were suffering from a condition known to the Scots as the 'whisky hunger'.

Oskar set sail immediately; he had no intention of curtailing or altering his programme to suit the hunger pangs of his two companions. In any case, the quicker they were home, the quicker they would be fed. Also on his mind was an appointment for the evening which he had every intention of keeping.

He decided to disregard the whims or desires of his companions and started the auxiliary engine. It was not long before he reached the jetty at Boness and said goodbye to Norma and Einer. Then on to the basin at Grangemouth where he decanted a very happy Emily and a merry, but hungry, Edward.

Chapter 19

The 'McGregor' was on the doorstep the following morning with a note from Sven. Emily's cousin had been a little concerned at missing the Sorensons, but as the note explained, Sven and Rory were anxious to contact Edward. They had something of importance to discuss with him and suggested a time and place where they could meet.

As Edward walked to the Sailor's Rest, his mind conjured up a convivial evening with his friends; on the other hand, Rory might not be too pleased to see him. He recollected the time that the Customs Chief had asked his support in supplying any information which came to hand concerning the smuggling of narcotics.

Later he had met Rory in Inverness and after hearing the harrowing details of the suffering of cocaine addicts, he had promised his friend he would do what he could in bringing those responsible to justice. He felt inadequate, he had done very little, other than concentrate his attention on the American, and even that had ended in near-disaster.

Although there was now some indication that Chancitt was involved in the drug scene, he wondered if the risk he had taken had been worthwhile. For him the night had ended in chaos with a knife just missing his vitals by an inch or two.

Although he felt duty bound to do something, there was one thing certain: in the future he would ensure to the best of his ability that Emily's potential child would not be fatherless.

As he entered the rendezvous, he looked for Rory, but his attention was drawn immediately to Steve Allrock and Punchy Rush enjoying their drinks. It was a pleasant surprise; he had not seen them since the pub brawl and cheerily greeted them in appropriate fashion.

"And what are the two conspirators planning this time?"

Punchy Rush replied sharply, "How we can prevent that desperado Edward Sorenson committing suicide next time round."

Edward put his arm around Punchy's shoulders and, pointing to their beer mugs, asked, "Regarding replenishment, it is my pleasure. Do you wish a repeat?"

As they smiled, they shook their heads and said that a beverage purely Scottish would suffice. Steve opted for a glass of Glenmorangie and Punchy an 'Antiquary' to remind him of his profitable hobby.

It was natural they would talk about what had happened during the disturbance at the Melodian Bar and any subsequent developments. Edward had little to contribute, feeling that his ignominious departure from the scene of mayhem and subsequent realisation that a father-to-be should not involve himself in further similar escapades obliged him to apologise for the negative part he had played.

But Steve and Punchy would have none of it, they did think Edward had been daft to approach the American when protected by his gang of four. Punchy thought his effort at survival was quite unique.

"If you hadn't kicked the knife man in the balls you would not be here now, sonny boy."

Edward, appreciative of his mate's views, was still of the opinion that he should have stayed and not run away. Punchy, versed in matters martial, thought Edward's departure a good move; two of the antagonists left in pursuit, thus reducing the odds and allowing Steve and himself to bring the matter to a successful conclusion.

"You were the target, Edward," he said, "and a moving target is difficult to hit."

As Edward hesitated, Punchy gripped his arm and reassured him.

"Remember, we were the ones who told you to run."

Before he could reply, Sven appeared and invited him to join Rory and his nephew in the lounge.

As they entered, Rory stepped forward and shook his hand, then introduced his nephew, none other than newly promoted Detective Sergeant Alistair McIllwraithe. Although taken by surprise, he reacted swiftly and replied, "How clever of you, Detective Sergeant, to have selected such a substantial uncle as Rory."

Rory ignored the flippant remark and, signalling Edward to sit beside him, asked, "What will you be haffing, Edward?"

As they drank together, he was relieved that Rory seemed in a good mood, but was still curious regarding the necessity of a special meeting. Rory asked his nephew to outline what had happened after the fracas at the Melodian.

According to the young policeman, four men had been charged and imprisoned for having a considerable quantity of cocaine in their possession. Two were local men, the other two hailed from the North of England and were hardened criminals.

Looking directly at Edward, the young Detective Sergeant told him that the two fingers of the man known as 'Tinker Tam' had yielded prints and the police forensic department had revealed that Tam, alias 'the knife', was wanted on a murder charge.

It appeared that the gang of four would be in a state of incommunicado for a considerable time as far as decent society was concerned, the two professionals for a period of years, the 'knife' possibly removed from life terminally.

The police were now investigating the part the American might have played in the smuggling of cocaine; they could only hope that he would surface in the near future to help them with their enquiries.

Rory intervened. "Customs and Excise also want to talk to Mr. Chancitt and we felt that you, Edward, could play a significant part by helping to unearth him."

Edward could not resist a facetious reply. "You mean, gone to sea and you expect me to fish him out."

Rory was in no mood for a silly aside. "Surely you can do better than that, Edward?"

Edward agreed the remark was silly, but that was the way he felt. After all, he had been reckless in the way he had approached the American, but if society as a whole had benefited, then he had no regrets.

Rory grinned and accepted that Edward could occasionally appear to be rather naive, but he knew he was no fool and, whether by accident or design, that he had caused the riot in the Melodian Bar, the end result of which had put four criminals behind bars and had certainly curtailed the smuggling of cocaine in the district.

Edward laughed and gave his reaction. "I'm certainly not a hero, but if I can help in tracing Chancitt or stopping cocaine smuggling, I will do so, provided my wife is unaware of what is happening. In other words, it is my intention to keep my eyes and ears open and leave the action to those equipped with the proper weapons."

Rory acknowledged his view and told him that his chief, Mr. Pringle, had asked him to convey his thanks and hoped he would continue to interest himself in the fight against drug abuse.

Rory, understanding that, with Sven being Emily's cousin, it was necessary to be discreet, terminated the discussion on a diplomatic note.

"I understand how you feel, Edward, and thank you for what you have done. Let's say in the future that you might be inclined to consider yourself as an undercover agent."

Edward nodded agreement, but thought it was time they concentrated on more pleasant matters. Rory conceded and, as a token of his desire for a happy social relationship, he produced a bottle of Allborg akvavit.

After a sip, Edward toasted the company, agreeing that Rory had indeed told the truth, but wondered how he had managed to acquire the rather special brew. Rory was not too forthcoming, but his reply was significant.

"You are not the only one who has an influential friend on one of the butter boats."

For the next half an hour only harmonious and peaceful subjects were allowed on the agenda. Then Rory and Alistair left, indicating that they were 'haffing to resume their respective official duties'.

Left to their own devices, Sven and Edward concentrated on matters familial. As usual, Sven was eager to have news of his cousin Emily and Edward, sensing that his friend was concerned regarding his ability to act responsibly, tried to side-track him by asking how he and Felicity were faring. But Sven had no intention of being diverted from the truth concerning Emily's welfare. Never one to encourage negative pursuits, Edward decided to end speculation.

"I know you think I am rather irresponsible at times and, consequently Emily could be unhappy. I suggest you come home with me and find out for yourself."

Sven hesitated before replying. "I wouldn't say you were irresponsible Edward, but ..."

He got no further, as Edward interjected, "Of course you wouldn't, but you have, you silly Swede. Now get your coat and let's go back to Grangemouth. Emily will be pleased to see you and I will be happy to tolerate your presence."

Emily was pleased to see her big cousin, not having seen him since the day of the wedding. It was natural she wanted to tell Sven about the wonderful things she had experienced since she last saw him.

It was Edward's turn to cook, he said; and, after all, he was sure they would need a considerable time to discuss family affairs.

The exuberance and enthusiasm surprised Sven, who had always thought of his cousin as a shy young woman. But this did not deter him from adopting a big brother attitude and delving deep to ensure that she and Edward were on target for a long harmonious association.

Emily laughed, then gently chided Sven for believing it could possibly be otherwise; surely he knew Edward was a good man; as far as she was concerned this was the happiest time of her life.

Sven smiled indulgently, nodded his head, but made no effort to reply. She was slightly annoyed and decided it was about time that Sven was brought down from what he considered to be the ethical standards of marital bliss to earthly reality.

She admonished him for being prudish in his approach, then asked him if it was his intention to marry Felicity, provided there was a mutual desire. Feeling out-manoeuvred, Sven hesitated, but Emily pressed her advantage, telling her cousin that she questioned his amateurish attempt to save her marriage, but he could feel free to ask her advice should he himself contemplate marriage in the near future. Accepting defeat gracefully, Sven apologised.

"You must have thought I was like some inquisitive female prude the way I questioned you, somebody like Aunt Matilda."

While he spoke, she looked at his strong handsome face, his expression was so serious she felt compassion for his dilemma, but it was the mention of Aunt Matilda that upset her equilibrium and caused her to laugh in a most unladylike fashion. Sven seemed crest-fallen as she erupted into peals of laughter.

It was Emily's turn to apologise.

"I am sorry if I appear rude, but you must admit that you do not look in the least like Aunt Matilda - you are tall, well built and handsome, while Aunt Matilda is short, squat and nosy in more ways than one, she also has a moustache."

He immediately relaxed, realising his statement had been both ridiculous and comical and accepted it as such. The corners of his mouth twitched upwards, the grin expanded to a broad smile and was followed by a gale of laughter, in which Emily happily joined.

As the laughter subsided, Emily had an afterthought and reminded him that their Swedish Aunt could talk with more authority than either of them. After all she had gone through three husbands and was marrying the fourth just before she herself had left Gothenburg to explore the world as a ship's stewardess.

Sven admitted that one in a lifetime was surely enough, he had no intention of emulating his Aunt Matilda, but it would not be long before he enjoyed the status of a married man.

Edward had heard the merriment as he entered with the pre-dinner drinks and asked if he could be put in the picture. Emily responded quickly, conveniently forgetting to mention the Swedish Aunt, she had no intention of blotting the family copy book.

"Sven has just told me he intends to marry in the near future."

Lifting his glass, Edward toasted his friend. "Skol, Sven, may you live in harmony with your chosen mate for the rest of your life. I trust I am right in offering my congratulations to Felicity, your intended?"

As news such as this merited special attention, Edward decided that the steaks he had been given by Harry MacSween should be used for dinner; having taken up residence in the cold cupboard, it was about time they played their part in the food chain. A substantial steak dinner was called for; after all, if Sven had decided to marry, it was essential that he should be fed for the job.

That evening a very well fed and happy Swede left for home. After bidding Emily farewell, Edward accompanied him to the door. Just as he was about to cross the threshold, Edward restrained him and in a low confidential voice, advised him, "If you require advice on any marital problem, I am at your service."

It was the following day that Edward met Oskar at the Shore in Leith. Having posted a sea stock order to Harry MacSween, he accepted an offer to join his friend on a little fishing trip. They tried their luck a mile out from the mouth of the River Almond, but, dissatisfied with the catch, they decided to cruise and explore.

Peace, perfect peace, is reclining in a properly designed deck chair, on a small well-equipped yacht, sipping a mature cognac, enjoying the aroma of a good cigar as it rests temporarily on a tray a bare arm's length away, having dined on lobster sandwiches expertly mayonnaised. To enjoy such an experience with a like-minded companion on board a sailboat gliding over a calm sea, while luxuriating in the warm rays of a temperate sun, is surely a recipe for contented minds.

It was Oskar's rapid movement that jolted him from his reverie and had him wondering for a few moments if something critical had happened. When he saw Oskar casually examining Inchkeith through binoculars he felt relieved, but annoyed that his day-dreaming had been so rudely brought to an end.

"And what is peeping Oskar looking at?" he asked.

Oskar shook his head and patiently observed, "I've always been interested in birds, Edward."

Edward had a serious, but rather wicked look when he offered his view that Oskar, like most bachelors, was probably more interested in curvaceous bosoms than coloured beaks. Oskar looked despairingly at his companion, indicating that there was little point in attaching sexual symbols to his viewing of the island; after all, apart from any observations regarding flora or fauna, there was historic value attached to it in the military sense.

But Edward, determined to be mischievous, indicated that M.O.D. would not be keen to allow him to view any fortifications that might be on the secret list. It might be a good idea to quit the area immediately and explore instead the coves and caves of Fife.

Oskar laughed and agreed to the proposition, knowing full well that Edward had hinted more than once that he was keen to explore the Fife coast from the sea.

The sail was lowered, the engine throbbed into life and Oskar set course for Kinghorn and from there they travelled leisurely up the coast. They passed the small port of Kirkcaldy, famous or infamous, dependent upon nasal sensitivity, for its smell of linseed, the product so essential for the manufacture of their well known linoleum, and, for those interested in history, the ruins of Ravenscraig Castle.

Almost immediately they drew abreast of Dysart harbour where small craft were landing their catch of fish. Using Oskar's binoculars, Edward could see lined up on the wharf, lobster pots or traps, a nostalgic reminder that his father was probably at that moment engaged in lobster fishing. He felt guilty, he knew he should have written by now to his father.

Keeping as close to land as safety would allow, they passed Wemyss, renowned for its caves and geological peculiarities and latterly, what could be described as the picturesque efforts of stone age man.

Passing the docks and yards of Methil, they reached Largo bay, where Oskar raised sail to take advantage of a breeze that would blow the Tivoli back to Newhaven in double quick time.

He explained that although he had planned to sail further up the coast to visit the colourful fishing villages of Pittenweem, Anstruther and Crail, he had an appointment in the evening which he intended to keep. Edward understood and was quite supportive, thanking him for the trip and wishing him every success in his quest for happiness.

As Largo disappeared rapidly astern, Oskar informed him that Largo was the birthplace of a sailor called Selkirk, who had been marooned on an island for many years and was immortalised by Daniel Defoe in his novel Robinson Crusoe.

As they sped towards Newhaven, Edward offered the opinion that Selkirk must have been a man of heroic proportions to have been able to survive on a diet of coconuts and fish, while denied the solace of wine, women and song.

It was at the point where they entered the shipping lanes that he asked if he could have the binoculars. For almost an hour, Edward played around with the glasses, gradually coming to the conclusion that Oskar had somehow managed to acquire an extremely efficient spying device.

Questioning his companion, Oskar admitted that he had paid a German captain more than three hundred kroners for what had been described as 'the best binoculars made in Germany'. Although he knew the binoculars were expensive, he felt that Oskar was exaggerating or had made a mistake in the deal. He felt he should comment.

"You may be a good purveyor of exotic foods, but as a teller of fairy stories, you leave a lot to be desired."

Oskar looked disdainfully at Edward and in a voice feigning authority, replied, "Just see to it, Edward, that the binoculars don't fall overboard or you will most certainly follow them."

Edward smiled and reassured his seemingly serious friend.

"I will look after them as if they cost you one thousand Danish kroners."

As they neared Inchkeith, he focused the glasses on a Portuguese merchantman heading for Leith or Granton, idly wondering if there might be some business when it berthed.

As he followed its tracks, he was surprised to see a small motor boat heading straight for the ship. The small boat was similar to his own berthed at Leith Shore and his curiosity being aroused, he wondered if the occupant might be a competing salesman.

For a fleeting moment he felt a grudging admiration for a potential competitor until the powerful glasses threw into relief the face of an implacable enemy. There could be no mistaking the malevolent features of Lucius Chancitt.

Some seconds later the motor boat passed the bow of the merchantman and was lost to sight. He waited, expecting to see it pass the stern of the ship, but there was no sight of it. He was sure now that the American had boarded the ship.

His feelings were a mixture of exhilaration and caution; excitement at the prospect of putting Chancitt behind bars and concern that an ill-timed move could complicate matters, land him in trouble and worry Emily unduly.

He knew he had no option, he had at least to investigate, but it had to be done sensibly. For a moment or two he thought of enlisting Oskar's assistance in capturing the American and then rejected the idea. If anything went wrong, he knew that his wife would hear of the incident from one of their Scandinavian friends. He decided he must go it alone, but there was something Oskar could do to help him.

He handed the binoculars back to his friend, asking him to look in the direction of the merchantman. Oskar grimaced as he put the glasses down in a position of safety and explained that he knew without looking that the merchantman was the S.S. Stenka Maru, a Portuguese trader.

Smell was a far more important sense as far as the Stenka Maru was concerned, for it plied its trade between South America and Britain carrying fertiliser.

Edward conceded that Oskar was more knowledgeable than himself regarding the background of the aptly named Stenka Maru, but smell or no smell, he was determined to board the ship once it reached its destination.

He asked if his friend would be kind enough to follow the merchantman till it docked. Oskar had a better idea: the sail was lowered, the motor started and a course set for Granton docks.

With the wind changing to head on, he had no intention of following in the wake of a stinking Stenka Maru when he could reach Granton a good half hour before the merchantman. Edward was curious: how was he so sure the ship would dock at Granton?

Oskar tapped the side of his nose and chastened Edward for his lack of faith, adding that some water agents would do anything for a shipping order. Also he advised him to be fair to Emily and proceed immediately afterwards to Leith public baths and thoroughly cleanse himself.

Edward seemed completely disinterested, he was engrossed in planning the elimination of Lucius Chancitt from decent society. For the moment, the malodorous cargo of the Stenka Maru seemed insignificant. Still, if he managed to achieve his target he might well come to consider the ship to have had the sweet smell of success.

Oskar wondered what the rascal was up to; he knew he would be wasting time asking Edward to clarify his intentions. He did know his friend, like himself, was determined to the point of stubbornness if he had decided on a certain course of action.

There was no conversation till they reached Granton, when Oskar shook his hand and told him he knew Edward was concerned with something far more important than a mere shipping order. But Edward was not forthcoming and made light of the matter. Oskar reacted angrily.

"I know you are up to something. If you need help, now is the time to tell me."

Edward declined the offer graciously, adding that he knew his friend would come if he was in trouble.

"I will shout loudly if I am in danger, Oskar," he assured his friend.

Oskar laughingly replied, "You will have to shout very loudly to attract my attention. I anticipate being in the Edinburgh shop an hour from now, after putting 'Tivoli' to bed at Newhaven. Incidentally, it will be another hour before the Stenka Maru docks."

Edward could not resist advising his friend that he should not talk in such endearing terms about his yacht in the presence of his Newcastle girlfriend.

Oskar reacted sharply. "If you're in trouble, Edward, don't shout for me."

In a last ditch effort he tried to appeal to the inner man, suggesting he should sail with him to Newhaven where they could enjoy a drink and supper at the Peacock.

Oskar had been right: almost an hour had passed before the ship docked. He knew he had to be patient and wait until customs clearance before he could act. He had never been good at the waiting game; more to the point, it was starting to rain and shelter seemed a priority. Some fifty yards away, almost opposite the Stenka Maru's gangway, was what looked like a rough wooden sentry box, to which he ran for shelter.

Reaching the structure, he realised it was a device used by railwaymen when shunting during bad weather; and having a seat, he found it most accommodating.

Quarter of an hour later, he decided that sitting and dreaming was not productive and some sort of action was called for.

Momentarily he felt deflated, there had been no sign of movement, he began to wonder if Chancitt had after all slipped away before the ship docked. Taking a card from his pocket, he toyed with it before deciding to approach the ship in the orthodox manner of a water agent seeking an order. If successful, good and well, it would at least give him an opportunity for a little detective work.

He walked leisurely round the upper deck twice and was in no way challenged to account for his presence. He decided to enter the steward's quarters to look around, ensuring his innocence by carrying his card of introduction prominently displayed.

Once inside the steward's cabin, he sat down to relax and prepare for the unexpected. He put his card down on the table and reached in his pocket for a cigar. As he snipped the end prior to lighting he knew he could be making a mistake. He realised the smell from the cigar could alert a potential enemy. Pocketing the cigar, he sat back to review the situation.

As he weighed up his surroundings, he knew at least four men had been drinking and smoking and one of them could be Chancitt, for the ashtray contained, apart from cigarette stubs, three half-smoked cigarillos. The foul smell in the atmosphere although not proof positive, gave a strong indication that the American was hovering around.

Directly opposite was a narrow doorway, the door was slightly ajar and his curiosity was aroused when he saw a narrow grille at the top. He knew this would be the steward's pantry, but wondered what might be inside apart from the normal comestibles.

Having been a steward himself, he knew the ploys that interested that particular breed. Smuggling spirits and tobacco had always been considered fair game, but was this a bad one who broke the rules and dealt in drugs?

He waited a few minutes, then decided to investigate, despite knowing that he was being illogical in taking risks, particularly after having pledged he would in the future behave like a sober and responsible married man.

Many a time his friends had warned him that his feline tendencies would land him in trouble. They told him, as did 'Eric' his inner voice, that it had been curiosity which killed the cat.

There were others, probably ill-disposed, who encouraged him to take risks on the basis that the cat after all had nine lives.

He knew that his speed of thought and action could land him in trouble, but on the other hand, his speed of thought and cat-like agility had allowed him to jump clear of danger.

Entering the pantry he left the door ajar and as he pussy-footed around, he listened intently to ensure that he was not caught unawares. He worked speedily, searching the nooks and crannies that a steward might use to conceal items for his eyes alone.

Suddenly there was movement and voices too near for comfort. He made for the door in an endeavour to get back to his original position, but had to change his mind quickly when he saw a number of men pass the cabin port-hole. Within seconds they would occupy the cabin.

The grating voice of the American did little to comfort him. He left the pantry door as he found it, hoping that no one would come through. As he looked through the grille, he saw them settle back in their seats and knew it would not be long before they started to drink.

A number of bottles decorated the pantry table not far from the door. Edward took the precaution of noiselessly shifting them nearer the door, just in case.

They were a querulous lot who seemed to take pleasure in being nasty to each other. They deferred, albeit grudgingly, to Lucius Chancitt, the paymaster of their illicit venture. Apart from the American, there were three of them and a mixed lot they were. Starting from the American, the first man was strongly built, tough looking, but spoke in a soft Irish brogue, neatly dressed and, in Edward's estimation, probably the steward.

Next to him sat a 'Bull-neck'ed man whose grimy appearance indicated a close association with the engine room or boiler house, and the third man was lean and wiry, his weather-beaten face a reflection of work on the open deck.

Just for a moment a nasty thought concerning what the four could do to him should he panic made him sweat. He knew that shortly they would replenish their drinks and this was a hazard he had to contend with - the bottles were atop the ice cupboard just inside the pantry door. Noiselessly he shifted them a foot nearer the door, trusting to the steward not noticing the change.

Luck was on his side, for the steward entered just far enough to collect the bottles and Edward, standing immediately behind, was hidden by the door. As the door closed he heaved a sigh of relief, but wondered just how long he might be confined to the pantry. From the grille he could see and, more important, he could listen in on their conversation - and very enlightening it was.

As he smoked his thin black cigar, the American outlined the master plan to his underlings and although they appeared to listen attentively, there were from time to time interruptions as the deck hand and the stoker attempted to increase their share of the action, while the steward remained quiet and waited patiently until the arguing subsided.

But it was the plan that alerted Edward. Despite his predicament, he was already taking notes.

The ship would return from Amsterdam and land at Granton in three weeks' time. When it discharged its cargo, twenty sacks of fertiliser would be laid aside to be collected by a company specialising in agricultural products; each sack would contain a bag of refined cocaine in its centre.

They were all given their instructions by a very nervous Mr. Chancitt; had Edward known the full facts, he would have understood why.

Pierre Blanc, alias Snowy, had connections in Amsterdam and had managed, through his organisation, to transfer a large consignment to that port and his accomplices had made plans for its transfer to the British market.

Snowy, having decided the East coast of Scotland was the best place to unload the contraband, had made Chancitt responsible for its transit between Amsterdam and Granton.

Lucius Chancitt knew only too well he was being tested and if he failed, Snowy would punish him severely. He cursed the day he had met Sorenson, the Dane had been a source of trouble ever since.

Looking through the grille, Edward could see the American studying a card lying on the table. Too late, he realised now he had made a mistake that could cost him his life.

Chancitt picked up the card for closer scrutiny, then, dropping it like a hot coal, bellowed, "Jeez's Christ, who put that there?"

The Irish steward looked at the card, then, putting a restraining hand on the arm of the American, replied, "Sure and it must have been the man himself."

The statement in no way pacified Chancitt. His long bony frame quivering in a mixture of hate and fear, he was adamant that Sorenson must have been listening to his plan. The genial steward made an attempt to pacify Chancitt, arguing that the American himself was the only one that had boarded the ship out in the Forth, that they had then proceeded to the fo'c'sle, so how could the man Sorenson have heard them?

Examining the card closely, the steward smiled and, pointing to the word 'water agent', offered the opinion that Sorenson had boarded the ship and entered the cabin while they were in the fo'c'sle. He knew from experience that any salesman would seek out the steward for a provisioning order; he had waited and then left his card and would probably come back.

The American leered at the Irishman and replied, "If that son of a bitch returns, I expect you and your two buddies to eliminate him, pronto."

Edward felt decidedly uncomfortable; how he wished that Punchy Rush and Steve Allrock were close at hand. Little Eric, his inner voice, chastened him severely. How could he be so foolish, to be influenced unduly by curiosity to the degree where he had forsaken and discarded so readily the mantle of responsibility which he had so recently worn?

For the time being he was trapped; he could only wait and hope that they would leave the cabin, but if discovered, he knew it would be a fight for survival.

As he peered through the grille he could see Chancitt studying the pantry door. Suddenly his claw-like fingers gripped the steward's arm and he croaked, "That son of a bitch could still be on the ship."

But the steward was not impressed. He laughed at the suggestion that Sorenson posed a threat, after all. If that had been the case, why leave a calling card? For a moment the American drew on his black cheroot and pointed to the pantry door.

"Sorenson could be in there listening to what we are planning."

Edward prepared for action - it looked like now or never. The American made a move towards the door, but the Irish steward stopped him.

"Sure, if this Sorenson man is such a cliver divel, he'll be in the fo'c'sle lookin at your samples."

The American had opened the door, but had not seen Edward, who was lovingly clinging to the back of the pantry. Accepting the steward's opinion, he swung round on his heel and ordered action.

"Back to the fo'c'sle," he ordered, "just in case that son of a bitch is around."

Within seconds they had vacated the cabin and were scurrying along the deck, the American as usual leading his men from behind.

Edward heaved a sigh of relief and praised the intelligence of the Irishman, who seemed to know just what was required. He waited patiently at the cabin door until Chancitt and his crew had disappeared down into the bow of the ship, then walked leisurely down the gangway and proceeded along the quayside to the dock gate.

Reaching safety, he gave thought to his next move. He knew the police wanted to question the American. On the other hand, would it not be better to wait and capture the American red-handed and eliminate once and for all that particular source of supply?

As he cogitated just outside the dock gates, a motor van drew up, the policeman on duty talked to the driver and then gave clearance. As it passed, he spied the hawk-like features of Chancitt, but what surprised him was the inscription on the van, 'Agri Products'. He made up his mind it was time for a pint and a little relaxation after what had been a nerve-wracking experience.

As he sipped the amber nectar, 'Little Eric' reminded him that there was always the tendency for fools to rush in where angels fear to tread, but as his propulsion was one of good intention, they had decided that, despite his meanderings, he was in spirit one of them.

Having given thought to what he had heard in the pantry and Chancitt's departure in the van, he felt that long term strategy was called for, as opposed to the immediate arrest of the American for questioning.

With this in mind he telephoned Sergeant McIllwraithe and arranged a meeting at Leith Police Station the following day.

Arriving home rather later than he had intended, he told Emily, who had been a little concerned, that he had accepted an invitation to go sailing with Oskar. Emily, good soul, was happy that he had the sense to accept the invitation to go sailing; after all, it was not a good thing to work hard all the time, health was more important than the acquisition of wealth.

Edward agreed with his wife, but smiled wearily as he considered the reality of the situation. Life was not that simple, he knew he had a social, as well as a family, responsibility, but also to tell his wife of his experience on the Stenka Maru would be pointless and worry her unnecessarily. Surely the time would come when Chancitt and any other villain that crossed his path would be summarily dealt with, leaving him free to enjoy life to the full.

In the morning he called in at Tam Richard's shop. It was his habit to call in most mornings, for although his work these days was predominantly as a water agent, they had an agreement that if the old man was unusually busy, he would be on hand to help out.

However, old Tam was unduly affable and greeted the young man accordingly.

"Butchering services not required, but shipping orders, particularly sea stock, very welcome."

Edward, always ready for a bit of fun, responded, "I would have thought that the number of orders I have given you these last few days would keep you going for at least a week or two. It was my intention today to relax and link up a few sausages."

The old butcher smiled and shrugged his shoulders, before replying, "Have it your own way, Edward, but Sergeant McIllwraithe rang me ten minutes ago and asked if you would meet him at the Sailor's Rest instead of the Police Station."

Edward accepted the message, indicating the police required help with some routine matter, probably a Danish sailor who had misbehaved and they required an interpreter.

Tam Richards laughed heartily and clapped Edward on the back. "Yes, and I know who that sailor is."

It was obvious the old man had already heard of the incident in the Melodian Bar, the news must have travelled very quickly from Leith to Grangemouth. He maintained a low profile as Tam Richards tried to ferret out information and satisfy his curiosity.

It appeared the old man already knew the whole story and Edward could only hope that Tam was not a gossip. He voiced his concern to the old butcher regarding the story reaching the ears of his wife Emily. Tam looked gravely at Edward before advising him.

"Take care, son. When you become involved in any way with bastards like yon Chancitt and his ilk, you can expect a knife in your back or a bullet in your brain."

He assured the old man he would certainly take precautions, but was still worried that Emily would learn of the Melodian brawl and the part he had played.

The old man was adamant that he had no intentions of spreading the story. After all, he was the one who had warned him about Chancitt originally; as far as he knew it was only pub talk and, although there was no guarantee, men rarely made their wives aware of pub happenings.

Edward arrived a few minutes early at the Sailor's Rest and, having breakfasted sparingly, settled at the counter with his pie and pint. Being a keen observer, particularly of late, he kept his ears and eyes open and was rewarded when he caught sight of the small man.

As usual, he was moving furtively around collecting slips of paper and imparting gems of wisdom to his victims with his twisted mouth via the palm of his hand in the direction of their twitching ears. On balance he appeared successful, but several told him to clear off, or words to that effect.

Being a bookie's runner, it was normal that pieces of paper should circulate, but it was the prospect of small packages being exchanged that was foremost in Edward's mind. He caught the eye of the small man, but had the presence of mind to stare straight through him and then listened without looking, hoping to learn something to the small man's disadvantage.

As the small man mingled with the crowd, the young Sergeant appeared at the lounge door and beckoned him in. He listened intently as Edward outlined the events of the previous day. From time to time he intervened in a cautionary way, nodding his head when he considered Edward to have been correct in his behaviour and shaking it when he thought some irregularity had taken place.

It amused him that the young policeman should be such a stickler for proper legal procedures, particularly considering the type of thugs that were involved. Sergeant McIllwraithe congratulated him on having obtained valuable information and agreed with his action up to the present, but cautioned him concerning his methods; he would be sorry to see Edward land in trouble.

It was at that moment that Mr. Horsburgh, the proprietor, entered with what appeared to be an urgent call-out for the Sergeant.

As the Sergeant left, Mr. Horsburgh asked Edward to come through to his small office in the public bar. Edward accepted readily, knowing it was a vantage point where he could view most of the bar in relative comfort and secrecy. He had been there before and had quite enjoyed listening to Mr. Horsburgh's tales concerning his life from that of a docker to owner of several licensed premises.

Edward had even thought of writing a book concerning the man's exploits and prepared himself accordingly.

But the publican was on a different tack this time, he was anxious to know how Edward felt after the affray at the Melodian. Edward was willing to oblige; after all he had a perfect view of the 'wee man' and was prepared to move swiftly if required.

On the other hand the time factor was not all important; the landlord, having poured him out a healthy measure of Allborg akvavit, deserved attention.

Edward, kind soul, gave a performance that had him laughing, but sympathising with his dilemma on the Stenka Maru. Feeling he had gone too far, he felt it necessary to warn the publican that gossip of what he had said could be counter-productive from a social viewpoint.

The publican was serious now and agreed that caution was essential and, looking at Edward, could only say, "Edward, you're a helluva man."

Edward pondered before replying, "The last man that said that to me was Rory McLeod."

Mr. Horsburgh responded that Rory must have had a great regard for him, "and take my word for it," he said, "Rory has done a lot for the public good. You've no doubt read about the smugglers arrested up North."

Edward looked quizzically at Mr. Horsburgh, who assured him that Rory had been mainly responsible for the criminals being arrested and again repeated the advice he had given.

"Take it easy, but if you should become involved, don't be too independent; let Rory or young Mr. McIllwraithe know what you have in mind. I know they both have a great regard for you."

Although he had been listening, he had also kept watch on the wee man who had now been joined by a rough-looking character; he knew they were up to something shady. His back was to them, but he could observe their actions by looking into the big mirror at the back of the bar.

The rough character had delved inside his jacket and produced a newspaper-covered package, while Chancitt's messenger had taken vegetables from a paper carrier and placed them on the table beside their drinks.

As they drank, the rough one surreptitiously placed the parcel within the carrier and the wee man placed his vegetables delicately atop the mystery parcel. Knowing there was something afoot, Edward hastened to assure the publican that he would heed his advice, then, looking at his watch, he thanked his host for his hospitality and told him he would be leaving shortly as he had an appointment to keep.

Mr. Horsburgh nodded and as he rose to serve a customer, he winked and hoped it would not be too long before he again enjoyed his company.

As the small man left, Edward strolled to the door, trusting that his pace would not attract attention, and once outside fastened himself loosely to his quarry.

As they crossed the bridge some yards apart, the small man suddenly veered right along the shore, but Edward walked straight on, having seen Sergeant McIllwraithe coming towards him from Bernard Street.

He came straight to the point, outlining what had transpired in the Sailor's Rest and that it was his intention to trail Chancitt's messenger.

"Leave that to the police," Sergeant McIllwraithe advised.

Edward grinned, assuring the Sergeant that only a few minutes before Mr. Horsburgh had dispensed the same advice. It was certainly his intention to leave it to the police, but having sat the last hour in a pub, he felt it necessary to exercise his legs and trailing the quarry to its bolt hole could prove interesting, even rewarding.

Giving the Sergeant little chance to reply, he told him he would meet him, if he was interested, at the junction between Bridge Street and Sandport Street in half an hour.

Edward's hearing seemed to have been affected, he did not hear the Sergeant imploring him to be sensible and not become involved in something he could not handle.

As the small man kept to the waterside, Edward walked along the pavement, but, finding the pace of his quarry too slow, he decided to move ahead and trail him from the front.

Reaching the Tolbooth Wynd, he decided window shopping would be most appropriate. From this vantage point he could see Bridge Street without being easily spotted. It was most gratifying that the small man did as he expected; as he looked at the reflections in the big plate glass window, he could see the Leith worthies going about their lawful business, but, more importantly, he could now see his quarry creeping along, predictably, on his 'awful' business.

As he turned into Bridge Street, Edward knew he had to act fast. Within seconds he was only a few yards away when a big docker, crossing over from Coal Wynd, gave him cover had the small man given a backward look.

He turned right into a tenement entry and Edward followed discreetly and silently, moving like a cat, all his senses tuned to coping with the unexpected.

He hesitated when he reached the end of the dark corridor, knowing he would have to adjust quickly to the poor light. From experience he knew what to expect; he smiled when he thought of a similar tenement building just around the corner in Sandport Street. It was there he had lodged with Mrs. Brown and had happy memories of his association with Maggie.

As expected, the only light entering the gloomy stairwell was from a weather and bird-stained cupola on the roof of the four-storeyed tenement. Knowing the person above would have the advantage of the light, he edged carefully upstairs and noticed at the first landing what appeared to be two trousered legs - the stairway to the next landing hid the rest of the body.

Peering intently, he could see the heels of the shoes and knew that the man's back was to him and he was waiting to enter the centre door. Another two steps and he could see to just below the man's shoulders, if the man moved left to come downstairs, he would have to make ready for a quick getaway.

The next minute proved interesting: the carrier bag descended and rested against the left leg, the right hand lifted up the jacket and, plucking papers from the hip pocket, then transferred them after perusal to the left pocket.

Suddenly the door opened and a querulous voice commanded, "Stop fiddling wi yer papers, have yi got the stuff?"

The reply was inaudible, the trousers disappeared along with the paper bag and the door slammed shut. Edward moved up to the door which had just closed and smiled when he saw the name 'Napier'. He idly wondered if there could be any connection with the famous inventor of logarithms.

This was no time for speculation. He moved further up the stairs to familiarise himself with his surroundings. Should he have to take avoiding action, he would not be at a disadvantage.

Reaching the top flat, he examined a hatch door leading to the roof and found that by balancing on the banister he could, if required, leap onto the attic level and from there to the roof.

On the way down, he noted the name Nesbit on the door directly above Napier's house. He tiptoed as he drew close to the Napier residence, hoping to hear something to the disadvantage of the occupant. As he descended the last flight of steps, a shaft of light suddenly shone from an opening door. He hesitated, hoping to hear or see something worthwhile.

Again the trousered legs, but this time on the way out, the rough voice of the occupant giving what amounted to an instruction.

"Remember, it's Aberdeen a fortnight from today."

As the door slammed, the trousered legs moved. Edward decided to vacate number thirteen and do his spying from number eleven. After waiting five minutes, he pocketed the newspaper he had used as cover and contemplated his next move. Had the small man gone upstairs instead of down? It occurred to him that his quarry was known to many as 'the wee man', the small man and other names never used in polite society, but at the back of his mind he could recollect the name Nesbit being used.

He knew now that Nesbit had gone upstairs. He decided to stroll in the direction of the rendezvous he had suggested, hoping to meet the young police sergeant.

He met him quicker than expected, for the young policeman had been watching him from an entry not far from Sandport Street. He was pleased to see him and made reference to his punctuality. The Sergeant gave a prim reply.

"When a member of the public, Mr. Sorenson, informs me that something unlawful is afoot, we have no option but to investigate."

Nodding his head in agreement, Edward made him aware of what had happened from the time they had been in the Sailor's Rest up to the present moment. The Sergeant listened attentively, but seemed unimpressed, then looking wearily at him he expressed the opinion that his resumé of events was high in romantic speculation, but low in factual information that could lead to an arrest.

Edward was not dismayed, he knew the Sergeant would stick strictly to the rules, unless he could prove that a risk was worth taking.

According to the Sergeant, there was insufficient proof to apply for a search warrant. Edward agreed that such a course would be a waste of time and, as time was of the essence, he intended to prove that action would have to be taken immediately, or the prospect of catching the culprits would be lost.

He asked the Sergeant to remember that he had been instrumental, whether by accident or design, in helping the police and Customs authorities in thwarting and putting behind bars known criminals.

The young policeman nodded, but was still not impressed. Edward referred rapidly to three points, first the parcel being put to the bottom of the carrier bag, the handling of pieces of paper before entering the house of Mr. Napier and the last, and most speculative, but possibly the most important, the words 'remember Aberdeen a fortnight from today'.

Edward continued in slightly sarcastic vein.

"I suppose the parcel could have been something quite innocent. On the other hand, the American was now suspected of being a cocaine smuggler and the 'wee man', Mr. Nesbit, was definitely a messenger for Chancitt.

"The fumbling about with papers was probably the sorting out of betting slips prior to delivery, after all 'the wee man' had convictions under the Betting and Gaming Act.

"However, on the other hand, they could have been questions from university students to Mr. Napier, who hopefully, as a great mathematician, would provide them with correct answers."

Sergeant McIllwraithe's patience was beginning to ebb, but he was still calm enough to interject in a reasonable fashion, "I know you are being funny, Edward, but if this Mr. Napier is what you say he is, I imagine he is collaborating with Mr. Nesbit and they are sitting with the Sporting Pink calculating the betting slips that should be retained and those that should be unloaded on the local bookie."

Edward shrugged his shoulders and conceded to local knowledge, but felt the last point was worthy of further examination.

"Remember it's Aberdeen, a fortnight from today."

Although that statement could cover a wide field, it was feasible and constructive to consider it important; after all, Mr. Nesbit was the messenger of a suspected dope smuggler. To spur the police into action, Edward issued a reminder.

"It was your Uncle Rory only the other day who was successful in putting drug smugglers behind bars and that was in Dundee and Aberdeen."

The barb struck home. McIllwraithe had great regard for his uncle, but there was no way he was prepared to concede that the McLeods were in any way superior to the McIllwraithes. The Sergeant put his left hand up to his chin and massaged it gently, a sure sign that he was in deep thought, then, looking directly at Edward, gave his decision.

"Haffing listened carefully to all you haff said, Mr. Sorenson, I intend to investigate immediately, but it will haff to be done with great care."

To speed matters up, Edward asked a hypothetical question.

"If you could smell smoke coming from a house and upon investigation you found the door locked, what would you do?"

The policeman shook his head in sufferance and, looking disdainfully at Edward, retorted, "What I haff to do I will do properly and legally."

He beckoned forward two policemen and directed them towards Number Thirteen and then was about to follow when Edward interjected, "Is there anything I can do to help, Sergeant?"

The Sergeant glared at him, but there was a glint of a grin as he replied.

"If you are here when I return, I will arrest you for intent to mislead a police officer."

Edward went home happily to Grangemouth knowing the Sergeant was adequately equipped and trusting the end result would be well worthwhile.

Edward was even happier the following day when he read his newspaper. Although the article was on page two, it had been prominently displayed under the heading 'Cocaine Pedlar Caught'.

A Leith Sergeant of Police had been extremely resourceful and because of his diligence had been successful in arresting a dope pedlar.

The Sergeant and two constables had seen black smoke issuing from Bridge Street and had decided to investigate. They had entered Number Thirteen and on reaching the first flat, could smell smoke coming from the centre house. The Sergeant had called through the letter flap that they were the police and asked if help was required.

There being no response, he had immediately shouldered the door open, knocking the tenant, Mr. Napier, to the floor. As he lifted Mr. Napier from the floor, he saw a number of small parcels scattered around. Mr. Napier gathered them together and put them into a bag, indicating he had been in the process of taking them to the rubbish bin.

The Sergeant, wondering why a man so recently flattened to the floor should be so anxious to rid himself of the bag, decided an investigation was called for. Commandeering the bag, despite the man's protests, he discovered that the small parcels contained cocaine. Mr. Napier was arrested and a subsequent search of the premises revealed a considerable quantity of drugs. Mr. Napier is at present helping the police with their enquiries.

Edward smiled at the idea of using a smoke screen to warrant breaking into the premises of Mr. Napier; evidently there was more than one way of acquiring a warrant. There could be little doubt that Sergeant McIllwraithe was quite inventive, but that was to be expected - after all, the Scots are an inventive race.

He thought about his part in the episode and felt it had been a minor one. Still, if he had not persisted in trailing the 'wee man', Mr. Napier would probably still be plying his profession as a 'Narcotics Nasty'.

Some time later, as he read his newspaper, he put his level of importance on a slightly higher plane.

Four seamen, part of an organisation based in Brazil, had been caught smuggling cocaine into the port of Aberdeen. A journalist conversant with the street value of cocaine had estimated that the haul was, in money terms, at least a hundred thousand pounds.

An involuntary whistle escaped his lips as he thought of that enormous sum and realised that his part was of some significance. He hoped the smugglers were unaware of the part he had played.

From now on he would abandon the idea of playing detective and concentrate exclusively on making a success of his marriage to Emily.

Chapter 20

Within a matter of months the Sorensons had achieved a standing in the community which would normally have taken years and the word 'incomer' had never even been mentioned.

Edward Sorenson, first on the scene, had obtained employment as a part-time butcher and established himself as a Water Agent in the Firth of Forth. His aptitude for hard work and ability to make friends had served him well.

Emily had arrived a little later and had won the hearts of all. Her serenity, compassion for others and her naive way of expressing herself effectively, despite her limited knowledge of the language, endeared her to all she came in contact with.

Edward looked tentatively at Emily wondering if she had been told by some gossip or other about the newspaper headlines 'Police Capture Cocaine Criminals' and 'Drug Dealer Caught on Stenka Maru'.

Keeping his fingers crossed, he asked his wife, "And what would you like to do today, dear?"

She looked at him patiently before answering. "Surely you remember, we are expected at the Wevlings in the late afternoon, preferably before 4 p.m., if possible."

Edward could relax now and hastened to assure his wife that they would definitely arrive in time.

It was Norma's turn to entertain and, having acquired a surfeit of lobster, she had decided to extend the invitation to the husbands, together with their wives.

After dinner the guests retired to the lounge for coffee and liqueurs. The buzz of conversation centred on the amazing events of the past few days. The startling news had excited them and given cause for concern. The local police force had raided a ship at

Granton, a considerable quantity of cocaine worth thousands of pounds had been discovered secreted within bags of fertiliser.

The smugglers had been arrested and were now awaiting trial, a man believed to be an American, was being sought for questioning. It appeared that this man had arrived on the scene in a van. Seeing the police, he had turned round at speed, driven dangerously through the dock gates and crashed the vehicle into a wall in Upper Granton Road.

Oskar and Edward looked at each other but said very little, confining their remarks to stressing 'it was a terrible thing to happen' and 'it should be stopped'. But Mr. Thorvaldson, the shipping company director, was more specific. His company's good name had been put at risk by these criminals. He dwelt on a number of cases where his company had employed South American sailors, some of whom had later been found to have been cocaine smugglers and had not only affected the prestige of the company, but had been responsible for the deaths of other sailors who had become involved in their activities.

He quoted a case where a company ship en route for Florida had enrolled three Colombian seamen to make up a crew shortage. During the voyage the three Colombians, together with two Norwegians, decided to play cards. As the game progressed, one of the Norwegians had won a substantial sum of money at the expense of the Colombians.

One of them produced a small package insisting it was worth two thousand American dollars and he was prepared to bet this against the Norwegian's winnings on a cut of the cards.

The young Norwegian, unaware of the type of company in which he found himself, had laughed in a derisory fashion at the idea he should risk his winnings on acquiring a package of drugs that in his estimation was responsible for making people soft in the head and ending up becoming unhappy slobbering idiots.

He was on cue for saying much more, but the Colombian had swept aside a makeshift table and driven his knife straight up through the midriff of the young sailor.

All hell had broken loose and the ship's officers and leading seamen had rushed to the scene, but the young Norwegian was dead. Meantime, the other Norwegian, realising that action was necessary for survival, had picked up the table and belaboured the Colombians, rendering two unconscious and, although badly cut by the original assassin, had managed to get to grips and was in the process of throttling him to death when the officers arrived on the scene.

It was at this point that Doctor Mathieson intervened, agreeing with Mr. Thorvaldson that drug smuggling, because of its very nature and the immense profit involved, could only lead to many lives being lost.

But far more important was the effect drugs had on society as a whole; although lives were lost in the smuggling and peddling of drugs, many thousands of addicts found life a living hell.

Although agreeing with the men, Jessie felt it was time a woman's view was expressed. In her estimation much of the evil in the world could be eliminated by proper educational methods: children should be taught from an early age that they could expect a miserable existence if they allowed drug dealers to influence them in taking drugs; and in the meantime everyone should help the police and customs in ridding society of such nasty criminals.

Norma, just returning from the kitchen, heard Jessie's remarks, agreed wholeheartedly and added that one newspaper had mentioned that a local man had been instrumental in laying the information that led to the capture of the smugglers. The police had indicated that the identity of the man could not be disclosed.

With the exception of Oskar and Edward, everyone present was curious, but each in their own way wondered who the local man might be. Oskar offered the opinion that the police were not only withholding the identity of the man to protect him from smugglers anonymous, but also to deny such criminals any information that would allow them to pursue their poisonous trade.

But Norma would not be denied, she liked Oskar and knew that, although he was considered a bit of a lad, he was also clever and shrewd.

"C'mon, Oskar," she said, "you always know what is happening. What's his name?"

Oskar smiled pensively, then, after a fleeting glance at Edward, told her that although he had an idea who the man was, he had no intention of naming him. The glance had not been lost on Norma, she asked Edward directly, "So you know the name of the man, Edward?"

Edward heaved a sigh of relief, at least he could answer the question without lying.

"Yes, I know the name of the man who gave the police the information which led to the smugglers being arrested and I have no intention of putting his life at risk."

Edward felt uneasy, but Mr. Thorvaldson rescued him.

"I am sure you are right, Edward. Idle speculation concerning the identity of the man who had the courage to expose that murderous gang could only assist them and make the work of the police just that much harder."

Greta Thorvaldson stood by her husband and suggested that the women could depart to their own den and allow the men to carry on the discussion if they so desired. As far as she was concerned, the women had more important things to deal with.

It was hardly an anti-climax; however everyone seemed happy they could do their own thing, with the exception of Norma who wondered why, as the hostess, she should be so uncertain while her guests were evidently quite relaxed.

As they travelled homewards, Emily questioned her husband regarding Norma's assertion that he knew the man who had helped the police. Having cleared the first hurdle, Edward had no intention of coming a cropper.

He explained it was natural that Norma should think in this way; after all, it had to be someone with maritime connections. The word agent had been used in describing the American who was a suspect; it followed therefore that any agent on the East coast could be the man who helped the police. He knew who the agent was and the only way to protect him was to keep quiet.

Emily refrained from asking the ultimate question, trusting to her man's ingenuity in keeping himself free from trouble.

When Edward left for Leith in the morning, Emily clung to him tighter than usual and as they kissed she murmured, "Take care, Edward, take care."

She hoped he would come early in the evening and as if to encourage him, she lapsed back to the Swedish.

"*Rodspotter i nat, Edvard.*"

He laughed heartily and replied that bribery was unnecessary, he would be home early.

The rodspotter, or red spotted flounder, was his favourite dish. Others could enjoy oysters or lobsters and other succulent shell fish, but give him a crisp fried rodspotter and he would be well satisfied.

As he walked to the station he had a feeling of nostalgia. He remembered his father, old Lars Villem, shipping lobsters to Frederikshavn. Although partial to a lobster, he persisted that the red spotted flunner, or flounder, was the food of the Gods.

There is a belief that Scotsmen encourage their sons to sup porridge so that they will grow up big and strong; similarly on the Danish island of Laeso it is essential that you should eat red spots if you wish to survive as a fisherman in those cold Northern seas.

There was a pang of conscience as he thought of his homeland; he had still not written to his father. He must write now and tell old Lars Villem that he had married; on the other hand, should he wait until the baby was born?

It was the clanging of the buffers as the train started that rudely wakened him from his reverie and introspection. He knew it would be another hour before he was in Leith docks searching for trade; enough time to relax, read his paper and discover what was happening on the Scottish scene.

After closely scanning the shipping news, he turned his attention to local items of interest. On reaching the sports section, he notched the scores and comments of the sports writers. After all, should someone show a particular interest, he would not be completely ignorant, it would be helpful to have some knowledge where the Hibs and Hearts stood in the Scottish football league.

Some time in the near future he hoped to attend a match and familiarise himself with the ritual involved.

Then, working from back to front of the paper, he passed with undue speed through the valley of death, spent a few moments in the marriage aisle and a little longer among the births; after all, it should not be much longer.

Passing through acknowledgements, he landed on page five and speculated airily what could be expected at the numerous garden fetes advertised. The holiday adverts intrigued him, they were honest insofar as they lauded the scenery without guaranteeing the weather.

He was nearing his destination when he turned to page one, it had been a habit of his to leave the headlines to the last. Long ago he had heard that no news was good news, but he knew as a salesman that such an attitude did not sell newspapers. Sensationalism provided bigger profits for newspaper owners and invariably doom and disaster all too frequently fed their coffers.

It was no different on this occasion. Miners had been the victims of an explosion, but, true to form, the headline blasted forth 'Massive Mine Explosion', followed by the all too sordid details.

He read the page in a mood of gloom and despondency, wondering why the editor had used such words that must have been soul-destroying to any of the relatives who had the misfortune to read all about the way their men had died.

He was all set to throw the newspaper away in disgust when he saw a small header outlining the success of customs officers in Dundee and Aberdeen in forestalling the smuggling of cocaine. Acting quickly on information received, three men had been arrested and were now awaiting trial, a considerable quantity of drugs had been recovered and the police were anxious to trace the whereabouts of an American, believed to be the organiser.

His mood changed instantly from dismal brooding to excitement and anticipation that it would not be too long before the murderous gang leaders were flushed out and summarily dealt with.

He knew that his anticipation and imagination were running ahead of probability, but if he could do anything to speed the process of justice, he would do so. But it would have to be done on the basis that his brain took precedence over his heart, the other way round was rather hazardous.

It was not long before he was doing what he liked best, scouring Leith docks and stalking any prospective shipping orders. The past two hours had been meagre, but this did not affect his cheerful disposition for he had learned that one of the big grain transporters was due to draw alongside the main elevator.

Within the hour the ship had docked, he had been the first agent to board and the ship's steward, after gentle persuasion, had rewarded him with a sea stock order. The stock would be of the highest quality at terms, according to Edward, that could not be beaten by any competitor.

Before leaving the ship he felt generous and went out of his way to leave a card with the captain, advertising Einer Wevling's Emporium at Boness.

After telephoning Harry MacSween and ensuring the customer would be given five star treatment, he decided to spoil himself a little; after all, Mr. Horsburgh had said he hoped it would not be too long before he returned to the Sailor's Rest.

Mr. Horsburgh was pleased to see him and encouraged him to stay awhile, but Edward declined graciously, insisting that half an hour was his target for recreation on this occasion. He admitted to having set himself certain targets that could be recognised as appropriate for what might be termed the model husband. Mr. Horsburgh smiled, nodded his head, but said nothing.

As he travelled homewards, Edward thought of what she had said and was determined to 'take care'.

Emily was supremely happy, her marriage with Edward had been more successful than she had first anticipated. She had great regard for him as a man who was never deflected from any objective he had set his mind on. She remembered when he first suggested marriage, admitting it might fail because of a feeling of insecurity in a foreign country. But Edward had been kind and considerate, teaching her the rudiments of the language, ensuring that he was nearby when those awkward moments arose, instilling confidence during interludes of depression and, through his loving attention, trying to show her that life need not necessarily be such a serious business.

She felt now that Edward's persuasion had been mainly responsible for her overcoming her self-consciousness, enabling her to make friends more readily than she could ever have expected. In the course of a year, a miraculous change had taken place; from a good looking, gentle, but rather diffident young lady, she had become a strikingly beautiful woman, still gentle, but now more self-assured; her serenity and friendliness had captivated the hearts of everyone she came into contact with. No-one can expect perfection, but Emily thought in the main the process of fulfilment had been a wonderful experience.

In approximately two months' time, another Sorenson would join the human race. For the Sorensons it was only natural that this would be a momentous occasion, an important event which they would have to prepare for.

They approached the subject each in their own way. Emily had always been fond of walking and ensured she did her daily stint, but over the last month she had voluntarily cut down to concentrate on what she considered more essential, the knitting of baby clothes.

Edward's contribution consisted of spending more time with his wife, helping with the household chores and keeping an eye on his partner's health and well-being. It was a privilege and a joy to be with Emily as she approached motherhood.

These were happy days indeed, days of wonderment and pleasant speculation. The name of the baby to be was of great importance and after toying with some 'posh' names associated with the so-called social élite, they decided to stick to fundamentals and choose the family line.

Always the gentleman, Edward suggested it was a case of ladies first - the forenames of the distaff side should surely have preference. But Emily could not make up her mind. Her mother's name was Martha, her father, Johan. Edward's parents were Ruth and Wilhelm.

She could not envisage a lively girl being content with an Old Testament name. However, she was sure that the baby would be a boy, in which case she felt that Johan would be appropriate, he would be called Johan Wilhelm.

Although only too willing to agree, Edward was curious concerning his wife's certainty that the baby would be a son of Soren. Emily smiled indulgently, took his hand and placed it over her abdomen. Edward, conversant with what to expect, was nevertheless surprised at the intensity of movement. Emily gasped a little as the movement became erratic and, looking at her husband, she voiced the opinion that only a gymnast could move like that.

Edward waited till the gymnastics session finished and a quiescent period had been established, then asked if it was not possible that the baby might be a potential lady gymnast; after all it was known that the Swedes encouraged both sexes to participate in healthy exercise.

But Emily was not impressed, she had it on good authority that the baby would be a boy. Edward, having taken a great interest in his wife's condition from the beginning, could not recollect the doctor giving any indication that the child would be male. On the other hand Emily had now made women friends and although he could visualise a get-together discussing his wife's pregnancy, he felt she would not have been unduly influenced. There was only one person apart from the doctor who fitted the bill and that was old Mrs. McGregor.

Emily, smiling at his wonderment, recounted that Mrs. McGregor's mother had been a midwife and had imparted her knowledge to her daughter. Edward knew that to question such a powerful authority would be both time-wasting and unproductive.

In order to finalise the issue, he suggested he could be Johan Wilhelm and, should Mother Nature decide on a girl, she could be called Johana Wilhelmina. Emily laughed at the idea and agreed she would prefer those names rather than the dull names of their maternal relatives.

During the next two weeks the Sorensons visited Edinburgh for the little bits and pieces that would be required. Einer's Emporium in Boness was also visited. After all, Einer stocked some of the articles they sought and Norma and Emily were given the opportunity to talk about the forthcoming event.

As the womenfolk busied themselves with serious matters, the men were invited to make a rapid exit. According to Einer this was no hardship; it would be a relief, he assured Edward, to allow the women to develop their views on the hazards of motherhood.

As a novice, Edward had little option but to listen to the older and more experienced man. Asking Edward to sit back and relax, he promised to enlighten him regarding the 'signs'. First on the agenda would be morning sickness or nausea, then an insatiable appetite for certain foods and confections. This, he stressed, was considered normal and healthy, after all the potential mother was eating for two.

There are, however, spoilsports who aver that over-indulgence is probably the main cause of morning sickness. But pregnant women dismiss this theory with contempt; too many of them who have never over-indulged were still visited by a mysterious nausea in the morning. The over-indulgence theory they ascribed to propaganda disseminated by jealous spinsters.

Edward sighed as Einer heaped on the agony. There was also, of course, the leg swelling or 'kitchen sink syndrome' caused by standing too long in one position, washing, laundering and cooking for His Majesty the male.

Edward had listened long enough; he had heard it all before, but it did not equate with the healthy and happy pregnancy that Emily was so far enjoying. He scolded Einer for wasting his time.

"I know you are only attempting to pull my leg, Einer, but you might have chosen a subject where we both could have a good laugh."

The look on Edward's face convinced him he had been too loose in his talk about pregnancy. Einer's face was serious as he apologised.

"Blame the akvavit, Edward. I am sorry if I disturbed you unduly, but I'm afraid that Norma, having had two abortions, has made me a little cynical."

Edward smiled ruefully before replying. "Don't mention it and don't use the word 'abortion' again or I shall be very cross with you indeed."

Einer, saying nothing, took Edward's arm and ushered him into the front shop. As they walked into the emporium, he pointed towards the lifelike figure of the gold-braided captain. On this occasion the right arm was pointing towards a rather neat oak casket with a fine brass handle, which folded in to an insert when not in use.

"It's called the 'mariner's mate'," he said.

Seeing the look of puzzlement on Edward's face, he explained that the box contained all the tools and texts which ensured that an intelligent apprentice ship's officer could rise to the bridge in record time.

Edward knew he was expected to evaluate the sales potential of the new line, but he paid scant attention, he was more interested in a man outside the shop staring in at them. He voiced his thoughts.

"I wonder where I've seen that man before?"

Einer was annoyed and puzzled by his companion's off-hand attitude, but when he saw the man peering through the shop window, he understood the reason for the statement, but felt that Edward's motive was only one of diversion. Edward felt compelled to tell Einer that the man seemed more interested in them than the mariner's mate.

It was a surly and disconcerted Einer who replied that he couldn't care less, he had never seen the man in his life before.

The man was of medium build, he looked like a fit-at-fifty type and seemed to exude the confidence of the successful businessman or bookmaker. Even from a distance of thirty feet Edward could see that he had blue twinkling eyes, eyes that he had seen before, not so long ago.

As he tried to place the man in his mind, the man waved merrily towards him and then was gone before Edward could reach the door.

On the way home that evening, Edward's thoughts were preoccupied with the man who had demonstrated friendliness towards him, yet when he had moved towards him, the man had made a rapid exit. He wondered if it was someone he should have recognised. He recollected having seen him when Emily was shopping in Princes Street. Just as they were leaving Jenners, the man and his smile passed them on the way in

For some obscure reason he still thought about the man as he lay in bed. It was early morning before he remembered that the man with the smile had first materialised one day as he crossed Bernard Street on his way to the Sailor's Rest. He found this a little unnerving. Was this man someone operating on behalf of the drug smugglers, possibly detailed to keep an eye on his movements?

Almost immediately he discounted the idea. Surely if the man was engaged in such nefarious activity, he would not draw attention to himself the way he had - apart from the smile, his clothes certainly attracted attention. A man such as this could only be a friend. He decided to erase bad thoughts from his mind, pledging to stop the man next time he saw him and solve the mystery once and for all.

Mrs. McGregor appeared just after breakfast to tell him that Sven had missed them when they were at the Wevlings. Sven had left a message that he would be in Leith the following afternoon and would be happy to see Edward if it was convenient.

Curious to know what Sven had in mind, but not too keen to leave Emily, he asked her if she would like a trip through to Leith to see her cousin. She laughed and admitted she would like to have seen Sven and talk about the family back home, but she had already agreed with Mrs. McGregor on a bakery experiment. As the old woman nodded her head, Emily explained that for a long time she had asked Mrs. McGregor to show her the secret of real shortbread in exchange for know-how in making Swedish *clenetor*, a product which required similar ingredients.

Edward smiled wanly, as a good steward he was always interested in the preparation of food, but unlike the infant in the song, he did not love shortening bread, nor did he relish spending the afternoon possibly being involved in passing comment.

Had the subject been the preparation of dishes derived from protein such as prime steak, mature venison or succulent lobster, then he might have been interested. As it was, he felt that Emily and Mrs. McGregor would probably appreciate being left to their own devices, while he contacted Sven and spent the afternoon in a constructive fashion, such as imbibing beer and reminiscing about their days at sea.

Looking coyly at her husband, Emily expressed the opinion that he, as an expert, might like to see the result of their endeavours; in the meantime someone had to meet Sven and she hoped Edward would represent them both - he could always sample the end product when he returned.

Edward wore that solemn resigned look and then, realising he might have overplayed the part, smiled to his beloved and replied, "No problem, dear, I shall give your regards to Sven."

When he arrived at the Sailor's Rest, Sven, Rory and Sergeant McIllwraithe were already seated in their favourite corner. He had barely sat down before Sven had taken his order and left for the bar. Rory, a peculiar mixture of the solemn and the bluff, was at his heartiest as he greeted Edward.

"I am pleased to see you so happy and contented, Edward Sorenson. What haff you been doing these last few weeks?"

Edward smiled towards Rory, but seemed in no great hurry to reply, but the young Sergeant felt the urge to intervene.

"It seems he is reluctant to tell you, uncle."

Rory glowered at his nephew. "Haud your wheesht, gie the man time to sit doon and think."

As Sven returned, he explained that, not having seen Edward or Emily for some time, he had felt it appropriate to leave a note with the old lady. Unfortunately, he had mentioned it to Rory, who had expressed a desire to be present. However, he hoped Edward would tolerate the presence of the Scots.

Edward responded enthusiastically and, after a toast to the company, reassured Sven that his cousin was in good health and looking forward to the miracle of motherhood.

Turning to Rory, he answered his question, outlining that over the past month he had spent as much time as possible with Emily making plans for the future. They listened patiently, complimenting him on his behaviour, but it was towards the end when they were being too sympathetic that he became suspicious.

Had he known what was to follow, he would certainly not have been so frank. The rather exuberant and irreverent sympathy that he was now being subjected to was, to say the least, annoying and childlike. They sympathised with him on the basis that a young man suffered sympathy pains relative to his wife's condition. Did he, for example, suffer from morning sickness and what about his diet? Had he an insatiable appetite for toasted cheese?

Edward tolerated the laughter, even though it was at his expense. He knew he could win a contest based on repartee, but felt such a prolongation was demeaning to Emily and that he would not tolerate.

Producing a newspaper and spreading it up in front, he allowed the questions and laughter to continue, minus his participation. It was not long before Rory asked in a voice meant to be heard, "Something special in the paper, Edward?"

Edward had a radiant smile as he lowered his paper. Folding it neatly, he returned it to his pocket before replying.

"Nothing special in the paper, but what did you think about the three characters sitting round this table a moment ago, laughing and burbling such idiotic nonsense? Where they are now is indeed questionable, but I must say that it is comforting and a relief that my friends have returned."

As they sat there wondering, Edward good soul, rescued them from their mental confusion. "I see that your glasses require recharging."

When he returned, he could see the look betwixt amusement and amazement on their faces, telling him that he could now initiate the change in conversation that suited him. He took his time when setting down the drinks and, pointing to the glass in front of Rory, told him that although he knew his favourite tipple was from his own glen, he thought that on this occasion he might tolerate a 'dram of Buie'.

Rory, conversant with Edward's type of humour, appreciated the gesture and its description - the famous liqueur was certainly one of his favourites. He wondered at the resilience of the young Dane and knew now that the newspaper act had been solely engineered to make them think about the impropriety of their remarks.

He knew the young man had the knowledge, the linguistic ability and wit to have blasted them verbally; instead he had chosen a clever and friendly way to achieve his objective. Rory liked Edward and had every reason to do so; apart from his frankness and friendliness towards him, there was also his enthusiasm in helping Customs and Excise put the cocaine smugglers behind bars.

He had been prepared to take risks not expected from a civilian and had even inadvertently, through a misadventure, been responsible for the imprisonment of drug smuggling thugs.

This apart, he recognised that his friend was an unusual man, a man of character despite his all too often flippant attitude. Rory felt an appropriate toast was required.

"Here's to you, Edward Sorenson, you're a fine honest man."

Edward agreed that Rory only spoke the truth, but flattery would not divert him from enquiring what Rory had been up to those last few weeks. Rory looked at him solemnly and asked, "Surely you would not haff me give away state secrets?"

Edward's reply was thought-provoking. In his opinion, Rory was too honest to be in any way connected with state secrets, so called. Too often the term 'state secret', or 'for reasons of security', had been used 'patriotically' by corrupt politicians and greedy financiers as a cover for their anti-social activities.

Rory seemed ill at ease, but before he could reply, Edward continued.

"Neither you nor I are greedy or dishonest enough to have any appreciable effect on that rather sordid condition known as state security."

His main concern was for Rory's welfare; if he felt some items might place him in jeopardy, then he only required to keep his mouth shut. Rory seemed more relaxed now, he eased himself back in his chair, gave a little wicked smile and suggested they sit back, relax and he would tell them what had happened in the last two weeks.

He told them he would tell them everything, including state secrets, warts and all. As he told his story, he had Edward wondering if the big Highlander had after all been pulling his leg.

He had been appointed a co-ordinator in the fight against cocaine smuggling. Being the Chief Narcotics Officer in Leith Customs, he was expected to be in constant touch with fellow officers all the way from North Berwick to Inverness. As usual, the government expected maximum cover with the minimum number of men.

Manning difficulties apart, there was the tedium and boredom of the job, such as having to continually question suspects on board ships and in dockland pubs. On the odd occasion it could become exciting and sometimes extremely dangerous.

Often he worked in liaison with the local police, but found their legal code restrictive and too slow when dealing with slippery individuals. However, he realised they had a job to do and had instructions to do it their way; but on the other hand, the information he had received from a certain police source had ended in a number of drug smugglers being incarcerated for a long stretch.

He looked dotingly in the direction of his nephew as he spoke. He referred to a number of incidents that had proved rather hazardous and one in particular that had annoyed him immensely.

It concerned a successful rounding-up of five smugglers after a raid, in which more than one hundred kilos of cocaine had been unearthed. As the culprits were being led away, Rory was questioning the second steward of the Argentinian steam ship. Although Rory's linguistic ability was limited, the second steward had decided he was not to blame for what had happened, had whipped out a knife and made a slash at the Highlander.

Trying to parry the assault, his right arm had become a victim. His reaction had been fast and furious, he had kicked up in the direction of the South American's groin. Unfortunately for the attacker, he had fallen backwards into the hold of the ship. Although immobilised for several months and his sex life probably destroyed, Rory had little sympathy for him. It was not so much the gash in his forearm that had incensed him, it was the irreparable tear in his tweed jacket. He gave vent to his feelings.

"It wass my Aunt Morag who weaved the cloth specially for the chacket. Heavens, what she will say if she ever finds out!"

But there had been brighter moments when the police and customs had combined to question suspects diligently and peacefully, ending in admissions of guilt and smugglers sent off in the Black Maria to their fate.

Rory deplored the lack of public interest in drug addiction, stressing that little interest was shown unless the problem landed on their own doorstep.

Looking at Edward, he praised him for what he had done in combating crime. "I know you are an intelligent, but rather hasty individual, but you haff, either by accident or design, managed to confuse and scare our enemies into making mistakes. Believe me, I'm grateful for what you haff done, but for Christ's sake from now on, look after yourself. I want you to live a long and happy married life."

Acknowledging Rory's concern for his safety, Edward was still curious to know how Sergeant McIllwraithe had fared over the past few weeks. The Sergeant appeared reluctant, so Edward decided a little encouragement would not go amiss.

"I know you would not wish to boast, Sergeant, but having read of your exploits in the newspaper, I thought you might like to fill me in on anything interesting, particularly the Bridge Street affair, where I play; what might be called a minor role."

The Sergeant dithered and Rory impatiently intervened.

"Tell the man, Ian. After all, we've a lot to thank Edward for."

His tale was similar to the newspaper version and seemed devoid of the personal content that friends could have expected. Edward's curiosity was not satisfied, so he decided to up the tempo in his own fashion.

"Your report is rather colourless, Sergeant. Surely your friends could expect to hear something more personal and exciting?"

The Sergeant seemed rather prim as he replied, "Whether it be friend or foe, Mr. Sorenson, I always question impartially and report back accurately."

Edward was quick to accept that the Sergeant would conduct his business in a legal sense, but he was also sure he had the intelligence to use his own methods in achieving what he wanted and still keep within the law.

Before the young policeman could reply, Edward outlined the scenario as he saw it.

'Intelligent civilian observes suspicious character entering 13 Bridge Street, has reason to believe person concerned could be involved in illegal activity. Informs Police Sergeant, who is interested, but cautious, knowing he should acquire a search warrant.'

'Knowing that time is of the essence, evolves a method of entry which could be considered legal. The saving of life being paramount, he is distressed when he smells smoke. Having been informed that suspicious person had entered door named Napier, he concluded that it would be most convenient for smoke to emanate from that area.'

'Shouting 'fire', he breaks down door and finds place full of smoke from cigar of occupant, a Mr. Napier, who is concentrating assiduously on making up small packets of destructive dope.'

The Sergeant, who had tried to keep a straight face throughout, laughed and interrupted Edward's spiel.

"I would agree that civilian concerned is intelligent, but his view on what happened is pure fantasy."

Edward turned to Rory and asked, "As I was so rudely interrupted by your nephew Rory, I ask your permission as Chairman to carry on?"

Rory waved his assent and Edward proceeded. "Having caught his fish, he then grilled it carefully and set it upon a plate for his superiors."

Rory chuckled and gave his verdict. "Edward seems to know more about you than you know about him."

Ian smiled graciously and replied, "I haff already admitted that Edward is an intelligent civilian, but to infer that some type of third degree was used is ridiculous."

But Rory was enjoying himself and would not be denied.

"Come off it, young man, give us the hoary details, how you used the rack and pinion and the thumb screw to make the bugger confess."

But Ian paid no attention to his uncle's provocative remark. Instead he turned to Edward and asked if he had now satisfied him concerning the Bridge Street incident.

But Edward wondered what had happened to the wee man and was surprised when Ian pointed to a table just behind him. And there he sat, a diminutive miserable morsel of inhumanity, reading the Sporting Pink. The Sergeant spoke to him.

"I see Mr. Horsburgh has allowed you back into the lounge, Mr. Nesbit. I hope this means you haff decided to lead an honest life in future."

Mr. Nesbit's reaction was a nod of the head, accompanied by an ugly leering grimace. It disturbed Edward somewhat that the wee man might have heard their conversation. On the other hand, he was probably too cautious, for his companions seemed not in the least concerned.

Sven, who had played a minor part in the conversation, thought too much time had been absorbed in police politics and parochial affairs, when he was anxious to impart some news from the Scandinavian scene, particularly for Edward's benefit.

Rory nodded acknowledgement, admitting that Sven had arranged the meeting, but he had to take into consideration that any event in which Edward was involved could, to say the least, prove unpredictable.

Sven spent some minutes on general news from Denmark and Sweden, but when it came to family news from Sweden, he lapsed into the Swedish language. Suddenly he realised that Ian and Rory were talking in a different language. He apologised for being rude: after all, real friendship was surely based on everyone speaking in a language all could understand.

"No need to worry, my friend," said Rory and then added, "we assumed you were both interested in news from home, so Ian and I used the time to haff a wee blether, in the Gaelic of course."

Shortly after, the two Scots left to take up their respective duties, leaving Edward and Sven to a Scandinavian 'up-date'.

The tail end of the get-together had been friendly, but slightly boisterous and Edward had hesitated to fix a future date, saying he had not intended seeing them before the expected birth. It had ultimately been agreed that as the birth was expected at the end of July, it would be safe and proper to meet again on July 25th.

Although Edward had reluctantly agreed, he would have been more disturbed had he known that the wee man, Mr. Nesbit, had, while sitting behind his Sporting Pink, notched the date as something his superiors would be extremely interested in.

Chapter 21

It was Sunday, it was June and Emily's time was drawing near. Right from the moment she had told him she was expecting a child, he had spent more time with her and less time business-wise.

Surprisingly Edward's earning power had increased, it was his belief that having less time to operate, he had been more selective in the orders he pursued. Whatever the reason, he was satisfied that his income was rising and Emily was happy with his company.

Being a restless man, however, he felt he should be more active, not just relaxing and trusting that the Gods would continue to look upon him and his kin as a protected species. Edward could not tolerate spare time, time was there to be used, he had to be doing something, something special and Emily had to be part of it.

Emily was happy now. There had been moments of despair when she felt she would never learn the English language, but love, patience and Edward's linguistic ability had plotted a course that had enabled her to learn the rudiments of the strange new language.

Edward felt the Highland honeymoon had laid the base for a happy marriage in the land of the Scots. Meeting the Scandinavians and their Scottish friends had convinced Emily that this could be a happy land.

However, Edward considered this was no reason for sitting still and, feeling that a widening of their horizon would prove interesting and enjoyable, his thoughts turned in the direction of a short holiday. With an eye to the future, a trip towards Perth and then over to the East coast could be just what Emily required; to familiarise herself with life so near their home.

As Emily walked towards the kitchen, Edward asked her brightly, "Would you like a hand with the dishes?"

She turned, smiled and gave a throaty chuckle. "I think you'd rather go fishing, Edward," she said.

Edward, always ready to encourage his wife to think positively, agreed readily and set off immediately for Boness. As he cycled towards Einer's Emporium, he gave thought to the logistics of a mini-holiday. Travelling by bus or train could mean much wasted time transferring luggage from transport to the hotel, or bed and breakfast. The only solution appeared to be the transportation of Emily, himself and their requirements by automobile.

An ironic smile played around his lips as he thought of his attitude towards the petrol-driven car a year ago. His aversion towards the smell of petrol and exhaust fumes had made him dub that type of motive power the 'infernal combustion engine'.

Since then, however, he had found the acquisition of a small motor boat had given him the edge over some of his competitors. Einer was interested, but surprised when Edward told him it was his intention to acquire a car for holiday purposes. He was amused at Edward's reaction and reply when he asked if he had ever driven a car before.

Edward informed him, quite blithely, he could see no problem. Apart from the basic knowledge required, he cited the remarks of Oskar, Harry MacSween and the landlord of the Sailor's Rest. They had all encouraged him to purchase a car and thus increase his earnings; they would not have done so had they thought there would be any difficulty in driving it.

He smiled at Edward's attempt at being naive. "Come off it, Edward," he said, "you are trying to inveigle me into giving you free driving lessons."

Edward was unrepentant and replied breezily, "How right you are! When do we start?"

Einer gave a sigh of resignation, shook his head and indicated it could absorb a bit of time, but as it was Sunday and most pedestrians were in church, this was probably the best time to start learning.

Edward looked quizzically at his friend and replied that with Einer's expert tuition the possibility of knocking down a pedestrian was extremely remote.

Einer stopped the car some miles from Boness on a road overlooking the Forth Bridge and, pointing to a train crossing over to the Fife side asked Edward if he could differentiate between a railway engine and a motor car. Edward gave the expected answer: the size and power of the steam engine was far greater than Einer's car.

Einer persisted that he wanted an answer relative to the task in hand. Edward shrugged his shoulders and cheerily admitted defeat. But Einer was serious and advised his friend to listen carefully, insisting that at all times he must recognise that the car, unlike the train, did not run on a fixed line system and therefore his hands must remain on the steering wheel.

On the second test Edward did quite well, he could recognise the magneto, the carburettor, knew how they worked and was conversant with the position of the clutch, brake and accelerator pedals. To say that he passed with flying colours would indeed be an exaggeration, but after three hours Einer was satisfied that Edward would concentrate on safety and was prepared to trust him with his car.

He must have felt confident indeed when he offered to loan his car for five days. Edward protested that his friend was too kind; surely it would be better if he hired a car, after all the hire company would be adequately insured.

Einer insisted that he should take advantage of the offer and gave him his first instruction.

"Drive me home safely now, Edward. The car is your responsibility; if you fail to return it in five or six days, I will retain your bike as security."

Edward could not resist the riposte, "Your car will be returned in good time and shape. I could never face Tam Richards if I lost him his all-weather Sunbeam."

Emily recognised the Wevling's car, but was mystified and concerned when she saw no sign of Einer. The essence of diplomacy is knowing when to keep the mouth shut. As an adjunct to this, the telling of the truth should be rationed relative to the expected happiness of all concerned.

It was a hesitant Emily who asked, "I did not know you could drive, Edward?"

Edward was most reassuring. "Yes, I can drive, Emily - at least Einer thinks so. After all, had he thought otherwise, he would not have loaned us his car."

Although he had originally decided to hire a car, Einer had insisted that they should make use of his car; he had little option but to accept the kind offer, they would of course repay him for his kindness in the near future.

The following morning a relaxed and happy mother-to-be sat beside her smiling, but rather introspective husband, as he drove the car very carefully towards Stirling. As the miles went by the more confident he became, but he bore in mind to concentrate and remember that although he had control, he had to be ready to take evasive action should he be unfortunate enough to be placed at hazard by another motorist driving in a dangerous fashion.

By the time they reached Stirling, Edward felt he could now claim to be a motorist of sorts, while his wife looked at him with pride and complimented him on his smooth driving.

A visit to Stirling Castle and the Wallace Memorial gave Edward the opportunity to relax and examine his potential as a car driver, while Emily, much to his surprise, seemed to know more about Scotland's hero than he could possibly have expected. As they left Stirling, Emily admitted that Lady Margaret MacKaskill had talked quite a bit about Scottish history.

It was late in the afternoon when they reached Crieff and Edward, although satisfied that the journey so far had been trouble-free, felt apprehensive when he saw the narrow streets and parked cars and carts through which he would have to manoeuvre in search of a bed and breakfast.

Common sense dictated he should park the car and seek lodgings on foot, but vanity prevailed. He stuck grimly to his task and delegated to Emily the important task of informing him when she saw a reputable looking B and B.

As he threaded his way between tradesman's vans and private cars, he saw down a side street the magic sign 'Visitors Welcome'.

Travelling slowly down, he passed a number of well-kept cars, an indication that the hostelry could well be worthy of consideration. His skill as a driver was now called into question and with Emily acting as pilot, he decided to reverse into the courtyard. Starting off with a jerk, his mind flashed back to Einer's lesson on the three point turn; he immediately attuned his feet accordingly and swung sweetly through the opening, coming to a stop a full foot away from the back retaining wall.

Emily was relieved, but proud that her man had achieved such a remarkable manoeuvre and Edward summoned up a broad smile, assuring his wife that as the holiday progressed he would get used to the peculiarities of Einer's car.

Ensuring that Emily felt safe, he approached what hopefully might be a safe haven for the night. The entrance to the establishment was in the main street and boasted, appropriately for an agricultural area, the sign 'The Plough'.

On entering he was agreeably impressed. The place was spacious and clean and, as might be expected, the public bar was occupied by local workers and farm servants just finished their stint on the real plough, while at the top end sat the farmers and businessmen on their bar stools.

After the affable landlord greeted him, he asked if he could provide a comfortable night's rest and sustenance for his wife and himself for the evening and the following morning. Pointing to a room marked 'jug bar', he advised Edward to enter and ring the hotel bell, he was sure that Mrs. McNab, his wife, would be able to accommodate them.

Mrs. McNab, a jovial buxom woman, seemed attracted to the rather shy good-looking Mrs. Sorenson and was eager she should come upstairs and examine a room that was available for the night. Emily was indeed satisfied and complimented Mrs. McNab on the cleanliness of everything in the room, particularly the bed sheets, which she examined carefully.

Edward said nothing, but thought back to the time when courting Emily; Sven had warned him that Emily could be very fussy. Fussy or not, the two women seemed to have something in common, they chatted cheerily, there appeared to be few language difficulties, their rapport was such that Edward felt he was merely a spectator.

Never one to waste time, he felt it necessary to intervene and, excusing himself for interrupting, he asked the good lady if she would be able to provide an evening meal. Folding her arms across her ample breasts, she beamed him a smile and told him she would not only provide an excellent meal, she would serve it in the comfort and privacy of their own room.

Emily's reaction puzzled Edward: although she had thanked Mrs. McNab, she had stressed there was no need to hurry, two or three hours hence would be time enough.

As Mrs. McNab left, Emily caught sight of Edward's look and hastened to inform him it was her intention to have a bath and then leisurely pay attention to some small items she required in the near future. He was learning now that when women are involved in making a decision, mere man is like a child to be seen but not heard.

Apparently, when women showed signs of exchanging confidences, a man was an even bigger nuisance and should contrive to make himself invisible. Being a true democrat, he excused himself, attended to the luggage and sought information to facilitate a smooth journey on the following day.

Having armed himself with the ingredients so essential for blissful relaxation in a man's world, he proceeded to a small table at the top end of the bar and sat back comfortably in a well-padded chair. As he quaffed his beer and sipped his whisky, his thoughts turned to the overall organising of the holiday. Einer had supplied him with maps and holiday brochures to assist him in planning his route, but he felt a little local knowledge would not go amiss.

Scanning the bar, he knew there was someone who would be only too pleased to oblige. Returning to the bar for a refill, he asked Mr. McNab if there was anyone near at hand who could give him the information he desired. Nodding discreetly in the direction of a young man speaking to a group of farmers, he informed Edward that Mr. Ross was the very man to ask.

He settled back in his chair, awaiting the opportunity to button-hole the smartly dressed Mr.

Ross. Slowly the group dispersed until only the young man was left. As Edward started to rise, Mr. McNab called to the young man, spoke a few words, pointed in his direction and the young man came towards him.

It appeared that Mr. Ross was the Scottish representative of a chemical company dealing in fertilisers and other agricultural products and was well qualified to comment and advise on places that should be visited.

Having acquired the information he wanted, Edward felt he should display an interest in the young man's profession. Mr. Ross was only too pleased to tell him about his negotiations with farmers. Like many salesmen, he inserted the odd anecdote, but on one aspect he was very serious: he considered he was extremely fortunate to have been chosen to work among the hills and dales of a country that, in his estimation, was the most beautiful on earth.

Edward discovered that his operational base was in Edinburgh, but it was the mentioning of the place Ferry Road that brought forth an involuntary cough from him.

Mr. Ross, a rather smart chap, realised that Edward had distinctly reacted to the mention of Ferry Road and came straight to the point.

"Tell me, Mr. Sorenson, what is your particular interest in the Leith area?"

Edward knew he had to be equally frank and referred to the Stenka Maru affair where a local branch of a national chemical firm had been compromised when cocaine had been found in sacks of fertiliser.

Before Mr. Ross could reply, he told him he was fully conversant with what had happened and, as a fellow salesman, he was in possession of information that an American adventurer was the real trouble-maker. The young salesman smiled ironically and expressed himself positively.

"You can say that again! That bastard Chancitt, or Chalmers as we knew him, caused the company no end of trouble."

Determined to voice his opinion of the real character of the drug traffickers, he cited the case of his young brother, an engineer, who in common with many other time-served engineers had left their native land to seek a worthwhile recompense for their skills in foreign parts.

Although his brother had been rewarded for his skills, his experience of life in Colombia had soured him somewhat. The abject poverty and appalling conditions in which the coca workers gathered in the beans so essential in the manufacture of cocaine, had sickened him. Anyone who had the temerity to stand against the cocaine cartel was soon eliminated.

It was against this background that Mr. Ross praised the individual who had been brave enough to supply vital information to the police. What he said then was the last thing Edward wanted to hear, particularly as his mind had been occupied with ensuring that Emily would enjoy the short holiday.

"As I was saying, Mr. Sorenson, I am happy that Yankee has been exposed and I hope the police will see to it that the man who had the courage to expose him will be protected from that murderous gang."

There was little doubt that Emily was happy, she was singing her favourite Swedish ballad softly to herself as she entered their room. She had immensely enjoyed bathing in the big beautiful bath, relic of a more leisurely period, installed when the building had been the manor house of the local laird, who, no doubt determined to enjoy all the creature comforts, had seen to it that only the best materials had been used, commensurable with his high office.

Emily had stepped from the elegant bath in a state of near ecstasy, had crossed over to their rather special room and lowered herself lazily into the back of the large comfortable sofa facing the log fire sparking away in the fireplace.

Emily, a Swedish country woman coming from a healthy but rather austere regime, felt that this was just the time to luxuriate when surrounded by the trappings of an opulent past. Having accepted Mrs. McNab's suggestion that the evening meal could be served in their room, she knew she had still an hour to relax and dream.

As she combed and dressed her hair, she took stock of her surroundings. Directly in front of her the sparks from the log fire were prevented from flying freely by a brass screen. A closer examination revealed that fine brass gauze ensured that no embers could reach the deep pile of the carpet. She was attracted to the artistic decoration of the fire guard. Embedded in the interstices of the brass was a circle of white metalled Scottish thistles and in the centre an enamelled coat of arms consisting of two crossed claymores, surmounted by a picture of what a Scotsman might concede to be the Monarch of the Glen.

Returning to the sofa, she lay back and conjectured that the sight of the magnificent fully grown deer probably indicated that the original owner of the house had at one time been a Baron whose lands included a deer forest.

Looking upwards to the ceiling, her eyes followed the ornate cornice decoration; although both were coloured sky blue, the beauty of white Grecian figures were thrown into relief by the white margin above and below the cornice itself.

Even the ornate oak panels at the windows and on the doors belonged to a period some two hundred years before.

But it was the bed that intrigued her most. It was the biggest she had ever seen; it had four posts, seven feet in height; at the top of each could be seen brass rings, a clue that told of nights when an awning had been stretched over the top with curtains completely enclosing the bed.

She remembered having seen a picture of a similar bed in which, as the caption would have it, slept a beautiful Russian Tsarina. The picture had been painted in the latter part of the eighteenth century and illustrated in detail the rich colours and texture of the brocades and other textiles that had enveloped the bed.

This bed was devoid of such fripperies. Instead it had a plain quilt cover, a blanket and a clean white sheet. She was apprehensive when she turned back the covers, having heard that the nobility were always feather-bedded. She gave a sigh of relief when she felt the firmly sprung mattress instead of the claustrophobic, unsupportive mass of feathers that she associated with spinal deformities, mites and fleas, depending on the value the occupants placed on personal hygiene.

When Edward entered she was still singing; happy and excited, she outlined to him the main features of their room. From what she had seen, she had formed the opinion that much of the furniture and decoration was at least two hundred years old. Pointing to the large four-poster, she invited him to examine it closely.

Edward smiled at his wife's exuberance, but did not move fast enough for Emily. A trifle impatient, she took him over to the giant bed. As he stood there silent and still smiling, she felt compelled to take action. Placing the palms of her hands on his chest as if to caress him, she gave a little wicked smile as she pushed vigorously, sending him flying backwards onto the bed.

As he bounced up and down she fell on top of him, to prove, as she said, that the bed although old, had a modern dynamic spring about it.

Edward cradled Emily firmly in his arms, agreeing that the bed was big, beautiful and indeed bouncy, wondering if the honeymoon would have been better served in such a remarkable four-poster. Emily kissed him passionately and agreed that one good turn surely deserved another.

He accepted the logicality of female thought in the sphere of love and affection, but added he would have to be fed for the pleasant task in hand. Laughingly Emily pushed him aside, saying that Mrs. McNab had promised to serve dinner in half an hour.

Edward left and five minutes later returned with their pre-dinner drinks. As they toasted each other, he noticed his wife's thoughts were elsewhere and when he asked what was troubling her, she confessed that Mrs. McNab had told her that dinner would be served by a waiter who was dumb and as far as she knew this probably meant the poor man was also deaf.

Although amused, he was sensible, knowing that he had initially to reassure her that she was probably having difficulty with the language and told her that after dinner he would show her she need not have been in the least concerned.

Shortly after, a beaming Mrs. McNab entered and set the table, followed almost immediately by serving mussels from, as she said, the Royal Burgh not far from their own home. But it was not Musselburgh that jogged Edward's memory, it was Mussel Meg from Newhaven dispensing the succulent bi-valves from her small cart at the Tron in Edinburgh.

As he toyed with the molluscs, his mind flashed back to the first time he saw Meg emerging from the sea, her gorgeous figure wet, but so inviting. The long walks and glorious times they had experienced would remain with him for a long time. His scarlet reverie was interrupted by Mrs. McNab enquiring if there was anything wrong with the mussels.

Caught unawares, he felt sheepish, but managed a smile and told her he considered Scottish mussels to be the perfect hors d'oeuvre and had been taking his time enjoying the flavour to the full.

After a dinner of Scotch Broth, legally acquired salmon poached à la McNab, haggis, tatties and neeps, the Sorensons relaxed, contemplating whether a sweet was really necessary or should they just finish with a cognac and coffee.

As Mrs. McNab cleared the table, Edward thought the time opportune to further Emily's education. After complimenting Mrs. McNab on the excellence of the meal, he asked her if she would be kind enough to show Emily the dumb waiter she had referred to earlier in the evening.

Emily, taken aback, protested mildly, feeling that the deaf man's dignity could be adversely affected, but Mrs. McNab's attitude and reply reassured her slightly.

"Come through with me to the restaurant, my dear, and let me show you our dumb waiter."

She led them over to a picture some three feet square; the picture consisted of a scroll listing a number of McNab's gastronomic delights, accompanied by the current price. Turning to Emily she explained.

"As you can see, this waiter does not speak, the customer can read at leisure and order accordingly."

The centre of the picture showed a basket of fruit, allowing the landlady to grasp an apple in one hand and an orange in the other, pull and 'hey presto' two panels swung out exposing a space three feet square by three feet deep. Resting on the base was the remains of the Sorenson dinner. Mrs. McNab explained that the waiter had to be manually operated, pulling on a rope she sent the crockery off down to the bar.

Edward intervened and asked if she would be kind enough to order coffee and cognac for two and she did just that using the speaking tube connected to the bar.

It was an abashed and happy Emily who was relieved to know that she would not have to converse with a dumb and deaf person. But Mrs. McNab was not finished, she felt the urge to elaborate. Pointing to the serving hatch, she told her that in the old days food and drink had to be carried upstairs from the kitchen and empties returned via the same route. Yes, the dumb waiter had a number of advantages, one of which was it never spoke back, hence the name the 'dumb waiter'.

Back in their room, Edward's suppressed laughter gradually oozed out and while Emily chided him, he encouraged her to try and see the funny side; after all, he had assured her that there was no real cause for concern. He was not laughing at her, but at the human situation which had arisen; there was no malice and he hoped she would laugh with him.

She responded and they were still laughing when Mrs. McNab entered with the coffee and cognac.

It had been a wonderful experience for Emily, even remarkable in a way. She had been agreeably surprised at her husband's ability to drive the car so smoothly and thought he deserved a special commendation for the efficient way in which he had reversed the car into the courtyard of the 'Plough'.

She had enjoyed every minute sitting in front with him watching the sun-speckled East Scottish scene roll by. As a farmer's daughter she could appreciates that Scottish farmers were efficient; this she could see in the state of the land, the lush meadows and the healthy animals.

She loved in particular the magnificent horses. The rather squat Swedish Dalarna horses compared unfavourably when judged alongside the bigger and better-proportioned Scottish Clydesdale.

A fine day in the country had ended successfully when they had the good fortune to enter 'The Plough'.

From the beginning, Emily and Mrs. McNab had established a friendly rapport, each seeing in the other qualities they admired and respected. During her inspection of the room, she had come across the hotel tariff and knew that their landlady was intent on treating Edward and herself as special guests.

Edward agreed with his wife's summing up, but had certain reservations concerning his skill as a driver. Although in a way confident that he could drive, he had no intention of mentioning to Emily his reservations concerning his heavy responsibility in ensuring her guaranteed safety.

Consequently, he saw little of the scenery, his full attention being given to driving at an average of twenty miles per hour and not taking his eye off the road for more than a second at a time. His mind could not encompass the efficiency or otherwise of Scottish farmers, he was too absorbed with the do's and don'ts of automotive engineering.

At the halfway stage with the engine purring gently, Edward had felt momentarily relaxed, until he thought 'what if the engine stops, what then?' Einer had certainly given him a crash course on what to do should an emergency arise, but he felt the twenty minute lesson on the function of the magneto, the carburettor and transmission did not equip him to deal effectively should a mishap arise.

He knew he had neither the knowledge or the expertise to diagnose the simplest malfunction. Basically an optimist, he had decided to forget about things he might not be able to handle and concentrate on the road ahead. It was imperative he should avoid sharp objects which could puncture the tyres. At least he knew how to change a wheel and should the car stop, he knew how to check the petrol level.

He reckoned that until he acquired the knowledge to tackle all emergencies, he had no option but to trust to good old providence. Having emptied his mind of any dross of despair, he decided to relax and enjoy the holiday.

Having finished his drink, he lit a marcella and instantly apologised to Emily for having lit his cigar in what, after all, was their bedroom, even if it was only for a night. Emily smiled benignly at her man and told him not to concern himself unduly with social manners and bedroom hygiene; after all, the bedroom was so spacious that their house in Grangemouth could have been fitted in and would still leave room to spare.

Pointing to the big four-poster almost twenty feet away, she said that it was their bedroom and where they were sitting was the living room for the time being. Edward nodded agreement and puffed away contentedly and, on seeing her empty her glass, asked if she required a refill. She was about to accept, but when she thought it would entail Mrs. McNab providing further service, she shook her head.

But Edward had read her thoughts and asked her to relax, then levering himself from the depths of the comfortable sofa, walked to the far end of the room, opened the door of the massive built-in wardrobe, disappeared for a few seconds and then came back to his wife carrying a bottle.

"No problem, Emily," he said, "we have glasses and we now have a bottle of the best French brandy."

She agreed he was indeed an efficient steward, that she would accept one more refill for the rest of the evening and encouraged him to smoke his cigar. She liked the aroma of a good quality cigar and felt it would complement the atmosphere of such a splendid old room.

She sat back and savoured the experience of living, at least for an evening, in the style of a rich and privileged lady of the eighteenth century, with the added bonus of modern plumbing and boudoir hygiene.

Edward, having already imbibed in the bar down below, was 'unco' happy and agreed that their temporary quarters were reminiscent of pictures he had seen of baronial splendour.

For the rest of the evening they talked about their good fortune in having booked in at Mrs. McNab's hotel and their future programme. Edward outlined what had taken place in the public bar, how he had met a young salesman who had provided useful information for the following day. It was his intention, if Emily agreed, that they could travel in the direction of Pitlochry, he was sure she would be interested in the trees of the area.

Emily smiled her agreement, stretched her arms lazily backwards, then rising gracefully, she approached her husband and putting her arms around his neck, kissed him and said only one word, "*Seng.*"

Edward accepted the invitation with the decorum and degree of enthusiasm it merited.

There could be little doubt that the magnificent bed held centre stage; its stout oak frame had supported many players over the past two hundred years. Over the years many actors had descended upon this bed and played their particular parts. Be it comedy, tragedy, farce or fiasco, the whole gamut of human emotions had reverberated through its strong oak timbers.

The Scandinavians stretched themselves full out on the well-sprung modern mattress, hoping and trusting they would experience a restful, serene and happy night. They started with fingers just touching; then, grasping hands, they edged closer, the holiday conversation gradually phasing out and pillow talk taking over. Endearments flowed back and forth while Emily lay cradled in Edward's arms. The amorous exchanges were interrupted when Emily asked a very delicate question.

"When you were eating your mussels, Edward, you had a look of bliss on your face. Surely they were not all that good?"

He knew he had to be economic with the truth.

He admitted it was pure coincidence; the mussels had made him think of the sea and against the background of the sea he had a vision of a very beautiful woman. She stirred uneasily, but before she could react he reassured her that she was the woman.

As she melted in his arms, he felt a stab of pain in the solar plexus, the region known to romantics as the soul, but so far unidentified by anatomists. His inner voice ('Little Eric') had certainly dealt him a hefty blow and was still castigating him for his lying and cheating.

He looked at Emily and could see she had accepted his story. She smiled sleepily, curled closer and a minute later fell fast asleep.

But sleep for Edward was still some time away, his inner voice was still nagging him. He was relieved that his immediate problem had been smoothed over and Emily was fast asleep; she looked so innocent, his heart grieved at his behaviour in having lied.

His thoughts then turned to the earlier part of the evening and his conversation with Mr. Ross, the young salesman. He had reminded him that Chancitt's employers would be gunning for the informer who had interfered with their plans and cost them dearly in profits.

He fervently hoped they had contracted an advanced state of amnesia and had forgotten his very existence. And then there was the man who always smiled and disappeared - was he friend or foe?

Edward realised that such negative thinking would prevent sleep, but he knew from experience that pleasant positive thoughts would ensure ultimate tranquillity and sleep would surely follow.

He started at the beginning. He remembered his mother as a loving, serious and religious person; he once heard his father say she was the milk of human kindness. Having been breast-fed, he could hardly disagree, but as a very young child he felt his mother could have been less stern and demanding, particularly when she upbraided him during any lapse in personal hygiene.

He realised later that his father had in mind the good work of his mother in looking after and caring for others in the fishing village who were, in her estimation, some way disadvantaged. His more recent memory was her kindness and anxiety when he had to leave the island and join the Danish Navy. He wondered if she would have in any way been assuaged had she known he would be rubbing shoulders with the Crown Prince of Denmark.

Thereafter came the sailing days to places with strange sounding names. It had been a hard but eventful and rewarding experience aboard the big sailing ships, conditioning him to look and observe the mysteries beyond their ports of call.

Love, life and learning had dominated his thinking and although a competent seaman with a knowledge of navigation higher than average, he had no desire to emulate Columbus in a modern sense; he would rather trace a path in the fashion of Darwin.

He focused not so much on animal evolution, more on man's development and behaviour within his own environment. His love of life and happiness was conditioned, as he saw it, by a state of mind. When greed and power were the motivating force, then man could expect the power of evil to take over, presaging destruction, death and ultimate disillusionment. But when need and the dignity of the human race were paramount, then the foundation for eternal happiness became a distinct possibility.

Knowing that an attempt to solve world problems could keep him awake all night, he decided to short-circuit and switch over to man's relationship with his natural mate.

Edward liked women and was happy that most women liked him; his friendly manner, his smiling eyes and obvious frankness captivated them. They felt at ease in his company and appreciated his desire to converse in their language or dialect. With Edward no subject was taboo; although much of the time was absorbed in chatting gently about the real meaning of life and love, there could be little doubt that the best time to learn was when Edward was around.

As he stretched out on the big bed, he wondered why he had been so successful and decided to file it back in his memory bank for future consideration. The immediate exercise being one of recording pleasant thoughts, he considered some of his more amorous moments.

Appropriately it had been in the Friendly Islands that he had fallen in love with a dusky maiden. The romance had lasted two full days before being whisked back to sea. For six months he remembered her, then sailing ships changed to steam and a new era was born.

Joining an American steamship as steward, he had made friends with Sven, who was second engineer. They had become as thick as thieves and stuck close together, particularly on shore leave. The ship had berthed in a Turkish port and they had set out to explore the local scene. They had ultimately ended up in a bazaar chatting up two sisters who, between them, managed the main textile and sweetmeat stalls.

Edward, having convinced them that he and his companion were interested in Eastern culture, were invited home to meet the family.

The Patriarch sat sucking his hookah, his dispassionate eyes betraying no sign of what he thought of the two handsome young men who had escorted home his two beautiful daughters. He was naturally suspicious; after all, seamen were a transitory tribe and they were also infidels. His womenfolk had to be protected, he had no intention of allowing developments to arise whereby he would be obliged, in nine months' time, to accept two young infidels into the family circle.

However, as a Moslem, he was polite and treated them as honoured guests. Edward could be very convincing, although his Turkish vocabulary was limited; he inserted Arabic quotations to fill the gaps and it seemed to work.

The old man smiled at his linguistic gymnastics, but was impressed by his frankness and sincerity in wishing to know about the customs and economy of the country.

As the conversation developed, it appeared the daughters played a significant part in the family business. On alternate days, they worked at the market and then at the family orchard and small textile factory.

Always interested in languages, Edward's attention had now been drawn to the body language of the young women. The taller of the two seemed attracted to Sven and, as her beautiful eyes met his, she inclined her head slowly and gracefully towards the door and with a 'Mona Lisa'-like smile, smoothed out her skirt in the region of her thighs.

It was Edward's turn now and he was pleased it was the vivacious sister who had decided to attract his attention. He had to be careful, he was sure the old Patriarch would not welcome an atmosphere of laissez-faire as far as his daughters were concerned.

He held the old man's attention, but from the corner of his eye he could see her body language hotting up by the second. He seized his opportunity when the old man found it necessary to do a bit of plumbing maintenance on his hookah. Turning swiftly to a potential source of Eastern promise, he gave her a flashing smile, winked and nodded approval and she replied with a 'come hither' eye and a slight gurgle of delight. Edward hoped earnestly that the old man would consider it to have been a gaseous gurgle from his smoking machine.

It was at this stage that Edward was diverted from the path of righteousness and tempted by eroticism afore-thought. He initiated a ploy to satisfy the demands of the flesh.

In true entrepreneurial spirit he outlined to the Patriarch that he and Sven, as potential exporters and importers, had considered for some time that there could be a growth market for Turkish sweetmeats and rugs in Scandinavia. The old man, envisaging valuable Swedish kroners flowing in his direction, was only too willing to allow the two young men to visit the family enterprise.

However, as much as he would have liked to accompany them to the farm and the factory to assess the profitability of the venture, his legs were acting up. Would they therefore be prepared to accompany his daughters who, after all, had been running the business and they could then discuss the feasibility of a joint effort?

Edward's audacity had taken the wind out of Sven's sails and being an engineer, not experienced in sailing close to the wind, the latter left it to his companion to make the decision.

Edward felt a trifle mean, but assuaged his conscience when he considered the old man's readiness to risk his daughters' integrity and possibly their virginity in his quest for wealth, surely it would be better to leave the decision to the women.

Looking directly at them, he asked if they would be prepared to allow two foreigners the honour of accompanying them to their place of work. The tall one looked at Sven, averted her eyes and then, smiling demurely, nodded her assent. Her sister was more positive, sheltered from the gaze of her father, she winked to Edward and enthusiastically agreed.

The orchard and the carpet factory nestled in a wooded grove at the foothills of a mountain range some three or four miles from the port. It was a warm and relaxing day; to have conducted business under such conditions would have been the height of irresponsibility, it was definitely a day meant for enjoyment.

Edward floated the idea that the weather and the magnificent scenery were so idyllic that it would surely be wrong to spend time indoors at the factory or wandering around the orchard.

Surprisingly, it was the more reserved sister who suggested they walk a mile further into the adjoining forest. They followed the course of a swift-running stream until it opened out to a glade of flowering shrubs, in the centre of which a deep pool gurgled slowly and peacefully.

Something happened then that the two could not have expected. As they walked Edward was aware of her playing up to Sven. She talked in her own language, assuming that he, like Edward, would understand.

Edward interjected in Swedish, telling Sven to watch his head; if the reply was to be yes, he would nod his head; if no, it would be side to side. Would he like to see the very special place where she worshipped her God? Sven, ever watchful, nodded his head vigorously and she smiled her approval. In imperious fashion she asked them to stand still while she paid obeisance to her God.

Sinking slowly to her knees she muttered something which to Edward seemed unintelligible. He could only assume that as a Moslem she was praying, as she faced in the direction of Mecca.

Then standing up straight, she stripped herself naked and advanced to the edge of the pool and assumed a posture of invocation. With her arms outstretched towards the sun, she asked that Islam should recognise her intention to cleanse her body and soul.

The men, not particularly concerned with religious ritual, were intensely interested in its earthly manifestation.

At that moment Svelta, for that was her name, appeared, at least to Sven, like a Goddess. Her elegant and beautifully-proportioned body was a delight to behold; her skin a light bronze colour highlighted by the sun, shone like gold.

Having hopefully assuaged the Deity, she dived into the cool clear water. Some seconds later, while still in a trance-like state, the men were alerted by a splash, the younger woman having joined her sister.

It would have been most impolite not to join them and seconds later the women were deciding who their respective partners should be. Svelta's eyes were fixed on Sven - at that moment he was the perfect companion, tall, blond and handsome, with an aura of studious dignity about him. Both were good swimmers and swam together in a synchronised fashion, much to the amusement of Edward who, although recognising their aquatic skills, felt that this was no time to swim up and down the pool a few yards apart; surely they should be in close contact, enjoying each other's company, at least that was his view.

It was the look of disdain on Svelta's face that convinced Edward that she was either a devout disciple of Plato or an adept tantalizer.

It had been a disturbing experience to have their hopes raised and then the prospect of delight so readily dashed. He felt cheated, there was no way he could believe that platonic friendship could be deemed compatible with nude bathing. Never one to hypothesize when nature called, he swam over to Svelta's sister, knowing she would probably look with favour at what he was about to suggest.

As they trod water, he told her he liked her and he had a plan. Did she like him and would she like to know what he had in mind? She nodded approval and they swam back towards the bank until they could stand upright.

It was here that Edward went through the formality of proper introductions. He knew she had already learned his name, but he had not been granted the privilege of knowing her name. She looked at him coyly and told him her mother and father had decided she should be known as Ekkstra.

He put forward his arms and, resting his hands at the level of her breasts, he looked into her hazel eyes and in her language told her she was very beautiful and he liked her very much.

She smiled, gave a little gurgle of delight and threw her arms around his neck. In her excitement to reach his lips she propelled him backwards. As they submerged, he gripped her round the waist for support and, finding the experience very pleasant, held onto her longer than he should have for safety.

When they surfaced she giggled and spluttered, reassuring him that she was quite capable of staying under water for a considerable period of time. Pointing to the other two swimming sedately up and down, Edward asked if she wanted to copy them or was she interested in knowing what he had in mind?

Glancing at the swimmers, Ekkstra crinkled her nose, a sure sign that she did not approve. She was sure he could offer something more exciting.

He pointed to the river bank and suggested they should sit down and discuss his idea. Levering himself up, he encouraged her to join him. She made a ladylike attempt, but fell rather short and, as could be expected, Edward was ready to rescue his maiden in distress.

Sitting safely on the bank, he put his arms round her waist and drew her close so that she more readily might hear what he had to say.

Variety being the spice of life, he had various ideas in mind. First the diving competition, where the one who dived the furthest before grounding would be judged the winner. Next, the first swimmer would dive in and swim to the opposite bank, three seconds later the second swimmer would set out to catch up before the bank was reached and if successful would be adjudged the winner.

There followed other suggestions, one considered rather controversial called water leap frog.

Each category would have a prize or a forfeit which would be mandatory. Ekkstra asked what was meant by the word forfeit and was told that it was the price paid by the loser of the competition to the winner. Seeing she was still bemused, he explained the forfeit could either be a coin or a kiss.

She laughed engagingly and agreed that kisses were far more acceptable; after all, coins reminded her too much of working in the bazaar.

A natural extrovert, she accepted his challenge in her own vivacious fashion. Stepping to the edge of the bank, she dived out as far as she could and Edward dived before she reached her target. As she came up to record her distance, she heard a movement behind her and there he was, his arms outstretched, grinning and indicating that he was ready to receive his prize.

She shook her head and swam back to the bank, complaining that he must have swum under the water, therefore he was disqualified and she was the victor. Edward agreed that she was correct and therefore he was the one who had to pay the forfeit.

He enveloped her in his arms and gave her a resounding kiss. She gasped for breath, admitting it was a bigger prize than she had expected. Should Edward win next time, she assured him she would reciprocate accordingly.

In the meantime, she required his assistance for the bank was too high and Edward, recognising that only a few yards away the bank was much lower, decided to enter into the spirit of the game and acted accordingly.

Asking her to face the bank, he submerged and then rose up so that she straddled his shoulders, then gripping her heels, he asked her to push with her legs. She did and, with assistance from Edward, shot onto the bank, rolled over and then lay eerily still.

Feeling a little concerned, he sprang up beside her and, leaning over her still body, wondered if he had been just a little too rough. Suddenly she came to life, throwing her arms and legs around him, drawing him down and laughing at his discomfiture. He had reciprocated in like fashion and chastised her for playing possum.

He held her close so that she might not struggle free, but need not have concerned himself for she relaxed in his embrace and smiled mischievously towards him.

Ekkstra complimented him on his game of forfeits. She felt it significant that in a game where there could be no real losers was surely a recipe for happiness.

The next half hour was spent in aquatic pursuits, Edward skilfully devising games requiring a minimum of athletic performance, but a maximum of body contact, and they both enjoyed every minute of it.

They lay sunning themselves on the river bank and barely noticed Svelta and Sven making tracks for the carpet factory. Ekkstra and Edward had other plans: hand in hand they journeyed further into the forest until they reached a bridge which beckoned them over to the higher bank.

Taking him by the hand, she led him up a path almost hidden by tropical flowers. As they climbed higher the vegetation was so dense it obscured the path completely, but Ekkstra seemed unconcerned, evidently knowing where she was going.

Shortly after, they broke through the undergrowth into a clearing of short grass enclosed by shrubs and small palms. It was here that she called a halt, explaining that she had known of this place since childhood and had always considered it to be her own very special retreat.

Seeing the look in her eyes, he decided he would do his best to ensure that this would become a very special day for both of them. As she lay back in his arms, he amused her recounting his adventures in many lands and she, in serious mien, told him he had indeed been fortunate; as a woman she had been denied the opportunity of travel, and as the youngest daughter had been assigned the most dreary domestic tasks.

As he sympathised she said nothing, but gave a little smile as he admitted his surprise that such an intelligent and exuberant woman had been able to tolerate the thraldom of a male-dominated Turkish society. She clung more firmly to him, knowing his sympathy was genuine.

In a matter of hours they had become firm friends, feeling they could trust each other. Anxious to please her, he asked if it was her intention to go back to the orchard. She laughed and tried to shrug him off, declaring that she had no intention of going to work; after all she had decided on a day off and in any case he, as a sailor, would soon be off to sea.

But now that he had mentioned it, there was a fruit he might be interested in, but first of all he would have to relinquish his grip. He apologised for restraining her and as she rose to go, he hoped sincerely that she would return.

Assuring him she would be back, she asked him to be patient for the next hour. He relaxed, knowing she would return, but as the hour passed and the minutes ticked by he became concerned.

Just as he thought he might have to search for her, she returned carrying a multi-coloured cloth, which an hour before had encircled her waist. The corners of the cloth had now been pulled up, making it into a bag in which rested wild berries and dates.

Having gathered the fruit in a secret grove, she had washed them in a mountain stream.

Edward had agreed it was a feast for the gods and, having eaten their fill, they journeyed further up stream until they reached a small bridge. It was here they had to decide whether to travel further up the mountain or return to the coast.

Ekkstra opted to cross the bridge and return down the opposite bank to the pool where they had bathed earlier in the day. She linked her arm in his as they journeyed down towards their venture playground.

Once they reached the pool, Ekkstra beat Edward by two seconds in entering their aquatic paradise. By the time the nude bathers emerged, the sun was dipping low and they were pleasantly tired and happy to just lie down and dry off.

Edward asked his companion if she wished to visit the orchard on the way home, but she was not interested; apart from reminding her of work, she felt that probably they both had consumed enough fruit for one day.

In a hot country it only takes seconds to disrobe and plunge into cool water, but after drying off, it takes some minutes to dress.

As they stood up to dress, the time factor became insignificant, all artificial inhibitions had disappeared, she saw in front of her a man from the North, his skin was fair, his blue eyes twinkled merrily. He had the muscular body of an athlete, strong legs and healthy

449

looking reproductive equipment that would no doubt respond positively if suitably encouraged.

What she saw she liked, she smiled her approval.

In turn, he saw glistening dark hair, beautiful eyes full of eastern promise, the elegant neck of the water carrier, breasts that were full and firm, a slim waist that flowed into substantial hips, the whole supported by generous thighs. Catching his admiring glance, she had asked coquettishly, "I please you?"

Extending his arms, she responded joyously and as he enveloped her she thrust herself forward against him. As he held her firmly she smiled and told him that the berries they had eaten were considered an aphrodisiac. He knew what she wanted.

Picking her up bodily, he took her over to the long grass and put her down gently.

Thinking about her now, he realised she had been aptly named, she certainly had been endowed with that little bit extra; to him she had been his Turkish delight.

He knew now that his intention to promote sleep through beautiful thoughts had become an aberration, thrusting him into a sexual limbo.

What a fool he had been to equate salacious escapism with beauty, when lying beside him was the most beautiful woman he had ever seen.

Feeling that true beautiful thoughts could still induce sleep, he confined them to the woman he loved, the woman who would be his partner for life. A few minutes later, he was fast asleep.

Chapter 22

In the morning Mrs. McNab insisted that she would set them up properly for the rest of the day. The full Scottish breakfast should be enjoyed in a leisurely fashion, she said, and the Sorensons saw to it that tradition was observed.

As they started out, the early morning haar had still not dispersed and Edward felt uneasy as he drove slowly in the direction of Blairgowrie. Fortunately the sun broke through, allowing him a clear vision of the road ahead and pleasing Emily, who was enjoying the unfolding Highland scene, happy in the knowledge that her husband could well be trusted to drive with care.

Reaching Blairgowrie, he stopped for petrol. He had already made up his mind to make frequent stops at garages and pubs, knowing that these were the places most likely to provide information concerning local beauty spots.

The garage attendant was most forthcoming and, pointing to the right, he uttered his piece of local wisdom.

"Gae doon that road tae Perth and yi'll see the biggest hedge in creation."

Remembering Mr. Ross had told him not to miss the opportunity of viewing this phenomenon and knowing Emily would be extremely interested, he had no option but to make an adjustment to his original plan.

Where trees were concerned he was no expert and it was not long before he saw in the distance what looked like tall poplars packed close together. It was not until he was a mere hundred yards away that he realised he was on course for the historic hedge.

Emily could not contain herself and, gripping his arm, asked him to stop the car. In a shot she was over at the greenery examining the hedge in detail. Her eyes were glistening with excitement when she returned to Edward and told him that she had seen what was probably the biggest hedge in the world.

She encouraged him to accompany her on a walk along the full length of the hedge. As they walked hand in hand she told him about a Swedish forester, a relative who had taken the trouble to teach her about trees and shrubs, and as a consequence she had acquired a worthwhile knowledge of the subject.

The more she saw, the more she enthused about this vigorous creation. It took a considerable time to walk and talk its full length, a half mile at least, Edward thought.

As they walked back to the car she told her husband that the hedge, in her estimation, was at least thirty metres high and still growing. Edward smiled, looked upwards and, visualising in his mind's eye the height of the masts of the tall ships, agreed she was probably correct.

Then she surprised him, announcing that the hedge was between one hundred and two hundred years old. It was his wife's view of the life of the hedge which astonished him, remembering Mr. Ross telling him the local laird had planted the hedge shortly after the 1745 Revolution.

Making allowance for legend and loose talk, it appeared that Emily certainly knew what she was talking about.

As he turned the car and made for the East coast, he marvelled at the talents of Emily, her knowledge of animal husbandry during the 'drunk cows' episode and now the wisdom of the forester. What next, he wondered?

Emily settled back in her royal carriage, smiling serenely as she surveyed the Scottish scene floating by. And why not? She had been regally entertained the day before and having spent the evening amid the exquisite furnishings of a Scottish baronial bedroom, had lain down in the majestic four-poster and in a matter of minutes had fallen asleep in her husband's arms. And now her love of nature, particularly trees, had been satisfied.

She had witnessed with her own eyes what she considered must be the tallest hedge in the world. The healthy state of the hedge indicated it had still not reached its zenith, something to look forward to in years to come.

Life indeed was good and it all seemed so natural with a clever husband like Edward around.

As Edward headed for Montrose something happened which forced him to alter his planned route. Nearing Forfar he drew up to a garage and it was here the attendant convinced him he should make for Glamis Castle. The man's enthusiasm was infectious and his historical description seemed interesting enough to warrant a look.

The Sorensons, having travelled widely, had seen many castles in the past and had quite recently viewed the famous Edinburgh Castle, but Glamis seemed at first sight a bit of an anti-climax.

Feeling he had to justify himself, Edward pointed to the square central tower, indicating it was probably built in the tenth century and Malcolm the Second had died there in the year 1034.

Showing proper respect for the dead, Emily decided instead to comment on the structures that had spread out from the original stronghold. The massive buildings either side could be the wings of a very large mansion or hospital, it was certainly not castellated in the orthodox fashion. She was prepared to concede that the foundations of the original castle might well be a thousand years old, but the buildings either side, in her estimation, would not be more than two hundred years old.

She was curious and wondered if it was still a royal residence. Edward was unsure, but of the opinion that a Scottish noble family were at present living in one of the wings.

Emily said nothing, but thought it very sad indeed that society was prepared to countenance and allow a small family, noble or otherwise, to live in such a privileged fashion. With a little organisation, surely the buildings could be used for useful social purposes, such as a hospital or other social amenity.

Acknowledging that his wife was not too enamoured with Glamis and what it represented, he pointed to a big sundial some distance ahead and asked her if she might be interested. She smiled knowing that he was doing his best and, drawing his attention to the beautiful flowers surrounding the estate, she showed her preference.

It was Emily's turn to entertain and she did it well. Taking him by the hand, she led him carefully between the flower beds, stopping now and then to name the flowers and persuade him to smell so that in the future he would be able to recognise and hopefully appreciate nature's bounty.

Interested in pleasing his wife, he resigned himself to strolling among the flowers. If Emily was happy, then he was happy. In any case, the slight haar that now surrounded Glamis Castle made objective viewing difficult, but there was always another time.

As they wandered through the estate, Emily enthused about the flowers and trees, lauding the horticulturist responsible for such a magnificent display. Her enthusiasm was such that they had travelled unwittingly outwith the estate and were now examining the hedgerows of a side road. Edward felt obliged to inform his spouse that there was the possibility of being run down by a passing automobile.

Emily apologised, but stressed that she had been so preoccupied studying the surrounding floral beauty that she had not realised she was now walking on a roadway. Edward was courteous enough to recognise that it was only natural that her great interest in flowers made her oblivious to any danger. After all, he was there to look after her and, in any case, as the driver he was surely expected to keep his eye on the road.

It had been Edward's intention to set course for Montrose, but when Emily confided that she hoped the next bed and breakfast would be something akin to the 'Plough', he hesitated and thought again. He remembered Einer praising the Wheatsheaf Inn in Arbroath, their ale and fish had been something rather special and sleeping accommodation had been first class.

He reached a fork in the road leading to the East coast: ahead was Montrose, to the right Arbroath. He hoped he had taken the right road, after all he had always wanted to taste an 'Arbroath smokie' and, being further down the East coast, it would allow more time to concentrate on the 'East Neuk' on the other side of the River Tay.

Next morning he thought Einer was indeed a wise man. The Sorensons had enjoyed every minute of their stay and set off for Dundee fortified by the legendary Scottish breakfast. He decided that from now on, a pub suitably vetted would supply their bed and a proper meal to start off their day.

Edward kept as near to the coast as he could, hoping Emily would enjoy a seascape as much as she liked the natural beauty of terra firma.

As they approached Dundee, the seascape diminished and the agricultural scene merged into the industrial. Keeping close to the estuary bank, they witnessed the maritime life of the city. It interested both of them in different ways. She listened attentively to

Edward's discourse on what to expect in the port of Dundee: the wharves, the loading cranes, the warehouses and, most important of all, the ships that shuttled people and goods between the ports of the world.

Emily had seen it all before, most recently at Leith, and it awakened in her a feeling of nostalgia, it had been a critical episode in her life. More poignantly in her mind was the sight of passengers ascending gangways as they looked forward to going home or travelling to their own particular island of pleasure.

On reflection, she was happy in the knowledge that she had chosen to share her life with Edward.

It was natural that Edward, being a water agent, would view the scene from a mercantile viewpoint. The tonnage of the ships, the flags they flew gave him some idea of the cargoes they carried and the potential ship supplies to satisfy the appetites of hardy seafarers.

Placing her hand gently on his arm, Emily murmured, "I like Leet better."

He nodded approval, he was happy she was signalling she was quite content to move to Leith if he thought it wise to do so.

Suddenly it dawned on him that if time was really of the essence, then he had undoubtedly squandered it in an extravagant fashion. Instead of cruising around Dundee's dockland with avarice afore-thought, he should be seeking out seascapes and trees. How foolish of him to think of work and allow it to interfere with the holiday.

Apologising to Emily, he admitted he had made a mistake in travelling from Arbroath to Dundee by the main road, thus missing a part of the coast. It was his intention now, if she approved, to travel back to Monifieth and get as near to the coast as possible and from there travel inland through the Sidlaw Hills and thence to Perth.

The other alternative was to travel direct to Perth through the city of Dundee.

Emily greeted the first option with enthusiasm and then they were off to the coast and the hills via, as Emily said, 'Monifeet'.

As they neared Monifieth Edward spied what he considered to be an ideal spot to view the coast and the open sea. Stopping the car, he clambered up a steep slope at the side of the road in an effort to establish the best spot for optimum viewing.

Emily, although unsurprised at the speed of her husband's ascent, wondered why he was now standing so still. Against the sky his silhouette appeared like a Viking helmsman from the dim past peering through the mists of time.

Feeling that he had been standing and looking for an inordinately long time, she decided to investigate. As she opened the car door to step out, he suddenly turned and beckoned her up to his view point.

As she started to ascend, he told her he could come down to help her, but she waved him back, indicating anything he could do she could do just as well.

The sheer joy on his face told her he had been viewing something rather special. Although her sea-going days had been happy, she knew her husband's love of the sea was more intense. As she looked out beyond the pleasant coast line, she could see a variety of vessels, colourful fishing boats, merchant ships steaming in and out of the Firth of Tay, but it was the beautiful sailing ship that held her attention.

It was an anxious and excited man that awaited her verdict. Feeling it hard to harness his patience, he almost blurted out,

"Well, what do you think, Emily?"

She knew what he expected and was able in all honesty to reply that it was the finest sailing ship she had ever seen.

Edward was enjoying himself now; his wife had given him carte blanche, or so he thought, to expand his knowledge on sailing ships. As they looked out to sea he told her about the Cutty Sark and similar ships that traded between London and China carrying cargoes of tea. They were known as tea clippers and were the fastest vessels of their time.

He was of the opinion that the ship they were looking at had been designed as a clipper, it was approximately two hundred feet in length and was probably travelling at ten knots, at full speed it would travel twice as fast, provided the wind was favourable.

They were witnessing the making of history, looking at one of the last tea clippers to sail the oceans; from now on steam would be the cargo carrier.

She felt happy for Edward, his enthusiasm was infectious, but it was the way he expressed himself that disturbed her. As the ship drew further away he turned to her and gave his opinion in a way which indicated he had still a lot to learn.

"She is the most beautiful ship I have ever seen! How I wish I could have sailed in her."

Emily, bless her, smiled, but wondered why men should refer to, ships and women as if they were interchangeable. Having made up her mind to spend the rest of her life with Edward, she hoped he would in time be more considerate.

But Edward's intense love of the sea gave cause for anxiety, colouring her judgement. She had a fleeting thought of envy and jealousy fluttering through her mind. He seemed to read her thoughts, clasped her round the waist and reassured her.

"Relax, Emily, I'll never sail again, unless you are with me."

From the environs of Monifieth they travelled inland and passing through the 'Sidlaws', ultimately picnicked in a wooded glen on the outskirts of Perth.

Leaving Perth they made for Newburgh, Edward's intention being to hug the East coast all the way back to their home in Grangemouth.

At Newburgh they were fortunate enough to find a friendly pub in which they spent the night. The following morning the Sorensons discussed their immediate plans during breakfast. The evening before, while enjoying a pre-dinner drink, they had become involved in a conversation with the local Headmaster and his wife, who was also a teacher. The Headmaster, a local worthy, held centre stage as his profession warranted. He had, to the best of his ability, ensured that the Scandinavians were provided with information that would allow them to enjoy their brief sojourn in the Kingdom of Fife.

As they left Newburgh, Edward held hard left and reached a small road high above the River Tay. They had a panoramic view stretching some ten miles or so, as far as the Tay Bridge. They remembered the school master referring to it as the 'silvery Tay'. Edward had seen many rivers in his time, some brown, some green and even yellow, all in the main dependent on the discarded foliage of nearby trees and sometimes coloured by man's destructive industrial processes. But the word silvery could apply to many crystal clear waters, particularly to Northern rivers. What, he conjectured, made the Tay so special?

His attention was drawn to the river bank and he noticed, as far as his eyes could see, a light golden colour. To him it looked like sand or couch grass, a weed associated with cornfields, or possibly a mixture of both. Whatever the truth of the matter, it impressed him.

Suddenly it came to him, the colour was that of gilt and its lustrous reflection in the clear water, aided by the sun, made it look like silver. At least that was how he interpreted it. Some day, if the opportunity arose, he would ask the schoolmaster.

On reaching the bridge they kept close to the sea, hoping to view the Bell Rock and other features connected with the Tay Estuary.

After passing Tay Port, Emily reminded him that the headmaster's wife had told her they should make for Tentsmuir Point and consider a walk in the forest of that name.

Edward did his best to locate a suitable road, but found the automobile was limited in what it could accomplish, particularly where farm and forest roads were concerned. Emily was sympathetic, realising the car was not designed for the terrain they were trying to penetrate and suggested they go no further and return to a suitable road.

He agreed, but was taken aback when she indicated that before they returned they should at least explore a part of the forest.

Although agreeing, he was nevertheless concerned that they could get bogged down and use up much of their time extricating themselves from trouble. She looked at her husband and smilingly assured him that although he knew more about navigation than she did, she had at least completed a few orienteering exercises in Swedish forests and felt she could get back to square one without too much difficulty.

As Emily led the way, Edward looked surreptitiously at a small compass he had secreted in his pocket, just in case. She was the leader and he was happy she was enjoying herself.

There was no visible sign of a track as far as he could see, but Emily seemed quite happy and unconcerned as she delved through her beautiful trees, showing no signs of apprehension on her part.

An hour later Edward felt more secure, he could smell the sea not too far away and a look at his compass assured him that all was not lost. Minutes later they emerged from the forest and were greeted by the sea.

While Edward reconnoitred the beach with a view to establishing future plans, Emily contented herself with looking for shells that could prove useful for decorative purposes.

Looking north, Edward spied Monifieth and Carnoustie where he had been the day before, and looking south he located St. Andrews and the East Neuk of Fife, places he soon expected to visit.

Leaving Emily to gather her shells, he walked north looking for a small forest path or road that could take them back to the car without having to risk going back the way they had come. Almost an hour later, he returned unsuccessful to find Emily waiting to greet him with a Swedish smorgass she had prepared the evening before in their bedroom at Newburgh.

As they ate their sandwiches and drank their pilsner, the next move became their topic of conversation. Emily was in no great hurry to leave what she called 'those beautiful trees'. Edward agreed their surroundings were pleasant enough, but if they wished to secure bed and breakfast for the evening, then it was imperative they should make for St. Andrews within the next two hours.

Being a tourist centre, he reckoned that to ensure a booking anywhere near the Kingdom's seat of learning could be quite time-consuming. Emily conceded, but pointed out that it had taken only an hour and a half to reach the beach, it would only take the same time to get back to the car.

Edward was not so sure, he complimented her for having led the way from the car to the beach despite there being no visible path, but to get back to the car might not be quite so simple.

Emily gave him a warm smile and assured him that she could complete the exercise in reverse.

As they approached the fringe of the forest, Edward looked anxiously for the point of their original exit, but could see no sign of it. Sensing his discomfiture, she told him it was not essential to go back in exactly the same way, then, walking straight into the forest, she started threading her way between the tall trees.

Edward kept some ten yards behind her, looking from time to time at his compass. The reading was westwards and varied very little from the original, but he did give a surreptitious glance on the odd occasion. It comforted him to know that his wife seemed to be treading a relatively straight path, despite the denseness of the forest.

One and a quarter hours later they emerged from the forest and there it was, Einer's automobile, only fifty yards away.

Edward was astonished, but delighted at such accuracy and on reaching the car he congratulated Emily and asked her how she had managed it.

She smiled sweetly and softly replied, "I tink dey call it intuition, it iss no problem, Edvard."

The expression 'no problem' was one he had often used himself; for his wife to use it now gave him food for thought. One thing was certain, Emily was no dumb Swede, he was proud of her. One look at her innocent face convinced him that she considered her achievement quite normal.

She thanked him for being patient in allowing her to explore the forest, she knew he had been concerned regarding the rough road and agreed the sooner they reached a normal highway, the better for both of them.

Edward drove forward until he reached a turning space, then drove slowly back towards Tay Port.

After three miles he turned left up a farm road, leaving behind a scene that could have been a source of trouble and ahead of him lay an open rural landscape.

As they approached a farm, they recognised the rich potential of the surrounding land. It was the healthy state of the cattle that caught Emily's eye, while Edward, although appreciative of the bovine species, was primarily excited at the spectacle of two enormous horses cavorting in a nearby field. He stopped the car so that they could savour this very special moment.

The farmer, having spotted them, walked over to the car and asked if he could assist them in any way. He was told that they were Scandinavians who, having settled in Grangemouth, were now exploring the nearby countryside. They were interested in animals and had stopped the car to study the cattle and horses in more detail.

The farmer smiled his approval, indicating he would be pleased to help them. Edward expressed surprise that the Clydesdales could be so frisky, his experience was of such big horses pulling heavy loads in and out of the docks at Leith. The farmer could see that Edward was genuinely interested in the Scottish horse and hastened to give his opinion.

He insisted that the city horse was, by comparison, sorely exploited, plodding all day long up the slopes between Leith and Edinburgh and when its task was over, it was incarcerated in its stable till the following morning when the carter collected his horse and prepared for another day of dreary, monotonous plodding.

He pointed to the big horses still frolicking around and explained.

"If the city horses could be set free into a green enclosure after their day's toil, then they would be just as frisky as Nick and Tam over there."

Edward nodded his approval, then, thanking the farmer for being so kind and patient to curious strangers, indicated that they were now bound for St. Andrews. But it was now the farmer's turn to be curious, which was only natural; after all they had come up the road from the forest and he knew that many ramblers and walkers were keen to complete what was known as the 'Forest Trail'.

The 'Trail', it appeared, was some twenty miles long and took approximately seven or eight hours to complete and consisted in the main of keeping close to the forest perimeter from start to finish.

Edward admitted that he and Emily had insufficient time to be quite so adventurous; they had in fact left the car and walked straight through the forest to the sea and had returned much the same way in just under three hours, possibly a distance of six or seven miles.

The farmer grinned widely, thinking the foreigners had misunderstood the question, but was soon disabused as Edward produced a map pointing out the approximate point of entry and exit of their forest walk.

The farmer found it hard to believe that this could have been accomplished; after all, there was no recognised trail across the forest. He gave an instance of a couple who, after travelling some eight miles around the perimeter, had decided to shorten the trip by cutting across the forest to the roadway. It had all gone horribly wrong: there being no obvious path, they had lost their way and after five agonising hours they emerged almost at the spot where they had entered.

Edward and Emily were sympathetic, they could well understand how the couple must have felt. Edward admitted to being fortunate that his wife, having learned lessons of orienteering in Swedish forests, had led them safely through from start to finish.

The farmer, a true son of the soil, used to working in open fields, tending farm animals and organising seasonal crops, found it difficult to believe that a woman could find her way through the dense wooded maze of Tentsmuir Forest.

However, Edward's frankness convinced him that, despite the lack of a recognised pathway, the Scandinavians had indeed negotiated the forest with the minimum of trouble, but how was a mystery. He addressed Edward directly.

"You were fortunate, mister. Your wife is a remarkable woman."

Happy that Emily's prowess had been so kindly expressed, Edward rejoined, "I would have thought that you, as a Scotsman, would have called her a wee gem."

The farmer laughed and, looking fixedly at Emily, replied, "I'm sure she is a gem, but she's no so wee."

Emily blushed at his controversial judgement and, although she felt the term 'gem' to be acceptable, she knew that the negative of wee in Scottish inferred something big and felt at a disadvantage. Was he referring to her height or her condition of pregnancy? Even Swedish women are diplomats - she smiled demurely, assuming his observation to have been made in the kindness of his heart.

As they drove away, the farmer advised Edward to turn left at the main road - there was no sign, he said; if they turned right, they would be back on the road to Dundee. Edward could not resist a passing shot.

"No problem mister, my wee gem will look after me."

Having enjoyed a restful evening in a small tavern on the outskirts of St. Andrews, they set off in the morning to explore that centre of education and golf. As tourists, it was essential that they should visit the University, the castle and the cathedral. The headmaster at Newburgh had already briefed Edward regarding many famous Scots who had been educated at the University, but for the life of him, Edward could not remember their names; but with a supreme effort he was able to tell his spouse that the seat of learning had been established in 1412.

Emily knew that although he had appeared interested whilst the teacher rattled off names, he had kept the conversation flowing while probably planning for the morning. Little did she know that his mind process had been shunted into reverse: he was still wondering how she had crossed the forest so accurately without the aid of a compass.

After leisurely viewing the chapels, colleges and other adjuncts of the University, they left the quadrangle of St. Mary's and travelled through the town in the direction of the shore.

The cathedral and the castle would be their next stop. Built in the twelfth and thirteenth centuries, they had now reached the stage known as magnificent ruins. The cathedral had, in medieval times, been recognised as the biggest church in Scotland. While she seemed interested in the ancient church, his attention was drawn to the remains of the old castle which faced the North Sea.

Remembering the date of founding was approximately 1200, he wondered if the raiders attacking its bulwarks had been English or rather late Vikings. After a little thought, he gave precedence to the English, realising that his ancestors had been on the rampage some two or three centuries before the construction of the castle. In any case he should have known better; after all, his kinsmen came from Jutland in the North of Denmark and they, together with the Norwegians, tended to rule the roost in the North and West of Scotland, whilst the Danes in the south concentrated their nefarious activities on the Scottish and English East coast.

He felt better now: no-one could say that his ancestors had plundered the East coast.

He knew he was indulging in a little day-dreaming and that led to thoughts of home and in particular to his grandfather.

He remembered the old man telling him stories about the Vikings. Like all stories told by men to young males, he had stressed that without the adventurous spirit, the world would be a very dull place indeed. Although told in realistic fashion to young Edward, he realised now that fiction had played a bigger part than fact.

The story of Soren, the god head of the Sorensons, had intrigued him. It appeared that having established a base in the Western Isles of Scotland, he and Eric the Red had explored the Atlantic and finally discovered the continent that would ultimately be labelled America. Eric and Soren had called it Vinland; whether it was the luscious grapes that grew from the wild vine, or the wine it produced, his grandfather had never been quite clear. To him the rugged old seaman was someone very special.

Just before his sixth birthday, a tragic event took place that he could never forget. The old man, dissatisfied with his catch, had left the waters of the Kattegat and made for the Skagerrak, despite a warning that a storm was on its way. Evidently, according to him, he knew better; as a fisherman with half a century's experience he felt the risk was well worthwhile.

In the early evening he had just sailed beyond Skagen, the most northerly point of Jutland, when the storm broke. Within minutes the waves had reached mountainous proportions and the fishermen who had heeded the early warning were berthing or had berthed in comparatively safe harbours.

What had motivated the old 'Viking', Edward would never know. He had a vast experience of cold Northern waters and must have known the risk, yet still he had sailed serenely out. What had been in the mind of his grandfather he could only conjecture, one thing he knew was that the old man must have battled ferociously to reach a safe haven and after a night of terror had managed to beach his boat on a remote part of the island of Laeso, had dragged himself over the gunwale of his boat and fallen exhausted into the sand.

The next morning he was found frozen to death. Knowing the area and the skill of his grandfather, Edward wondered if, in some mysterious way, he had set sail for Valhalla.

The sudden shock of losing his beloved grandfather had been intense, it had taken him a long time to come to terms with it - even now he could feel like crying. As he looked out over the North Sea, he imagined a mist was developing, but the mist was in his eyes. He knew now he had to prepare himself, but too late, a tear drop rolled slowly down his cheek.

Standing by his side, Emily saw the tear roll towards his mouth. She pulled his arm and asked him what was wrong, and as he turned he assured her at there was nothing wrong; he had been straining his eyes in an effort to discover the nationality of a ship some five miles out at sea and the moist air of the developing mist had made his eyes run. He knew he could not tell her the truth, there was no point inflicting his misery on her.

Feeling he had defused the situation, he felt it prudent to consider their next move. Pointing seawards, he informed her that the moist wind hovering around could be called a type of mist, but the Scots knew it as haar.

She smiled and, knowing now there was no immediate problem, took him to task for straining his eyes in a quest for shipping orders; after all, they were supposed to be on holiday. Accepting the rebuke cheerily, he put his arm around her waist and escorted her to the Royal & Ancient.

It was not his intention that they should play golf, but the least they could do would be to familiarise themselves with the rules, the skills and ritual of that ancient game so beloved of the Scots.

Trust a woman to notice quickly a sartorial change. Nudging Edward, she pointed to people she considered must be golfers. It was not the long leather bags with the tools of their peculiar pastime rattling that intrigued her. Instead of trousers, they wore what looked like long baggy knickerbockers. Edward enlightened her: the strange garments were known as plus-fours.

Emily giggled, then excusing her levity admitted that mathematics had never been her top subject; whether they be plus or minus fours, she was not likely to know the difference.

They circled the course, keeping close to the sea and avoiding the shouts of 'fore', ultimately ending near the sociable nineteenth hole. It was here that Edward met a man who closely resembled Mr. Blackwell, the Leith Master Butcher. Taking a calculated risk, he approached the elderly golfer and, introducing himself as a foreigner wishing to know something about the game, he asked if he was being too presumptuous in hoping that a player of the game might have enough time and patience to explain the essentials of the game.

The old golfer's answer was in the affirmative, and why not? It was a glorious day and he had just knocked three off his handicap, so why not accept the opportunity of talking golf with a very polite and engaging young couple?

Handing Emily a golf ball, he explained that the clubs were designed in such a way that, striking the ball with a smooth action, the ball would travel for distance or height relative to the club used. He smiled wryly as he explained that the ball had to be projected towards a hole in the ground some hundred yards away.

This required that the golfer lined his swing in the direction of the hole, making due allowance for intervening terrain and changing atmospheric conditions. Having reached this stage, he addressed the ball, hoping that after a smooth controlled swing, the club head would propel the ball towards the proper address, the hole.

Edward could see from the demeanour of the old golfer that he felt he had a captive audience, but he also realised that Emily, ball in hand, was becoming restive. Feeling acutely responsible for having started the educational process, he felt he had little option but to bring matters to a conclusion as quickly and as politely as possible.

Taking the ball from Emily, he handed it to the old golfer and apologised for having absorbed so much of his time in explaining the fundamentals of golf. The old man, feeling a little disconcerted, protested that he had barely touched on the subject.

Edward intervened to assure him they were grateful for what he had told them, but they had no intention of imposing on him and in any case, his wife who was Swedish, had been given enough information to absorb her attention for quite some time to come.

Before the old man could reply, he stressed that it was possible they might meet again, but would he be kind enough, before they parted, to explain why golfers wore plus fours. The old golfer, who was also a doctor, gave a kindly look at Emily and now understood that what he had thought to be unseemly on the part of the young man, was the anxiety of a young husband ensuring his wife was not subjected to an experience that added to her self-consciousness.

Concentrating his attention on Emily, he demonstrated why plus fours were essential. Taking a club, he addressed an imaginary ball and having straddled his legs, he pushed his posterior backwards, explaining that if this was not done, there was the probability that the body would fall forwards during the drive, full thrust would be lost and the direction of the ball would be pure guess-work.

Pointing to his baggy plus fours, he told her that trousers were too restrictive, hence the necessity of wearing nether garments that gave complete freedom.

Being a physiologist, he was interested in body posture and emphasised that plus fours allowed the body to adopt a proper stance. Making sure he had her attention, he pointed to his plus fours and indicated that trousers could be a damn nuisance when walking through wet grass or heather.

Turning to Edward, he asked him if he thought his wife would now understand why plus fours were essential for golf. As Edward nodded, the doctor referred to the suggestion that they might meet again some time and introduced himself as Doctor McNab, general practitioner in the East Neuk of Fife and resident in Anstruther.

Edward hesitated and then apologised for being slow on the uptake. After introductions, the doctor, in jovial mood, no doubt due to a reduction in his handicap, was keen to impart his knowledge of the game.

If in the near future the Sorensons wished to contact him, he would be only too pleased to see them. He could invariably be found at the Royal and Ancient, or if they were in Anstruther, just ask anyone, they would soon be directed to his surgery. Edward thanked the doctor for his kindness, assuring him they would consider carefully all he had told them and as an afterthought asked, if they decided to play the game, could he advise them.

Doctor McNab smiled his approval and, touching Emily on the shoulder, said, "Skirts and plus fours are just the dress for golf and if you are thinking of participating, I would advise you to wait until four weeks after the child is born."

Then he disappeared in haste, no doubt to inform his friends of his three points handicap reduction.

Taken aback, the Sorensons had little time to react and could only stand and stare as the good doctor vanished into the club house with his friends.

Having lost the initiative, Edward felt slightly abashed and Emily, still blushing, was beginning to relax, knowing that the remark had been made by a doctor, who was only giving her friendly advice. They exchanged looks of wonderment at what had happened, then slowly the corners of their lips moved upwards and the smiles were followed by hilarious laughter.

Having been smitten by the laughter bug, they had little option but to let it run its course. There comes a time, however, when the intercostals have had enough, the ribs ache profusely and the happy sufferers are forced to desist. Having done with their boisterous exercise, they had time to think.

Emily asked her husband for his reaction and he could only sum it up in a phrase he had learned recently.

"I can only say, Emily, we have been well and truly 'ribbed'."

Next on the agenda was the East Neuk of Fife and Edward, looking forward to discovering the interesting and romantic small fishing villages, hoped his wife would be suitably impressed. Coming from the small Danish island of Laeso, an island of fishermen, he was looking forward to meeting his Scottish counterpart.

In the early evening they arrived at the fishing port of Anstruther. Emily, having spied what she considered to be a respectable bed and breakfast house, decided to investigate on her own. Ten minutes later she informed her mate that she had examined the bed linen, also the premises, and had arranged their dinner and accommodation for the night.

Edward was pleased that she had taken the initiative in booking them in; it appeared Emily was becoming more conversant with her new language and intended to play a bigger part in their future plans.

After an excellent meal, he suggested an evening stroll along the sea front, followed by a nightcap to round off a most satisfying day. She smiled, knowing full well he was thinking of beer and akvavit if he could unearth it. She suggested he could, if he wished, walk down to the harbour, have his carlsberg and talk to the locals. She, on the other hand, had decided it was time she washed her hair.

By the time he reached the harbour he felt a little tired and knew he had little option but to pass through the portals of the Sailor's Rest, wondering as he did so how it would compare with its Leith counterpart.

Names can be very deceptive. He had envisaged sailors sitting quietly smoking, drinking and probably shuffling dominoes while they discussed the day's catch. Certainly up in the corner he could see some of the older men playing cards, but the others, to say the least, were extremely boisterous. Most were standing near the bar gesticulating or shouting the odds, while two hefty sailors were doing their best to break each other's wrists in an arm-wrestling contest.

Suddenly there was an ominous silence as the supermen reached the peak of their power. Then a howl of delight as the successful gamblers claimed their winnings and a moan of despair by the almost gallant losers. The battle of the giants being over, all eyes turned in the direction of the incomer. It almost seemed they were daring the stranger to comment on what had just taken place.

Fancying himself as an expert in hand-wrestling and having a knowledge of the finer mechanics of the game, he felt tempted, but realising that money and pride were involved, he decided it would be more prudent to keep his mouth shut.

Instead he raised his glass of whisky to all in the bar and in a voice loud enough to be heard by all he gave the Scandinavian toast of 'Skol'. Although some seemed taciturn and unresponsive, most of the seamen smiled their appreciation. There was a buzz of conversation and then a young sailor made his way towards Edward: it seemed the crowd had chosen their delegate.

"It's been a fine day, mister," he said, then a little self-consciously added, "we were wondering if this is your first time in 'Enster'."

Edward replied that if he could be made aware of the whereabouts of Enster he would only be too happy to answer the question. The young man, apologetic to a degree and realising the stranger required a little local education, informed him that Enster was the name locals used for Anstruther.

Edward nodded, recognising that local people had the right to use their own name and outsider had no option but to use the map for reference. The young man thought the incomer was obviously English, but when he learned that Edward was a Dane he seemed relieved and pleased. It appeared that anyone from England had to be treated with caution.

Conversant with the 'auld enemy' syndrome, Edward understood how the young man felt; after all, many Danes considered their neighbours the Swedes in the same fashion. Still, this was no time to try to resolve national differences; his objective was to learn something of life in the East Neuk.

When the young man learned Edward had been born and brought up on Laeso, an island of fishermen, he was delighted and asked him to join his friends.

Half an hour, two pints and three whiskies later, Edward reached the stage where his new-found friends were still encouraging him to tell them all he could about the prospects for fishermen in Scandinavia. His original intention had been to learn as much as possible about the East Neuk, particularly about the fishermen, but he was now finding that the canny Scots wanted to know more from him before divulging the state of things in their part of the kingdom.

However, he found out that herring catches were considerably greater than he had anticipated. It certainly appeared the Scottish fishermen had good cause to name the herring their 'silver darlings' and anyone who had participated in a successful drave, or season, would enjoy a profitable return.

Although the Scots and the Scandinavians fished for herring, Edward was of the opinion that while the Scots fished primarily for herring, the Danes and Norwegians were more interested in cod, ling and haddock.

Egged on by his new-found friends, he deigned to admit that in his area, Jutland and Southern Norway, flat fish were more often on the menu. He referred to the large port of Frederikshavn where the local dignitaries had christened their town 'Rodspotter Bu', which translated indicated that they were proud to announce that Frederikshavn was the home town of the red spotted flounder.

Having eliminated the different species of fish from the agenda, they concentrated on the mechanics of their trade, such as the size of mesh, the type of material used for lines and a description of the tools in common use.

There comes a time when workers, even fishermen, decide to depart from the mundane and show an interest in the humanities. Every pub has its philosopher, politician or religious fanatic and, mercifully, someone interested in recreation.

It was significant that the incomer, having admitted he was on holiday, would be questioned concerning his thoughts on Fife. His short exploration of Tentsmuir Forest passed with little comment, but as soon as he mentioned St. Andrews, the sporting fraternity at the bar asked if he was a foreigner who had come over especially for the golf.

They were disappointed when he told them he had never played golf, but their mood changed when they knew he had visited the Royal and Ancient and had been fortunate in meeting a Doctor McNab, who had been kind enough to teach his wife and himself the fundamentals and importance of golf in Scottish history.

He held their attention as he described how the doctor had demonstrated the importance of addressing, aligning and keeping an eye on the ball during the swing. There was silence as he spoke; he knew from the attitude of the fishermen around him that they all had a great respect for Doctor McNab.

He finished by telling them that should he or his wife decide to take up golf, the doctor would be delighted to teach them.

In the general buzz of conversation that followed, they vied with each other in expressing their appreciation for what Doctor McNab had accomplished on behalf of the people of Anstruther.

Not only was he an excellent doctor from a patient's view, his knowledge of preventive medicine had obliged him to crusade continually against ruthless employers, lackadaisical government officials and other dross of the establishment, as he called them.

It was the oldest sailor in the bar who was given the floor to illustrate what he knew and thought about the good doctor of 'Enster'. It appeared that Doctor McNab, concerned at the mounting injuries and deaths of fishermen at sea, had boarded a trawler as an observer as it set out on a drave. The seas had been rough and the doctor, although suffering sea sickness, had persisted in staying on deck.

At the height of the storm a mountainous wave had swept a man overboard. The doctor had reacted immediately and dived in the direction of the fisherman, minus a lifeline. Although a powerful swimmer, it had taken a supreme effort to reach the man before he descended into the deep. It had seemed an interminable time before the skipper had managed to manoeuvre the vessel into a position where a lifeline could be thrown over the men in the sea.

But it had been done, the seaman, supported by the doctor, had been hauled aboard and his rescuer, although frozen stiff, had found the strength to empty the lungs of the victim, and give him the kiss of life; and he refused to leave his side for the next two days. The doctor had nursed the man while at sea, ensuring that his patient could walk ashore at the end of the drave.

The whole bar was silent as the old man finished his story. It reminded Edward of the atmosphere he had experienced in a cinema in Hamburg, where in the film the local hero returned after slaying the dragon and all lived happily thereafter. But here there was real drama, the rescued fisherman had stared into the jaws of death and the good doctor, having saved him, had ensured that he could enjoy to the full the happiness of life. The old man looked directly at Edward and admitted, "Yes, I was the man Doctor McNab rescued from the sea and to me he is an extremely brave and exceptional man."

He would have said more, but his compatriots were determined to have their say; it was obvious the good doctor was extremely popular.

A young fisherman summed it up on behalf of his friends. "Aye there's nae doot Doctor McNab is Enster's hero."

Edward left shortly after, but before crossing the threshold one of the fishermen, a golfing enthusiast, gripped him by the elbow and advised him breezily, "Tak ma advice, see McNab, he'll improve your golf."

The Sorensons started off early the following morning. Edward, having decided to allow only an hour to explore the harbour area, hoped to have sufficient time to enjoy viewing the East Neuk fishing villages in a leisurely fashion.

But Emily was adamant that they should view the Chalmers Memorial Church, not because she was interested in churches, but she had promised the landlady she would do so. After all, the landlady had been very kind to them and had stressed it was an important tourist attraction, adding that as it was situated on top of a hill, it was a sight that should not be missed.

He agreed readily, knowing it could be seen from the harbour, and stopping the car asked her to step out; as she did so, he pointed upwards.

"There you are, my dear," he said proudly, "the Church, no problem."

She dug him in the ribs, laughed and demanded a closer look. Being a dutiful husband he did her bidding and after some minutes pottering around an Anstruther show piece, he asked if she was ready to visit the romantic villages of the East Neuk.

She smiled her approval, he swung the starting handle and seconds later Einer's automobile rolled steadily towards Pittenweem. Within himself he knew there would be insufficient time to accomplish all he wanted and resigned himself to what he hoped would be an enjoyable pilot scheme. Some day in the future he would come back and explore Crail to Largo.

Entering Pittenweem, he swung the car down towards the sea. The roadway was narrow, twisting and steep, a rain shower had made the cobbled surface extremely slippery. He knew he had to be cautious and drove accordingly, while Emily, appearing not in the least concerned, asked him to look at the quaint houses lining each side of the street.

It was the sight of a big whitewashed, craw-stepped building that was almost his undoing. The sun reflected from the building dazzled him, while Emily's call of

'Look at that' caught him completely by surprise. As a consequence his foot resting gently on the brake momentarily slipped off and, in trying to adjust, he pressed the accelerator by mistake.

The car shot forward some thirty yards or so before he could re-locate the brake and although he attempted to discipline the movement the contact was far too hard. The car wheels locked and a rapid skid towards the harbour developed. To brake or not to brake, that was his dilemma.

His early training in the craw's nest had taught him to anticipate potential disaster, but his horizon was only a hundred yards away and it was a very wet one. At the bottom of the hill and almost straight ahead was a long stretch of wharf. Unfortunately two big fish-carts barred his way, and to the left a big warehouse obscured his view, giving no comfort, for the sweep of the wharf was leftwards, leaving no room for manoeuvre.

Edward felt his only hope was to use his brakes effectively on the last fifty yards, for this part, being open to the wind and sun, had dried out. He prayed as he trod on the brake and swung the tiller to the right just as he reached the end of the wet stretch; the car swung one hundred and eighty degrees and shuddered violently as it hit the dry surface.

Miraculously it stayed upright. It was now travelling backwards towards the edge of the harbour and the brake seem impotent. There was only one thing left to do, press the accelerator and trust to providence.

The tyres squealed as if in pain, the car again shuddered. It was slowing, but would it be enough?

It seemed an eternity, but it had stopped and looking through the windscreen Edward could see the bonnet of the car rising slowly up the hill from which they had just descended. It was a horrible sensation: could it be that after all they had gone through the car was now poised to fall backwards into the harbour?

He thought of Emily, who seemed dumbstruck, and, although concerned, he was slightly amused when he thought of her outburst some seconds before. He realised a shift of weight in the car could prove disastrous and caution was essential. He spoke in a casual fashion to Emily.

"Would you just open the door, Emily, and when you get out, come round to my side and tell me what you see?"

She gave a rather wan smile and did as she was bid. She was distinctly happy to report that there was a foot or two to spare, but hoped he would not consider reversing.

As he looked in the direction of the sun god that had prevented his slip to disaster, a red faced fisherman raced to his side.

"Good Christ, man, this is Pittenweem, no Brooklands!"

Taken aback, Edward was dumbfounded for a few seconds and then, understanding that a pedestrian might have been badly injured, apologised to the angry man.

After explaining what had happened the fisherman cooled down, but was still determined that the incomer would obey local rules regarding the parking of vehicles. Pointing to the car and then a notice board, he advised Edward to shift the car to another parking place before the Harbour Master's beady eye focused on it.

It was an uneasy moment for Edward, he felt he should do something to gain the man's confidence. His ability to extricate himself from awkward situations came to his rescue. He introduced himself and then asked the fisherman his name. The man, although taken by surprise, responded quickly telling Edward that he was Bob Grant, the owner of the big warehouse Edward had just passed during his quick descent down the brae.

Edward thanked Mr. Grant for his patience and understanding and asked if he would be kind enough to suggest a safe parking place. The fisherman agreed he could park the car adjacent to the warehouse and assured Edward he would keep an eye on it.

It was inevitable that Edward and Bob Grant would discuss their fishing backgrounds - Edward saw to that. It appeared Mr. Grant had a particular interest in lobster fishing; it followed therefore that, with Edward's father being a lobster fisherman, they both had a common interest.

It was arranged that Mr. Grant would boil two lobsters, to be collected by the Sorensons after a short walking tour of Pittenweem.

In Pittenweem they were about to discover that all the East Neuk fishing villages had something in common. The main coastal road skirting Fife is, as one might expect, on a decidedly higher plane than the villages it serves. Unfortunately, as Edward had experienced, the entrances and exits are rather steep and can be disconcerting for the amateur touring motorist.

But they were walkers now and could explore, in a pleasant leisurely fashion, Pittenweem and its immediate environs.

The older houses, in which many of the working fishermen lived, had either been whitewashed or 'ochred' to camouflage and prevent erosion over the years. They were a pretty sight; it appeared in many cases that bright yellow ochre was the 'in' colour of the decade. Emily was particularly taken with one house, coloured yellow; it had blue windows and a blue door, even the craw-steps were coloured blue.

"Surely it wouldn't be because it was painted in Swedish colours?" Edward teased Emily.

As they travelled upwards gradual changes took place, colours and shades became more conservative, till they reached the stage where architecture dated the change from vibrant human activity to that where the more prosperous people could live in comfort, in modern villas and mansions designed to their own particular requirements.

It was only to be expected that successful fishing captains, astute business people and others atop the social ladder would occupy, as soon as feasible, premises reflecting their advancement. The villas varied in size and design and according to the architectural requirements of the professional strata and their ability to foot the bill.

These more modern structures were a delight to behold, made from stone hewed from Scottish quarries, in the main granite and red sandstone had been used, with some combining both to reflect strength and beauty. One such structure, bigger than its neighbours, probably a small mansion, was well worth close examination.

It was entirely surrounded by a four-foot wall, inside of which grew a well trimmed hedge a foot higher. Access to the house was through a stone portal on which was hung an ornamental wrought iron gate, its centre piece, made of brass, displayed a laurel wreath; within which two sets of initials could be seen.

Twenty yards up the garden path they could see the same initials inscribed in the stone lintel of the main door. Just above the lintel the date 1850 was clearly seen. Although the date and initials intrigued him, Edward was surprised that a house built more than sixty years before looked as if it was only a few years old.

Emily drew his attention to the lintel and questioned the date. In her estimation the building, which she considered quite magnificent, must surely have been built within the last year or two. He agreed the structure was in superb condition and indicated, as it seemed Aberdeen granite had been used, then its longevity might well be considered as normal.

Emily was not so sure, but enthusiastic, feeling their short survey had been rewarding. She was still curious concerning the initials on the lintel. Edward had referred to the initials as adding a touch of romance to the building. Emily agreed that irrespective of age, it was a fine building, but could not visualise its connection with anything romantic.

As they made their way back she told her husband that she had enjoyed the walk and thought the village most picturesque, in some ways a little quaint, but very alive and very charming. He agreed the village was certainly alive, but then how could he think otherwise, coming as he did from fisher-folk himself.

He told her he had seen in his travels similar houses in the Dutch sea villages and had learned from some of the seamen in Anstruther that many centuries ago Dutch seamen had settled in the East Neuk, bringing with them their ideas of architecture, and legend had it they had been instrumental in introducing something more romantic than the craw-stepped gables: it had become known as the marriage lintel.

Reacting coolly, Emily informed him that although she was willing to learn, she was still to be convinced that there was anything romantic in letters carved out in stone.

Edward had a grin on his face as he escorted her to a house at the harbour level and, pointing to one of the oldest buildings, he asked her to look closely at the inscription above the door. The figures chiselled in the stone lintel above the door were R.S. and V.P., the date was 1751.

Edward's eyes twinkled merrily as he offered the opinion that Roderick Stewart had proposed by letter to a maiden of the name Violet Porteous. Having asked politely for a reply, she had accepted and they had married and the inscription was a contract in stone.

Knowing her man's potential for story-telling, she assumed the names to be imaginary, but Emily was a little quicker this time and surprised him, indicating she had sufficient knowledge of French to know what R.S.V.P. meant. Although agreeing with his theory of a marriage contract, why should the man's initials come first, surely that was undemocratic and therefore, could not be called romantic.

Edward feigned puzzlement while listening to Emily's viewpoint.

It would have been fairer and more romantic had the man suggested that his wife's initials should figure first on the lintel.

A wicked little smile played around his lips as he agreed with his wife and then found it necessary to explain that times had changed over the past 160 years and, being a believer in equality of the sexes, he declared that should they decide to acquire or build a permanent home, then he would be only too pleased to see her initials carved first on the lintel.

Emily laughed as she informed him that although he was a good salesman, he could not consider he was doing her a favour, particularly as both of them had exactly the same initials.

"Oh," Edward expressed surprise, "so they are."

She could have laughed outright at his feeble attempt, but restrained herself, knowing he was doing his best and after all, he was her good man. As Edward hesitated, she followed up by proclaiming he was probably sixty years behind in his attempt to change the system.

His look of puzzlement this time was genuine. Laughingly she asked if he had examined in detail the mansion at the top of the hill, the one he had extolled as a masterpiece of Scottish architecture.

Before he could reply, she reminded him that the brass relief work on the gate indicated within the laurel wreath that E.S. and E.S. had occupied the building in 1850. He could only grin and bear it, as she told him that a good romancer had to have a good memory and also an eye for minute detail.

However, she had no right to complain; so far it had been a marvellous holiday, full of interest and delight. She felt it would not be too long before they returned to explore the East Neuk in depth; what she had seen so far had been captivating.

It was not long before St. Monans came into sight and here Edward, mindful of his experience at Pittenweem, drove warily through the village, stopping only at either end to view the beautiful seascapes.

Much the same procedure was observed on arrival at Elie and from there it was on to Largo.

After tea and viewing the Robinson Crusoe statue, they rested awhile at a spot overlooking Largo Bay.

In the late afternoon, as they approached Leven, Edward could see not far off what appeared to be a small forest. As they drew nearer he saw it was an estate, but there was no sign to indicate whether it was public or private. The entrance consisted of two large square stone pillars with rusted door attachments. The door, it appeared, had either been knocked or taken down some time in the dim past.

Before entering he had seen a small stream, or burn, and wondered if it ran through the estate. It was as well he had given this thought, for almost immediately the car started to slide towards the right. Slowing to walking pace, he veered cautiously to the left. Even then he could see the car was only two feet short of sliding into the burn some six feet below.

After fifty yards of extremely slow driving, he reached a clearing and seized the opportunity of reversing the car so that they could extricate themselves should they meet some unseen hazard.

Having agreed that this was the time for leg-stretching, they set off on a mini-exploration. They started off briskly, but it was not long before they were forced to slow down: the path ahead was overgrown with weeds and fallen leaves, making negotiation slow and arduous. The path cleared as they swung up past the tall trees and it followed the course of the stream, coming to an end at a small bridge.

It was make-your-mind-up time and Edward was uneasy as they emerged from under the canopy of the trees; the sky was darkening, the atmosphere was oppressive and thunder seemed not far away.

Whether to cross the small bridge or go back the way they had come, that was the question. Having spotted a bridge not far from the start of the forest, Edward was of the opinion that the path would take them down the other side of the stream and then they could cross over to the car. Emily felt sure he was correct in his assumption, but even if a storm blew up she knew she had nothing to fear. After all, Mrs. McGregor had convinced her that as she was not made of sugar or salt- she would not melt.

By the time they reached the car the sky had brightened considerably and their spirits had adjusted accordingly. When Edward told Emily that he expected to reach Grangemouth in the early evening, she became quite excited. Although it had been a wonderful holiday, she was happy she was going home, the urge to plan for the baby's arrival was strong within her.

Still hugging the coast, they passed through the town of Kirkcaldy, the smell of linseed a potent indicator they were now in the linoleum capital of the world.

Just before entering Aberdour he swung the car leftwards to the renowned 'silver sands' and, parking the car, they walked up to a promontory looking out on the Forth. As they looked out to sea, Edward pointed in the direction of the Firth of Tay, indicating roughly how they had travelled during the last two days. Then directing attention to the coastline directly opposite, he reminded her of the time they had cruised the Forth in Oskar's yacht.

Shafts of light from the sinking sun penetrated the lowering clouds, throwing into relief a large stretch of the Lothians. The Port of Leith could be clearly seen against the silhouette of Arthur's Seat and Salisbury Crags.

Looking towards the Forth Bridge, they could see in the background, nestling below the arches, the burgh of South Queensferry.

It was when Edward mentioned it would not be long before they reached North Queensferry and would be able to cross over to the other side that Emily became a little concerned. Would he, she asked, be able to drive onto the ferry boat or would there be someone to perform what she considered to be a rather hazardous task? Acknowledging her concern, he promised there would be no problem.

As they returned to the car there was a rumble of distant thunder, an indication that an inconvenient atmospheric change could well dampen their homecoming. Fortunately, they were safely ensconced in the car before the East Lothian skyline disappeared into a funereal black hole, followed rapidly by a lightning strike of such intensity that what had been night, was now eye-searing daylight.

The thunderous roll that followed gave a clear indication that local authorities could anticipate full reservoirs for some time to come.

Safely ensconced in Einer's car, they could only sit and watch the display of pyrotechnics and try to forget the drum beat of rain that threatened to flatten the roof of their temporary haven.

It was natural that Emily should be nervous, but Edward, a combination of the romantic and the adventurer, was quietly contemplative.

Some minutes later, after the initial storm had eased, he spied two fires in what he considered to be the Prestonpans and Port Seton area and hoped fervently that no-one in the fishing community had been harmed; in particular his thoughts centred on Mussel Meg, who often visited her aunt in that locality. Had he known what had taken place during the storm, he would have had reason to fear more for his own safety than that of others.

Within the half hour the storm abated and the Sorensons were homeward bound. Although many roads were flooded, they were fortunate enough to be travelling on a road that was relatively trouble-free.

Crossing the ferry, the amateur motorist felt like a professional as he drew up safely at Einer's Emporium in Boness.

Einer and Norma were delighted to see them and insisted they should stay the night. Exuberant as ever, Norma grasped the young mother-to-be in her arms and tentatively asked her if everything was going to plan.

Einer accepted Edward's hand in a casual fashion, but after a sidelong glance at his prized possession and after establishing that it had been returned in good condition, his grasp became decidedly cordial, praising Edward on his motoring skill.

Norma insisted they should stay the night, stressing that Emily should be spared the chore of making supper after such a wonderful holiday.

The Sorensons were pleased to accept the invitation and a happy and memorable occasion it proved to be. There could be little doubt that the highlight of the evening was the champagne and lobster supper, everyone agreeing that Pittenweem would well be worth visiting in the not too distant future.

Chapter 23

The thirteenth of July 1913 was a day the fisher-folk of Port Seton and Musselburgh would want to forget. During the afternoon, dark storm clouds had started rolling over the Pentlands, expanding rapidly and turning day into night as they approached the East Coast.

The atmosphere was humid, heavy and distinctly ominous. Suddenly there was an ever-increasing rumble as the dark clouds jostled for ascendancy. There could only be one outcome to the friction of storm clouds battling for space in the sky.

An eye-searing bolt of lightning flashed earthwards, unloading its immense power directly into the harbour area. Within seconds the unnerved people of Port Seton were witness to several small fishing boats sinking and the main curing shed burning like a giant torch.

As they looked despairingly at the carnage, the ear-splitting sound of thunder reminded the optimists that light presaged sound and the worst was probably over. But too many were not so hopeful. They were not necessarily pessimistic, but they remembered that after the thunderbolt they could expect the waterfall and, having survived the fire, did not relish the possibility of drowning.

The rain that hammered the East Coast unnerved even the most resolute. Fortunately no one was either killed or drowned, this despite a repeat performance some minutes later.

Mercifully the casualty list was much smaller than expected, but during phase two an unoccupied house on the outskirts of the 'Honest Toun' of Musselburgh was burned to the ground and a farm hayshed not far from Port Seton suffered a similar fate.

An attentive young policeman had noticed a wisp of smoke near a corrugated structure about a quarter of a mile away and decided to investigate to ensure that any inflammable material inside had been rendered safe during the storm.

Finding the building closed, he had approached the adjoining house, which appeared to serve as an office. The man who answered the door was extremely co-operative. It appeared that the owner, a Mr. Maxwell, had departed in the morning on a business trip to Edinburgh. He was sympathetic to the policeman's role in the storm and assured him he was quite capable of dealing with an emergency.

Being in charge, he convinced the policeman he understood the hazards and should he require assistance he knew he could rely on the police and the fire service to give any support that might be required in an emergency.

The young policeman was impressed. After all, there was no reason to believe that the dapper, smiling man, clothed in a neat grey suit, was not a responsible citizen who recognised the invaluable service provided by the police and fire service.

He departed feeling he had done his duty, but unaware that the smiling man in the grey suit was a confidence trickster who had passed A.1 in the University of Duplicity many years before. His assignment on this occasion was to ensure that four enemies of human society ensconced in the house were not disturbed as they planned the possible demise of an individual who did not agree with unrestricted private enterprise, particularly the freedom of the public to acquire cocaine at bargain prices.

'Smiler', for that was his name, returned to the inner sanctum and informed the leader that the police were no longer a threat. Pierre le Blanc, alias Snowy, or Peter

White, as he was known down in Carlisle, nodded his approval.

Having achieved his task, Smiler looked at Snowy and asked to be kept informed regarding any work requiring his special skills. Snowy waved his hand in a dismissive fashion, but was polite enough to assure him that he would be in touch. Smiler departed, happy in the knowledge that he would not have to be present in the company of criminals who were completely devoid of any social standard.

Pierre was extremely angry, he had not wanted to come up to Scotland, but Lucius Chancitt, alias Mr. Maxwell, had made such a mess of things that the Scottish branch of Cocaine Distributors Anonymous was threatened with closure.

Normally he would have seen to it that the meeting would have taken place discreetly in a hotel room, but the police were closing in fast, so a legitimate venue, so called, had been chosen. Some years before he had acquired a small fertiliser and agricultural products business and it was within the house of the original owner that they were now sitting.

Unfortunately, he had not made provision for the vagaries of Scottish weather and was not amused by the sudden violent display of pyrotechnics, his ardour being significantly dampened by the rain storm that followed.

Anticipating the necessity of using force, he had arranged that two of his heavy squad would meet him at Maxwell's Agricultural Products. The two men had just escaped from prison, an event that had been engineered to some degree by Pierre himself. Having spirited them away from the attentions of the police, he had sent them North to the present rendezvous.

But time, tide and thunderstorms still elude the control of man and throw the best laid plans into utter confusion. The storm as such had had little effect on Pierre le Blanc, but the subsequent arrival of the Fire

Brigade and Police at the burning hayshed only a few hundred yards away had a dramatic effect.

Knowing he could expect a visit from the police or fire service, he had directed his hired spy and confidence man to reassure the authorities. Smiler had certainly done a good job and had given him valuable time to reorganise if required. He shivered at the prospect of what could have happened had the police entered the room in which they were sitting.

The Strangler and his mate lacked the intelligence and finesse to convince even a 'rookie' police officer that they were farm labourers and Lucius Chancitt had become so demoralised in the last few month that he would probably have excused himself as he made a dash for the lavatory.

Pierre le Blanc had no intention of allowing two of his zombies and Lucius Chancitt to interfere with his style of life. It hardly bore thinking about that he, Pierre le Blanc, or Peter White, a noble pillar of high society in the North of England, could be in any way associated with three criminals on the police wanted list.

Although Chancitt had at one time been one of his companions in crime on the South American continent, he felt nothing but contempt for him now. He had given Lucius his chance and he had failed miserably as his Scottish distributor of cocaine. He had no option but to come North to re-establish or lose all the potential profits.

He had wondered at first if his journey was really necessary, but having decided, he still had a feeling of frustration. He pondered his assets and cursed Lucius for placing them in hazard.

Apart from the profits accruing from international cocaine distribution, he had reached the stage where he could relax and enjoy the life of a respected entrepreneur whose talents included the successful operation of some of the country's most popular hotels.

He also owned the most prestigious restaurant in Carlisle, which adjoined the notorious art and leisure centre.

There are many views concerning what can be described as art, or for that matter, pornography. Some of the top social columnists seemed to agree that although the artistic qualities displayed were at least equal to anything in Europe, there was however the tendency to compare certain aspects more with the courtesans of the Orient.

A well known social editor had referred to Peter White's art and leisure centre as nothing more than a five star brothel and the goings on as 'harem-scarum'. Such vapourings did Pierre no harm and in the long run increased his trade. Many of his patrons and customers being judges and heads of state and, more importantly, the Chief Constable, who was also a client, would surely in the interests of free choice protect his democratic rights.

As always, there was the common element who described the brothel operation as expensive prostitution for the favoured few. Such a delight had to be protected with all the means at his disposal.

He grilled Lucius Chancitt mercilessly to reach the base of the malaise, but Lucius seemed in a dream and could only babble, "Sorenson, Sorenson."

For an hour Pierre delved and came to the conclusion that in the main it was Chancitt's inept handling which had been the main source of trouble, but he indicated a reprieve for Lucius, provided that within the next three months the Scottish account reflected a substantial figure in the black column.

Looking at his distraught agent, two words were uttered. "Or else!"

Lucius Chancitt quivered with fear as Pierre le Blanc slowly raised his hand, put his fingers to his throat and drew them dramatically across, a sure indication that

Lucius could expect to be cut off from any further interest in life.

Pierre had learned from his spy Smiler that although Edward was not in the pay of the police or Customs, he had nevertheless passed valuable information to the authorities. The result had been disastrous for Cocaine International and it was now essential that Edward Sorenson should disappear permanently.

In the past Pierre would have done his own dirty work, but he was more mature now and wealthy enough to employ assassins; but he would have to be careful, he could have wished for a higher level of intelligence in his gang; knowing he would have to oversee the operation himself.

Having issued his instructions, he warned Chancitt that this was his last chance and, peering in the direction of the Strangler, he asked the ruffian to look after him.

Twelve days later, Pierre le Blanc, known as Snowy in the profession, but registered as Peter White, gazed from his window in Edinburgh's Caledonian Hotel. He was looking in the direction of Leith Docks a few miles away, trying to visualise the background against which his evil deed would take place.

Being an influential man in the hotel trade, his every comfort had been catered for. Crossing the suite, he entered the bathroom and started to shave. While shaving he thought of recent events, wondering where he had gone wrong.

In the early days he had led an eventful and dangerous life, he had built up an exceptionally profitable and illegal business from the coca plant. In the subsequent cocaine wars he had eliminated many tough competitors, so why should he concern himself now?

Surely a young seaman who had become a water agent and had stumbled unwittingly, as it appeared, on information that alerted the police, could easily be dealt with.

Still, he had to be careful; it was one thing to kill a competitor in South America where the authorities were, in the main, corrupt; in Scotland he would have to ensure that Sorenson disappeared without trace.

Not far away, Edward Sorenson had just breakfasted and was enjoying a cigar before setting off for Leith. It was a warm sultry day, the conditions were similar to those which preceded the thunderstorm that had enveloped the Lothians twelve days before.

It was the twenty-fifth day of July 1913, a day he was destined never to forget. The atmosphere was oppressive, in no way conducive to the efforts expected from a progressive and enterprising young water agent.

Emily, although relaxed, was in a state of wonderment, speculating on what to expect when the critical period of pregnancy arrived. She had been having slight bouts of nausea lately and abdominal pains were on the increase.

Edward's diary indicated that he was expected at the Sailor's Rest at two o'clock to meet his friends, but whether he kept the appointment or not was contingent upon the state of his wife.

The doctor had told him the day before that the birth could be expected probably in five days' time, but Edward, having acquired some knowledge on the subject, felt that the time of launching could well be five hours.

But Emily was adamant that he should keep his appointment; after all, she wanted news from Sven concerning what was happening at home in Sweden. She accepted that his concern for her was natural, but she still felt he was far too fussy; exhorting him to travel forthwith to Leith and enjoy himself.

It was a special day in the Port, all work had ceased at 12 o'clock. Whether the dockers and carters had organised some annual event or not, he did not know, but it gave him time to walk leisurely through the docks that were to become a major part of his life.

Leaving the dock area, he walked along the shore thinking, as he passed the various establishments, how he would operate his agency. Should he accept the old butcher's offer to work as a temporary butcher in Sandport Street when shipping business was slack, or should he seek premises and set himself up as a ship's chandler?

The second option appealed to him, but then he realised that, apart from the capital expenditure of building up stock and controlling it, his life would become too static; he could, in effect, become a prisoner within his own shop.

This was unthinkable. Far better, he thought, particularly after their motoring holiday, was the prospect of buying a car and travelling the East Coast acquiring shipping orders. In his mind he could envisage daily or short term orders being commissioned through Tam Richards, Einer or the old butcher in Sandport Street and the big sea stock orders could be dealt directly with Harry MacSween.

As he crossed the bridge, he was still dreaming of the future when he saw the man that smiled coming towards him. 'Smiler' was fifty yards away, he waved his hand and as Edward moved rapidly towards him, he jumped on a tramcar and waved a farewell. Edward, stymied on the wrong side of the road, could only wonder what the 'Will o' the Wisp' really represented.

He was hailed enthusiastically by three of his friends when he entered the Sailor's Rest, for Sergeant McIllwraithe had joined his Uncle Rory and Sven and they were curious and eager to hear if the holiday on which Edward and Emily had embarked had proved exciting.

Edward's rather languid attitude, as he explained that Einer had allowed him the use of his car, had them laughing in rather an unseemly manner. He waited until their laughing subsided before reproaching them for maligning Einer's car.

"I can say categorically that the car functioned in an extremely efficient fashion."

Sven intervened diplomatically. "You must excuse us, Edward. I'm sure that Einer's car would be capable of functioning properly; what we did not know was that you had acquired the skills necessary to use it in a safe and efficient manner."

Edward looked at his best friend with feigned disdain and replied, "I have never heard such nonsense! That my friends should even question my ability to perform such a simple task is beyond belief."

Rory and his nephew nodded knowingly, while Sven seemed lost for words. But Edward, never one to waste time, was already on his way to order the next round of drinks. Edward asked his friends to sit back and imagine that they were in Einer's car and, when relaxed, he would take them on a journey full of East Coast promise.

His method, as could be expected, was a little unorthodox. Not having maps and other aids to illustrate his tour, he felt obliged to use the tools at his disposal. Using bottles, glasses and beer spilled from his carlsberg, he carried his audience as far as Crieff, then his beer finger travelled eastwards.

Suddenly, he remembered a detail which merited elaboration and looking directly at Sergeant McIllwraithe, his eyes twinkled as he told them that, on 'information received', he had backtracked to enable his wife to enjoy a rather unusual experience.

Edward asked his audience to imagine an enormous giant doing a pruning job on a line of tall trees almost a mile long, halfway between Perth and Crieff. With his gigantic shears, he trimmed the tops and shaved the sides and there, within minutes, was revealed the magical hedge of Meiklelour. It stood one hundred feet high and wise men had proclaimed that it was the highest hedge in the universe.

Recharging his glass, he asked his friends to refrain from applauding until he had finished his narrative. The beer trail was still eastwards and after passing Montrose, wended it way leisurely and squiggly down the East Coast. Feeling his time was limited, he spared them his observations on the Tay Estuary, but felt impelled to demonstrate his enthusiasm on having sighted one of the old 'tea clippers'.

He spent little time on the scholarly interlude in the Newburgh pub, but admitted they had been given information that could prove valuable in the future. He skimped a little on the Tentsmuir Forest incident, but focused attention on their visit to St. Andrews. Concentrating on the personal as opposed to the academic or historic, he stressed that meeting Dr. McNab had been a chastening experience.

Then on to the East Neuk and their short sojourn in Anstruther, but he had to admit that the ten minute stop at Crail was far too short, particularly when he recalled the charm and atmosphere of that small fishing village with its almost medieval-style dwellings; looking as if they had just been built.

Anstruther had impressed him and, having spent a considerable time in a pub frequented almost wholly by fishermen, he had heard from that impeccable source that 'Anster's' (or was it 'Enster's') fortunes swam in harmonious unison with shoals of herring.

Next morning as he left Anstruther cold and sober, he knew that his friends of the evening before had told the truth. The solid mass of vessels that packed the tidal harbour were not boats for pleasure, but represented working craft ready to sail, hopefully to embrace those 'silver darlings'.

The near disaster at Pittenweem seemed to pass without comment, not one of his audience had laughed, smiled or made a definite remark for the last five minutes and he wondered if he was becoming a bit of a bore.

There had been a smile on Rory's face when he had mentioned the hero-worship of Dr. McNab by the East Coast fishermen, but did that smile mean he was really interested, or was he just tolerating the efforts of an entertainer, so called, running out of steam?

To Edward, the very thought that he was being a bore was anathema and that definitely called for action. Gathering up the empty glasses, he made for the bar, excusing himself.

"Be back in a moment, gentlemen. Driving over a period can be wearisome and most definitely a thirsty business."

As he left, the merry laughter of his friends was music in his ears. He did not consider himself 'musical' but could differentiate between the two types: he knew they were laughing with him. As they settled down with their drinks, he asked them to be frank and voice their observations on his story telling.

The young are invariably impatient, it was Sergeant McIllwraithe who was first to offer an opinion. He had found Edward's version of the holiday enjoyable and interesting, but took issue with him concerning his hand illustrations, he insisted that a motorist must always keep his hands on the wheel.

Edward conceded the point concerning safety, but still felt he should prove the feasibility of alternative steering. For a fleeting moment, the fertile story teller's brain conjured up the picture of a car guided by remote control, something akin to an automatic pilot system being tested at that time on a Swedish motor ship.

Edward turned towards the young policeman to assure him that there was no reason for him to be apprehensive; after all, there were alternative ways of guiding vehicles.

Meanwhile Sven had been studying his friend and decided to intervene before Edward developed a bizarre scenario; it almost seemed he had read his thoughts.

"As a qualified electrical and mechanical engineer, I can assure those present that Einer's car is not fitted with a remote control device - that system is yet to be invented. It is natural, however, that Edward, always ahead of his contemporaries, should think like this. What matters, my friends, is that he has, in one hour, taken us on a most interesting motor trip and brought us safely back."

Rory laughed, clapped Edward on the back and congratulated him on a performance that had outshone any travelogue he had attended; the beer trail, he felt, had made it more authentic.

Rory McLeod had every reason to be happy having, in the last fortnight, succeeded in trapping a number of top drug smugglers and he was looking at the man who, through his stubborn determination to rectify an injustice, had started a train of events which had ended in the imprisonment of some extremely dangerous criminals.

Edward's amateur detective work had yielded results that made him a firm favourite with Rory McLeod and his nephew, Sergeant McIllwraithe. Rory chose this as an occasion for thanking him and making him aware of something rather personal.

The operation in Aberdeen having proved successful, he had decided to reward himself with a short stay at St. Andrews. His eyes twinkled as he informed Edward he had met an old friend and played golf with him and at the nineteenth hole they had been joined by a colleague of his friend.

In the course of conversation, Edward's name had been mentioned and it appeared that Edward, despite his youth, was becoming known as a character.

"Does the name John Broad mean anything to you?" Rory asked.

Edward replied instantly, "It does indeed, if you prefix it with the word doctor, who it would appear is a colleague of your friend, Dr. McNab."

Rory smiled agreement as he told him that Dr. Broad had been kind enough to affirm that Edward was a delightful companion. To Edward this was praise indeed and as if to accentuate the importance of such approval, he made reference to the great doctor's work in pioneering successful research in his own particular field.

Rory nodded sagely, appreciating Edward's reaction, but stressed that Emily's potential had also been raised in a positive fashion. It appeared to Dr. McNab that Emily was an intelligent and good looking young lady, whose placid approach to life would stand her in good stead should she decide to enter the world of golf.

But Dr. Broad, although conceding she would probably prove a good golfer, felt it would be a shame if her orienteering and athletic potential was marginalised by being channelled into that pleasant, but sometimes rather frustrating pastime of sending a small white ball towards a hole in the ground.

Rory conceded, however, that Dr. Broad had given his opinion on Emily's ability to keep up with him when hill walking in the Applecross area; he also had been surprised at her orienteering skills and shared her love of trees.

Sven, having sat passively during the conversation, suddenly joined in when his cousin's name was mentioned. He felt he had to intervene and play a significant part in the proceedings and recalled how

Emily, as a young girl, had been extremely athletic, had a passion for trees and had on numerous occasions beaten many older children in forest orienteering competitions.

He was sure Edward would agree that Emily had acquitted herself well during the hill walk with Dr. Broad. Edward could indeed vouch for his wife's ability to carve her way through a forest. What had intrigued him was her ability to achieve her task speedily, without appearing to rush. But, Edward stressed, it was time for others to hold the platform, surely the Sorensons had been on the agenda too long.

His friends had other ideas and insisted that he, as a father-to-be, had an onerous responsibility and they were determined to help him in every way possible. He thanked them for their interest in the forthcoming event, but unless they had the appropriate credentials in midwifery, he was not interested.

But his friends were persistent and carried on the banter to the stage where he knew he either sat and suffered in relative silence, or took the initiative and attacked.

He thanked them for what he called their negative contribution; they had been given the platform and had abused it with their amateurish suggestions on 'fathercare'.

Although sadly disillusioned, he was determined they should be given the privilege of learning something of fatherhood from an aspiring, but intelligent, novice. He had already made plans for the child's education and would try and instil in the child's brain the absolute necessity of thinking for himself or herself. To consider and treat others in an honest and friendly way and expect others to reciprocate in the same fashion.

As the child developed to student age, he would encourage the potential adult to pursue a field that would generate a happy fulfilment; if it proved profitable in a financial sense, then that might be a bonus.

He would not unduly influence the young person, but if there was any evidence of mental deficiency, such as considering Customs and Excise or the police as a career, he would have little option but to advise his progeny of the social stigma attached to those non-productive organisations.

The reaction of Rory and his nephew was almost one of horror, to think that a friend could treat them like this was almost unforgivable. But Edward was not finished yet. How could a set of bachelors be expected to advise him, a potential father who had fully accepted his responsibility, unless of course they were fathers or expectant fathers without the recognised marriage certificate, in which case he might still listen attentively.

No one claimed the dubious honour, but Rory and Sergeant McIllwraithe felt it necessary to remind him that the Customs and police had been good friends to him. Edward grinned widely and admitted that there was always the exception. The young Sergeant stressed there was one occasion in particular where police intervention had been readily welcomed.

Edward flippantly replied, "You are referring, my young friend, to the time when two bloodthirsty ruffians pursued me to my temporary residence in Sandport Street."

The young Sergeant gripped his arm tightly. "We've been fooling around too much this last half hour," he said.

Taken aback, Edward did not reply, his silence recognised that the young man had something very serious on his mind.

Looking Edward straight in the eye, he told him that those criminals would be only too pleased to welcome his demise. He stressed quite vehemently that Edward should, in future, distance himself from any interference in the smuggling world. What he did not tell him was that the Strangler and his mate had escaped from prison three days before.

Rory supported his nephew, hoping Edward would consider the warning seriously. Edward realised that banter and fooling around was over and that his friends were extremely concerned for his safety. Raising his hands above his head, he surrendered, telling them that he really meant it and was prepared to take aboard seriously any advice offered.

According to Rory, Edward had unfortunately acquired a reputation among the drug dealers of knowing and informing the police of their movements. He lectured a little on the serious aspects of espionage and counter-espionage, while Edward, playing it cool, felt that Rory was overstating his importance.

Rory was adamant and annoyed, informing him that the drug smugglers now knew he had been the spy on the Stenka Maru. He was also sure that the cocaine gang had a spy secreted somewhere in the police or customs' organisation.

Having done his best to warn Edward, he insisted that he should inform him personally if he suspected anything unusual. He gave him a number to ring. Should someone other than himself answer, he should ask the name of the person, take a note of the time and ask that Mr. McLeod ring back.

When Edward asked if all this was really necessary, Rory replied that it was crucial; after all, he could be talking to a spy in the pay of the smugglers.

Edward felt a cold chill at the prospect of having to look constantly over his shoulder and at the reflections in shop windows, take a note of anything the least suspicious, operate a system of codes. How long before he would be wearing a bullet-proof vest?

He agreed to Rory's terms, but felt that watching for someone to harm him was rather negative; surely moving around would make him a more difficult target and give him some chance of eliminating a potential assassin?

Rory smiled, shook his head and said, "You promised, Edward."

Edward took his hand, squeezed it heartily and replied, "I always keep a promise, now let's talk about happier times."

They did just that, reminiscing in a light-hearted fashion about incidents they had experienced in the past. Rory's story raised the biggest laugh.

He admitted there could be a deal of truth in the saying that confession is good for the soul. He confessed that he had suspected a seaman of smuggling a bottle of perfume. A box containing nine bottles of exceedingly expensive perfume had been unearthed in the forecastle of a ship.

The box, indicating 'dix parfum' had been interfered with and he felt sure the small missing bottle was secreted on the person of the seaman. The seaman had happily agreed to be searched. There being no sign of the bottle, Rory had apologised to the seaman.

However, later that evening as he hung up his jacket, he felt a hard object in an outer pocket. He knew instantly, the cheery seaman had cheekily switched the bottle as he frisked him. There can be little doubt that when you confess, your mates will laugh with you; should you not, they will most certainly laugh at you.

The time had come for Rory and his nephew to resume their duties, they were reluctant to leave, but were anxious they should all meet again in the very near future. Both men, knowing that the Strangler and his mate had escaped from prison, were afraid for Edward's safety, but knew they dared not show it, particularly when parting. Shaking his hand, they indicated that the next time they met, hopefully, they would be baptising a young father in his favourite akvavit.

It was time for a Scandinavian up-date and Sven was only too pleased to inform Edward of Swedish family affairs and in return looked forward to hearing how his favourite young cousin was faring.

During their mutual exchange, Edward noticed a small decrepit individual sitting in the far corner reading a rather careworn sporting paper. From time to time he looked in the direction of the small man, knowing he had seen him before, but failed to put a name to him. It was when Sven pulled on his wrist that he realised he was being rude. He apologised for his lack of concentration and when he discreetly pointed to the far corner, Sven smiled and put him in the picture.

It was none other than Mr. Nesbit who, apparently under civic pressure, had been forced to alter his way of life and consequently had deteriorated physically and was now prone to periods of sullen silence.

Although assured by Sven that the man was indeed Mr. Nesbit, he was appalled at the change that had taken place. He felt sorry for the small man and then, remembering what he represented, he dismissed him and concentrated on conversing with his friend.

Some minutes later Sven, remembering he had an appointment with Felicity, became restive, feeling he was in danger of being late and said that he had to leave. Edward, as an understanding friend, sought to comfort him.

"Tell your lady friend that you have been in my company, I'm sure she will understand."

Sven sighed and replied, "I'm sure she will."

But, knowing what she thought of Edward, he was not comforted and Edward, invariably the optimist, asked Sven to transmit his felicitations to his loved one.

However, this time Edward had gone too far. The smile on the big Swede's face to say the least was sardonic and his reply was anything but friendly.

"Your sarcasm and wit, so called, are not appreciated. You know damn well Felicity thinks you are a bad influence and I'm thinking she may well be right."

Edward, knowing he had been too flippant, promised in future to behave in the normal manner as far as social niceties were concerned. As Sven accepted his apology, Edward put forward his hand and Sven grasped the opportunity to apply significantly more pressure than required for a friendly handshake. Edward, well versed in the art of hand-wrestling, was prepared and, absorbing the undue pressure, waited his chance to return the compliment. Sven knew Edward was strong, but had not expected him to emerge as an equal in the test.

Edward complimented Sven in his own peculiar way. "I'm happy we are friends once more. The firmness of your handshake is a welcome token of your sincerity."

Sven burst out laughing. What else could he do when dealing with a character like Edward?

As they parted company, Sven advised him to heed Rory's warning concerning the potential danger of considering the drug smugglers as a spent force. Edward assured him he knew there could be danger, but had no intention of living the life of a hermit.

Having time to spare, he decided to relax and read his paper, but seconds later the paper was discarded as his thoughts focused on Emily. Had he known that not long after his departure Emily was experiencing strong contractions and Mrs. Mackenzie had summoned the doctor, he would have discounted rail travel, unearthed his bike and travelled hell for leather back to Grangemouth.

Ignorance is bliss, everything had been taken care of, he would have time to buy flowers for her in the Kirkgate before boarding the train.

He retrieved his paper and pretended to scan it, but he had another ploy in mind. Turning the pages over slowly and looking up and down the columns, he was able to observe Mr. Nesbit, trusting that the wee man would not be unduly suspicious.

He was amazed at the physical deterioration, remembering him originally as an ugly man who was reasonably sprightly in his movements, but displayed a deviousness that Edward abhorred. He seemed even smaller now and was ill-kempt, his clothes dirty and hanging loose, an indication of a considerable loss of weight and interest in personal hygiene.

Although Sergeant McIllwraithe had told him that the wee man had been cleared by the police regarding drug offences, Edward was sure he was still a tool of Lucius Chancitt. He was obviously an unhappy man. The ugly lines of despair on his twitching face told the story of someone living in a hell that he had largely carved out for himself. Although feeling sorry for the man, he was still suspicious and thought he should keep an eye on him.

It all happened during a lack of concentration; he had been flicking over the pages of his newspaper mechanically when he saw a small white parcel float onto Nesbit's table. It startled him; there was an involuntary jerk of his head as he saw standing there the man who always smiled - but this time the glance was one of malevolence and it was directed at him.

He could only stare as a potential enemy departed through the lounge exit and giving a quick look at the table, he realised that the small parcel had also departed.

At first Edward considered the whole episode as much ado about nothing, but on reflection wondered why a man he did not know should display such enmity.

Was the parcel all that important and if so, who had placed it on the table in the first place? After some thought he decided Mr. Nesbit had not placed the parcel on the table, he was too wily a customer to be sold the old newspaper cover trick. On the other hand, that smiling mercurial character could well have entered the bar and placed the parcel on the table, assuming that the person behind the paper was only interested in the two-thirty racing result.

On balance, he decided the parcel was now in the possession of Mr. Nesbit. What he did not know was that the whole charade had been enacted not for his benefit, but ultimately for his destruction.

Edward felt he had no option but to weigh things up behind his paper, trusting that his indifference to Nesbit and his peculiar friend would be taken to heart.

In the meantime, he would have to consider the situation and decide on the action that might be required. The main point was the parcel and what it contained, if it was a bundle of betting slips then he was certainly not interested.

He knew Nesbit had already been convicted under the Gaming Act, but there had been no evidence in connection with drug smuggling. Edward had already seen packages exchanged between Nesbit and Lucius Chancitt in a most surreptitious manner.

It was also significant that after the pub brawl, the Strangler and his mate had been arrested and a quantity of cocaine had been found on them during a police search. As Nesbit and the two thugs were hirelings of the American, it followed, as far as Edward was concerned, that Nesbit was a cocaine pedlar. He felt now that the parcel contained something more deadly than betting slips.

He reckoned that betting slips would not have had any significant effect on the 'bookie's runner' sitting in the corner. But this man was in a bad state, he was breathing hard and shivering, he was involved in something that was overwhelming him. The mysterious parcel was also on his person, of that Edward was also sure. He reasoned that if 'smiler', lately the man with the malevolent look, had taken away the parcel, he would also have taken away a load from the mind of the wee man.

He knew now what he had to do, but he also knew that he had to move with extreme care. Looking over his paper, he was just in time to see Mr. Nesbit make for the door. As he passed through he looked in Edward's direction, but Edward did not respond.

Edward moved rapidly over to a window facing the Water of Leith. He saw the dismal and bedraggled figure of Nesbit walking slowly over the bridge towards the shore. Having more than an hour to spare, he decided to shadow him.

After crossing the bridge, Nesbit carried straight on along Bernard Street with Edward wondering if it would all amount to much ado about nothing. Remembering the sorry state of some of his shipmates who had become addicted to cocaine and the harrowing tales of suffering and death recited to him by Rory, he knew he had a moral duty to perform.

The wee man turned left and headed for the Edinburgh dock gate and Edward followed discreetly, contemplating his next move. Keeping in mind the warnings of his friends, he asked the policeman at the gate if he knew of the whereabouts of Sergeant McIllwraithe. The reply was in the negative, but he did know that the Sergeant was expected to visit the dock within the next half hour.

Keeping in mind his promise, he asked the policeman to relay a message indicating that he, Mr. Sorenson, had vital information and could be found in the vicinity of the Edinburgh dock area.

Turning towards the Elevator, he could see Nesbit almost two hundred yards ahead and, knowing he had to be cautious, he made for a line of railway wagons running parallel with the road. Then, jogging along, he kept the wagons between himself and his quarry, stopping from time to time whenever a gap gave him the opportunity to spy out the land.

Nesbit was only a few yards ahead now, his legs could be seen on the other side of the wagons, with the last wagon only twenty yards away, Edward seized the opportunity to shelter in a conveniently placed shed door. From here he could observe Nesbit's movements as he drew near to the big grain elevator. He watched him move over the railway line and disappear round the side of the building before he followed as discreetly and silently as conditions allowed.

He had to move quickly to maintain the initiative and knew he had little option but to come out far enough to see the full length of the dock. Being a holiday, he had not expected to see anyone other than Nesbit.

The big shed doors on his left were closed and to the right there was nothing to be seen other than a gigantic loading crane, the big grain ships having departed the day before. The crane was some fifty yards ahead, Nesbit was probably behind it; there was also the possibility that the wee man had company and that could prove troublesome.

There being little point in pussy-footing around, he made straight for the crane, preparing himself should action be called for. When his quest proved negative, he was annoyed that he had wasted his time. He backtracked, wondering where and how the wee man had disappeared.

Should he pursue his chosen objective, or behave as a serious father-to-be and make haste back to Grangemouth and Emily? Had he been in possession of a magic crystal ball, he would have chosen the latter option, for Emily at that moment had reached the critical stage, with the birth expected within the hour. Had he known, his zeal for solving the world's problems would immediately have evaporated.

It was a fateful moment indeed. Thirty yards from his starting point he discovered an enclosed wooden stairway and realised the elevator, a wooden structure, had to have an entrance. He knew now that Nesbit could well have been ascending the wooden stairway while his attention had been focused on the big crane.

Still having a half hour to spare, Edward speculated if he should continue searching or call a halt, or pass over his information to the police. Curiosity overcame his better judgement and despite 'Little Eric's' warning, he started his ascent into the unknown.

Another feline trait emerged as he moved noiselessly, two steps at a time, to the top of the stairway. This was now a difficult time for Edward, knowing he had to remain absolutely still and concentrate on listening.

For a few minutes he controlled his impatience, then, opening the door a few inches, he peered and kept listening. Then throwing caution to the winds, he pushed the door open wide.

And there he stood on a wide platform not far from the door - that miserable wee man, Mr. Nesbit. As Edward strode towards him, the door shut with a resounding bang. As he turned, his heart sank a little when he saw the Strangler and his mate grinning at him.

It was time for action, but what could he do? He could see just behind Nesbit a protective banister about four feet high, erected, it would appear, to prevent workers falling into the grain well. He could make a dive over the barrier into the grain, but could he be sure of locating the exit and what were the chances of not drowning among thousands of tons of grain?

Time seemed to stand still as he pondered his dilemma. The two ruffians were still there and still grinning. Could he convince them that physical violence would not necessarily be to their advantages? He was just about to ask them if they'd had a nice day, when they moved towards him in an unfriendly manner; but a cultured voice with a slight French accent stopped them in their tracks.

"Go back to the door, gentlemen, this man will be with us for quite some time."

Pierre le Blanc had emerged from a small office on the left and was standing with a revolver or pistol in his hand.

Edward had little option but to stand still, while 'Little Eric' lambasted his soul for allowing vanity and sub-normal intelligence to influence his earthly actions.

Pierre looked at Mr. Nesbit and told him he could now cease shivering and join the Strangler and his mate, then waved the man known as Smiler to join them.

Still covering Edward with the gun, he uttered the word 'Lucius' and Chancitt made his entrance from the wings and joined his master.

Edward, although in trouble, could not resist laughing; he had little idea that he ranked so high in the struggle twixt good and evil.

Pierre le Blanc was not amused and castigated Edward for his interference in his cocaine business and ended the diatribe with a threat.

"For someone who will probably be dead in a few minutes, I would have thought that prayers would be more appropriate than laughter."

As he railed at him, Edward cursed himself for having fallen so easily into what now appeared to be so obvious a trap. He felt he had let people down, friends such as Rory, even the police and customs officials he had been in contact with, but in particular, the most important person in his life, his wife, Emily. He was angry now, knowing the child Emily was bearing would be born fatherless, unless he contrived a disappearing act of magical proportions.

As the French Canadian ranted on, he thought deeply concerning survival and made up his mind on what he had to do. Although trembling inwardly, Edward knew it was vital he should remain calm and play it cool. As le Blanc finished his hateful diatribe, Edward asked if, as a condemned man, he would be allowed to speak. When Pierre nodded, he asked, "Some minutes ago you said I would probably die and, as you are the one holding the gun, I would like to know who you are. It could be most insulting to be killed by a homicidal idiot."

Pierre, a handsome, intelligent, but greedy man, reacted according to type.

"Bravo, mon enfant," he replied, "at least to that you are entitled."

Edward managed to hide his feelings as Pierre preened himself in front of his serfs and told him he was Pierre le Blanc, known in England as Peter White, an extremely successful business man in the field known loosely as 'artistic entertainment'. But more to the point, he had established a cocaine distribution network that supplied an insatiable market, which had made him a millionaire.

When he finished his introduction, he left Edward in no doubt regarding the treatment he could expect.

"You will have gathered, Mr. Sorenson, that I am a very rich man and to remain rich and protect my way of life, I have no option but to deal with people like yourself in a ruthless fashion."

Edward smiled wanly on hearing the word option, knowing that all he could do was to slow down the pace of events and pray for a solution.

"I assume you know, Monsieur le Blanc, that the penalty for murder in British law is death by hanging."

Pierre's white teeth flashed, his face was wreathed in a devilish smile as he informed his captive that it was his intention to ensure that no evidence of murder remained. It would be a simple task to dispose of his body in the North Sea, or for that matter it would be simple to set a torch to the grain elevator.

But Edward was persistent.

"Can it be, Pierre le Blanc, that your spies have not informed you that my association with the Leith Police is a cordial one and I have not been dismissed from their attention. At this very moment they could have their force concentrated on this very building?"

Pierre seemed unmoved, but did betray a degree of caution.

"Have a look, Smiler," he said.

As Smiler moved towards the door, Pierre pointed his gun and motioned Edward in the direction of the banister. It was time for the final assessment of the forces lined up against him.

As Smiler passed through the door, the Strangler and his mate positioned themselves on either side of what seemed to be the only exit. On his left stood Lucius Chancitt, his eyes filled with hate, and to his right, the miserable figure of Mr. Nesbit.

Straight in front, some ten feet away, the handsome but menacing figure of Pierre le Blanc took casual aim at Edward's head. He smilingly assured Edward that he was not yet ready to despatch him, but warned, "Should you shout, or make a fuss, I shall keel you at once and keep in mind, Mr. Sorenson, that no one will hear the shot being fired: this German pistol is fitted with a clever device known as a silencer."

Edward thanked him for the invaluable information he had been given, but asked him to give thought to the real reason for the drastic fall in profits. Still playing for time, Edward seemed keen to bargain.

"If I give you information regarding a certain weakness in your organisation and prove it is not I, but members of your own gang that are responsible for the downturn in your financial affairs, would you then consider commuting my sentence?"

Pierre le Blanc looked almost angelic as he fingered the gold crucifix hanging around his neck and smiled as he proclaimed, "I swear on the cross that, should you prove to me that what you have just said is true, I will certainly consider setting you free."

Edward knew that Pierre was lying, but it did give him a little more breathing space. Just then Smiler returned, shook his head and Pierre nodded his approval.

Edward knew now that he was entirely on his own. To attempt an escape through the doorway was out of the question; if he included the wee man in the equation, he would in some fantastic way have to do battle with five and a half men. He could expect a bullet between the eyes if he did not in some way disarm Pierre le Blanc.

He gave a wry smile as he contemplated his only remaining option, he knew it was suicidal. Some might have said that it was against the grain - he could only hope the grain would be kind.

Over the centuries it has been said that as man is confronted by danger, his senses react more acutely. Although he had little time to explore the chemistry of nature, he did smell the overpowering stench coming from the enormous tonnage of grain stored almost to full capacity.

Being a hot and humid day, the expansion and contraction friction of grain particles had resulted in an increase of temperature with the danger of a combustible gas increasing by the minute.

After a few generalities concerning the weakness of Pierre's organisation, the French Canadian raised the pistol and, pointing it at Edward's head, gave him a final warning.

"You have one minute to give me something specific; if not, then I pull the trigger."

Edward's response was slow, but deliberate. "Your second in command cannot be trusted: I learned while I was on the Stenka Maru your plans for at least a month ahead."

Lucius Chancitt was desperate and angry and snarled, "Kill the son of a bitch, 'Snowy'! You know I would never let you down."

But Pierre was not so sure; he wanted to hear more. After all, he might have to pull the trigger twice - Lucius had already made too many mistakes lately. While Pierre instructed Chancitt to keep quiet, Edward exercised his toes, hoping he still retained some of the gymnastic ability of his teens. The pistol was still aligned too close to a point between his eyes; he knew this would be his ultimate attempt to upset the plans of Monsieur le Blanc, with the very remote possibility of surviving the ordeal.

"Ask Mr. Chancitt," he said, "why he took no action after finding my calling card on the steward's table of the Stenka Maru."

As he flexed himself for a back somersault, he pointed to Chancitt. Under the circumstances it was a valiant but rather clumsy effort, his buttocks scraped the protective banister in his backward leap and as he turned in the air he felt an agonising pain in his ear and wondered if that side of his face still existed.

As he twisted sideways into a mass of grain, he heard a deafening explosion and for a split second he cursed the perfidy of his enemy.

Silencer indeed, he thought, but at that instant he saw a ball of flame and knew the gas rising from the grain had been ignited by the firing pistol.

Within a second, the ball of flame had expanded, filling the entire roof space. Then a second explosion, more terrifying than the first, blew out the roof of the granary. The wooden platform on which all had been standing was now a blazing inferno.

Even in his desperate position, he thought of his enemies. They had either been blown to hell or were now negotiating entrance into their own particular heaven, contingent of course on their record while on earth.

Irrespective, the poor bastards were now passing through the hell of incineration. Which reminded him, he had no option now but to claw his way deep into the grain to save himself from being burned alive.

Having burrowed some three feet below the burning grain, he felt he might survive the heat, but a minute without oxygen convinced him he had to seek a method of obtaining oxygen without being incinerated.

He knew clambering upwards was impracticable, indeed impossible; the burning grain in any case was moving slowly downwards, reminding him just too vividly of an unstoppable volcanic river.

Threatened by extinction, his mind raced rapidly, mirroring the hazardous and important events of his life. He recalled the time when the crew panicked in a fo'c'sle fire; he had saved the situation with the ship's extinguisher. Unfortunately this time it looked that his life would be extinguished, but the words of Nils Olsen rang in his mind.

Olsen, a young seaman attached to an Arctic expedition, had survived an unexpected avalanche and had recounted to Edward how his survival had been based on keeping calm and using a swimming stroke as he was swept downwards.

He had never made the grade as a swimmer, but remembered the essentials he had learned as a young seaman in the Danish Navy. In any case, death by drowning in hot grain would be preferable to incineration on the blazing surface.

He decided to swim for it, trusting and hoping that somewhere there existed an exit towards salvation. With flames licking around him and red hot grain showering his back, he submerged and started to swim. His befuddled brain told him if he swam in the direction of the road loading bay he might be successful.

Unfortunately, he soon discovered a number of factors that were not in his favour. To swim at all within the grain required great strength and, apart from exhaustion, he realised he would only end up in the bottom of the granary with many tons of grain on top of him.

It was a dilemma, but he knew now he had to swim upwards if he was to hold his position in the descending grain. Battling courageously, he just managed to surface for air, only to find the burning grain and encircling flames searing his back. His desperate attempt to gulp in air ended with the hairs in his nostrils burning and his lungs still gasping for air. He felt nature could be very cruel: to stay alive he had to breathe, a supply of oxygen was vital.

Unfortunately, the same applied to the fire, even the portion of oxygen he required was being consumed by the greedy flames licking over the surface of the grain. He knew now his choice was one of incineration or asphyxiation, but still he fought, although it seemed he was doomed.

Although seemingly damned, he felt angry that he had failed Emily in her time of need and surfaced for what might well be his final gulp of air. It was a harrowing experienced: his intake was one of fire that seared his lungs. With lungs bursting and burning, he submerged again for what could be the last time.

He was almost unconscious now, at the stage where the human animal speculates on the feasibility of an after life. Was he a candidate for heaven or hell? Only time would tell.

With his brain still functioning, he brought his hands together and pointing them upwards, hoped and trusted he would not sink into the depths of the granary.

It was as if he was praying, but he felt on balance he was tempting providence and, having heard of limbo, wondered if it was an extension of the earthly hell through which he was now struggling; and if so, was he a prospective candidate for permanent residence in Hades? He knew he was dying and hoped fervently that his good deeds on earth might now be recognised, however tenuously, by Heaven's authority. As life ebbed, there was a singing in his ears. Could it be that angels were pleading his case?

Suddenly, an earth shattering explosion blotted out all feeling, the heavy loading bay doors and a considerable part of the building blew out, sending tons of grain into the street below. Caught in the blast, he was propelled upwards and out from the cloying and suffocating mass - he felt he was floating. All around was the dazzling colour of blue. He knew he was in Heaven and then he was no more.

Chapter 24

Back in Grangemouth, Mrs. McGregor was happy and relieved that her very good friend and neighbour, Mrs. Sorenson had, after a wee bit of an ordeal, become mother of a bonnie bairn.

It had all started just after ten o'clock when she had looked in on Emily.

In the middle of their coffee break, Emily had gasped with pain: it was the first of her contractions, signalling the birth could well be a week prior to the doctor's estimate. From the time of the first sign, Mrs. McGregor had been in a constant state of anxiety, her feelings alternating between concern and anger.

Having attended and assisted at a considerable number of births, the old woman knew that this would probably be the day. As the contractions increased, her concern for Emily kept pace, as did her disappointment and anger with the doctor and Edward. She felt the doctor had been lax in his judgement and was angry that Edward had shown too little concern at such a critical period.

An hour later she knew she was in for a stint of nursing. She hid her feelings and gave succour to Emily in a kind and intelligent fashion. By three in the afternoon she had assembled, discreetly, all that would be required and feeling certain that Emily's time was not far off, sent a neighbour for the doctor, stressing that the call was urgent.

Already out on his calls and his time being absorbed in treating a stroke patient, he had relayed a message that he would attend Mrs. Sorenson in approximately one hour's time. As the minutes ticked away, the old woman busied herself with last minute preparations.

As she tied a towel at each end of the bed headrail, Emily nervously asked what they were there for. The old woman placated her saying that towels were always needed and hanging them thus, they were less likely to fall on the floor and become soiled. Emily smiled weakly, and before she could reply a violent contraction had her gasping and moaning.

Mrs. McGregor was really worried now, she hoped fervently she would not be left to deal with the task of bringing forth the child on her own; she felt she was now too old to accept readily such an important responsibility.

She knew it was time to initiate Emily into the expulsion stage. In a voice as casual as she could muster, she asked her co-operation.

'Tell you what, Emily, I'll tie these towels a little tighter, then you can hold them and the next time you feel it coming, grip tight, push hard with your belly and yell out if you feel like it."

Two yells later, it was a distraught Mrs. McGregor that heaved a sigh of relief as she saw the doctor advancing up the garden path. It seemed opportune that Emily, although never one to subscribe to unnecessary noise, should just at that moment indicate to all and sundry that she had something inside her determined to get out.

The doctor knew he had a job on his hands - Mrs. McGregor's admonition was ignored as he demanded towels and hot water. The old woman snapped back, "Everything is ready - I hope you are, Doctor!"

The critical period had certainly arrived, the embryo-cum-infant had started his journey, causing the mother added stress as it battled from the claustrophobic womb towards the big world outside.

The doctor nodded to Mrs. McGregor and she responded, knowing what she had to do. It was not long before he knew that the delivery would be a difficult one and was considering if surgery would be required.

Mrs. McGregor could hear him muttering under his breath and knew there was trouble ahead. She thought she heard words like 'it's ahead of its time' and wondered if he was having trouble locating the child's head or was unconsciously reprimanding himself for forecasting the birth a week adrift.

When he took the instruments from his bag, she knew things were very serious. The good doctor, an accomplished practitioner, more concerned with practicality than bedside manner, wondered how the wee beggar had managed to get so far off course, particularly when the father had a sound reputation in the field of navigation.

With extractors, forceps and a peculiar silver tube that looked like the periscope of a model submarine, he first explored the deep inner scenario. Time was of the essence and he wanted to avoid a caesarean, knowing it would mean a trip to hospital with the intervening time militating against the patient's survival.

He encouraged his almost exhausted patient to keep pushing as hard as she could and he, examining and manipulating, ultimately manoeuvred the child into the proper position for birth.

Then with retractors already in position, he inserted the forceps and gripping firmly, held any gain made by Emily, who was now in a parlous state.

The penultimate contraction gave him the safe grip he required for success. With a last desperate gasp, Emily pushed and the doctor brought forth a rather placid and easy-going boy. It surprised the doctor, considering the boisterous behaviour of the infant during the earlier stages of labour.

He had spoken too soon. A few seconds later, bloodied and scarred by the forceps, he bellowed his disapproval at being pulled so rudely from his mother. Just for an instant the doctor felt a little concerned, but after cleaning and examining the head he knew they were merely scratches, he felt that he and his patient had done exceedingly well.

Leaving Mrs. McGregor in charge, he turned to her in the doorway and in confidence expressed his thoughts.

"You know, Mrs. McGregor, these Vikings have very big heads!"

An hour had elapsed and the old woman, having finished her immediate chores, decided to rest. She was happy for Emily, although she had been apprehensive at the start of labour, she was pleased with the way things had worked out, now was the time for a wee chin-wag with the young mother.

Settling down in the chair at the bedside, she looked at the sleeping mother, wondering how long it would be before the patient would be ready to speak. The baby seemed settled, but she was becoming restive as she observed the pallor on Emily's face.

It was an absurd state of affairs: she wished to converse with Emily in a rather intimate way, but was inhibited by her friend's appearance. It looked as if she was in a deep sleep, in which case she should not be disturbed; on the other hand, her lack of colour could be serious, an indication that professional attention might be required. It worried her that Emily did not seem to be breathing.

Rising from her chair, she stood by the bed and, seeing no sign of movement at chest level, she decided to investigate. She knew she could solve the problem by feeling the pulse, but wondered if she could still do it properly. Circling Emily's wrist, she felt with her fingers for the movement that might relieve her tension.

Feeling no movement, but still keeping a grip, she discarded niceties and took the plunge and in a stage whisper she asked her friend, "Are you all right, Emily?"

For a critical half minute there was no response and then she felt her own hand being squeezed and Emily was smiling to her.

The young mother nodded her head, put a finger to her lips and said, "I'm tirsty."

The old woman handed her a glass of water. After a few sips Emily handed it back and, before Mrs. McGregor could question her action, she blithely explained, "I'm tirsty for coffee, Mrs. McGregor."

The old lady, although taken aback, was delighted that her patient had made such a rapid recovery. Over their coffees, they relived the last hours and both in their own way agreed that the end result had been well worthwhile, an experience they would remember. Emily made light of the pain involved and Mrs. McGregor steered clear of mentioning her anxiety when the doctor had to resort to the use of instruments.

"What about the name of the wee laddie?" Mrs. McGregor asked.

"Johan Wilhelm Sorenson," was the reply from a proud, but very tired, young mother.

It was natural the old woman would be curious to know how the first names had been arrived at. When she heard he had been named Johan after his maternal grandfather, she smiled approval; but Wilhelm, or Villem, from Edward's side, did not impress her. In her mind, she saw the heavy fierce bristling moustaches of Kaiser Bill, known as Villem to the German aristocracy and Villain to many Scots of that period.

She felt it a shame the infant should be saddled with such a heavy responsibility just after birth, but she had no option but to smile and hope the first name would always be used.

Emily was tiring now and Mrs. McGregor felt that holding the fort was becoming irksome. Where on earth was Edward? It was high time he was home looking after his wife.

Supportive of her man, Emily instanced that labour had commenced a week before the projected time and, had he known, she was sure he would never have left her side. The 'McGregor' had made up her mind.

"I'll be leaving you for half an hour, Emily," she said, and added, "if you feel you are safe."

~

The butcher was surprised to see the old lady.

"You're late today, Mrs. McGregor. What can I do for you?"

Mrs. McGregor left him in no doubt what she expected him to do. "Get in touch with Edward Sorenson and tell him to come home immediately, his wife has just had a bairn and needs his support. God knows why he should be gallivanting in Leith at a time like this."

Tam Richards was sympathetic, but what could he do? Edward was a free agent; he had no idea where to contact him.

But Mrs. McGregor was more positive; she knew what should be done and told him how she expected it done - after all, his shop telephone was surely more than an ornament.

Mr. Horsburgh, proprietor of the Sailor's Rest, had just escorted two rather obstreperous persons from his premises when his head barman came out to the street and informed him that a Mr. Richards was on the telephone. Mr. Horsburgh was inclined to be brusque until he learned that Mrs. Sorenson had given birth to a son, and, as Edward was somewhere in Leith, could he help in tracing him and if possible, expedite his return to Grangemouth?

Tam Richards was relieved when the publican assured him he would do his best to find the rascal and speed him homewards. Horsburgh remembered that

Edward had been drinking with three friends an hour prior to the call. He sent a messenger over to the Customs House and telephoned Sven and the police, telling them that Edward Sorenson was required immediately at home in Grangemouth.

Rory, Sven and Sergeant McIllwraithe, having been alerted, proceeded to search for their friend. Fortunately, the Sergeant was in Leith Police Station when the telephone message came through, just when he was about to start a shift down in the docks. Recollecting Edward's tendency to make a bee-line for any potential shipping order that might be on the horizon, he decided to make for the Harbour Master's Office.

He walked along the shore, keeping a close watch, hoping to spot the missing father. Reaching his first duty call at the dock gate, a short distance from the Edinburgh Dock, he curtly addressed the constable on duty and was set to move on when the constable stopped him in his tracks.

"A man called Sorenson asked me to tell you he had some information for you and if you were interested, you might find him down near the elevator."

The Sergeant, caught unawares, could only exclaim, "Are you sure, constable?"

Before the policeman could reply, there was an earth-shattering explosion and the sky seawards was on fire. They both ran forward and there to their right they could see the elevator engulfed in flames.

"Phone the fire service, constable, tell them it's a major fire, then stay where you are, I'm on my way to the elevator."

The pale blue sky darkened ominously as he hurried towards the fire, a brisk wind whistled in from the sea, feeding the flames and scattering burning embers in all directions. His mood, keeping pace with the weather, darkened as he gradually neared the fire, wondering why Edward was so inconsiderate, going missing at a time like this.

He had started out quickly, but the cascading debris blown by the wind was descending too near for comfort and obliged him to travel now at a snail's pace. A piece of blazing timber knocked off his helmet and the spiralling sparks stung his face, threatening to blind him.

The ever-darkening sky and peals of thunder from the south were not reassuring, unless, of course, the rain from a probable thunderstorm dampened the ardour of the gigantic flames enjoying at present their pyrotechnic party.

Meanwhile, McIllwraithe, having rescued his helmet, advanced with extreme caution. He was now only a hundred yards away from the inferno and prepared to retreat should the enemy increase its intense fire power.

As he hesitated, an ear-splitting explosion rocked the ground under his feet, forcing him to dive for cover behind a high-sided railway van. From a relatively safe position, he was just in time to see a large part of the building blowing out, sending concrete and burning timbers skywards. For some seconds he cowered behind the van, trusting to providence and good fortune that he might be spared.

Cautiously he looked back and saw a mountain of grain spilling forth, like a giant waterfall from what, seconds before, had been the loading bay of the elevator. He knew he could go no further - the river of grain had already reached the boundary wall. There was no way through now, he would have to go back and make his report.

But then he saw on the moving mass what looked like two outstretched arms and part of a head - but there was no sign of life. He was undecided; whether to investigate or not was his dilemma - it could well be that the conditions were affecting his judgement. He knew the intense heat would prevent a close examination, but as it appeared a fellow human was involved, it was his duty at least to investigate further.

As he started forwards, he was assisted by the elements. The threatening thunderstorm broke loose, a ferocious rainstorm followed, cooling the atmosphere, and a flash of lightning showed clearly that the object floating towards the roadway was at least part of a human being.

The rain having cooled the atmosphere, he moved quickly towards his objective, arriving just in time to establish that only the hands were visible now, but the encroaching grain was threatening to swallow up anything in its path.

There was no time to waste, he delved deep into the scalding grain, scooping away to the level of the head, searching desperately for a grip on armpits, trusting that they still existed. He pulled hard, the restricted arms fell, an indication that there was at least a torso.

Gripping below the armpits, he pulled again, but the grain showed little signs of loosening its grip. The Sergeant had mixed feelings; he had hoped he might be rescuing the body of an unfortunate docker who was still alive, but now he felt the poor man was dead and extricating him from the sodden mass would be a more difficult, unrewarding task.

A Scottish Highlander faced with a crisis can be a fearsome sight and the Sergeant was no exception. Being also the anchor man for the Leith Police tug-o-war team, he was well equipped for the job in hand.

Gripping the torso tight and digging in his heels, he pulled. But, having over-estimated the power required, he shot backwards along the greasy road, holding a body in his arms.

Gaining his feet, he carried the man to comparative safety, then turning his mind to possible resuscitation, he adjusted the body for First Aid and sought a pulse. While considering his potential as a paramedic, the rainstorm had intensified and washed away the grain sticking to the clothes and face of the rescued body. He could feel no pulse and when he looked at the face, his heart sank - it was the face of his friend, Edward Sorenson.

He felt like crying, but knew that a waste of time could be crucial. He cleared the mouth, pinched the nose and used the mouth-to-mouth procedure, but felt he was getting nowhere. As he adjusted his position to put pressure on the chest, his hands slipped and he fell heavily on his friend. Wiping his hands on his tunic, he cursed his ineptitude.

He carried on with the chest pressure procedure and on the fourth movement he thought he heard a slight gasp and groan. He thought at first it was his own reaction to failure, but knew he had no option but to continue.

With the palms of his hands, he again pressed down on Edward's chest; then, releasing the pressure, made ready for the next push. Just as he was about to apply pressure, Edward coughed violently. It so upset the Sergeant that his hands slipped and he again fell heavily onto his friend.

The sudden gasp of pain from Edward alarmed him; he hoped he had not irreparably damaged him. As he sat back on his haunches, he contemplated his next move and was delighted when he saw his friend's chest moving, but was unprepared for what followed.

Edward sat bolt upright, smiled sweetly at his rescuer and thanked him for his attention.

"I must compliment you, Sergeant McIllwraithe, on your punctuality. Had you been a little later, I'm afraid I would have been unable to enjoy your company."

The Sergeant was in a quandary. It was not so much what Edward had said that concerned him; he was used to his friend treating serious questions or events in a mundane or even frivolous manner. Having witnessed Edward's horrific expulsion from the grain elevator after the massive explosion, he was at a loss to understand how Edward could have survived what must have been a terrifying experience.

As a Police Officer he knew he would be expected to send for an ambulance and take appropriate measures to prevent shock. Meanwhile Edward, having absorbed as much oxygen as his lungs could extract from the smoke-laden atmosphere, struggled manfully to his feet. Steadying his friend, the Sergeant admonished him for his sudden movement, advising him to take it easy while he summoned an ambulance.

Edward expressed surprise that the Sergeant should want an ambulance.

"I know you must have expended a great deal of energy hauling me out of the grain, but you look fit enough. I would hardly have thought you needed hospital treatment."

Knowing Edward, the Sergeant had expected resistance to his suggestion, but he had not anticipated such a fatuous reply, even from Edward. Angry at Edward's lack of sensitivity, he blasted him.

"The ambulance is meant for an idiot who has caused me more trouble than he is worth."

Edward knew he had gone too far and apologised sincerely to his friend for his rather senseless remarks, but still he insisted he was fit enough to move under his own steam.

Suddenly, the Sergeant remembered he had something to tell him and wondered if in the telling, he could convince him that he should at least attend Leith Hospital for a check-up. Putting his arm around Edward's shoulder, he addressed him in a fraternal way.

"Have it your own way, Edward, but I would have thought that a man who had just become a father would react in a more responsible fashion."

It had, of course, the opposite effect. Edward's eyes glistened gleefully and then he was serious, plying his friend ceaselessly with questions concerning the birth.

Assuming the doctor to be correct in his timing, then the baby was premature; in which case, did he know if Emily was all right, at what time did the birth take place, was it a girl or a boy?

The Sergeant assured him his wife was safe and his source of information was Mr. Horsburgh of the Sailor's Rest. It appeared the publican had received a telephone call from Mr. Richards in Grangemouth, who had been asked by Mrs. McGregor to find Edward Sorenson and instruct him to return home immediately, as his wife had given birth to a baby boy.

Edward laughed outright, telling his friend that, even if he had agreed to attend hospital, he would have had no option but to go home at once; after all, Mrs. McGregor was the type of person who, having made up her mind, would make things uncomfortable for anyone who opposed her. In any case, he was responsible for what had happened, it was essential that he reached Emily without delay.

Sergeant McIllwraithe however made Edward aware that as a Police officer he had to make a report to his superiors concerning what had happened. Edward was quite light-hearted - the brave Sergeant had rescued an unconscious man called Edward Sorenson from grain that was threatening to suffocate him. McIllwraithe was certainly not happy, he wanted to know what had happened prior to the rescue. But Edward was adamant, he would only tell the Sergeant what he considered to be enough, he had no intention of telling the full story and then finding news-hungry reporters prowling around his home, disturbing his wife during a critical period and making a general nuisance of themselves. Before the Sergeant could reply, the clanging bells of Fire Engines approaching warned them to stop speaking and make for the nearest place of safety. Two Fire Engines thundered by as they approached the Police box at the dock gate. Although Edward was determined to protect the privacy of Emily and himself, he realised he had no option but to give McIllwraithe sufficient information for his report to Head Office. As they walked towards the gate Edward had an idea as he remembered the story of a seaman who had been the victim of a shipwreck in the South Seas. During a storm an enormous tidal wave had carried him landwards, ultimately dumping him onto a rocky ledge. For days he had lain semi-conscious until rescued by a passing ship. He had survived the ordeal but lost his memory. Attempting to mollify the Sergeant he pulled on his sleeve and told him he would give him information and it would be in the presence of an official witness. As the young constable came forth from his box to report to his Sergeant Edward seized them initiative. Turning to McIllwraithe he indicated that he thought he had seen the Policeman somewhere before, not so long ago. The young constable smiled and agreed.

"You saw me about half an hour ago, sir. You asked me to pass on a message to Sergeant McIllwraithe."

Edward was delighted and responded accordingly.

"How pleased I am - it looks as if my memory is slowly returning. I wonder if you saw a small rather shabbily dressed man passing by a few minutes prior to my arrival?"

The young constable, obviously in line for promotion, had been very alert. "Yes, you are correct, sir, he preceded you by about two hundred yards."

Edward put his hand to his head - it was all returning now. He remembered following Mr. Nesbit, having reason to believe that he would be meeting someone connected with drug smuggling. He had seen Nesbit disappear around the corner of the elevator - after that everything was a blank. When he regained consciousness it was to find that the brave Sergeant had saved him from suffocation. Feeling he had adjusted the situation in such a way that his friend would now be able to submit a report to the Police authority he bade him 'farewell'.

"I'm off to Grangemouth now. I will contact you in the next few days, and hopefully I will have overcome what I think can only be a temporary state of amnesia."

On his way to the railway station he realised that his personal appearance was socially unacceptable. His clothes smelled of scorched grain, he was soaked to the skin and felt dirty despite his drenching during the thunderstorm, and knew he could not go back home in such a dishevelled condition. He swung right and headed for Sandport Street, knowing he had left a suit hanging in a cupboard in Ove's place. He was interested in how he looked, and seeing a chemist shop with a large mirror frontage he stopped. What he saw startled him: at first glance he was wearing a blood red collar with white streaks. It took some seconds to recognise that his white collar had become saturated with blood from his bleeding ear.

On close examination he could see the bullet had nicked out a small piece of that delicate organ. He trembled a little when he remembered that the man he was looking at had just survived a most hellish experience. As he turned from the mirror the man disappeared and he felt thankful that it had just been a nightmare. But if it was a bad dream, why was he not in bed? Why was he standing fully dressed in front of a chemist's shop window in Bernard Street?

He turned back to the window and there was the man again. For a moment he almost panicked, then he smiled and the man smiled back; then he sighed, knowing his sanity had returned.

When he reached the shore, he knew it was decision time. Should he change his mind and turn left for the hospital, or carry straight on to Sandport Street? His friend had advised the hospital, no doubt having in mind the possibility of shock after his ordeal. Edward reckoned that the chastening experience at the chemist's window was a big enough shock and, having survived it, he decided to go straight ahead.

As he crossed the bridge two amply-portioned women came towards him. Always the gentleman, he stepped from their pathway down to the tram lines, slipped and almost came a cropper. Regaining his balance, he gave them an affectionate smile, but the two matronly figures paid scant attention to his diversionary ploy - they were more concerned with his appearance. The one nearest to him turned to her neighbour and expressed her feelings.

"Did ye see that man, Aggie? What a smell o' drink."

Her companion concurred and added her visual comment.

"Aye! but did ye notice he'd been fechtin and his throat's cut?"

Edward, although recognising the legitimacy of their remarks, was in no mood to allow their observations to deter him in his drive to arrive home in a respectable state.

He set about the first stage of rehabilitation, discarding his blood-stained collar, washing his neck and face, finally spraying eau de cologne over his clothes to camouflage the ale house stench. Taking the clothes he required, he parcelled them up and made tracks for the Commercial Hotel at the foot of Sandport Street.

He knew he would be welcomed by the proprietor, Wolfgang Richter. He had met the German some years before in Hamburg and although they had only been in each other's company for three days, they had become firm friends. Wolfgang, in his youth, had been attached to the paramedics in the German Army and this had influenced his way of thinking. His contribution to the classless society was to encourage all he came in contact with to adopt the principles of Syndicalism.

He had been arrested, imprisoned for two years and then discharged and ultimately, escaping the attentions of the Secret Police, had found his way to Scotland.

The hotelier, though pleased to see Edward, was disappointed that his friend would not be booking in for bed and breakfast. Edward pointed to his clothes and replied that all he required was a hot bath, a change of clothes and then he would be off, post-haste, to Grangemouth to see his first-born.

Wolfgang complimented him and then, making reference to his appearance, asked, "How come you look like a 'drookit hen', as our Scottish hosts might say? And smell like a brewery, with just a touch of *parfum a la brothel*? Not to mention the tip of your ear, which she seems to have bitten off."

Edward sighed visibly, and countered, "Just come outside before I explain."

Wolfgang agreed readily, knowing that Edward was really serious.

When they emerged from the hotel, he was astonished to see that a large part of Leith dockland was ablaze. He knew now that Edward had been involved in something unusual, probably dangerous, but hopefully within the law.

When Edward explained that he had been a victim of the fire and subsequent thunderstorm, Wolfgang realised that his friend was telling the truth, but the story that flying debris had damaged his ear seemed rather questionable. Still, one should never doubt one's friends.

Edward lay back in the big bath and gave a long sigh of contentment. The last hour having been the most eventful of his young life, he felt he deserved some minutes of perfect peace. As he dressed, he consulted his railway timetable and felt slightly deflated when he discovered it would be another two hours before a connection to Grangemouth would be available. Wolfgang Richter tried to inveigle him to stay for dinner.

"I started a Swiss chef two months ago - why not let him cook you one of his specialities?"

Edward declined gracefully, but promised he would return with his wife and son.

Wolfgang pointed to his ear. "Before you go, at least let me attend to your war wound."

As he treated the ear, he reminisced. 'The last time I fitted a plaster on an ear was during an exercise with live ammunition. The paramedics were being put through their paces, they had to rescue the wounded and bring them back to base. One poor lad's ear had been nicked in the process, his injury from a stray bullet was almost identical to your own."

Taken by surprise, Edward gasped, wondering if Wolfgang had guessed the origin of his injury. But his friend, like all good medics, was totally absorbed in his work.

Having finished dressing his ear, Wolfgang offered him schnapps, which he gladly accepted. Then, thanking him for his attention, he left with the intention of reaching home as quickly as possible. If he took the train, he would be home in three hours; if he unearthed the bike in Sandport Street, he could make his target in less than two hours. Speed was of the essence and there was another alternative, but it meant a call at the Sailor's Rest.

When he entered, Mr. Horsburgh greeted him like a long-lost son. "Where have you been, Edward? We've had a search party out looking you. Do you know your wife has given birth to a son?"

Edward assured him he had been made aware of the happy event by Sergeant McIllwraithe - and if it had not been for the action of the good Sergeant, he would not now be talking to him, but that was a story for the future.

He reminded the publican that on one occasion he had advised that the use of a car as opposed to a bike could prove more profitable. The astute Mr. Horsburgh smiled broadly; being a canny Scot he knew what was coming next.

Before Edward could ask, he intervened. "So you think if I loaned you my car you would get back to your wife a wee bit quicker?"

Edward reacted brightly. "What a wonderful idea! Why didn't I think about that? I would be extremely grateful if you put your car at my disposal."

Mr. Horsburgh, although happy to oblige wanted to ensure that Edward could drive the car in a safe and proper fashion. After citing the five day trouble-free holiday in Einer's car, the publican agreed. If Einer, whom he knew, could risk his car, then he was quite prepared to let Edward have the car for the next five days.

Edward was overwhelmed by the publican's generosity and indicated that he could return the vehicle the following day.

Mr. Horsburgh gripped his hand and assured him that he would rather have Edward looking after the car for the next five days. Looking around the bar, he lowered his voice and told him that for the next five days he would be joining Dr. Broad at Applecross and hopefully the fish might be biting in the sea lochs.

'The responsibility of looking after the car, Edward, will belong to you."

Always ready for action, Edward was restive as he awaited a move from Mr. Horsburgh, but the publican was still curious, wishing to know what had happened during that vital interval. Edward assured him the whole story would be told when he returned with the car; in the meantime, Sergeant McIllwraithe was free to divulge what he knew, but his story could not be told until he had overcome his temporary amnesia.

Mr. Horsburgh knew he would have to wait, but as a genial host he wished him well. "Have a snifter, Edward, before you go."

But Edward, always alive to his responsibility, replied, "No thanks, remember I am driving."

As he drove towards Grangemouth, he knew from experience that his neighbour, Mrs. McGregor, would be attending to Emily's needs and he expected to be chided by her for not being on the spot during the birth.

What he had not bargained for was the frosty reception he was accorded by an old lady who had nursed her wrath to ensure that a self-indulgent husband was given the scolding he deserved for being senseless, wasting time in Leith when he should have known that his wife could be placed at hazard at their home in Grangemouth.

"Edward Sorenson, you should be ashamed of yourself! You knew Emily was expecting, you should hae been here to help her."

Caught by surprise, he could only stand and stare vacantly at the old woman. He was at a disadvantage and felt she was being unfair, but on the other hand he understood from her attitude that the birth had been a difficult one. This was no time for excuses or clever explanations, he was too anxious to know what had happened to Emily.

He raised his arms in supplication, clenching tightly in a fist a bunch of flowers he had just purchased for his wife. Standing there, he looked incongruous and his admission was given short shrift.

Mrs. McGregor was still very much in charge. "Give me the flowers, Edward, before you kill them. I'll put them in water and bring them to the bedside."

The infant was sleeping and Emily had just been propped up when Edward entered the bedroom. As he kissed her, she noticed the rather neat dressing on his ear. When asked what had happened, he dismissed it as nothing of significance, he had suffered more trouble when shaving, he was far more concerned about what had happened to her since leaving home in the morning.

It had been a rather dreary and painful experience, there had been complications and she only wished the doctor had been more accurate in his forecast, so that they both could have been together at the time of the birth.

She was happy that he was with her now, she felt that in a week's time the birth could have been even more complicated. She would be able to look back then and rejoice that the travail of conception was over.

As Edward looked at his son, he saw the marks of the instruments on the child's head and felt sad and impotent that he had not been able to influence the end result. He knew he would have to be careful when he talked with Emily concerning the appearance of their son.

As he looked at her she smiled, she seemed to know what was on his mind. "Well, what do you think, Edward?" she said.

He leaned forward, kissed her and replied, "He looks healthy and strong, his high domed head indicates an exceptional brain."

Her answer shook him. "Let's hope the marks from the instruments have no ill effects."

Before he could reply, she continued, "I heard the doctor speaking to Mrs. McGregor and he thinks the marks will be gone in less than a month."

Edward marvelled at her attitude, she seemed so self-assured; even light-hearted, despite an experience he guessed must have been harrowing.

He held her hand and talked about their son and his future. She pressed her fingers against the palm of his hand and asked conspiratorially, "Now tell me what really happened to your ear."

He thought that to tell the truth to his wife could be devastating; on the other hand to tell lies would be self-destructive and contagious. He chose the middle path of being economic with the truth. He told her he had made his way to the docks, there had been an explosion, the big grain elevator had caught fire. Sparks, debris, even grain had been flying all over the place. How he had received his injury he could not tell, but cited the case of Sergeant McIllwraithe, whose helmet had been knocked flying from his head by a piece of blazing wood.

At that moment Mrs. McGregor entered with a vase of flowers, giving Edward the opportunity he required to dodge the really hazardous part of the story and concentrate instead on the generosity of Mr. Horsburgh who, having loaned him his car, ensured that he arrived home two hours earlier, not having had to wait for a train.. Emily was delighted that he had shown such determination and initiative in arriving home so speedily.

For the next few days the Sorensons decided to enjoy being housebound. Emily's recovery was swift, but gave Edward sufficient time to fuss around the house and plan leisurely for the future. The infant's behaviour was exemplary, a delight to behold. As they slept soundly, the young Johan Wilhelm-to-be did likewise.

On the third day, Edward organised an outing in the car, feeling it was about time the Sorensons paid a visit to the outside world. Emily was happy, she looked forward to seeing her Scandinavian friends. Although she was grateful for the attention and ministrations of Mrs. McGregor, she was looking forward to meeting women nearer her own age group.

Edward drove with extreme care and attention; he had no option, Emily having insisted that she and the infant should sit beside him. It was his intention to follow the coast and after passing the Forth Bridge, to head inland towards the rural area.

Realising she was passing through Boness, Emily suggested that it would be rude not to visit the Wevlings, particularly as they were barely a quarter of a mile from the Emporium. He was shrewd enough to know he had little option, guessing that Emily had in mind that it was Norma's turn to entertain the ladies.

Norma, delighted to see them, welcomed them in her usual hearty fashion. Edward had guessed correctly: waiting to see them was Jessie Mathieson, Greta Thorvaldson and their husbands. He was agreeably surprised to see the men folk and happy to know he would not now be solely in the company of women.

It seemed inevitable that Johan Wilhelm would reign supreme. They all paid their respects to the newcomer, the ladies in particular admitted to the proud mother that they had never, until now, seen such a perfectly formed child.

Unaware of the importance of the occasion, the infant yawned most of the time and Norma, the perfect hostess, recognising that his majesty was desirous of sleep, arranged a cushion on the sofa so that he could safely sleep without the hazard of bouncing to the floor.

As the womenfolk talked excitedly amongst themselves, Einer Wevling signalled to his wife. She smiled, nodded her head and he discreetly led his companions to the inner sanctum.

As could be expected, the wetting of the head of the bairn, a phrase used by Doctor Mathieson, was accomplished in the form of drams of Antiquary doled out by Einer from his own secret whisky store. As they toasted the well-being of the newly born, they acknowledged, after some light-hearted banter, that Edward had proved his prowess in fathering a fine boy.

As the women concentrated their attention on the new arrival, the men focused attention on business and current events. Thorvaldson, a director in Norske Fiskeri, was happy there had been a significant increase in whale catching over the last few months. On the other hand, Doctor Mathieson was pessimistic, there had been an alarming increase in respiratory cases during the same period. Einer was pleased that Thorvaldson was having a whale of a time and sympathised with the doctor in his fight against bronchitis and other conditions of the lungs.

It had not escaped Edward's attention that the conversational pendulum was swinging inexorably towards him. Having done his stint, Einer Wevling looked in his direction, indicating that it was his turn.

"And what have you been up to, Edward?" he asked.

"Oh, things have been rather quiet," Edward replied. He outlined that although business had been slow, the preparation for the birth had so absorbed him and his wife that social activity could be described as minimal. As expected the birth of a son had been an exciting and rewarding experience.

As Edward hesitated, Einer teased him. "Yes, you must be a happy man, but I'm surprised that your business in the docks has been so humdrum."

Shrugging his shoulders, Edward indicated that the word humdrum was not applicable, but the last visit to

Leith had not shown a profit. Einer laughed heartily and praised him for his understatement.

"Before you involve yourself, Edward, I should tell you that I was in the company of Sergeant McIllwraithe late last night; he is a friend of mine, you know."

Edward smiled approvingly and attempted to sidetrack the curiosity of his friend. "In which case you will know the gallant Sergeant probably saved my life during the fire which engulfed the elevator. How I came to be there has still to be established and when my amnesia has been conquered, he will be the first to know. Until then it would be unfair for me to make further comment."

Einer and Thorvaldson still coaxed him, but Edward did not respond. Einer persisted that he knew that some dead men had been recovered, also he knew that Edward had been at risk.

Doctor Mathieson intervened. "I think we should let him be, chaps. I'm sure he will tell us all when circumstances permit."

The chest surgeon admitted that his knowledge of the condition known as amnesia was limited, but knowing Edward, he was sure that he would overcome it.

"I am sure," he said, "he has undergone a terrifying experience and has wisely decided to say nothing until he is sure that his wife would not be adversely affected."

Edward seized the opportunity to thank the doctor for being considerate and expressed the view that he should add psychology to his other merits. He did admit that his amnesia was a ploy, set in motion to stave off the newshounds during Emily's confinement, but the critical period was over now and a report would be made to the Sergeant and then the truth could come out at a time when Emily was not at risk.

When the Sorensons arrived home in the late afternoon, Mrs. McGregor was there to meet them and, after fussing around Emily and the bairn, she told Edward that Tam Richards had received an important telephone message and that Edward was to ring back Leith Police Station.

As he saw her to the door, she turned and in a rather nervous voice, asked, "What have you been up to now, Edward? It's a Police Sergeant that wants to speak to you."

Edward put his arm around her shoulders in a comforting fashion and assured her that the policeman concerned was a friend of his who was probably needing information from him concerning the elevator fire in which they had both been involved.

Mrs. McGregor's brow furrowed and her mouth puckered as she admitted that she might have been a little hasty in scolding him, but she still felt it necessary to tell him that if Emily or the bairn were put at risk, he could expect to get the sharp end of her tongue.

As he smiled, he thanked her for what she had done and told her that when she learned all the facts concerning his late arrival, he was sure she would forgive him.

Never guilty of wasting time, he made tracks for the butcher's shop and was just in time to prevent Tam Richards putting up the shutters. Tam seemed cagey and a little concerned - something was obviously worrying him.

"A Sergeant in the Leith Police rang the shop two hours ago, he wanted to speak to you, I think his name is McIllwraithe."

Edward placated him. "Not to worry, Tam. McIllwraithe was first on the scene during the elevator fire and as I had to leave suddenly due to my wife's pregnancy, he no doubt wants to clear up a few points regarding the possible cause of the fire."

As Edward telephoned the Sergeant, Tam listened intently to the conversation. When finished with the

Sergeant, Edward turned to the butcher, knowing he had probably heard some of the Sergeant's remarks.

"You might like to know, Tam, that I am not suspected of smuggling, but some corpses have been found inside the elevator and it seems they might well have been cocaine smugglers using the elevator as a secret rendezvous."

The butcher appeared surprised and reacted accordingly. "Jesus Christ, well I never!"

Then, as if to ensure that Edward would not consider him a complete fool, he attempted to summarise a possible chain of events. He told Edward he had learned from friends in Leith that he had been involved some time ago in a pub brawl that had put the police on the trail of an American suspected of dealing in drugs. Some time afterwards, the police captured a number of smugglers and a large amount of cocaine.

As the butcher paused for breath, Edward remarked, "And so?"

There was a crafty look on Tam's face as he continued. "I well remember the police were successful due to the information given them by a certain person."

Edward gasped, "You don't say."

"Aye, ah do," replied Tam.

Again he hesitated and as Edward did not react, he pointed his finger and finished dramatically, "And I jalouse that you were that man."

Edward appeared perplexed and asked, "What does the word 'jalouse' mean, Tam? To date, my vocabulary does not encompass it."

The butcher reacted testily. "You know damn well what I mean, as a student of languages you might have preferred the fancy English word 'deduce'."

Edward laughed heartily before replying. "You are free to jalouse or deduce whatever you wish, but there is one thing you must not do and that is to tell Mrs. McGregor about your deduction."

The butcher slapped his thigh and laughed. "I knew I was right," he said.

Edward again cautioned him that he should not, in the course of blathering with Mrs. McGregor, inadvertently make his views known in case Emily was alerted to a danger which no longer existed.

The butcher tapped the side of his nose, a significant sign of worldly wisdom and proclaimed paternally, "Leave it to me, son. I know how you feel and by the way, I'm proud of you."

Chapter 25

Emily, happy and fulfilled, waved cheerily to Edward as he left in Mr. Horsburgh's car for his assignment with Sergeant McIllwraithe in Leith. As he drove slowly and cautiously, his mind travelled back in time. It seemed to have slipped past so effortlessly, yet so much had happened during the last two years. He felt as though he was reaching the end of a chapter in his life and already preparing for the next.

Although he appreciated that Tam Richards had given him a start, he had repaid the investment handsomely in shipping orders, giving a far higher profit level than the bluff butcher could have expected.

It was time for a change. He knew from experience that Leith offered him a glorious opportunity of establishing a profitable ship chandler's business. He also knew that he still required to increase his earnings before he acquired the necessary capital for such a venture. It appeared to him that Mr. Blackwell, the butcher in Sandport Street, should be the first person he contacted.

He drove first to the Sailor's Rest. After parking the car as advised by Mr. Horsburgh, he set out on the next chapter of his life in Scotland.

For some minutes he stood staring at the Water of Leith, then a little smile flitted across his face as he remembered the night when, overcome by the usquebaugh germ, he had boasted he was in a fit enough state to walk upon the water, but good old Sven had warned him that his faith in Christ was inadequate for such an onerous task.

Turning his back on the Shore, he walked leisurely towards Sandport Street. On reaching the Commercial Hotel he felt duty bound to walk in and thank the owner for the assistance he had rendered after the elevator fire.

Wolfgang Richter, having just accepted a case of akvavit from an unknown source, implored Edward to sample a glass and give an expert opinion. As he could hardly refuse such a kind offer, he sampled the liquor and passed it as first class.

Next stop on his list was the butcher's shop just around the corner and, hopefully, an interview with the old man himself.

Almost immediately he knew he would have to postpone the interview, for outside the shop was parked a big van; standing beside it was Harry MacSween. It was an inopportune moment, he would rather have spoken with the big man later, but was not given the option, he had to respond to Harry's cheery and effusive greeting.

Harry pointed to the van. "I remember you telling me some time ago that you would do your best to channel some big orders my way, so that I could buy a new van."

"It would appear that we have both been extremely successful," was Edward's reply.

Harry dug Edward gently in the ribs and, after the riposte "You can say that again", he outlined what had happened over the last few months. Profits on sales had been high enough to trade in three small vans and replace them with the latest new design and a bank loan had given him the opportunity to acquire a custom-built four-ton transporter for the really big carcasses.

He proudly informed Edward that his latest acquisition could transport six sides of beef if required and, as many of the bigger animals weighed in excess of a ton, he was sure Edward would appreciate that business was booming.

Being stymied in his desire to contact Mr. Blackwell, Edward was restive as he pondered his next move. At that moment, Ove emerged from his small shop at the top of Sandport Street and Edward, realising he had to move fast, tapped Harry on the shoulder and asked him to look up the street.

As Harry looked, he was told that the man with the seaman's hat was a friend he had been trying to contact for some time. Would Harry excuse him as it was important he should contact Ove before he disappeared from sight.

Harry laughed loudly and replied. "On your bike, Edward, and catch him. Then come back and have a snifter, you know where, when you're finished."

Ove had almost reached Bridge Street before Edward caught him up. He was delighted to see Edward and insisted they should go back to the shop and exchange their experiences over the last few months.

It was to be expected that the two men, coming as they did from similar backgrounds, should have something in common. For almost an hour they exercised their power of recall and some fancy stories were told.

Although enjoying the camaraderie, Edward realised he was lagging behind with his timetable and felt he should admit to his friend what he hoped to achieve. Ove was magnanimous.

"Go to it, Edward," he said. "We can always swap yarns at a time more suitable to both of us."

The interview with the old Master Butcher was a qualified success. Holding a high position in the Master Butchers' Association, he was adamant that, should Edward make a move, he had to guarantee that Tam Richards knew in advance what was happening and that there was no possibility of his employer voicing a plea of unfinished business.

The old butcher accepted his assurance and Edward set out to deal with the next item of his itinerary.

Next en route was Leith Academy, a fine school overlooking the Links. After making enquiries regarding the education of his son, he visited local house agents concerning the possibility of renting accommodation in a neighbourhood adjacent to the docks.

Now was the hour he had prepared himself for. Having promised his friend Sergeant McIllwraithe that he would tell all, he felt happy he could at last unburden himself. It had been a nightmare re-living his hellish experience in the elevator and knowing he could tell no one until Emily was safely through her confinement.

The four men who sat in a private room in the Sailor's Rest each speculated in his own way what Edward Sorenson would say and how it might affect them. Sergeant McIllwraithe, who had convened the meeting, hoped and trusted that Edward, on this occasion, would provide information that would raise his status as a competent investigator and stop his immediate superiors pestering him.

His uncle, Rory McLeod, was quite confident that his friend would, with his wit, wisdom and wile, provide an entertaining and informative afternoon, hopefully spiced with some controversial material.

And Sven, knowing Edward, hoped his friend could remain serious enough for long enough to prove he really was an asset to the Scottish scene.

But Inspector Mackintosh of Scotland Yard, having been sent north to investigate the mystery of finding six badly burned corpses within the burnt-out elevator, was in an extremely serious mood, particularly when it had been established that it had been a Port holiday and no one, with the exception of a watchman, should have been on the premises.

When Edward entered, Mr. Horsburgh took him aside and advised him.

'Young McIllwraithe is in the private room along with your friends, but watch your step, a London detective from the 'Yard' has just joined them.'

As he entered the room, Rory McLeod and Sven Sjogren acclaimed him like a hero returned from the wars, whilst Sergeant McIllwraithe sighed with relief that Edward had at last arrived, and the man from the Yard's secret squad nodded sagely.

The Sergeant introduced the stranger to Edward.

"Inspector Mackintosh from Scotland Yard has asked to be present when you outline what you know of any events that took place prior to, and if possible during, the fire that destroyed the grain elevator at Leith."

Edward looked directly at Inspector Mackintosh and asked, "Forgive me for asking, but are you the inventor of that world acclaimed waterproof?"

The Anglo-Scot replied breezily, "No, that was my father and I can only hope and trust that you have a waterproof case regarding your innocence in any event that led to and ended in the conflagration at the Leith grain elevator."

Although slightly unnerved by the Inspector's attitude, he made it crystal clear that he had come at the behest of Sergeant McIllwraithe to give him information of what he knew about the elevator fire and if Inspector Mackintosh was conducting an enquiry or investigation on behalf of Scotland Yard, then he had no objection to him remaining in the room, provided the Sergeant agreed.

The Inspector frowned, the Sergeant said nothing and Edward started his story. They listened in rapt attention as the plot unfolded. Even the 'Yard' man was impressed and the Sergeant saw fit to add the important part he had played in the latter stages.

Edward admitted that, through sheer stupidity, he had been led into a trap set by the cocaine smugglers. He outlined how a man who introduced himself as Pierre le Blanc had dominated the proceedings.

Hopelessly trapped and held at pistol point, he knew he was doomed to die, but through guile and flattery, he managed to procrastinate long enough to give himself the possibility of a suicidal attempt to cheat death.

Six men and a loaded pistol covered his escape through the elevator door, but a backward dive deep into the grain gave a remote chance for survival. He had dived, the pistol had been fired and as far as he knew, the flash had ignited the gas from the sweltering grain.

How he had survived, he would never know. Suffocating, burning and dying in the Stygian morass, a blinding blue light had put an end to his torture - he had assumed he was in heaven. He knew now there had been a second explosion and he had been carried out in a river of grain.

For almost a minute there was silence in the room. Then Rory came round to Edward, clapped him on the shoulder and gave his verdict.

"I'll say it again, Edward - you're a helluva man!"

And Sven commiserated, "It must have been a terrible experience, only a hero could survive."

Edward laughed at the idea that he was a hero; he had been a very frightened man; the real hero was the Sergeant sitting opposite him; had it not been for the Sergeant, he would not be speaking to them now.

Looking directly at McIllwraithe, he asked if what he had said would now allow him to complete his report and the Sergeant, with half an eye on his interloping superior from the south, proclaimed, "I haff all the details I require, Mr. Sorenson."

But the man from down south, although appreciating Edward's testimony, was unsure that it met his requirements.

"I have listened carefully to all you have said, Mr Sorenson, and I am sure you have been helpful in reducing narcotic offences, but as I have been assigned by Scotland Yard to investigate the deaths of six men found within the burned out elevator, I would appreciate your assistance."

As Edward nodded approval, he asked him to describe what the men looked like and Edward indicated he could, but he had no intention of wasting time; the Sergeant, no doubt, would provide all the information he required in the case of four men who already had local criminal records.

He was, however, prepared to describe the other two. For a moment the Inspector seemed perplexed, then he smiled and nodded his head and Edward gave a description.

Facially, the man with the permanent smile looked very like the Inspector himself, but would probably be about half his weight and was no bigger than five and a half feet. The professed leader of the gang, who had held Edward at pistol point, was a commanding figure. He was at least six feet tall, well proportioned and well dressed and had all the airs of a successful man. He was a product of the French middle class.

The Inspector felt he had to intervene.

"Although you are a Scandinavian, Mr. Sorenson, it appears you are acquaint with the character Sherlock Holmes."

He looked plaintively at the detective and agreed he had heard of Conan Doyle, but his observations were not fanciful, they were based on his own linguistic potential.

The Inspector persisted with the investigation. "Can you prove, Mr. Sorenson, that you were in the elevator when the fire started?"

Edward sighed before replying.

"I'm afraid that six burnt out corpses are hardly in a position to support my story, although I might suggest that one body might have two fingers missing from his right hand and the leader of the gang might still have a necklace round his neck, despite the intensity of the fire, and a German pistol with a silencer somewhere near the body."

The Inspector, although impressed, stuck to his task, but the Sergeant felt it necessary to bring the Inspector down to earth.

"When I arrived on the scene, Inspector Mackintosh, I was in time to see the blast out from the loading bay and shortly afterwards, as the grain poured out, I could see an arm pointing sky-wards being swept along by the outflow of grain. I ran towards the outflow, hoping that the person attached to the arm was still alive.

"The arm had all but disappeared by the time I reached what was now a river of grain. Fortunately, I was in time to pull Mr. Sorenson clear and probably saved him from suffocation."

Edward could not contain himself.

"Bravo, Sergeant," he exclaimed, and added, "it would appear, Inspector, that your question has been satisfactorily answered."

The man from the Yard grinned and explained that he was duty bound to search for a motive where life had been lost. Edward agreed readily, as in his estimation his own life had taken top priority. As far as he was concerned the elimination of himself, a water agent, who in all innocence had interfered with the plans of a cocaine boss, had surely to be above suspicion. He hesitated, then asked the Inspector if he should continue.

The Inspector assented. "By all means, Mr. Sorenson. I'm sure you have something interesting to tell me."

Knowing his life was at stake, Edward had gambled on the assumption that many so-called successful men are inordinately vain. He had provoked Pierre le Blanc, telling him that if he had been efficient, he would have sacked Lucius Chancitt before the ineptitude of his second-in-command had allowed him to learn so much of the French Canadian's plans.

Pierre, secure in the belief that Edward would soon be dead, had boasted that he was probably the most successful business man in the North of England, owning first class hotels and a leisure centre in Carlisle that was frequented by civic leaders and others of international repute.

For a full minute they waited for the Inspector's reaction to Edward's summation, and to speed things up Edward concluded, "If you have no more questions, I could offer an opinion that I feel could be helpful to the police."

The Inspector pursed his lips, but still said nothing and Edward felt compelled to continue.

"You were looking for motives. The person with a motive was Pierre le Blanc, alias Peter White, who hoped that, by killing me, he would eliminate someone who was spoiling his plans. It was poetic justice that the plan backfired and that he would self-destruct in the process. On the assumption that Peter White was telling the truth, it should not be difficult to trace his assets and contacts."

Edward grinned as he theorised.

"I can see you now, Inspector, acquiring the necessary search warrant to delve into the private affairs of Mr. White, who had died suddenly in extremely suspicious circumstances. Warrant for Search would also be required where the initial investigation proved that certain important figures had been involved with the said Peter White, alias Pierre le Blanc, in his illegal activities."

The Inspector did not reply. Rising from his seat, he walked over to Edward and stood facing him, his hands resting on his hips. For a moment or two he looked quizzically at the young salesman and then observed, "I have never met a person quite like you before, Mr.

Sorenson - you are a very interesting and remarkable man. You have obviously undergone a traumatic experience. I can only advise that in future you choose your company with much more care."

Edward nodded his head and, pointing directly at his friends, he agreed.

As the Inspector made his exit, his voice was barely audible. "Present company excepted, of course."

Inspector Mackintosh, known as 'Macsiccar' to the constabulary of London, grinned all the way to the Central Station in Leith. He was a happy man, knowing he had been fortunate in meeting Edward. The information he had received was valuable; even the suggestion that Edward had pinned on at the end of his testimony showed an astuteness he admired.

Like a true Scot, he had been canny with his own information and had deemed it unnecessary to inform Edward that the forensic squad had discovered one skeleton with two fingers missing, and in the hand of another, when the fingers were prised open, a partially melted gold crucifix was revealed, the name 'Pierre' was barely visible.

Having heard from colleagues in the North of England about Peter White, a French Canadian, who had prospered as a business man, but was suspected of having criminal contacts, he knew he was on to a winner. He remembered the expression 'artistic pursuits' and remembered the story of a famous politician being caught with his pants down in Peter White's palace of pleasure.

As the Inspector stepped onto the train, he blessed Edward for having guided him in the direction of righteousness.

Meanwhile, back at the Sailor's Rest, the four friends felt free to enjoy themselves. Sergeant McIllwraithe apologised to Edward and asked forgiveness - had he known that Inspector Mackintosh would appear on the scene, he would have warned him. As Edward dismissed it with his usual 'no problem', the Sergeant added that Mackintosh would certainly make full use of the information and the idea Edward had provided.

Edward shrugged his shoulders, acknowledging that an intelligent Scot would not only understand the value of his statement, but would realise that his idea did 'warrant' attention.

For a moment nothing was said, then the Sergeant and Edward looked at the other two, as much as to say, 'We've done our bit, now it's your turn'.

Rory, a big strong West Highlandman, had all the attributes of his countrymen: intelligence, inventiveness, patience and resourcefulness; all the qualities required when dealing with dangerous and greedy drug traffickers. He had watched Edward's attitude during the Inspector's interrogation and admired the way he had handled the situation.

Rory liked Edward, had done so from the first time he had met him, an affection which had increased as the young Scandinavian had volunteered his services and had been instrumental in exposing cocaine smugglers to the Customs and the Police.

Rory coughed gently, a sure sign that he was about to make an important statement.

"I applaud your determination, Edward, to win against the powers of evil and may good fortune attend you in all you strive to accomplish, but I feel it necessary to warn you once more that life is far too short to take the foreseeable risks you seem to consider normal."

Before he could reply, the Sergeant intervened, hoping he could influence the proceedings.

"You are quite right, Uncle, but what can you do with a man like Edward? We've warned him on numerous occasions."

Edward accepted their views philosophically and assured them that, as a father, he had no option now but to slow down, agreeing that, in retrospect, his life had been just that bit too bizarre.

But Sergeant McIllwraithe still felt he was not treating the matter with the seriousness it warranted and voiced his reservations in a manner that suited him.

"At school on the Island of Skye, when a hand shot up, the teacher would not proceed until the question had been suitably dealt with."

Edward smiled encouragingly, but made no comment and McIllwraithe continued.

"As I approached the elevator I saw this hand pointing sky-wards. When the grain spilled forth I knew I had to answer the question. Had I known it was the hand of Edward Sorenson, I would have gone back to school for further education."

Edward assured the Sergeant that he had passed with honours and should not demean himself. As the verbal fencing showed signs of continuing, the rather staid Sven thought fit to intervene.

"If the two protagonists will desist, I would like to enlighten a fellow Scandinavian concerning what is happening in his wife's original back yard."

Clapping him on the shoulder, Edward assured him that he would like to hear, but insisted that first and foremost drinks had to be assembled for a very important toast.

Glasses filled, Edward toasted Sergeant McIllwraithe. "This toast is to a very remarkable man, who, remembering his early school days, followed a raised hand through a sea of grain. He solved the problem and saved my life, for which I shall be forever grateful."

Following the toast, Rory and Sven voiced their approval of the young Sergeant's bravery, while the centre of their attention sat staring into space, appearing embarrassed, wondering what to say. Rory thought fit to encourage his nephew.

"Come on, laddie, have your say."

There was a whisper of a smile on the young policeman's face as he spoke in his soft West Highland dialect.

"I was chust doing my duty, the chob for which I was trained."

The three men reacted spontaneously. Rising from their seats, they clapped him on the shoulders, applauding his selfless attitude towards life and his fellow man.

From that moment normal service resumed, with the four of them exchanging views and ready to vie with each other in the telling of interesting happenings or tall yarns.

It appeared that Sven had collected letters that afternoon from the Sailors' Home in the Shore and he thought his friends might be interested in what amounted to certain developments in Scandinavia.

A letter from a man called Per Axelson concerned the ongoing debate between Norway and Sweden and the changes taking place since Norway's independence. It appeared that Axelson had taken advantage of a Swedish Government training scheme and had ultimately qualified as an expert in the construction and maintenance of the modern Swedish motor-ship.

Axelson had shown a great interest in such craft and was now commuting regularly between Christiana and Gothenburg as a design expert on behalf of the Swedish Government.

Rory intervened from time to time, asking for more details and when Sven hesitated, Rory encouraged him to continue, adding that any improved method of transport which brought the maximum number of people closer together, was surely worthwhile.

Sven smilingly nodded agreement and was about to start again, when Rory recalled he had a cousin called Sandy Grieg who had left Clydeside and travelled the world as a ship's engineer. Some years later he had married a Swedish stewardess and ultimately, reaching Stockholm, they had disembarked and taken up residence in a flat owned by the stewardess. He had obtained employment as an engineer and after mastering the language, he had advanced rapidly and was now a lecturer in Stockholm University.

Edward could not resist joining in. From what he had heard, there was a distinct possibility that at the present moment Axelson and Grieg were toasting their combined success in designing the perfect motor-ship in which they were now ensconced as it moved silently and serenely through the Norwegian Fjords.

McIllwraithe started to laugh at Edward's romanticising, but Rory put up his hand and asked for silence, then, in seeming contradiction, smiled broadly and, unable to contain himself, burst out laughing and declared that Edward, as usual, was the world's best storyteller.

As Edward acknowledged the rather dubious compliment, Rory persisted that there was an unconscious element of truth in Edward's story. Just yesterday he had received a letter from Sandy Grieg, referring to a meeting between himself and a man called Axelson, which had taken place almost a year ago. They had both been commissioned by the Swedish Government to come up with a design that would be helpful to the Scandinavian economy.

Sven was quite excited and indicated that he would write to Axelson and they would soon know the truth of the matter.

Becoming restive, Edward thought fit to interject.

"Just you do that, Sven, in your spare time. At present the only cousin of yours that I'm interested in is Emily."

Sven took the hint and produced a letter from Emily's family. He looked at Rory, who laughed and waved his hand in agreement, then added, "There's no stopping Edward when his mind's made up."

Sven appeared rather diffident as he started to read the letter, then, realising he was reading out loud in Swedish, he apologised for being so rude. Rory signalled Sven there was no need or desire for an apology; in any case, he and his nephew could always use the time discussing family business. There was a glint in his eye when he indicated they might elect to use the Gaelic.

However, Edward had another idea and suggested that the three of them should enjoy themselves in doing whatever took their fancy and he would content himself reading the letter from Sweden.

Looking directly at Rory, he warned him he had spent sufficient time in the West Highlands to have learned enough of the Gaelic to comprehend any salacious material that might unconsciously be revealed.

Before anyone could reply, Edward put his hand to his lips and asked if the present company would remain as quiet as circumstances permitted while he read the letter. The reaction from his friends was hardly complimentary, but Edward, oblivious to disparaging remarks, pursued single-mindedly the reading of the letter.

When finished, he handed it back to Sven, who questioned him concerning his ability to absorb all the information in such a short space of time.

"I think you must just have scanned it," he said.

Edward smiled encouragingly and replied, "No problem Sven. I have a photographic memory, my power of recall is such that Emily will be made aware of everything going on at home."

Questioning his friend's ability to absorb all the information in the letter, Sven took out his watch and pointing to the dial, indicated that three minutes was surely not enough time, even for Edward, to have memorised all its contents.

As Edward looked at the watch, his face crimsoned. He was perplexed and concerned, his appearance deteriorated almost to one of consternation, then he blurted out, "Are you sure your watch is correct?" Then, fumbling in his waistcoat, he brought out his watch and, looking at it closely, he sighed. "Oh, not again."

His three friends were now concerned. To them it was an extraordinary experience, to witness Edward in a state of anxiety.

Rory was first to intervene. "C'mon, Edward, tell us what is wrong, tell us what's needling you."

He smiled and thanked his friends for their consideration, then asked them not to laugh at his behaviour if he explained what had upset him. Before they could reply, he told them that on the day of the birth he had left his wife, indicating that although the event was expected in a week's time he would be back by five o'clock; just in case she was having trouble.

It so happened that while she was suffering the trauma of an early delivery, he had been involved in an adventure he could have done without. Learning of the birth, he had done his best to reach his wife in the shortest possible time.

Sergeant McIllwraithe, feeling closely related to Edward's dilemma, spoke up, relating how Edward, in very poor shape, had even discounted his advice to have a hospital check-up and, by his determination and a wee bit of ingenuity, managed to get home by the quickest means possible.

Thanking the Sergeant for his intervention, Edward added that if he did not move swiftly, he could fail her once again.

Rory rose to the occasion. "Drink up, lads, let's get this married man back home to his wife as quick as we can."

Five minutes later four men could be seen striding through the Kirkgate on their way to Leith Central Station. Their presence attracted attention as they strode along - three of them no doubt because of their size and the fourth, although of medium build, because he seemed, in a sense, to be in charge.

The three big men measured in excess of six feet and were in jovial mood, while walking briskly in front of them, the smaller man, who was extremely well dressed, appeared deep in thought.

Although bystanders were probably puzzled, it would not be difficult for them to visualise the four men in a military context. Although in mufti, the three big men were powerful privates enjoying themselves at the expense of the rather serious-minded corporal leading his men.

Before reaching their destination, Rory had disappeared among the bustling shoppers, leaving the other three to make their way into the station.

Almost immediately a miraculous transformation took place as Edward looked at the ticket to Grangemouth, knowing that within three minutes he would leave for home. Edward's jovial nature had returned, no longer was he morose, he was his old self now, thanking his friends effusively for their patience in tolerating his company when he thought things were going awry.

There was no sign of Rory. What had happened to him, Edward asked.

Sven and the Sergeant were uncertain concerning his exact whereabouts, but were sure he would turn up before the train left. Knowing Rory, Edward relaxed and agreed he would meet his friends 'as arranged' in a fortnight's time.

The big figure of Rory advancing towards them set the seal on their next meeting. Why should the big man coming towards them in such a portentous fashion be bearing flowers? Edward, forewarned, stood steady, awaiting any unorthodox assault on his sensibilities. The big beaming man pushed the flowers into his hands and Edward reacted in his own way.

"Thank you, Rory, but I didn't think you cared."

Rory blasted back, "The flowers are not for you, you idiot, they are for Emily, and hopefully she may allow you back to Leith fourteen days from now."

As the train drew away from the platform, Edward's friends started to cheer and continued their vocal exercise until the train was out of sight. The old man sitting opposite Edward in the carriage was obviously very curious.

"Your friends seem to think a lot of you," he said.

Edward smiled and offered the opinion that, as they had all been drinking, it was only natural that they would be a little rumbustious.

But the old man still seemed interested and offered an opinion.

"I'm thinking it wisna just drink that made your friends cheer. Sergeant McIllwraithe and his uncle, Rory McLeod, are weel kent as guid and serious members o the community. I'm o' the opinion they have a guid respect for you, mister."

Edward was quite happy to tolerate the old man's rather personal curiosity. "That sounds rather comforting, considering that I am a Dane seeking British naturalisation."

The old man was taken aback and admitted he thought Edward to be a man of letters; it amazed him that a Dane could speak English so fluently. As the conversation developed, he wondered if Edward might be a doctor, or possibly a lecturer at Edinburgh University.

"A was thinking you might be an M.D. or a P.H.D.," he said.

Edward felt he had to indulge the old man, after all, he seemed to crave company. "I am not a medical doctor," he said, "and I'm afraid the term P.H.D. escapes me."

The old man was quite elated and anxious to impart his knowledge. "It means that anyone with the letters P.H.D. after his name is a Doctor of Philosophy."

There was silence in the carriage as Edward cogitated and then a grin spread over his face as he admitted he was not entitled to be recognised as a Doctor of Philosophy. He was hardly old enough to be a Philosopher, but wondered if some people might judge him to be a philanderer; after all he had been a sailor until quite recently and there was the common belief that a sailor had a wife in every port.

The old man laughed at Edward's frankness, but felt he was demeaning himself and expressed himself in a definite fashion.

"You're a handsome, healthy lookin chiel, and I'm sure you get on weel wi' the lassies, but had you been on the philandering game, you would have had a broken back by this time."

As Edward considered his reply, the train slowed up. The old man left his seat and made for the carriage door and turning to Edward, expressed his feelings.

"I've enjoyed oor wee blether. I hope you dinna think I have been too curious, some of my friends at times think I'm a nosy bugger."

Edward could not restrain his laughter as he replied, "No offence taken, old man, and guid luck to you."

A big beaming smile spread over his face as the old man realised the foreigner had taken the trouble to answer in his own language. His departing remark gladdened Edward's heart.

"Aye, y'er a character."

As the train clippity-clopped towards the Falkirk interchange, Edward was a little bemused, conjuring up in his mind the meaning of the word character and how it applied to him in particular. His lips pursed, then moved upwards, signalling a grin as he contemplated the meaning of the old man's statement. Surely the old man himself could be called a curious character.

Rationalising his own position rather subjectively, he considered it possible that he might be known by his contemporaries as a studious character. What had been in the mind of the old man when he made his final comment? He had not prefixed the type of character, an indication that he thought Edward was an unorthodox or unusual person.

He wondered if the old man thought he was eccentric, or had he in mind his association with Rory McLeod. On several occasions he had heard Rory referred to as a character, no doubt due to his relentless pursuit of drug smugglers. His strength of mind and purpose when dealing with wrongdoers and his kindness to those less fortunate than himself was well known, particularly by the people of Leith.

It suited Edward's vanity to accept the old man's assertion that Rory would not be cheering him unless he thought him to be a worthwhile person. It was a comforting thought to feel he was being recognised as a character, it implied that he was now accepted as a member of the community and any unusual or unorthodox behaviour would be accepted in a friendly fashion.

He had started out early in the day, intent on fulfilling certain obligations and laying a foundation for the future, recognising that Leith could well become his base and home. In the main he had been successful, but the intervention of the man from Scotland Yard had left a bitter taste. Although he had dealt with the investigation effectively, he was annoyed that he had been forced to relive the most devastating episode of his life.

He smiled grimly, that part of his life would now have to be relegated to history, he had no intention of reliving it. He was happy now, his friends had stood rock solid beside him, they had even seen fit to ensure that he kept his word to Emily.

As the train sped towards Falkirk, he had time to take stock, time to examine his life in Scotland over the past two years.

Having visited Scotland some years before, he had fallen in love with the country and its people. The scenic beauty of mountains, glens, waterfalls and dazzling streams had won his heart and when his ship had berthed at Grangemouth he had seized the opportunity to become a part of the Scottish scene.

Using his linguistic and salesman talents he had succeeded beyond his expectations and felt he had done sufficient to warrant his acceptance as a person who could contribute constructively to the life of Scotia.

It never ceased to amaze Edward how he had crowded in so much in such a short period. His lifestyle had changed somewhat, he was more considerate towards his fellow man now, realising that they, like him, could be married and have to accept the responsibilities of marriage, together with its sweet advantages.

Deep down inside, he felt a change taking place; his approach to life and those he came in contact with was being mysteriously channelled into a slower steadier stream; his happy exuberant attitude was definitely softening, yet he had never been happier.

He was beginning to realise now that subtle changes in his life had started from the first day he had met Emily. The rapport between them had been rather unique, he being a ship's steward and Emily a stewardess having a love of the sea, but both seeking a new experience.

Edward had decided to pursue a course of action that would ultimately lead to the setting up of a profitable ship's chandlering business. Feeling she had been too long at sea, Emily had decided to relax for a short period and seek a post as a governess or something in catering that suited her abilities, but the language and her shy approach to strangers, particularly foreigners, made things difficult.

Alternatively, after a rest in Leith aboard ship, she could sign up and hopefully land back in Gothenburg, near to her family. But she had met Edward and he, after a lightning courtship, had convinced her that their mutual happiness would be in putting their roots down in Scotland.

As Edward, flowers in hand, crossed over to the Grangemouth connection, he had very much in his mind his responsibility and love for Emily.

As the train sped homewards, it was the wise words of his father on which he now focused his attention. He remembered the serious old Lars Villem as he told him, while still a callow youth, that vanity and fear were probably the most important factors in life.

Taking it to the extreme, women were often fascinated by beauty, many wishing to be considered as the most beautiful in their particular sphere, whereas the male hoped to be recognised as the most courageous and strongest amongst his contemporaries. It was unfortunate that the majority had to settle for second best.

So much for vanity, if we fall downstairs, we get up and dust ourselves down, assuring our fellow men that we are quite comfortable. We may have a broken leg or two, but that has to be tolerated if we wish to show we have not made an ass of ourselves.

Surely it is better to be honest and accept gracefully the kind ministrations of our fellows when *we* accident-prone humans make human mistakes.

But fear is something the whole human race must face with real courage and determination. It plays a dominant part and has to be conquered if man wishes to attain the state of mind known as true happiness.

His father had insisted on classifying the different types of fear. The fear of a man that he might lose his ability to provide for his family, through accident, misfortune or death. The fear of someone being brutalised by a corrupt authority. The fear of the death of a loved one and the fear of suffering agony before the death of oneself.

His father had admitted that when he was young, like Edward, he thought he had nothing to fear, but after his father had been found dead in his small fishing boat on the sandy shore of Laeso, he had been afraid to go to sea. He had overcome the feeling of terror and had always in the future, knowing the power of the sea, prepared himself physically and mentally for any foreseeable hazard, ultimately conquering his fear.

It was a sobering thought indeed; only now he knew that his old father had been speaking as a man with responsibility for a family and that he was his son, soon to set out on the sea of life.

A lump rose in his throat as he thought of old Lars Villem awaiting news from a son who was too busy carving out a career for himself in a foreign country. A letter to the old man was obviously a priority - he was entitled to know without delay that he now had a Scottish grandson. Looking back on all that had happened, he recognised the wisdom of his father.

It had been vanity that made him approach Chancitt and his thugs and demand repayment of his stolen commission. The end result had been an involvement in a hazardous adventure where he had to face death.

Only good fortune had favoured his survival, but the drug smugglers had been burned to death. In the future he would lead the life of a respectable citizen and ensure that family affairs were given precedence.

The old man's words concerning the death of a dear one had shocked him. Although knowing that death was inevitable, he had not, until now, given it serious consideration. His father's words had now alerted him to the fact that death had to be reckoned with, particularly now that he had a wife and son dependent on him.

It was the paramount fear in the life of man that had to be faced and handled with dignity. If death was inevitable, then surely the pursuit of happiness through the attainment of one's dreams was the driving force of life.

Descending from the train, flowers in hand, his thoughts encompassed Emily, their small son, himself and the desire to live life to its optimum fulfilment. Strangely, he had never felt more elated. True love, it appeared was a powerful force to be safeguarded fearlessly.

His heart was singing, he was walking on air, oblivious to all around him, thinking only of Emily. As he neared home, he descended from the clouds and returned to the real world.

Almost home, he met two young women coming towards him. Tipping his hat, he wished them a good evening, but as he did so, the flowers decided to go slightly askew and as he rescued them from a terrible fate, he stumbled slightly.

The women flashed friendly and comforting smiles. Feeling abashed, his senses now acute, he heard one remark to the other:

"That's Mr. Sorenson, he's a real character."

Edward was supremely happy. He was no longer an incomer, he was no longer a foreigner, he was now one of them.